The Hero and the Patriot

1775

HEART OF THE REVOLUTION
BOOK TWO

STEPHANIE MCRAE

For the dreamers who help us see
what our country was meant to be

Hide not your Talents,
     they for Use were made:
What's a Sun-Dial in the shade?

— POOR RICHARD'S ALMANACK

YORK
PORTO BELLO
WILLIAMSBURG
WILLOW HAVEN
THE GARDINERS' HOME
JAMES RIVER

A MAP OF THE
MOST RELEVANT PARTS OF
VIRGINIA PENINSULA
IN THE YEAR OF OUR LORD 1775
RIVER
YORK TOWN
N
S. McRae
2025

Glossary

This glossary is included for the convenience of the modern reader, who may be confused after typing "clothespress" into a search engine and being subjected to advertisements for small household appliances.

Athair—father

Barrister—a courtroom lawyer

Brief—a court case

Buckle—a sausage-shaped hairpiece that was "buckled" (or clipped) onto the wearer's hair or wig

Cabinetmaker—a woodworker who specializes in making furniture

Clothespress—a large piece of furniture for storing clothing

Case clock—grandfather clock

Christ's cross—a small cross marked the beginning of the alphabet on hornbooks. Children who learned their alphabet were said to have "learned their Christ's cross." In the process, the children learned to move their eyes from left to right, top to bottom, so the phrase evolved into the modern word "crisscross."

Coffin—a container made of stiff pastry. Coffins preserved meat fillings from spoiling for weeks or longer.

Colony, country, province, state—these words were often

used interchangeably in colonial times. Even though the USA was not a country in 1775, it is not an anachronism for a colonist to speak of love for their "country," by which they might mean colony or province

Delftware—fine blue and white pottery from Holland; similar in appearance to china

Dinner—the main meal, served around 2 pm

Dollars and jos—common coins in the colonies. "Dollars" refers to Spanish coins, which were sometimes cut into wedge-shaped pieces (pieces of eight). "Jo" refers to Dutch coin.

Dozen colonies—the number of British colonies attending the Continental Congress in 1775. Delaware would join later

Gloaming—twilight

Hoecakes—cornmeal pancakes

House of Burgesses—similar to the British House of Commons, the House of Burgesses was colonial Virginia's lower legislative body. Each county sent two burgesses who had been elected by the county's male landowners. The House created Virginia's laws, but those laws were subject to veto by the council and the royal governor

Hunting shirt—worn by longhunters and frontiersmen, the hunting shirt (sometimes called a frock) was the uniform worn by Virginia (patriot) soldiers early in the war

Humble pie—a humbling situation or forced apology

Huzzah—a joyous exclamation

Jacob's ladder—a toy with a series of blocks held together by strings or ribbons. When the top block is flipped down, the lower blocks appear to tumble downward as well

Kitchen—in coastal Virginia, the kitchen was typically an outbuilding. Separating it from the main house meant the cooking fires didn't heat the house in the summer

Ken—know

Linsey-woolsey—a coarse twill or plain-woven fabric with a linen or cotton warp and a woollen weft

Màthair—mother

Née—used to indicate a woman's maiden name

Old Dominion—a nickname for Virginia that is still widely in use. The story goes that Virginia was loyal to the crown during the English Civil War, refusing to acknowledge Cromwell's authority and insisting that Charles II was king after his father was beheaded. After he was crowned, Charles referred to Virginia as one of his dominions. It is old because Virginia was the first English colony

Ordinary—an inn

Petticoat—a skirt. During the eighteenth century, it could refer to any skirt, not just an underskirt

Pillory—a wooden frame that secured a person's hands and head in place for public scorn and humiliation

Pinner—an apron with a bib that pins to the bodice. Aprons with bibs were rarely worn by genteel women of mature age. They were frequently worn by young women, girls, and tradeswomen

Portmanteau—a round bag made of stiff leather

Put to bed with a shovel—an old saying meaning "to bury"

Queue—the classic hairstyle of the founding fathers: hair gathered back into a low ponytail or braid. Sometimes, "buckles" would be added

Redcoat—another nickname for British soldiers

Seasoning—those new to Virginia were often ill as their bodies adjusted to the climate and battled local illnesses, such as malaria

Settee—a wooden bench, sometimes padded; a sofa

Shift—a woman's knee-length linen undergarment

Shirtmen—a nickname for colonial soldiers whose uniform was a hunting shirt (sometimes called a hunting frock) worn over civilian clothing

Shortgown—the eighteenth-century equivalent of a woman's t-shirt. The shortgown was a T-shaped garment that ended between the hip and mid-thigh. It was worn over a petticoat, often with an apron and kerchief. This was the daily uniform of lower-class women. It was sometimes worn by women of middling and upper classes when they weren't expecting company

Stays—similar to a corset, stays were a foundational garment that gave the torso a conical silhouette

Sultana—a relaxed gown that wrapped around the figure and was tied with a sash. The predecessor to the kaftan

Switchel—before Gatorade, there was switchel. Variations of this nonalcoholic drink go back to ancient Rome. It was believed to be "invigorating and healthful," especially for summer laborers. One American recipe calls for five gallons of good water, half a gallon of molasses, one quart of vinegar, and two ounces of powdered ginger (see *Practical American Cookery and Domestic Economy* by Elizabeth M. Hall, 1856)

Syllabary—a list of syllables used for phonics instruction (i.e.—ab, eb, ib, ob, ub; ad, ed, id, od, ud)

Syllabub—a confection made with ·sweetened whipped cream mixed with cider or wine. Some recipes included beaten egg whites. *American Cookery*, the first cookbook published in America, mentions that a trifle could be made by layering broken biscuits, boiled custard, and syllabub. The trifle could then be garnished with jelly and flowers

Tapsalteerie—topsy turvy

Tester bed—bed with a canopy

Tête-à-tête—a French phrase that translates literally as "head to head," it means a one-on-one conversation

Tobacco notes—represented ownership of a certain number of pounds of tobacco from a warehouse stock. Could be used as currency

Wareroom—showroom for merchandise

One

A MORNING LIKE ANY OTHER

MONDAY, MAY 15, 1775

Emmeline Gardiner opened the door of the dairy. The small outbuilding stood in the shade of the apple orchard. Vents drew a circulating breeze to keep the milk and butter cool through the warm May days. She selected a crock of buttermilk that would join their spring vegetables in a pie Henrietta and Mama were preparing this morning, so they had something ready for supper that evening. In a few hours, her family would put on their Sunday best and go to town for the wedding. Until then, it was a morning like any other. There were the before-breakfast chores, the after-breakfast chores, and once those were completed to Mama's satisfaction, she would join Papa in the workshop where she assisted him until the midday meal.

Except, there was no need to prepare dinner today, as they would eat at the wedding. Her cousin, Charles Johnson, had left an hour ago in his best suit, his worldly goods packed in a trunk and a haversack. He hoped to deliver the trunk and still have a few hours at the office before the wedding ceremony that would bind him, heart and soul, to Miss Susan Bailey, an Englishwoman more elegant and beautiful than Lady Dunmore.

Emmeline yearned to have something new and elegant to wear to the wedding. Nothing so grand and frivolous as to be unpatriotic. Such things were far beyond their means. She had simply hoped for a new gown for her birthday last week—that had been the tradition every year as far back as she could remember—but with the ban on imports from England, anything but homespun was far too dear.

"Besides," Mama had pointed out, "your blue muslin still fits you fine, and you're getting too old to expect gifts just for being alive."

Those bracing words had brought her no comfort, but at eighteen, she was old enough to save her tears for when she was alone. The next day, she had been able to bear her little cross with fortitude. The blue muslin had once been her delight and joy. At the wedding, she would pretend the bodice wasn't fraying along the seams and that the starched hem was unstained from walking to church on muddy days. While the Good Lord hadn't blessed her with a life of affluence, He had blessed her with a robust imagination.

A striped orange cat darted into the dairy before she could close the door. He walked around the little space, flicking his tail, as if he owned every crock of milk and butter, then turned his green eyes on Emmeline. She tilted the crock in her hand until the buttermilk sloshed. Nutmeg's tiny pink tongue appeared, and he darted to her. While he meowed against her petticoats, she locked the dairy.

"Come along," she said, and the cat ran ahead of her to the kitchen, the only building that kept a fire all year long. The door was propped open. Nutmeg leapt up the two steps. Mama was rolling out a piecrust on a wooden table. Emmeline set a tin plate on the floor and poured buttermilk onto it. It was important to keep such a good mouser close to the kitchen.

"Have you completed your chores?" Mama asked.

"Yes, ma'am." Emmeline set the crock on the table.

"Then go help your Papa."

Emmeline had one foot out the door when Mama added, "But no painting. I won't have you arrive at Charles' wedding with paint splatters on your hands."

"Yes, ma'am." Painting wouldn't be needed today. She had painted enough toys this month to last them through May, and they had just received a commission for a black walnut dining set —a large drop-leaf table and a set of spindle-back chairs.

The back door to the shop was propped open to let in air and light. "Good morning, Papa."

He glanced up from his workbench. "Good morning."

The collection of roughly cut sticks leaning upright against the wall near the lathe had grown since she had helped him on Saturday. Papa trusted her to turn each plain stick into identical spindles for the commission of chairs they were working on. But that important chore could wait for a few minutes. She and Papa had a tradition.

Standing on tiptoe, she pulled the latest edition of the *Virginia Gazette* from a high shelf, where it had been securely wedged between a trade catalogue of Thomas Chippendale and the multi-volume *L'Art du Menuisier* by French carpenter André Jacob Roubo. She unfolded the *Gazette* and sat on her three-legged stool—the one she had painted with sunflowers, daisies, and roses. Each day, there was a blessed pause between the house and garden chores Mama gave her and the shop chores Papa gave her when she read aloud. She glanced over the first page of the supplement, which she had begun reading on Saturday. It had included another report from Boston. A British soldier was quoted to have said that "the militia had fought like bears," and that "he would as soon attempt to storm hell as to fight against them a second time."

A thrill of excitement ran through her as she read that line again. She was proud of her sister colony for defending itself with such courage, but she was also a little frightened by the reports of the dead and wounded. The battles of Lexington and Concord had happened last month when General Gage had tried to seize the magazine stores near Boston. That same week, Lord Dunmore, Virginia's royal governor, had succeeded in seizing gunpowder from the Williamsburg Magazine. She was angry he had succeeded so easily, but Charles and his friend, Mr. Quillan Morris, had been standing watch that night. If Virginians had been as ready to defend their arms as their sister colony, they might have died.

There wouldn't be a wedding today if Charles were dead and buried. Instead, Miss Bailey would be draped in black silk, sailing back to England, her salty tears filling the ocean destined to separate her from the grave of her true love. Shakespeare could have written a lovely tragedy about it, but Emmeline was grateful it wouldn't be written about her cousin.

At last, her eyes found the heading where she had left off, and she read aloud,

"Williamsburg, May 12—

"This day, about two o'clock, the Right Honorable, the Countess of Dunmore, with the rest of the Governor's family, who have for some time past been on board the *Fowey* man-of-war, arrived at the palace in this city, to the great joy of the inhabitants, and, we make no doubt, of the whole country, who have the most unfeigned regard for her Ladyship, and wish her long to live amongst them."

She glanced up at Papa, but he was too engrossed in his work to comment. After all this worry of war, surely returning to the palace was a good sign, though one she didn't understand. She looked back at the broadside. "Mayhap his lordship is ready for peace."

Papa grunted, and she had almost resumed reading when he spoke. "If the conflict were between Virginians and his lordship, mayhap peace could be achieved." At first, his words sounded like a cautious agreement. But the 'if' stuck in her mind like hoecakes in honey.

She attempted to voice what he had left unsaid. "But it's bigger than that."

"Aye, Emma. It's bigger than all of us."

What was he saying? Which part was bigger, and who was this between? "Bigger than one colony against one governor or—"

A bell rang, notifying them of a customer, and her mouth snapped shut so fast she bit the tip of her tongue. People came to the shop for what they made, not for what she had to say. Papa went into the wareroom, a room off the street where their finished furniture was displayed in all its polished glory: a tea table and settee fine enough for any parlor, a desk and document cabinet, a small coffin, and a pair of painted Windsor chairs. The paneglass window by the front door was where she displayed the toys she painted, made from scraps of wood: spinning tops, Jacob's ladder, Noah's ark, and the eclectic assortment of animals Charles had whittled.

She put the *Gazette* down and penciled guidelines on the would-be spindles. Every spindle in every chair had to appear identical; each bead and each cove had to be the same width and depth. She didn't notice Papa come back into the shop until he dropped a pamphlet beside her. She snatched it up and read the title, "A Summary View of the Rights of British America." The anonymous author was described as a native of Virginia and a member of the House of Burgesses. She glanced up at Papa.

"Colonel Hendriks said this pamphlet was printed quietly last summer and has been read by all the Tidewater planters. I bartered him for it."

She held the pamphlet like it was made of rubies. "What did he take?" There was a dark moment when she pictured the loss of Noah's ark, with its handsome couple and pairs of animals, far too valuable for an ordinary pamphlet. But this rare treasure had been exclusive knowledge for the wealthy planters. Not even the grandest toy would have been too much for this pamphlet

"A few of Charles' animals and one top."

She opened the pamphlet, but Papa's hand fell over the page.

"We'll be saving this for Sabbath reading so everyone can enjoy it."

Disappointed, she closed it and handed it back to Papa. He took it to the wareroom and shelved it inside the document cabinet, where it wouldn't be a temptation to read when they should be working. Her hands returned to crafting spindles. As she worked, her imagination flitted between the drama of recent battles and images of the finery Susan might wear as a bride.

Two

THE GROOM'S FAMILY

The Sign of the Eagle creaked overhead as Quill locked the office door. Most Mondays, Charles Johnson was quietly working in the same room, and Quill wouldn't dare leave so early in the day without a sound excuse. This Monday, Charles had spent the morning in a state of distraction before quitting the office at half-past eleven. Quill had attempted productivity for a few minutes more before abandoning his work with a smile. Weddings were delightful occasions, allowing a fellow to shirk his responsibilities in the most respectable manner. There would even be cake.

His sister's face appeared in the upper window of the rooms they shared across the street. Polly gestured for him to wait and vanished from view. It was a blessing that they had found rooms so close to the office, as she divided her time between acting as his clerk and keeping house, if one could call their quarters above the silversmith a house. There was no need for him to be escorting her back and forth during the workday when they lived across the street. He met her at the base of the stairs.

"Do ye have the ring?" Polly asked.

He patted his waistcoat pocket. "I do." There had been a moment of panic this morning when he had opened his lockbox and not seen it atop the jumble of dollars and jos. After upending the coins onto his bed, he found the gold band hiding under a crumpled tobacco note. He had promptly tucked it in the safety of his pocket.

As they walked the streets of Williamsburg, the sun was as warm and welcome as bread fresh from the baker's oven, and the breeze was as soft as thistledown. He could almost forget the rumors of war, if not for a pair of redcoats from the twenty-gun HMS *Fowey*, who emerged from the coffee house. The officers paused, frowning across the street at a man dressed in the coarse linen hunting shirt of the Williamsburg Volunteer Company. The shirtman answered their frowns with a cocky smile, his hand resting casually on the head of a tomahawk he wore tucked in his belt. When the frowns deepened, the shirtman grinned.

"Excuse us, officers," Quill said, tipping his hat. Then he turned to the shirtman and repeated the courtesy with a brief, "Sir," before daring to walk the wide road between them.

Polly's fingers dug into his arm, but she said nothing as they hastened between the enemies. Turning onto the next street, she let out a long sigh of relief.

Quill stared ahead at the carriage-lined road. "I thought the wedding was no' until noon."

"Indeed. We're early."

"Then why are there so many people here?" Weddings were supposed to be quiet, intimate affairs. Most well-wishers didn't arrive until after the ceremony was over. When Graves, the footman, answered the door, it was clear that poor Charles Johnson's wedding had become the society event of the year. The first families of Virginia were dressed in all their feathers and finery and gathered inside the Blue House.

He frowned. Virginia's gentry weren't there for the groom. Charles was a reclusive loyalist from a middling family. They must have come for the bride. Quill glanced around. Surely among all these people, someone had come to support the groom, but he was disappointed. Everyone, save Quill, was there for Susan.

Blast it all, it made sense that the bride's family couldn't come —they lived in England and one didn't cross an ocean for a wedding. She only had her widowed aunt, who lived in Williamsburg, and the brother who had escorted her to the colony. Charles, on the other hand, was born and raised a Virginian. His family should be here for him. But Charles' mother had passed away some years ago, and his father, while pleased with the connections his son was making in marrying above his station, was occupied with a new bride of his own.

The only family of Charles' who cared enough to attend his wedding wouldn't be wearing silks and lace. His father's sister had been raised to marry above her middling class and had disappointed the family by marrying a man in the trades—an honest, hardworking cabinetmaker. The Gardiners should have arrived by now, along with their eldest daughter, Miss Emmeline Gardiner, whom Charles loved like a sister. She had insisted her family would be here for the ceremony. Quill had asked her yesterday after evensong. And after morning service. And the week before. And the week before that. She was coming. Her family was coming.

Blast, bother, and bewilderment. Where were the Gardiners?

Polly greeted a friend, and Quill made his way to a lone figure in the crowded parlor who paced like a soldier anticipating his first battle. He slapped his shoulder in a cheery greeting. "Charles!"

The groom startled at the touch, then blinked, and recognition lit his anxious eyes. "Quill. You're here." He sounded relieved. Charles had always been more comfortable in social settings when Quill was present. It was flattering that, as a mature, soon-to-be married man of six and twenty, he still needed his old friend. "Do you have the ring?"

Quill patted his pocket. "Right here. Trust me." This wasn't the time to admit he had almost lost it.

"Of course." The groom straightened his collar and cuffs.

The banns had been read for the third and final time yesterday. The bride's brother, Isaac Bailey, had agreed to delay his departure just that long. The suddenness of the betrothal and wedding had been a source of merry gossip. Susan Bailey was well-liked by Virginia's gentry. They were happy to adopt her as one of their own. Her bold choice to marry and settle here was a bright spot amid the thundering rumors of war.

The front door opened, and the groom twitched.

"Steady," Quill murmured as Mr. and Mrs. Gardiner walked in, followed by Miss Emmeline Gardiner in the same gown she wore to church every Sabbath. Surrounded by a sea of silk, she looked as innocent as a daisy that had sprung up in a rose garden. A daisy Charles was determined to protect from the cruel thorns of the world.

A weight rolled off Quill's shoulders. "Your family's here." His relief turned to concern as distant friends of the bride, people who should have waited for the wedding supper to make their appearance, closed in, pressing Charles' poor relations against the wall behind the front door. Anger flashed like lightning from a blue sky. Who cared if the entire House of Burgesses was crowded into the foyer, their ruffles and lace crushed together? The Gardiners were Charles' family. They deserved to be here in the parlor. Charles deserved that much.

"Excuse me." He crossed the parlor and foyer with some effort. As he was shorter than most of the men and half of the women, he didn't part crowds with the same ease as Charles. He waved off several greetings before he reached the family. "Mr. and Mrs. Gardiner," he nodded to them, then turned to their daughter, who was nearly his height. "Miss Gardiner."

Emmeline Gardiner's wide gaze had been taking in the crowd around her. At his greeting, her blue eyes met his, and his breath stilled. She had a way of looking at a fellow as if she could see straight into his soul, and he found himself tallying old sins he had been saving for judgment day. Then she dropped her gaze to the floor and gave a demure little curtsy as she murmured his name. "Mr. Morris."

He addressed the head of the family. "You should be in the

parlor." He offered Miss Gardiner his arm. She stared at it a moment, then accepted his escort, her fingers feather-light on his arm. They had only made it two steps across the foyer when a hush brought him up short. The bride was coming down the stairs, escorted by her brother. Her generous figure was draped in a pink silk gown dotted with pearls and dripping with lace. The flowers in her hair were as white as the pearls at her throat and the slippers on her feet. She looked like an expensive confection. Miss Gardiner gazed up at her with open admiration.

The bride and her brother reached the bottom of the stairs, and the crowd parted like the Red Sea. Quill brought Miss Gardiner along in their wake and hoped her parents had the sense to follow. With all the ceremony of the occasion, Mr. Isaac Bailey handed his sister, Miss Susan Bailey, to the minister, who then placed her right hand in Charles'. The moment she touched him, his restlessness stilled, and his shoulders straightened. He held her hand as they exchanged the old vows to have and to hold, for better, for worse, for richer, for poorer, in sickness and in health.

There was a pause.

"The ring," Charles whispered.

Quill released Miss Gardiner and fumbled in his pocket, then handed over the ring.

Charles slid the bride's ring onto the fourth finger of her left hand. With his fingertips still on the ring, he looked his bride in the eye and repeated, "With this ring I thee wed." He blinked, and a tear slid down his cheek. "With my body I thee worship, and with all my worldly goods I thee endow. In the name of the Father, and of the Son, and of the Holy Ghost. Amen."

Quill swallowed hard as the groom wiped his eyes. Had he ever seen Charles cry before? He wore his feelings like a garter—always hidden from view. The couple knelt side by side, he austere in a gray suit and she extravagant in silk ruffles. The minister prayed over them, beseeching their Heavenly Father that they would live long lives full of godly love and see their children brought up in a Christian manner.

The ceremony complete, people pressed forward to congratulate the happy couple. Quill was caught up in greeting acquaintances. There were so many people around him, he almost didn't notice one bonny lass slip away from the crowded room. He turned to the groom. "Charles, the sooner ye feed the people the sooner they'll leave."

His friend appreciated the hint, and soon he and his bride led the company into the dining hall. Open windows were draped with white paper chains, bobbling in the breeze. Delft vases overflowed with white flowers. Orange slices floated in a bowl of punch. Maurice had prepared white foods: two beautiful cakes, whipped cream with berries, slices of white bread, pale cheese, and boiled chicken powdered with flour.

Miss Gardiner stood under the paper chains. The breeze toyed with curls that escaped her white cap while Isaac Bailey told her about his grand home in England. The bride's brother outclassed all of Virginia's gentry. He could have been talking to any of the women trussed up in silks and feathers. But the fabric of Miss Gardiner's gown molded and draped around her attractive figure in charming simplicity, unencumbered by the artifices of fashion. The muslin matched her blue eyes, which glanced up at Isaac enough to captivate his attention. Quill frowned. That lad was no hero. The Englishman would never fight for Virginia. So what if he'd served during Dunmore's War? He'd never actually fought. Being an errand boy took no special courage. He'd never done anything to earn her respect.

"Isaac," the second time the bride called his name, the lad looked up.

"What?"

"It's time." She glanced meaningfully at the punch bowl.

Isaac excused himself from Miss Gardiner and led the first toast. Quill led the second one. "To the happy couple. May they be blessed with prosperity, posterity, and punctuality." Polite laughter followed as the punch was sipped. Toasting continued with more and more distant acquaintances speaking longer and longer. When at last the words and punch slowed, the groom's cake was sliced and passed around. Miss Gardiner savored hers while watching the newlyweds. Charles was making cow eyes at his bride, and she liked it.

Miss Gardiner liked it, too. There was a soft, dreamy look on her face. Quill ate quickly, then moved in her direction, his progress slowed by the ladies' wide petticoats and the civil need to return cheery greetings. By the time he reached the window, she was gone. He continued his ponderous progress until he escaped through the back door.

He wasn't the only guest to move into the gardens. Some clustered by the roses, though the flowers were weeks from blooming, while a group of men discussed politics near the vegetable garden. Quill caught a flash of blue through the honeysuckle and hastened to the pergola.

Miss Gardiner leaned back into the trembling yellow blossoms. The scent was sickly sweet. Isaac towered over her, one hand on the post above her head, the other tangled in her curls. She winced.

The cake settled heavily in Quill's stomach. She was nothing to Isaac but a lark. An adventure to tell the boys about when he got home. He would steal a kiss amidst the flowers and not be there to apologize when she cried.

"Have I ever told you how pretty you are?" His words slurred even as his English accent deepened. He was tipsy if not outright sloshed. Any number of men could have told her she was pretty. It was a simple fact. A lass with eyes that sparkled like sunlight on the bay, whose rosy cheeks dimpled when she smiled; a lass whose face was framed with wild curls the color of honey, a lass like that couldn't help being pretty. It didn't give Isaac the right to be standing so close. It didn't give him the right to be the one telling her so.

Miss Gardiner eyed the lad warily. Score one for her. Score ten and twenty. She was too clever to be flattered by the sweet talk of an inebriated young man.

"You're the prettiest girl I know." He leaned closer. She shifted to the side.

If Charles came across this scene, his new brother-in-law might return home with a black eye. But Charles was too enraptured with his bride to worry about his pretty cousin today.

"Good morning, Miss Gardiner, Mr. Bailey," Quill interrupted brightly, bringing himself within easy distance of the two of them. His arms swung freely by his side, loose and ready. "I trust ye are well." He looked meaningfully up at Isaac. The lad took a step back, his hands falling to his side. He scowled down at Quill.

"I am." Miss Gardiner flushed but met his eyes, their gaze nearly level. "Thank you. And yourself?"

"Quite well. Mr. Bailey, when do ye meet yer ship?"

Isaac crossed his arms over his chest. "Late Tuesday."

"Tomorrow?" *Glorious grasshoppers.* That was soon. "Our loss." He cuffed his shoulder in a friendly way.

Isaac stumbled another pace back.

Quill stepped into the space he had created between Isaac and Miss Gardiner. "May yer voyage be smooth and swift. Do write when ye've arrived."

"I'll send a letter to Susan. I'm sure she'll pass it along."

Miss Gardiner's eyes darted to Isaac, then away. Quill clenched his fists. She had every right to expect her own letter after the way he'd been cornering her.

"Ye need coffee," Quill said sternly. "Go ta the kitchen. Maurice can sober ye up."

To his credit, Isaac stumbled toward the kitchen house.

Miss Gardiner twirled a tendril of honeysuckle vine on one finger. "The wedding was nice."

"It was, wasn't it?" He offered his arm, and they strolled the shady length of the pergola. A breeze blew through, stirring the sweet fragrance. Bumblebees hummed lazily. "I think they'll be happy together."

"They already are." A hummingbird darted past her. She gave

a little cry of delight and turned to watch it hover only a few feet away, its sliver of a beak deep in a flower. Her face lit with wonder and amazement, as though this were the first time she had ever seen a hummingbird up close, its feathers shimmering in the morning light. The wonder, to Quill, was that she hadn't lost her sense of wonder for something she had seen many times before. For a moment, he watched the light dance across her bonny face, highlighting a dainty nose, soft cheeks, and a smooth brow. Then, as quickly as it had come, the hummingbird left, disappearing into a distant tree.

She sighed. "Prettier than a peacock, but without an ounce of vanity. I wonder what the bard would have written, had he ever seen one."

"He would have compared it ta some sweet maiden—a bonny lass made all the bonnier by her manner."

Her face turned thoughtful. "I suppose you're right. How quickly you thought of it, too. I didn't know you knew Shakespeare so well."

He chuckled. She deserved the praise all the more for being blind to it. "Only as well as any gentleman of modest education." He waited for her to contradict him, to protest that any man who had graduated from William and Mary must be exceptionally well educated. Instead, she accepted his light self-deprecation as the gospel truth. Mayhap for good reason. Though he had, at long last, graduated, he had never been a model student.

Another young man, apparently weary of politics, entered the pergola. Quill drew Miss Gardiner closer. He would stay by her side until her family claimed her. That's what Charles would want. It was no trouble, really, looking after his friend's cousin for him. After everything Charles had done for him in his troublesome youth, he owed him little favors like this. Favors like keeping young men with amorous intentions from bothering Miss Gardiner.

Three

A CLOSED BOOK

TUESDAY, MAY 16, 1775

Emmeline swept the corners of Charles' old bedchamber. The mattress and curtains were draped over the back porch railing to air. Her footfalls echoed in the empty room. The wedding had taken two of her favorite people to the Blue House. She had known Charles would leave them to be with his bride. She hadn't expected him to take Jenny with him. They had almost forgotten she was an indentured servant, rescued from an unthinkable situation by Charles.

Jenny had insisted the change was nothing, that she owed him for his service. She was to work out the rest of her indentures by serving as a lady's maid to Susan Bailey—now Susan Johnson. In a fit of sentimentality, Emmeline had given Jenny her best hat as a parting gift. That had been a week ago. She had been to the Blue House twice since then and hadn't seen her friend. Servants didn't dine with the family or attend their weddings.

She reached the broom under the bed, stirring up dusty old feathers. If Jenny were here, Emmeline could tell her all about the wedding, how Susan had been a vision in pink and white, and Charles had surprised everyone by crying during the ceremony.

She wanted to believe a romance like that waited for her—one where she personified a bouquet of spring flowers and her true love was so full of adoration he was reduced to tears when he saw her.

Even her imagination couldn't achieve such a ridiculous fiction this morning. Mr. Isaac Bailey had been a pleasant companion at dinners and the Twelfth Night Ball. If life were a book, they would be star-crossed lovers, tortured by their looming separation. He would leave flowers where only she could find them, communicating his feelings through nature. And when he left, he would spend anguished hours writing love letters. Their love could never be, but at least they could express their dismay in a dignified manner.

And then he had to ruin it all by getting drunk.

He had loomed over her, reeking of alcohol. She had never been kissed before, but his intentions were plenty clear. He was going to kiss her. And he was going to buy that kiss with a cheap compliment. *You're the prettiest girl I know.* She hadn't been pretty to him until he had wanted to kiss her. Until he had drunk one too many healths to the happy couple.

Honestly.

It wasn't that she had never heard she was pretty before. She heard it once or twice a month when she walked into town alone on errands for her mother. The men who said it were strangers, often twice her age. It was always a preface to something inappropriate. An offer to buy her something that would leave her indebted. An invitation to a party with strangers.

Did all men think she had never seen her reflection? Or that she was too stupid to recognize what she saw? She knew every divot left from her battle with smallpox. Her hair was too dark to be angelic and too pale to be regal. She couldn't coax her curls into the plump sausages that every fashionable lady wore. Her eyebrows were too pale. Her clothing too plain. She rather liked her nose, but nobody else seemed to notice it.

She moved the dust pile to the top of the stairs—a narrow

space between the two upstairs bedchambers—and sneezed. It was time for the windows. She placed a rag on top of the bottle of lavender vinegar and tipped it until the cloth was saturated. Then she rubbed each window pane clean with tiny circles.

She wasn't so desperate for admiration as to abandon her good sense. No ships would be launched by the incomparable beauty of her face. No medieval troubadour would write ballads inspired by a vision of her loveliness. She rubbed her fingertips together. She didn't even have a lady's hands. Hers were calloused and sometimes splintered from constant work. Dirt had made its way under her nails. She sighed.

The same dirt darkened the rag she used. She folded it so the cleanest side faced outward and tipped more vinegar onto the cloth. As she wiped the film away, she saw every ripple and bubble in the glass. They were pretty in their way, catching and scattering light like a babbling brook.

It would be nice to be admired for something, whether that was beauty like a rose or wisdom like a sage. But between her mother's gruff counsel and Charles' protectiveness, she had grown suspicious of easy praise. The freer it came, the more she believed it to be false. The only praise worth having was the sincere expression of the heart. The only praise she trusted came after hard work, like a finely crafted table, by which time she already knew she had done well.

She hadn't expected Isaac to write her anguished love letters, but it would have been nice to pretend she could expect such things. She could have pretended a gentleman adored her. She could have imagined what it would be like to be the lady of a grand English manor. It would have given her something to think about while she weeded the garden.

Instead, he had cornered her until her skin had crawled, and she had been inching away. Then Mr. Morris had interrupted. The predicament he had found her in hadn't dampened his usual merry nature. Did her cousin's friend have no sense of delicacy?

She hadn't known whether to laugh or cry. But he had sent Isaac to sober up, so she couldn't despise him.

She sighed and opened the window, reaching her arm around to clean the outside. That's when she saw Mrs. Evans' carriage coming down the road. That was curious. It only came this way to collect her for dinner, but that wasn't until tomorrow. Then understanding came as clear as type on paper. Isaac had a boat to catch. He had come here to say goodbye.

Goosebumps ran down her arms. She had once imagined him coming like this to declare his love. Considering how to deliver her rejection had kept her amused through the dreary mending pile. But after yesterday, she didn't want to see him ever again. She stepped away from the window and beat the dust from her petticoats. If he had to come, why did she have to be wearing this old thing? Isaac was a wealthy gentleman. She was Charles' poor relation who was too proud to be seen streaked with dirt.

She crossed the hall to her chamber and fairly tore her pinner off and then the baggy shortgown, stabbing the pins into a heart-shaped cushion that hung from a peg by the door. Her entire wardrobe, and Henrietta's too, hung from that row of pegs. There wasn't time to change the kerchief that was pinned to her stays or the old petticoat she wore. She snatched her jacket off a peg. It was the one she wore when she went into town to dine at the Blue House or run errands for her family. She thanked God she hadn't done more than loosen the laces the last time she had removed it. She wriggled into it and was tightening the laces when Henrietta threw the chamber door open. "There's a man here to see Miss Gard-i-ner," she called in a sing-song voice.

"Hush." Heavens, she hoped Mr. Bailey hadn't heard her. This was humiliating enough without little sisters. She tied the laces in a neat bow and threw her shoulders back. If she couldn't reject him coldly as a fine lady, she would face him like a general. She would not show fear. She would not betray her discomfort. She was halfway down the stairs when she realized her head was bare. She returned to her chamber where her mobcap was on the floor with her apron and shortgown. She tucked her curls inside and went downstairs, her spirits lowered by the certainty that he had heard her scurrying footsteps. Would he have guessed that she had changed in haste? Her cheeks heated.

Mr. Isaac Bailey rose when she entered the front room, Mama firmly in attendance. He didn't quite meet her eyes. "Miss Gardiner."

"Mr. Bailey," she said, dismayed by her breathy voice.

"I was passing by on my way down to Hampton. I realized I hadn't properly taken my leave."

"Oh." She turned the words over, holding them up to the light, checking for hidden meanings. She found none.

"It's a fine day." He glanced at Mama, then met her eyes. "Would you show me your garden?"

The formal garden ran alongside the road between the house and the workshop. There were no clandestine nooks to be cornered into. Emmeline looked at Mama.

"Go along and show the boy the flowers. Don't worry about me."

"Yes, ma'am." She led Isaac to the front door. She wouldn't have dared to call him *boy*. He was nineteen and a gentleman. She led the way through a picket gate. Was that wrong? Should she have stood aside and allowed him to open the gate? Susan wasn't here to advise her.

The gate clicked closed, and she turned toward him. Now she couldn't meet his eyes. Tucking her lips between her teeth, she studied the shrubbery. She made a terrible general.

Isaac cleared his throat. "I wanted to apologize if I..."

She looked up.

He was studying the roofline of the shop behind her. "Made you feel uncomfortable...yesterday."

Her brows rose. If there was anything she had expected less than a declaration of love, it was an apology. If she had been in his shoes, she would have hidden her face and run for the boat. "Thank you for apologizing. That's brave of you."

He scoffed. "Brave for admitting I acted the coward?"

"It's hardest to admit the things we're ashamed of." She smiled, attempting to commiserate. "Did Susan put you up to this?"

He looked sheepish. "Actually, it was Mr. Morris."

Could this day bring any more surprises? Mr. Morris had smiled like it was all a good joke. But he'd tried to fix things, too—sending Isaac to sober up and then to apologize. "I suppose Charles put him up to it."

"Charles doesn't know. Look. You're a fine girl. I hope you have a good life." His lips twisted wryly. "I suppose Susan will write me all about it. I just didn't want to leave things..." He swallowed. "Forgive me. Goodbye."

He touched his hat and stepped into the carriage, leaving Emmeline to resume her chores. As she worked, she waited to feel the overpowering effects of grief and separation. To her dismay, the day proceeded as dull and uneventful as any other. Isaac had been a small part of her life when he had been in Williamsburg. Now he was gone with the finality of a book closing.

Once Charles' bedchamber was clean and the curtains rehung, she joined her mother in the kitchen, making a large batch of vegetable pies for weary travelers who begged their hospitality. She sliced a mountain of carrots two at a time. "Life isn't nearly as interesting as books. Even goodbyes are duller than one imagines. And where are the heroes? We could use someone to—"

Mama, despite being a gentleman's daughter, snorted. "Don't be a goose. We don't need heroes. We need people to milk the cow and bake the bread. Books are well and good, but we don't live in them. We live here." She gestured around them. "What good is a hero in the kitchen? None. But what good is a man without dinner in his belly? Also none, but the world is full of men, not heroes, so that's what matters."

Emmeline bit her tongue. She hadn't meant to be a goose. But Mama was wrong. History books were full of heroes. When the Aequians had threatened to invade Rome, it was Cincinnatus who left his plow to lead them to victory. And now the colonies were threatened. They needed a great hero, a man of conviction, a great orator, someone to rise and lead the colonies to victory.

Four

JUSTICE & MERCY

As Quill locked the door to their apartment, he said, "There's a concert on tonight at the Apollo. I thought we might go."

They descended a flight of stairs. "I willna invite Susan," Polly said. "She would have ta bring Charles and they're too recently wed ta be fit company for anyone but each other."

"Aye. But we could invite some of yer other friends ta meet us: Miss Ray, Miss Carter, Miss Randolph—"

"Miss Gardiner."

"What?" Quill stumbled on the last step. He righted himself and stepped into the sunlight.

"Why not?" Polly asked, as they waited for a wagon to pass. "She enjoys music. And though she is a mite young, she makes an agreeable companion. And we never invite her ta anything, though she is Charles' family."

They crossed the road to the Sign of the Eagle. Quill had never seen Miss Gardiner at any plays or concerts. She had only ever attended one public ball, and Susan had arranged that. Her family had one old horse and a wagon for delivering furniture. It wasn't suited to convey the lass home after dark. She would have to walk the whole way. It wasn't impossibly far. Her family walked to church even in the cold of winter, but not when it was fully dark. And though the expense of admission was a trifle to a barrister, might it be an extravagance to a tradesman's family? He unlocked the office door. "When would ye ask her?" He hadn't expected to see her again until they met for dinner at the Blue House on the morrow.

"Oh," Polly said. "I hadn't thought of that." She knelt in front of her writing desk and pulled out the drawer under the seat. "Maybe another time."

Quill looked over his desk. The papers from three briefs were spread across it, and two books lay open where he had last been researching some legal minutiae that might benefit his clients. He separated the briefs into tidy stacks, then sat down to the books. He skimmed two pages of one, then five pages of another, looking for two things at once. He had finally found something useful and was trying to remember which of the three briefs he had meant to add it to when Charles walked in and hung his cocked hat.

"What are ye doing here so early?" Quill asked.

"Early?"

"I thought ye would at least take the morning off, since ye're newly married."

"I need to make money so I can buy a house."

"Ah." Quill made a note at the bottom of what he thought was the right brief. He returned to skimming the book and made it three pages when he realized he had picked up the wrong book. He shut it and tossed it on one of the briefs.

There was a knock at the door. "Enter," he called, turning in his chair.

A man of middling age opened the door. "I'm looking for a Mr. Morris. Is he here?"

Quill rose. "I am. How may I be of service?"

"I heard of your recent success in annulling an elopement."

"Yes, sir." Several months ago, a distraught father had come to see him. His fifteen-year-old daughter had been tricked into eloping with an older man. After his girl had been recovered,

Quill had helped him sue for an annulment. He had argued that the girl was not of age and had married without her father's consent. "I was glad to see justice served."

"Yes, well, I unfortunately find myself in a similar situation."

"My condolences to you and your family. Please, take a seat, sir." He gestured to the one extra chair they kept in the office for clients. It belonged to the set from his dining table, but there wasn't room for so much furniture in their small front room.

Polly shuffled her papers, setting out a fresh sheet so she could take notes while Quill interviewed their client. The man's eyes flicked to her.

"Forgive me. This is Miss Morris, my sister and clerk. And Mr. Johnson, another barrister." There was an awkward moment where he half-expected the man to protest against Polly's presence, but then he nodded. While it wasn't common for a gentleman's daughter to work alongside a barrister, it was common enough for women to work in the family business. Their arrangement wasn't so very different from the blacksmith's daughter shoeing a horse or the cobbler's wife selling shoes.

"Tell me everything ye can about this tragedy." When the man didn't reply, Quill prompted him with something more specific. "Have ye recovered yer daughter, sir?"

"Not exactly."

Quill sat back in his chair and frowned. That should have been the man's first matter of business, securing his daughter's physical safety. An annulment could take time. "Not exactly?"

"She refuses to come home."

Why would a father discover his daughter and then leave her in a compromising situation? If she wasn't already expecting a child that could change at any day, and make it more difficult to persuade the courts that an annulment was in her best interest. "I'm surprised ye didna simply carry her home."

"She's a mite big for that. Says she's in the family way."

Quill and Charles exchanged a look over the client's shoulder.

He had managed things very poorly. "How well do ye know the man?"

"Well enough. He was apprenticed a mile from our home."

"Did he run away from his indentures?" That might help their case.

"No. He completed them a year ago. He's been skulking around the house ever since. Caught him throwing rocks at her window more than once. Told him to stay away from my girl. Things were quiet for about a month, and I thought he was. Then one night, after everyone was in bed, I heard the front door. I grabbed my rifle and went out. He was sitting on the steps of my front porch with my girl in his lap, kissing her like his life depended on it."

The more the man talked, the less this sounded like an abduction and the more it sounded like a clandestine courtship.

"I held the rifle to the boy's chest and sent him running. Two days later, she was gone. I brought the note she left." He handed it to Quill.

> Dearest Father,
> Please do not be angry. By the time you read this,
> I will be married. You know who my suitor has been.
> Though you have not cared for him, I am convinced
> my greatest chance for happiness is with him. Give the
> family all my love. I know not when or if I will see
> them again, as we are traveling some distance to begin
> our lives together.

Quill frowned. This didn't sound like the voice of a naive fifteen-year-old. "Sir, how old is yer daughter?"

"She was twenty last month. She has another year before she reaches her majority. The marriage was performed without my consent."

"But sir, she's expecting a child. Shouldn't the man who caused that be responsible for raising that child?"

"The marriage wasn't legal. Therefore, the child was conceived in sin and should become a ward of the church."

Charles nodded grimly. The client's assessment was correct, legally speaking, even if his determination to act was misguided.

Quill attempted to counsel the man. "Sir, think carefully. If yer daughter was so determined ta marry this man that she ran away from home and ye havena yet persuaded her ta leave the man, what good do ye think an annulment will do?"

"Do you think my daughter would live with a man she wasn't married to?"

"I—" Quill broke off. The man didn't follow his own logic. And anyway, the lass clearly knew her mind. It may have been a foolish choice, but wouldn't she make the same one in a year when she was of age? What good would it do the man to bring his daughter home in shame? To have a baby when she wasn't married to the father? To have her child torn from her arms and raised as an orphan? Even if it wasn't the wisest marriage, wouldn't it be better to validate it?

Charles cut in. "The wedding couldn't have been legal without your consent."

Quill frowned at his friend. Didn't he see this was the time for mercy, not justice?

The man turned in his chair. "Exactly! That's what I mean. She's living in sin, but she won't see it. She won't listen to me. That's why I need a judge to tell her that."

This was absurd. Quill tried to dissuade the client once more. "'Tis unlikely the court will rule in yer favor."

"Likely or not," Charles said, "every man deserves a fair trial."

Quill couldn't argue that sentiment. His friend's devotion to justice had saved him from a lifetime of unrequited misery. But this trial would be nothing like the one Quill had faced as a young man. These young lovers had chosen each other. The parent could validate the marriage with greater ease than he could annul it.

Mayhap that was why Charles accepted the brief. He might have hoped to persuade the man to see reason and mercy during their next meeting. Or, mayhap Charles only saw justice because he had so seldom needed mercy. He had approached his marriage the proper way, securing permission from her father, even though legally, Susan was old enough to enter into a contract herself.

This girl had foolishly chosen between her family and her fancy. She had entirely forsaken her family to be with the man she loved. Now she would be forced by that family to forsake both the man she loved and her child. In a world where every good thing came from God, it only led to misery when people insisted on choosing one good thing at the expense of another.

Five

DOVETAIL

Emmeline blinked in the darkness. The first songbirds were orchestrating the sunrise. Too early. She reached to pull the blanket up to her chin and grasped at air. Fumbling in the darkness, she found it cocooned around her sister, Henrietta. She yanked her share back. Henrietta moaned and rolled over. Emmeline wriggled her shoulders deeper into the mattress. She didn't have to wake this early unless it was—

Today.

The thought clanged like church bells. She was only allowed to attend dinner at the Blue House if she finished her chores. And since Jenny had moved to the Blue House to work as a lady's maid, there were even more chores than usual. She slid through the bed curtains, feet first, her knees landing on the braided rug. "Dear Lord, give me strength." She could get that far out of habit. Her heavy head dropped against the mattress. *No.* She wouldn't fall back to sleep. "Amen." It was a blasphemously short prayer, but she couldn't think on her knees when the sun had yet to clear the horizon.

She dipped a washrag in the pitcher and lathered soap onto it.

Nothing woke the mind like washing with cold water. There would be no traces of sweat or dirt by the time she was done. No evidence of a life where she didn't wear lace every day of the year, read all day long, draw beautifully, recite poetry, and play a dozen instruments.

She tied her stays with the practiced ease of tying an apron. What would it be like to stand like a statue while a maid tied and pinned her clothing into place? *Delicate flowers wilt in the sun and shrivel in the frost.* Her conscience sounded like Mama. She shelved the daydream like a book that always fell open to the same worn place. A war was beginning. Soon, ships would blockade Chesapeake Bay just as they had done to Massachusetts. Coveting wasn't simply immoral. In times of war, it was unpatriotic. Lace wouldn't protect Virginia if troops were sent here. Music would feed no one if supply ships couldn't get through.

She tied her petticoats. There was no need for a maid. No need for daylight, even. There was no need to see a mirror as she pinned her shortgown closed. Those were all very sensible reasons to be grateful for her meager selection of apparel. She stepped softly into the hall. Charles' door was open, his room empty. Last night, she had accidentally set an extra place for supper.

She milked the cow, watered the garden, and unlocked the kitchen. She sprinkled wood shavings on the ashes in the hearth and stirred them with a fire poker. The slumbering embers came to life and consumed the kindling. She and Isaac had nothing in common beyond a nearness in age. She had imagined more to it— fancied herself capable of managing a grand house in England. She hadn't believed it. If she had gone, she would have found herself more at home in the kitchen than in the dining hall.

Mama came in. "I'll get breakfast on the table. You help Henrietta."

"Yes, Mama." Never mind that when she was her sister's age, she had been expected to manage her stays and hair by herself.

"Oh, that reminds me," Mama said.

Emmeline stopped on the threshold. "What is it?"

"When are you going to begin teaching that girl? The one Charles wants to turn into a governess?"

"Kitty? Not until he buys a house. Then she will live in town instead of at Johnson Hall."

Mama made the kind of grumpy noise she would never have allowed Emmeline to make. "That could be months from now."

"Indeed, it could."

"Well, when it does, you might take over teaching Henrietta, as well."

"What?" She didn't know how she would find time to teach Kitty, much less her sister. The days were already too short. Books were read by stealing paragraphs when Mama wasn't looking, the guitar mocked her lack of accomplishments, and Granny's basket of lacemaking sat in a drawer, waiting for a day when she could practice her rudimentary skills.

Of all the many things she wished she could devote more time to, teaching was not one of them. Widow Wager had taught thirty children at once, and who remembered her? But when Charles had asked her to teach the little slave girl who cared for their grandmother, to give her a future where she could work as a tutor or a governess, Emmeline had agreed. There had been something earnest in his request that had inspired a vision of something greater. Combined with the honor of having her cousin, a respected man of business, entrust her with something he valued, she found she could not refuse.

There was neither vision nor honor in Mama's demand, but she couldn't refuse it, either. Honoring one's parents was so important a commandment that it was written on Moses' stone tablets, alongside "thou shalt not kill" and "thou shalt not steal." If she failed to submit to her parents, she would be like the Israelites who had wandered in the wilderness for forty years and died before their children saw the promised land. She already had a land flowing with milk, honey, and apple cider. But the specter of a life wasted in wandering, a life with no purpose, was enough to keep her feet on the straight and narrow, even when the dreariness of the world clouded her view of eternal joys.

"We might take on an apprentice," Mama said, "for your papa. And I can get more done if I'm not teaching your sister."

An apprentice would slow Papa down until he had him trained. That could take years. Emmeline had used the lathe to turn the spindles on dozens of Windsor chairs—the painted kind that used up mismatched scraps of wood—before Papa had allowed her to help him with a commission from a discerning customer.

But Mama had that determined look in her eye—the kind she got at the beginning of cider season or spring cleaning. It didn't matter what challenges lay in her way. Mama had chosen a path and wouldn't turn back until she had completed it.

After breakfast, Emmeline hoed around the shrubbery in the front garden. It was a dull season for flowers. The tulips had withered away, but the roses were tight-lipped around green buds. The little oasis of formality had been one of the first improvements Mama had made to the property. She had been the one to purchase it, just before she and Papa married, with money from selling the land she had inherited when her father had passed away. There had been a little money left, so they had added a back room for dining with a wide covered porch, built the shop for Papa, and planted roses and boxwood in the front garden.

"Lady?"

She turned. Standing in the road was a tall man in trousers. His deep tan was shocking against pale blond hair. He was a sailor. Mama didn't like sailors, but who else would fill the shelves in town?

"Leetle Lady, ver ees Villemsberg?" His accent was heavy. For a moment, she thought he had spoken in Dutch.

"Williamsburg?"

"Ja."

She pointed north. "This road."

He looked where she had pointed. "*Ik raak altijd verdwaald op het land*." The words slipped around her ears like water through her fingers. He bowed. "Dank you."

"Wait, sir." She formed a cup with her fingers and tipped it to her lips. "A drink?" He might be a sailor, but his courtesies pleased her. He deserved hospitality as much as any traveler.

He brightened. "Ja. A drink."

"Wait here." She was back in a moment with the old tin cup.

He drank it in one gulp and handed the cup back to her. There was kindness in his hooded eyes. He bowed again. "Dank you, leetle lady. Good day." His long strides took him north.

At last, her house chores were completed, and she read the *Gazette* to Papa. After the thrilling supplement and the allure of the new pamphlet, other news fell flat, and she was soon content to turn her attention to spindle making. Time flew with the woodchips as her foot rocked the treadle that kept her wood spinning, and the skew carved out the coves and rounded up to the beads. She had hoped to finish enough spindles for one chair before dinner.

One spindle, two spindles, three spindles done. She wasn't halfway through her work, and the sun was past its zenith. Only once before had she not been ready when Mrs. Evans's carriage came to collect her, shortly after Twelfth Night. But the garden was so much bigger now, and there was a cow to milk. "The Lord helps those who help themselves," Mama always said. There were scarcely enough hours in the day to accomplish the work set out. Emmeline hadn't opened a book since Sunday. And she was going to miss dinner at the Blue House anyway.

She blinked hard and put another slender piece of wood on the lathe. Her calves burned from working the treadle, but she started pumping again. Soon, the sharp edges of the wood blurred as it spun, and she gently pressed the skew against it, blinking away the sawdust.

Papa looked up. "Isn't it time for you to go?"

"I'm not finished."

He sighed and looked at the results of the morning. "You're a good girl. Go get ready for your friends."

Emmeline's foot slipped off the treadle. "Truly?"

"Indeed. You're a gentlewoman's daughter. Go act like it."

"Thank you, Papa."

She raced up the stairs to freshen up. She removed her work clothes and her mob cap, then bent over, rumpling her curls as sawdust fell to the floor. Then she washed her face and arms until the skin glowed pink and put on her best petticoat and town jacket. She studied her reflection in a hand mirror. The glass was broken into several large pieces. If she held it fully upright, it might slip from its frame, so she had to bend her head to see her fractured reflection. She took a pinch of pomade and smoothed the curls that framed her face, and put on her best cap: snowy white with the blue ribbon Susan had given her.

On the whitewashed wall was a flowery landscape painted by Aunt Vina. She had told Emmeline of all sorts of riches she had planned to leave to her—silk gowns, pillowcases with lace edging, jewelry, and books with delicate illustrations—but the painting was the only one she gave before she passed away. Uncle Charles had had little interest in his wife's wishes when she was alive. Upon her death, grief moved him to install a stately little head-stone at the church cemetery before forgetting about her altogether.

"Emmeline!" Henrietta shouted up the stairs. "The carriage is here."

She hurried downstairs and leapt through the open door as though afraid the carriage would turn into a pumpkin if she waited any longer. It lurched into motion, and she sighed. She had made it. She pulled a book from her pocket. Until they collected the other passengers, her only companion would be *A Midsummer Night's Dream*. She was lost in a fairy world when the carriage stopped. She glanced out the window. No one from her party waited under the Sign of the Eagle. If she were lucky, they wouldn't be ready for another five minutes. She turned another page.

The fairy queen was asleep in her bower when the mischievous Puck squeezed the juice of a magic plant into her eyes. When she woke up—

The door opened, and Emmeline jumped in her seat. Polly Morris slid in beside her and squeezed her hand. "I'm glad ye're here. I'm afraid Susan is going ta be a wee distracted." She glanced meaningfully at Charles as he took the seat opposite them.

Mr. Quillan Morris sat beside her cousin. His friendly face was freckled from his cravat to his auburn hair. He touched his cocked hat in greeting. "Miss Gardiner."

"Mr. Morris. How do you do?"

"I'd be better if I hadna been stuck in the office with him all morning." He nudged Charles with his shoulder.

"What did I do this time?"

"Now that ye're married, ye smile all the time. Miss Gardiner, married men are happy, and happy men are unforgivably dull. They canna be teased."

She smiled and shook her head. Mr. Morris was the most absurd gentleman of her acquaintance.

"Only think," he continued, "if every man got married, the world would be as bland as ginger cakes with no ginger."

She shook her head. How could Charles be such good friends with a man who made light of marriage?

Charles settled back in his seat with his chin high. "Well, as only one of us can be married to Susan, the rest of the world can never be as happy as I am."

"It's been a long morning," Polly muttered.

Emmeline fumbled for something to say. She couldn't discuss their shared morning together as she had only just joined them. Susan had once counseled her to speak only of matters of general interest, but nothing in her life was of general interest, unless one counted the things she read. She didn't dare discuss matters of politics in mixed company, and Charles had informed her that fiction belonged in books, not conversation, so Emmeline sat there hating herself for being such a dull, mousey creature who could say nothing but bland civilities. She deployed one of those civilities to her cousin. "How is her health?"

Charles sobered. All immigrants had to endure the seasoning eventually. Susan had finally begun it a few weeks ago. The worst was over, but the fever could come and go for months. "The color isn't back in her cheeks yet. She takes chill too easily."

"Now that ye're married, canna ye fix that?" Mr. Morris was as impish as Puck on a midsummer night. "I imagine ye could warm her up with a wee bit o'—"

"Quill!" Polly jerked her head toward Emmeline like she were a child. The rejection stung like the blow of a mallet. They couldn't even pretend she was a natural addition to their party. She was a charity case, a poor relation who needed improving. She accepted Susan's invitations out of a desperate need to learn the world her mother had descended from and an optimism that poise and manners couldn't be any harder to learn than the craft of applying veneer to a chest of drawers.

Mr. Morris blushed as red as a cardinal's wing. "Apologies." He rubbed the back of his neck.

A tense silence filled the carriage. It would have been less awkward if Polly had allowed him to finish his sentence. Emmeline wasn't a child, and it wasn't so scandalous to tease a newly married man about kissing his wife. She pursed her lips in thought. Kissing was too bland a word to finish a phrase that began with as much flavor as "a wee bit o'." It must have been sparking. The word suggested more warmth than a simple kiss, and Emmeline placed a hand to her cheek, grateful she didn't color as easily as some people. The stain had faded from Mr. Morris' complexion, leaving him as pale as pinewood with a complex inlay of mahogany freckles.

The carriage rocked to a stop across the road from the Blue House. Emmeline folded her hands in her lap and waited while the gentlemen exited the carriage first. Learning when to sit and be quiet had been the easy part of emulating the manners of a gentlewoman. Learning when to speak was proving much more difficult. Mr. Morris stepped down from the carriage and was turning around when Charles stepped down, nearly bowling him over.

"Sorry, Quill," Charles said, then crossed the road without waiting for the rest of his party.

Quillan Morris blinked in surprise as though this were the first time in his life he had been nearly bowled over. Mayhap it was. Some men carried themselves with the elegance of a church steeple, but Mr. Morris, short and stocky, carried himself with the sturdiness of a powder magazine.

Polly laughed at her bewildered brother's expression as she exited the carriage with all the practiced grace of a gentlewoman. "They say marriage changes a man."

"I wouldna say he's changed. He could be blunt and ill-mannered as a boy." Mr. Morris smiled up at Emmeline and offered the firm support of his hand. She rested her delicate hand on his. In truth, it was the calloused hand of a tradesman's daughter, but resting it on his broad one made her feel delicate in contrast, as if she were Titania, Queen of the Fairies. In a moment, she lost the fairy story elegance when her second foot, instead of joining the first on the unseen step, tangled in the hem of her petticoat. She gave a little cry as she lost her balance, but her escort moved quickly, and she landed, not in a puddle of disgrace on the filthy street, but with her other hand on his broad shoulder and his other hand at her waist. They remained like that for a moment—he as steady as a brick wall and her heart fluttering from the fall.

"Are ye well?" Polly asked. "Did ye turn an ankle?"

Emmeline pulled her hands off Mr. Morris as if he were a hot skillet. Susan had neglected to tell her how to smooth over a moment of public clumsiness. Then again, Susan was never clumsy. Emmeline rolled her ankles, one at a time, her calves tight against the stretch. "My ankles are fine." The only thing she had turned was her pride. In one moment, she had gone from the ethereal Queen Titania to the crude and ludicrous Bottom. She tried to brush aside her embarrassment by continuing their conversation as if nothing had happened. "Was Charles ill-mannered? He never pushed me over."

Mr. Morris chuckled as he offered his arm. "Pushing a lady is *beyond* ill-mannered." It was the second time in one day that she had been called a lady. The benign flattery made sense coming from a Dutch sailor who needed directions. Mr. Morris hadn't needed anything. The word rolled off his tongue with the forgetful ease of buckling one's shoes. He wouldn't remind her of her misstep any more than he would remind her of the reasons she didn't belong here. It was just the balm she needed after the embarrassments of the afternoon. She accepted his arm, and he led them around the horses and in clear view of the parlor window, where he stopped and gave a low whistle.

"Oh, dear," Polly said in polite shock.

Charles had his arms around his bride, their lips sparking like flint and steel.

Their escort turned them away from the intimate scene. "I fancy a turn about the street before dinner."

"Aye," Polly said.

Emmeline squeezed her escort's arm in agreement. Romance was pleasant to read. It was not pleasant to watch. She would have been content to grow to a bent old woman without knowing her reserved cousin could be a passionate lover. At least Mr. Morris was the same as ever. Nothing upended his playful equanimity. After a turn down the road, he tapped on the front door. In a low voice, he asked Graves, "Is now a good time?"

The footman suppressed a smile. "I'll announce you."

Susan was blessedly alone in the parlor. Her cheeks were a rosy color, and her eyes were bright. "It is good to see you. Charles will be back in a moment. He went to get me a shawl."

Polly put a hand to her forehead. "Have ye caught a chill?" It was such a mild afternoon.

"It's nothing. Come, I've been longing to play with some-one." Susan sat at the harpsichord and arranged the music. It was an old song. Polly didn't need to see the music. She stood on the far side of the instrument by her brother, singing with a bell-like voice that could have lured sailors from their ships. Emmeline felt a twinge of envy. Her accomplishment with the guitar was middling at best, and she had never had other music lessons.

Charles returned to the room. He arranged the elegant shawl around his wife's shoulders.

From two steps back, Emmeline admired the tableau. Susan, not missing a note, looked lovingly up at her prince, whose hands rested on her shoulders. Polly was the lady-in-waiting. Mr. Morris was the court jester. But what was Emmeline?

So much of a person's life was dictated by who their parents were and what they did. The children of a printer would be raised in the business. The sons of the gentry attended the College of William and Mary. As the daughter of a cabinetmaker *and* a gentlewoman, Emmeline was too refined for some circles and too coarse for others. If only she could dovetail the sides of herself as neatly as she could dovetail a drawer.

"Emmeline," Susan pronounced her name like poetry, "come sing with us."

She obediently joined the others around the harpsichord, as out of place as a three-legged stool at a tea table. The song was a familiar one to everyone but her. She whisper-sang, first following the melody, then the harmony, but her singing voice was neither bell-like nor velvety rich, and she faltered. Mr. Morris nodded his encouragement, but his tenor was as bold and bright as a trumpet, something she could never achieve.

When at last the song ended, she escaped to the privacy of the window. Across the road was a large maple tree, its lacy green fingers brushing the sky. There was something thrilling about a fine old tree. Their roots were deep, their trunks strong, but the branches swayed with the grace of the muses. Her fingertips touched the glass, and she whispered, "Love, whose month is ever May, spied a blossom passing fair playing in the wanton air."

"Shakespeare?" Mr. Morris was nearly at her elbow.

She pressed a hand to her chest, willing her heart to slow. She had avoided public recitations since that incident with her uncle. "Yes. Shakespeare." She bit her lip. "May is a fine month for trees, don't you agree?"

He glanced out the window. "Aye. The best. By August, ye forget the trees spend so much of the year barren. In May ye canna take it for granted."

"True. May is the glory of spring. There isn't a trace of winter left, but summer hasn't begun her oppression, either."

Mr. Morris glanced at Charles. "And a few lucky men do find love in May." His eyes, a curious mottling of brown and green, returned to hers. "The rest of us get ta watch."

"We cannot all be storybook heroes. Not at the same time."

"Heroes?" He twisted his lips ruefully. "Is that what it takes, Miss Gardiner?" He shook his head. "Then we common folk have no hope."

"You're as bad as Charles." She wouldn't have dared to scold anyone else. But Mr. Morris, who took everything as a joke, could hardly be hurt by it. "He thinks I cannot discern between ancient myths and modern living. If a man rode down that street today in knightly armor, he would be ridiculous. But our country does need men of conviction who are unafraid to protect our liberties."

A shadow flickered across his face.

"What are you two discussing?" Polly asked, alone on the far side of the harpsichord. Charles stole a kiss from his wife.

The shadow was gone, replaced by a Puckish gleam. "Miss Gardiner was schooling me on love."

Emmeline's mouth dropped open, but his amusement was contagious. "You horrid man." Her voice shook with laughter, and she fought back a smile. She lifted her chin and walked over to Polly. "I was doing nothing of the sort."

Six

HEIRLOOMS

Quill sank into his chair and rested his forehead in his hands, his elbows propped on his desk. The office was unnaturally quiet this afternoon. Charles had taken his work home with him as if he could get anything done with his new wife in the same room. After dinner, Polly had gone to visit her friend, Miss Ray. Quill should be able to get more work done now that he had the office to himself, but dinner with Miss Gardiner had left him as tapsalteerie as a block tumbling down a Jacob's ladder.

His first tumble had begun because he had blushed in her presence. Nay, he had blushed because of her presence. If only he could hide his discomfort like a grown man. Màthair insisted freckles and red hair were blessings from the Creator, but she could not persuade him that blushing for all the world to see was anything but a curse. He could no more hide his mortification from a pretty lass than a schoolboy could hide his hands from the teacher's lash. He rubbed a thumb across old scars, the faded white lines criss-crossing the backs of his hands.

His next tumble had come when she had tripped from the carriage and into his arms. He shouldn't have been holding Charles' cousin. He hadn't planned to. He hadn't dreamed she would fall into his arms. Nay, though he would never admit it to his friend, he had dreamed it, but he hadn't expected it. He had, however, enjoyed it. For one beautiful heartbeat, he had fancied that she was his lass and had longed to be in his arms. Then she had leapt back as though stung by a bee. The reaction told him everything he didn't wish to know. She did not want him. He was forced to watch her roll her trim little ankles with the conviction that there was a reason she hesitated each time he offered his arm in escort. Whatever her dreams were, they did not include touching him.

The final tumble that had knocked him to the bottom of the ladder had come when she had begun talking about heroes. If that was what she dreamed of, there was no hope for him. He wove his fingers into his hair. He shouldn't be thinking of her like this. Shouldn't be wishing the moment he had held her had meant something to her. He owed it to Charles to keep his cousin safe— to drive away unworthy suitors and to catch her when she fell. That was all this could be—all this should be.

As a barrister, he often found himself defending the guilty. He was no white knight, crusading for justice and liberty. What would she think if she knew he was preparing to defend a boy caught stealing sausages? There was no question of guilt. There had been plenty of witnesses. Quill had taken the case out of pity, hoping to soften the verdict. He shook his head, forcing his eyes to focus on the text before him. He was no hero, but he had responsibilities.

There was a tap at the door.

"Come in." He marked a page with his thumb and straightened to greet a client. The door opened. A tall man stepped into the office, his shoulders nearly as wide as the doorframe. "Athair! What brings ye here?" Even after Quill had surprised everyone by growing three inches when he was nineteen, he still had to tilt his head back to meet his father's eye.

"I dinna need an excuse ta see my son, do I?"

Quill's smile was wry. Had Rabbie required so many letters to and from school? So many tutors? So much work in a failed attempt to mold him into a man his father could be proud of? "Nay. I'm always happy ta see ye."

Athair glanced around the empty office. "Do ye have business, now? There's something I'd like ta show ye."

Whatever plans he'd had for the afternoon slunk out the window like a cat on a hot summer day. "I'm all yers." He locked the door and hurried along in his father's shadow.

"Where's Polly?" Athair asked.

"She's visiting a friend." She often spent the afternoons with women of her acquaintance.

"And Rabbie? Have ye seen him of late?"

"Aye, a few days ago, at church. He was well." Quill was surprised his father had come to see him first.

"I understand his business is struggling. 'Tis noble of him to support the ban."

Was his brother being noble when the Committee of Safety ensured each merchant supported the ban? Rabbie was too conscientious to accept smuggled goods, so he relied heavily on what could be grown and made at Willow Haven to fill his shelves. A casual customer wouldn't suspect the merchant behind the abundance was so reduced in his circumstances that he had given up his rented room and now slept on a pallet in the storeroom loft. They were all doing what they could to make it through the ban, though the merchants were most hurt by it. "Was smuggling common when ye were a lad?"

"Aye. The coasts were home to patriotic free traders risking their lives to keep money in Scotland, when England demanded it in taxes. The most dangerous smuggling came during the 'Rising. A man caught smuggling gunpowder would be sent straight ta the gallows."

Quill released a low whistle, grateful his brother wasn't so reckless.

"They were dangerous times," Athair continued. "Anything ta

do with what England called rebellion could get a man hanged for treason."

"Fighting," Quill said, recalling his father's tales of the old country.

"Aye, fighting, but also refusing ta send tax money along ta England or even advocating for armed resistance. Words were dangerous. The right letter in the wrong hands could get a man hanged."

Quill shivered. "Then why do it?"

"Why do it?" There was fire in Athair's eyes. "For the love of yer home and yer family. Or for fear of the alternative: standing by while Englishmen slaughtered yer clan and countrymen."

They continued in silence. Quill had grown up on adventurous stories of the Jacobite Uprising. That's all they were: stories from a different land and a different time. Things like that couldn't happen in Virginia. They just couldn't. His parents had escaped Scotland for the safety of Virginia. They were safe here. He couldn't bear to believe otherwise.

Athair entered the livery stable. Quill followed him past the stalls of horses for hire. He only came here when he needed a nag to visit clients. His father, who bred the finest horses in Tidewater Virginia, would never ride a nag. "Did ye purchase a new horse?" It would explain his eagerness.

"Nay. I've more than I ken what ta do with." He stopped in front of a stall with a handsome gray gelding. He had a sleek hanging mane and moved with the energy of youth. "He's yers."

"I—sir?" He must have misunderstood.

"I've just worked it out with the livery. I'll pay for his keep here and ye can ride him whene'er ye please."

"That's mighty generous of ye." He held his palm out. The gray gelding nuzzled his hand. Even *he* might look heroic riding a horse this fine. Pride swelled in his chest.

"Ye've been generous yerself, taking care of yer sister. And I fancy Gunpowder will be more fit for a gentleman than the old nags ye've been hiring."

"Gunpowder?" His pride burst like a pig bladder on New Year's Day. The Gunpowder Incident had proved he was no hero. The horse's name was salt in the wound.

Athair chuckled. "Pretentious name for a gelding. Yer sister chose it when he was a wee one. Just send word ta the stable and they'll have him saddled whene'er ye need."

Quill didn't trust his voice, so he nodded. He couldn't refuse such a fine gift from his father.

"There's something else," Athair said.

Quill looked up. His father pulled a handkerchief from his pocket and unwrapped it, revealing a tangle of metal so tarnished that if it had fallen in the hearth, there would have been no gleam to distinguish it from the ashes. He set it in Quill's hand. It was heavier than it looked. The splotched silver was cool to the touch. He traced a finger over two intertwined hearts and then across the single crown they shared.

"It was yer màthair's betrothal brooch."

"But—Rabbie." An heirloom like this should have gone to the oldest son.

Athair shook his head. "When ye were born, ye were such a wee bairn we feared we would lose ye. She pinned it ta yer blankets for luck. She would have wanted ye ta have it, ta give ta yer betrothed. 'Twill need some polishing. Yer màthair never trusted anyone else ta do it. After she passed...well...neither did I."

His betrothed. Quill nearly laughed. He wasn't like Charles, pining away for the same woman for a whole year. On occasion, Quill had a fancy overtake him for several weeks, rising and ending suddenly, like a paper catching fire and burning out. He wasn't fool enough to propose marriage during these times. He had few ideas of what he wanted in a marriage, but that was one thing he was sure of—he wanted a love-fire that would never grow cold.

"I kept waiting ta hear ye were courtin' a lass afore giving it ta ye, but it seems ye're more of a chaperone. The ladies are all about ye and ye dinna favor one or the other. There may be a bit of luck left in it. Enough ta bind a heart ta my lad."

Quill took the brooch, wrapped it in his handkerchief, and put it in his pocket for safekeeping. It was a treasure he wouldn't be needing anytime soon. It hadn't been polished in years. It wouldn't hurt to put off polishing it until he had a lass to give it to. The horse, on the other hand, would need regular exercise. It would need to be taken beyond the congested roads of Williamsburg. There was a scenic country lane just south of town that would be perfect for putting a fine horse through its paces. He might even look heroic while doing it.

But did the blasted horse have to be named Gunpowder?

Seven

GUNPOWDER

THURSDAY, MAY 18, 1775

Guilt was an uncomfortable emotion, and Quillan Morris disliked being uncomfortable. "This war would have happened anyway." The House of Lords had sent troops to Boston *before* the raid on the Williamsburg Magazine.

"Mmm." Polly was copying a letter, but there was no one else to talk to. They were alone. Charles was coming in late again.

Guilt prickled like a thorn he couldn't reach. "No one else would have stood another's watch."

Polly looked up. "No one blames ye."

"Miss Gardiner does."

"She said so?"

"Ye were there. At the dinner Charles missed."

"'Twas nigh a month ago. Why are ye defending yerself now?"

"Gunpowder."

Polly laughed and shook her head. "The horse? 'Twas named years ago. Dinna take it so personally."

Quill couldn't think about the horse without remembering his failure at the magazine. "'Twasn't even our watch anymore. Our relief never showed up. Charles and I were right admirable

47

staying on as we did in the middle of a storm. Not even Patrick Henry blamed us for moving ta the tavern window." They had braved the storm for two hours after their assigned watch had ended before moving to the window inside Chowning's Tavern. And a lass who had never stood watch in her life had accused him of abandoning his post.

"Does she blame Lexington and Concord on ye as well?"

"Nay." There was no way he could have prevented that. Even if there had been a way to prevent Virginia's royal governor from raiding the gunpowder and arms in the Williamsburg Magazine, those battles would have happened. The battles had been the same week as the raid on the magazine. No one believed the timing was a coincidence. If Quill had stayed out in the storm, would he have delayed the inevitable attack by one night? Or would he have been the first casualty of war in Virginia? It was easier to see himself as an inconsequential pawn than as a mythical hero.

He glanced at the window. If only Charles were here. A little teasing would do wonders to lift his mood. As he sharpened his quill pen, a faint tune pierced the thin walls. The door swung open and Charles sauntered to his desk, whistling merrily to himself.

Married life agreed with the man. Charles settled behind his desk with a smile that could only be described as smug. "Good morning," he said.

Quill flicked an imaginary speck off a paper. "Ye missed enough of it."

Charles sighed contentedly. "Domestic felicity." He drew the words out luxuriously, the way one might savor Spanish chocolate. "You should try it."

Polly flushed red to her copper hairline and hid her face behind the letter. Quill wasn't embarrassed. He was too... annoyed? Jealous? Not of Susan. But curmudgeonly old Charles had found himself a wife who adored him. Why couldn't he?

Quill had long been telling himself that if he was patient, love would find him. At moments like this, he wondered if love was even looking. Or mayhap it was looking, just not for a short man with a heavy accent and an abundance of freckles. It was cruel of Charles to remind him of what he was missing.

"Did I mention I have a horse?" He was eager for a change in conversation.

"'Tis a fine horse," Polly offered. She had seen it yesterday.

Charles frowned. "You don't have money for that kind of extravagance. You haven't been gaming agai—" he turned to Polly. "He hasn't been gaming again, has he?"

Polly stared at him. "What are ye talking about?"

She was two years their junior. She wasn't privy to the time when he was sixteen and wasted the next year's finances in a short two months. The calculations at the card table had touched his intellect in a way school had failed to. Unfortunately, the thrill of the game had blinded him to the consequences. It had taken the combined efforts of Charles and Athair to save him from himself.

Quill placed one hand on his heart and raised the other. "I havena touched a deck of cards in ten years." Anyone who so thoroughly lost control of himself at the card table had no business gaming.

Charles looked at him in a shrewd way, as though he could see falsehood if he looked hard enough.

Quill put his hands down. "I promised I wouldn't. So I didn't. Polly, have ye ever seen me gaming?"

She cocked her head. "Are we including horse races?"

Traitor.

"Horses are not cards." Besides, it had been years since that had been a problem. Did she have to dredge it up?

Charles waved him away and addressed Polly. "Do tell me about the horse races."

"Our father breeds horses," he cut in, in a final attempt to sweep the topic under the rug. "So there may have been the occasional wager at races."

Polly gave an unladylike snort. "Occasional? 'Twas an obsession. Sneaking away from yer studies, applying yer life savings ta a losing stallion."

Charles had just left for England. Quill had been eighteen and despised law books. And it had only taken three or four races before he'd come to his senses. The wagers affected him the same as the card table. And he couldn't trust himself there. "I learned my lesson. Surely eight years of prudent finances prove that."

Charles looked as though he was considering asking to see a record of Quill's finances covering the last eight years. As his records only went back as far as Polly had been keeping him, Quill changed the subject. "Have ye settled everything about the lessons? Has yer cousin begun?" Before the banns had been read, Charles had persuaded his father to allow Miss Gardiner to teach Kitty, but Quill had heard nothing of it since.

Charles glanced at Polly and back at Quill, annoyance in his eyes. He thought Quill had been indiscreet with the family secrets. Quill shook his head. Polly knew nothing.

Charles relaxed at the inarticulate assurance. "We haven't arranged that. I haven't seen my father since his wedding. I was going to wait until I bought a home in town and could better supervise her comings and goings, but it feels urgent. The less time she spends near my father's wife, the better. I don't want her to think she has a right to Kitty's help. I'm afraid the woman will put up a fuss and change my father's mind. The less opportunity she has to use the girl, the more confident I am of her future." He unlocked his desk and sighed. "I'm getting behind on my work."

"I could do it," Quill said.

"What?"

"I have a horse, remember? It needs exercise. Tell me what ye wanted ta say and I'll go this afternoon." He had been hoping for an excuse to traverse the country lane that ran by the Gardiners' home. An errand to Johnson Hall was perfect. Even Polly wouldn't question his motives. And, with any luck, a certain young lady would see him pass her home. She might even admire how heroic he looked on his fine steed.

~

IT WAS A DELIGHTFUL DAY TO BE ON HORSEBACK. Riding the same roads he usually walked allowed him to see the world with fresh eyes. May was his new favorite time of year. The trees were green. The birds sang. He was neither too hot nor too cold.

A fine horse was as good as a new suit of clothes. He held his head taller. His shoes stayed clean. Several people had nodded approvingly at him as he'd ridden by. He had made too much of the name. Not one person had asked what his horse's name was. They simply admired it.

He was on his way back to town when he saw a familiar face. "Miss Gardiner!" He tipped his hat and was rewarded with a smile above a stack of dirty dishes.

"Mr. Morris. Excuse me a moment." She disappeared into an outbuilding.

Quill adjusted the white cockade on his black hat and brushed a hand across his jacket..

"That won't be necessary." Her voice carried from the kitchen and across the garden. "It's only Mr. Morris."

Only Mr. Morris. Nothing more. He slapped at his breeches, dispelling a cloud of dust. She might have said, "You should see what a fine figure Mr. Morris cuts on horseback."

She came out of the kitchen carrying a tin cup. The gesture was nothing personal. Just the Gardiner hospitality. It was also nothing personal the way he watched her move through the ornamental garden with the grace of a wildflower. It was polite attention for his friend's cousin.

Every lass deserved to be out for at least a year or two before settling down to the responsibilities of marriage and childbirth. Miss Gardiner had been out for only a few months. She had been invited to dinners at the Blue House and had attended only two balls, where she had innocently broken several hearts. She didn't owe him her admiration. She reached over the picket gate to hand him the tin cup.

"Thank ye, Miss Gardiner." He took a sip of cold cider seasoned with nutmeg. "'Tis a fine day."

"Indeed." She glanced about the garden. "The wildflowers must be blooming down by the creek."

"What creek?"

"Hmm? At Johnson Hall. Aunt Vina loved the columbine."

Quill sobered. "Charles' mother?"

"The same. She taught me everything I know about flowers."

Johnson Hall would never be the same without her soft touch. "She was a good woman."

"She was."

Quill finished the cider and cleared his throat. "I'm actually on my way back from Johnson Hall. Yer new pupil begins her studies a week from Monday."

Emmeline looked both flattered and confused. She would break a dozen hearts before the year was out. "My pupil?"

"Aye. Charles did talk ta ye about Kitty, did he not?" The man could be secretive to a fault. Charles would never tell Miss Gardiner that Kitty was as much her cousin as he was. But he should have discussed the role he hoped she would play in her education.

"He did, but *pupil?* It makes me sound like a schoolmaster." There was a lilt to her voice that made him smile. If only his schoolmasters had held his attention the way she did.

"I suspect ye teach better than several of mine did. Ye know the material and ye feel it. Any child would be blessed ta have ye as a teacher."

She blushed. Her coloring barely changed, but she dropped her gaze, and her cheeks dimpled. She was pleased, flattered, and a little shy, all because of something he had said. Her reaction made him pleased, flattered, and a little bold.

He leaned forward in his saddle. The curls that framed her

face danced in the breeze, as light as thistledown. Dare he reach out and touch one? She glanced up, and the moment passed.

He handed her the empty cup. "Thank ye for the hospitality."

"You're welcome. Thank you for bringing me news."

"It was no trouble. My horse needed the exercise."

Her eyes went to the gray gelding. "I didn't know you had a horse. I thought you always hired one."

"My father breeds horses. He insisted he had no use for another gelding and gave this fella ta me." He patted the broad neck.

"That was kind of him." She held the flat of her hand to the broad nostrils. The gelding nuzzled her so hard she fell back a step and laughed. "What's his name?"

Blast. Blast and bother. Quill shifted in the saddle, his eyes settling on the chimney. With resignation heavy in his heart, he said, "Gunpowder."

"Oh." That one little word had never experienced such a range of expression as Miss Gardiner gave it just then. There was a tense silence. "Well," she caressed Gunpowder's muzzle, "he's a handsome fella."

"At least one of us is." The gruff words escaped before he could catch them. She stared at him, mouth round in surprise and uncertainty. He grinned, playing it off as a joke. She gave a half-laugh. He swallowed a sigh.

How had it come to this? He'd known for months that she was a bonny lass with a fine mind. Capable. Dependable. Prayerful. But one stormy night, her virtues were no longer simple arithmetic. They had gone through a complex series of algebraic equations. Suddenly, with her, two and two was twenty.

He had gone to the Gardiners' house to meet Charles on the stormy night they were assigned to stand watch at the Williamsburg Magazine. She had answered the door, the picture of domestic felicity. Her mother's chatelaine hung against her petticoats, sparkling in the firelight while she poured hot cider into his canteen and wrapped it with a cloth to keep it warm through his watch. Her wide-eyed concern had pierced him to the heart. Concern for their country, for Charles, for *him*. He'd fought the impulse to kiss her brow and hold her close until the concern melted away. Instead, he'd quoted Shakespeare, and Charles had fumed. The most innocent of flirtations was forbidden where his young cousin was concerned.

Even if she were twenty-one, it would be folly to court her when her family disapproved. At barely eighteen, crossing her relations was a sure way to end up in court, and not as a barrister. He wasn't such a fool as that. Family, friends, and fancy were best enjoyed in balance. Forsaking one for another made everyone miserable.

He would not be courting Miss Gardiner. Nor would he die of heartache. Fancies like this passed as quickly as they came. The world was full of bonny lasses that wouldn't put him in opposition to his most loyal friend—lasses who wouldn't be forced to choose between family and romance. This consuming attraction would die out any day now. It had long overstayed its welcome.

Eight

NONSENSE & NATURAL RIGHTS

SUNDAY, MAY 21, 1775

Whispering in the balcony drew Emmeline's attention from the prelude music. A gentleman in half-moon spectacles ushered the William and Mary boys, dressed in black school robes, into their pews. She didn't usually pay them any mind, but Mr. Morris' phrasing had stuck with her. She would soon have a pupil, as if she were a grand professor or headmistress, respected in the community as the guardian of the wisdom of the ages. She was pulled from her lofty thoughts when one of the older boys caught her eye and gave her a saucy wink. Her jaw dropped, and he grinned in the most detestable manner. She lifted her chin and faced the podium with affronted dignity. At least her pupils would be girls. Boys were the worst.

Though she would have a small class with only two pupils, she felt the stirrings of enthusiasm in her heart. She had been entrusted to mold young minds, and the possibilities thrilled her. This was the beginning of something wonderful. She had seldom been so impatient for a sermon to conclude, so eager was she to make lesson plans.

After the final amen, the congregation spilled out the double doors and into the sunlight. The palace green was lined with open carriages waiting to escort the gentry home, including Susan and Charles. The women who stepped into these carriages looked as grand as peacocks. She really shouldn't be admiring things so worldly and unpatriotic, especially on the Sabbath, but she couldn't help the feeling of awe that came over her by such a wealth of beauty. She would never possess such fine things, yet it was somehow comforting to know they existed. One fine lady in a gown with more bows than bodice wore her silk hat at a dramatic angle by tying it behind her head instead of under her chin.

"Emmeline!"

She turned and saw Jenny running up to her, a hand on her head to keep her straw hat in place. It was the hat Emmeline had given her friend as a parting gift. She didn't regret the gesture. Not truly. For almost a year, Jenny had been a friend and sister to her. But it still hurt Emmeline's feminine conscience to be seen at church in the limp old hat she was left with. It was one more reason to wish her family would finish visiting and head home, so she could tear the ugly thing from her head.

"Jenny! How are you?"

"Homesick. There are no other young people at the Blue House. I have no one to talk to."

"Neither do I." It wasn't quite true. She talked to Papa in the shop and to Mama in the kitchen. But it wasn't the same as a friend only two years her junior. In the age-based pecking order of young women, Jenny was obliged to be a little in awe of everything Emmeline said and did.

Henrietta dashed between carriages to greet a friend on the green. Sundays were the only times she could see some of her friends. Many people were at their leisure, even more than had fit inside during the sermon, all enjoying a day of rest from their labors and time to exchange news. Mr. Morris was conversing with an elderly spinster in a friendly manner that Plutarch would have called democratic.

Lord Dunmore frowned at a man wearing a hunting shirt and

tomahawk over his Sunday best and gestured his family toward a closed carriage. The oldest boys took their seats beside the driver while their parents and younger siblings sought refuge inside the stuffy carriage. Emmeline frowned.

"What is it?" Jenny asked.

"Nothing. I just think it's too fine a day to be riding in a closed carriage. And Lady Dunmore used to take her time talking with people after church."

Jenny scoffed. "She never had a word to say to either of us, and we're people."

"Indeed, we are," Emmeline said, and resolved not to make the Dunmores' troubles her own. If she had to be stuck on the green in an ugly hat waiting for her family, she might as well enjoy time with her friend. She asked Jenny about her duties at the Blue House and bemoaned their inability to see each other except at church. Then Jenny excused herself to be with her aunt, and Emmeline went in search of her family. Papa appeared to be engaged in an animated conversation with Mr. Hay, another cabinetmaker. She was considering the merits of insisting Henrietta walk home with her now versus getting close enough to listen to Papa's conversation. Listening was all she would do. She wasn't a master cabinetmaker like her father. Mr. Hay wouldn't be interested in anything she had to say.

Mr. Morris interrupted her deliberations with a tip of his hat and a warm smile. "A merry Sabbath ta ye, Miss Gardiner."

She was so surprised she giggled. "Merry?" The word suggested bowls of punch, dancing, and games—things that didn't sound like the Sabbath at all. "I should hope not."

"Merry as the month of May. Happy, if ye prefer. The weather is too fine for gloom."

"Indeed." She cast about for an item of general interest to discuss. "Will you go out riding? Did you ride Gunpowder to church?"

At the mention of his horse, an unmerry shadow crossed his countenance. He must have been quite remorseful of the Magazine Incident if such a little reminder troubled him so. "I did not. It would have been unfair ta Polly who doesna have a mount of her own. I'll take him for a ride later. 'Tis too fine a day ta keep a horse stabled."

Emmeline tucked her lips between her teeth. She hadn't meant to cast gloom on his cheery conversation by reminding him of his Great Disappointment. Would it be better to ignore it or address it? "If I might be so bold—" She paused. Her voice was as timid as she felt. It was too much. She wouldn't say it.

"What is it?"

She shook her head. "'Tis nothing."

He studied her face as though he could see through her. "I'm afraid ye've piqued my curiosity. Will ye no' tell me what is weighing on yer mind?"

"It isn't truly my business, but I wish you wouldn't dwell on it."

"On what?"

"On the Gunpowder Incident. It would have happened eventually."

He gaped with an astonishment that puzzled her. Her assessment wasn't remarkable. She had assumed any reader of the *Gazette* would have reached the same conclusion. How had he not? Recovering his senses, he said, "Do ye believe it would have? Truly?"

She was not above appreciating the compliment of a man of business looking at her as though her opinion carried the weight of a jury's verdict. Her confidence grew, so she said more of what was on her mind. "It was apparent after the battles of Lexington and Concord, wasn't it? Parliament or the king, or maybe both together, must have ordered the confiscation of the best gunpowder stores in the colonies. Why else would the governors of Virginia and Massachusetts order such a thing the same week? If you and Charles had stayed by the gate all night, the king's men might have killed you to get inside. They killed the men in Massachusetts."

"Aye. We would have been martyrs for Virginia."

What a tragically poetic way to die, with the whole country in mourning and tearful maidens scattering flowers over the soft earth of a new grave. But Mr. Morris seemed to prefer a common life to a martyr's death. As for herself, she wouldn't have enjoyed such a grand funeral nearly so much if it had been for people she knew. She would miss her cousin's steady character. As for Mr. Morris, she would miss the bit of sunlight he scattered wherever he went. "I'm glad you are still alive. It's much more pleasant to talk to you than bring flowers to your grave."

His pale brows rose so high they disappeared in the shadow of his hat. Had she offended him? Then he chuckled and said, "I shall take that as a compliment."

"I-I meant it was one," Emmeline said uncertainly.

"What's a compliment?" Polly asked, joining their conversation without greeting them.

"Miss Gardiner prefers me alive ta dead."

Emmeline was appalled by the brash paraphrase, but was afraid that if she spoke again, she might make it worse. People often didn't hear what one meant to say. There was wisdom in silence.

Polly frowned. "How is that a compliment? I prefer everyone alive, even those I prefer to keep at a very great distance. 'Tis so uncomfortable to think of any acquaintance being dead, even the ones you dislike."

"Ah," said Mr. Morris, "but ta die a martyr is almost as noble as living as a hero, and as I have no hopes of earning the esteem of a hero, I must be quite pleased ta have my life valued above a martyr's."

"What nonsense," Polly said.

It was the best sort of nonsense as it gave Emmeline something to think over on the walk home. What was the difference between a martyr and a hero? One was dead and the other lived. But if that were all, then Charles and his friend were heroes by virtue of not dying. That wasn't right. They had left the gate. If they had kept the watch and defended the magazine without dying, they would have been heroes. Neither a hero nor a martyr walked away from the danger. They both risked everything for what they loved. So why did one live and the other die? Was it mere providence, or did a hero possess greater skill? Mayhap Mr. Morris was right. The hero was more noble than the martyr.

Safe in her bedchamber, she tore at the homespun ribbon that bound the misshapen hat to her head. It was tempting to put the ugly thing to bed with a shovel, but it was, alas, her only hat. She hung it from a peg as carefully as if it were covered in silk and feathers. Then she collected the books that had once belonged to Bray School and carried them downstairs.

She sat on the floor of the front room, pulling books from their shelves and sorting them into stacks. There was a whole tower of delicious little Newbery readers, and smaller stacks of history, Shakespeare, other literature, and mathematics. The single volume of science was flat and lonely beside the other subjects. Charles had reclaimed his old school books, so Greek, Latin, logic, algebra, and calculus were not represented.

She thumbed through *Mother Goose's Melody*. The playful old rhymes and maxims with their illustrations caught her attention like they had years ago. There was a tabby cat who might have been Nutmeg, standing on its hind legs and playing a fiddle to the tune, "High diddle diddle." Then there was Little Jack Horner with his old Christmas pie, and Jack Sprat still eating dinner with his wife. How joyful it would be to help a child read these for the first time.

Kitty would need to learn her syllabary before she could read words. How long did that take? Emmeline had learned to read so young that she scarcely remembered standing at Mama's knee and reading the hornbook with its letters, simple syllables, and the Lord's Prayer. It was only a page of learning. She would allow a week for that, then another week for the syllabary before introducing her to playful poetry. Reluctantly, Emmeline returned the Newbery readers to their shelves to await Kitty's literacy.

Henrietta had begun lessons several years ago. She could recite some histories of Rome and Britain. She could read aloud, stumbling over one word in twenty. She could multiply but struggled with fractions. She was a slow learner but was now, like Aesop's tortoise, miles from the start. How was Emmeline to deliver two separate lessons for two students of different ages and abilities?

She thumbed through Henrietta's history book. If they were reading aloud, might both girls study the same history lessons? Then they could share one subject. But Henrietta was halfway through the book. Should she start them both there or go back to the epic tale of 1066?

She was so lost in thought, turning the pages of the books of her childhood, with the fond sentimentality of encountering an old friend, that she didn't hear the table being set for dinner, or her stomach calling for it, until Henrietta stepped amidst the wealth of books open on the floor around her to call her to dinner.

After they had cleaned up from the meal, the family gathered in the front room. At last, the time had arrived to read the precious pamphlet that Papa had bartered for. Emmeline was allowed the honor of reading aloud. When Papa handed her the book, her eyes fell on the printer's name. Though the author had kept his anonymity, the printer's name was printed boldly on the cover: Clementina Rind. What would it be like to have a voice that all of Virginia listened to, even if that voice was just setting the type for another's writing?

A few more words declared this little pamphlet to be intended for the Virginia delegates to the Continental Congress. She sat a little taller. If the word was mightier than the sword, then she held the cavalry in her hand. "America," she read in a strong voice, "was conquered, and her settlements made, and firmly established, at the expense of individuals, and not of the British public. Their own blood was spilt in acquiring lands for their settlement, their own fortunes expended in making that settlement effectual; for themselves they fought, for themselves they conquered, and for themselves alone they have right to hold."

As she read, a fire filled her heart and forged conviction. America was not conquered by the Normans in 1066. This land, baptized by the blood of their ancestors, was theirs. Americans were the equals of the noblest man in England. They would not accept the rule of despotism.

The author was bold and brazen in his assertions, going beyond the polite and measured phrases in the *Virginia Gazette*. He claimed flattery belonged to those who feared and was not "an American art." Here was a courageous hero, leading colonial minds into the light where the sun shone on their natural rights.

"The God who gave us life gave us liberty at the same time," she read with reverence. Might God have preserved the lives of Charles and Mr. Morris for some divine purpose? She prayed God would be as generous in preserving the bounteous liberties he had blessed them with.

Nine

❧

THE UNEXPECTED ESCORT

MONDAY, MAY 22, 1775

"And don't talk to sailors," Mama said as Emmeline tied her straw hat in a bow at the nape of her neck. She couldn't manage the fashionable tilt of the brim without piling her hair high on her head, but at least she could manage her ribbons.

"What if sailors talk to her?" Henrietta asked.

"Then she says no. As long as a lady stays on the main road in broad daylight, the only weapon she needs is a firm no."

Charles and Mama disagreed on Emmeline's safety, but he could no longer run errands for the Gardiners now that he lived in town, and the only troubles she'd ever run into had been avoided by keeping her distance and saying no. She opened the door.

"Are you sure you don't want your cloak? The air is heavy."

It was May. By the time she had walked into town and back, she would just be carrying her cloak. "It isn't cold. I'll be fine." So she set off, swinging a basket from hand to hand as she considered the pamphlet she had read last night. The anonymous author argued that the recent acts against America were void because the

British parliament had no right to exercise authority over the colonies.

Papa, though a tradesman, had the proud privilege of voting. He explained that British landowners elected their representatives to the House of Commons, and Virginian landowners elected their representatives to the House of Burgesses. The two houses were independent of each other, and neither had the right to supersede the other. This truth had been understood and respected from the founding of the first British colony until Parliament had passed the Stamp Act. Since that time, Parliament had persistently threatened the natural rights of America.

Swinging her basket and contemplating the natural rights of her countrymen, she was halfway to town before she noticed nature's signs of an impending storm. A congress of crows had settled in a pasture. Robins and cardinals swept from low branches to the side of the road. Dark clouds were heavy with rain.

She made haste until she got to town, where she couldn't help slowing to admire the window displays: the ribbons and bonnets, silver and delftware, all the beauty the fingertips of man could create from the raw and wonderful resources the Creator had given. It was a joy to see the windows filled again. Dutch ships had taken goods from Holland to America, circumventing the almighty East India Company that parliament favored above its American colonies.

Then she saw The Hat hanging in a window, and stopped walking. It was a proper bergère—a finely crafted straw hat with a shallow crown ornamented with a garden of silk ribbons and rosettes. She admired every twist of ribbon and every pink rosette, so captivated by the beauty that she didn't notice a tall sailor approach her until he spoke in a heavy accent. "Leetle lady. Pretty lady. I buy you drink." He pointed down the street to the coffeehouse.

"Oh." She stepped back and looked up. It was the same vast Dutch sailor who had asked for directions a few days ago, with the same pale blond hair and deep tan. She felt as small as David before Goliath. "No, thank you." She gave a brisk curtsy and walked on, hoping he wouldn't follow.

She made it to the printer without incident and breathed a sigh of relief. This shop was like a second home with the scent of wet ink and new paper. Printing must have been a messy business, because George the apprentice had nary a clean spot on his apron nor his fingertips, which leafed through a book, searching for the Gardiner family's account. Her eyes devoured the titles on the shelves behind him. She had read some. The others beckoned to her like sirens called to sailors, but she was trusted to spend only enough to settle the family accounts and purchase a few household necessities. Tooth powder was essential. Fancy hats and new books were frivolous.

At last, George was ready for her coin. Once that account was settled, she visited the butcher and a dry goods store. Her coin purse was lighter and her basket much heavier as she turned toward home on a path that led her dangerously close to her cousin's office. The Sign of the Eagle swung back and forth on its hinges, ready to fly away on the wind. She passed on the opposite side of the street, hoping to escape Charles' notice. It wasn't her fault that Mama sent her to town unescorted. She didn't need to endure her cousin's concern—a concern that would multiply if he ever learned a sailor had tried to buy her a drink.

Her stomach rumbled, and she wished she were already home and sitting down to dinner. Her one comfort was that if she were hungry, then Charles had likely already left the office for dinner. He couldn't tell his wife that Emmeline had been all about town without an escort if he didn't know. She didn't mind doing the shopping, but she did mind being seen as a rustic by her genteel relations.

The wind pushed her petticoats faster than she could keep up with them. She shivered, looking up at the heavy, dark clouds. Mama was right. She should have worn a cloak. A cat hissed, its hair on end, and darted across the street and through a window just before it closed. Lightning flashed. A horse tossed its head restlessly, and a dog trotted down an alley and into a stable. Thunder rumbled. She quickened her pace, anxious to be home before the heavens opened. Scattered sounds, like acorns falling on a roof, drew her eye heavenward. Tiny white balls bounced on rooftops and fell to the ground.

Hail.

A small stone struck her shoulder. The beasts, wiser than humans, where comfort was concerned, had already cleared the streets. Belatedly, the people scattered. Emmeline needed to find shelter, but where? She was too far from home. The Blue House was several blocks away. Along this road, there were only the homes of strangers and businesses she couldn't afford to patronize. She had learned the folly, a year or two back, of entering a shop without money or object. Merchants watched her in the most unnerving way as she looked over their wares, as though they suspected she might pocket something.

The old shame of their silent accusations decided her. There was no help for it. She would have to brave the sting of hailstones and hope the storm passed quickly. She clutched her basket tightly and walked faster, the wind pushing her down the street. She sent a wordless prayer heavenward, grateful that the wind was at her back. The storm could be much worse.

Then the hat flew off her head and sailed down the street. She started to run after it as lightning flashed again. When the thunder rumbled itself out, the hail had lost its acorn-soft sound. A pane of glass shattered nearby, and she was pummeled by hailstones as big as Spanish dollars.

"Miss Gardiner!" A friendly voice shouted above the storm. She whipped around, squinting into the wind. Mr. Morris, his head ducked low, was running through the empty street. Barely slowing when he reached her, he threw an arm around her shoulders, protecting her bruised flesh from the sting of hailstones.

"This way!" He pulled her along.

"But my hat!"

He must not have heard over the thunder of falling ice, and she hurried along with him, head down, conscious, as he was not, of how this arrangement pressed them together. He threw open a door with his free hand and pushed her inside. A small crowd had gathered under this roof. Sailors mingled shoulder to shoulder with Virginians and sailors of every race and creed. He closed the door behind them, and the storm softened to a dull roar, the stones attacking the roof like a castle under siege. They were safe.

"Are ye alright?" His breath came short.

"I—I think so." She was a little shaken and surprised to find herself standing so close to strangers, so close to Quillan Morris, and dizzy from the aroma of baked goods she couldn't afford. She tried not to think of the nearness of food when her dinner was miles away. She brushed her shoulders and ran her fingers down her kerchief, finding a hailstone within the folds of fabric. It bounced when it hit the ground.

Mr. Morris caught her hand, turning her arm, which was bare below the elbow. "Ye're bruised." So she was. Most of the tenderness hid out of his sight, speckling her back and shoulders.

"What about you?" The image of him running through a hailstorm to reach her was engraved in her mind. How had she ever thought him lacking conviction?

"Nothing ta speak of. We Scotsmen may no' look like much, but we're sturdy." He cheerfully dismissed what it had cost him to run through the storm to pull her inside. He may have been built like a bureau—thick, square, and homey—but thick bones and broad muscles were under the skin. They weren't armor. He had sheltered her from the hailstones with his body and taken the bruises meant for her.

Lightning flashed through the windowpanes. The storm was just getting started. "I should have hastened my errands." She should have been nearly home. Her parents would worry. And when Mama worried, she scolded.

"Better ta be safe. We'll just have our dinner while we wait." He took her hand, pulling her past those using the bakery as shelter from the storm toward the counter, while her feet followed and her mind raced. There was a little left in the coin purse, but it wasn't hers to spend. It was the family's. Was Mr. Morris offering to pay? Should she let him? The Gardiners offered charity. They didn't take it. But he was a family friend. Surely that made this different. She couldn't reason out how, when her head was dizzy and her knees were weak from the aroma of yeast and flour.

At the counter, he released her hand. She almost wished he hadn't. There had been something like friendship in the gesture, something that had thawed the icy loneliness that had pelted her in the street. It was a simple comfort she hadn't known to desire, as simple and essential as a breeze in summer or a fire in winter. The next time her heart ached, she would long for Mr. Morris to hold her hand.

Her unexpected escort was considering the rows and baskets of baked goods while the baker struggled to communicate with a tall blond sailor. Emmeline shifted her basket and stepped behind Mr. Morris, watching the interaction over his shoulder.

The sailor pointed at a basket of small sweets. "Cookie." He held up three fingers.

"How many times do I have to tell you foreigners? That's a tea cake. Tea caaaaake."

"Ja." The sailor pointed again at his selection. "Tea cake cookie."

She stifled a giggle. The baker sighed as he took Dutch coin and handed the sailor three tea cakes. Emmeline's amusement vanished as the baker turned their way. "Mr. Morris," he said, "what will it be?"

"I'm still deciding." He turned to her. "What do ye fancy?"

"Oh." She twisted her hands about the basket handle. How much did everything cost? What could he afford? She would hate to accidentally select something priced too dear. "I'm not sure."

"Shall I choose for ye?"

"Yes, please." At least then she would know what he had meant to offer.

"Two meat pies," he told the baker. Then he grinned. "And two of those cake cookies. Put it on my account."

"Yes, sir." The baker flipped pages in an account book, then handed Mr. Morris the baked goods. He parted the crowd, leading her to a corner by the window. She stood backed up to the wall. Susan could say all she wanted about ladies claiming the space God gave them, but she wasn't sharing one room with half of Williamsburg.

He handed her a meat pie as big as her hand and leaned against the windowsill, the tea cakes beside him. The view of the street blurred as the hail melted and trickled down the windowpanes. She held the pie by the crimped edge of its golden crust. He took a large, savoring bite of his pie. She nibbled at the pastry. This was too good to be true. She had wanted food so badly that she had imagined it into being. But as her hesitant bites reached the meat and potatoes, she gave a little sigh of contentment.

"Good?" Mr. Morris asked around a mouthful.

"Mmhmm."

After that, they enjoyed their dinner in companionable silence as the weakening hail plinked against the glass. She finished her meal as contented as Nutmeg napping in a patch of sun. She ought to thank God in all the poetic glory of the prayer book for her exceedingly great blessings. There were so many beautiful hymns and prayers. If only the writers had included "A Prayer for Thanksgiving for Deliverance from Hunger and Hailstorm." She closed her eyes and composed a prayer pieced together from the beautiful phrases engraved on her heart.

"O Eternal Lord God, who spread the blue canvas of heaven and by thy word sends forth the wind, I give thee humble thanks for my deliverance. We went through thunder and hail, and thou brought us out into a wealthy place. My soul hungered and my body ached, but in thy tender mercy I have been filled with goodness. I beseech thee to continue thy loving-kindness upon me, through Jesus Christ our Lord. Amen."

An amen echoed hers, and she looked up at Mr. Morris in

surprise. She had thought her whispered prayer wouldn't be heard above the noise and commotion of the bakery. "I forgot to say grace," she said, by way of explanation. She ought to thank her mortal deliverer as well. He had been instrumental in her comfort. Before she could compose her gratitude, a voice caught her attention.

"Leetle lady." The Dutchman, standing in the middle of the room, head and shoulders above the crowd, had seen her.

"Oh dear," Emmeline murmured. Mr. Morris glanced from her to the tall man approaching her. The sailor smiled down at Emmeline. It would have been a pleasant smile if it hadn't been aimed at her. "Pretty lady, eat cake cookie?" He offered her one of his tea cakes.

She had refused to accompany him for drinks. That had been difficult enough. It felt more rude to reject a sweet when he was so cheerfully presenting it to her. But Mama had insisted she say no. How could she refuse politely? She glanced about, desperately, her eyes pleading with Mr. Morris. *Help me.*

He studied her a moment, then addressed the sailor, enunciating slowly. "*My* pretty lady. *My* pretty lady eats *my* cookie."

Emmeline held her breath. The Dutchman looked taken aback. He inclined his head toward her. "Sorry." Then he returned to his companions and said something in Dutch that made the men laugh.

She sighed. "Twice in one day. But I didn't mean to make you dishonest."

"Twice? You met him earlier?"

"Yes." She wrinkled her nose. "He wanted to buy me a drink. I said no, of course."

"He what?" Mr. Morris shook with laughter. "Sailors have a funny idea of how ta treat a lady. But back ta what ye were saying. 'Twas the truth." He handed her a tea cake. "Polly always called them pocket cakes, because that's where she tucked hers, but I like cookie."

Emmeline liked it, too, but only when Mr. Morris said the

funny word. She took a dainty bite. The flavor was subtle and elegant, with a hint of rosewater and cardamom, not like the ones she enjoyed at home, heavy with woodsmoke.

Mr. Morris watched her with dancing eyes. Then he leaned forward and said, "My pretty lady eats my cookie."

Emmeline flushed. "But I'm not—"

"Mine? Ye are my friend's cousin. Ye are mine in that sense, if no other."

"I meant pretty."

His eyes moved appreciatively over her wind-tousled appearance. "Indeed, ye are. And until this storm is over, ye're *my* pretty lady."

Heat crept up her cheeks. He wasn't drunk. He was no smarmy stranger. He was Charles' old friend. There was nothing he could want from her. So why would he call her pretty? And with such sincerity? There was only one rational reason. He was Mr. Morris, and Mr. Morris teased.

"And I'm yer freckle-faced Scotsman. 'Tis like a dance. We belong ta each other until the music stops. I'm honor-bound ta keep ye safe and fed. And ye willna accept gifts from other men. We'll enjoy a tête-à-tête and laugh at each other's jokes." He paused in mock-solemnity. "I apologize for no' taking the time ta ask ye properly. Under the circumstances, it seemed prudent ta rush that part."

"Under the circumstances, I appreciate the haste." Flirtation or no, he was still the same Mr. Morris: self-deprecating, playful, and safe. He hadn't just pulled her out of the storm. He had placed one brawny arm around her shoulders, placing himself between the danger and her. He could say all the nonsense he pleased. She was safe with him.

The hail, which had died down while they were eating, returned with renewed vengeance, hammering at the roof, the door, and the paneglass windows. Shattering glass—the sound Aunt Vina's hand mirror had made when it hit the ground— made her cry out and leap back. Mr. Morris, no more troubled than if a cat had been pawing for attention, looked behind him at a broken window pane. "That was unexpected." With one pane gone, the roar of the storm was louder.

"Are you hurt?"

"Nay, lass. I'm not tall, but I'm sturdy. It will take more than a few hailstones ta hurt me." He took a step toward her, angling himself between her and the missing windowpane.

"Morris!" A man with a sharp nose and thin lips interrupted their cozy tête-à-tête. "I almost didn't see you hiding in the corner with a pretty girl. Dashed inconvenient weather we're having. It's going to be a poor year for tobacco if this storm spreads out of town."

"Miss Gardiner, this is Mr. Patrick Henry of the House of Burgesses. Mr. Henry, this is Miss Gardiner, a friend of the family."

Emmeline, in her shock, only just managed a courteous greeting. This man in buckskin breeches was the greatest orator of the modern age, the one who had stirred Virginians' blood with his cry, "Give me liberty, or give me death!" His name appeared regularly in the *Gazette*. He was the man who had confronted the royal governor after the Magazine Incident, demanding reparations. He was part of the body of men who had selected Virginia's representative to the Continental Congress. He was a man she could now claim as an acquaintance, thanks to Mr. Morris, who was speaking to Mr. Henry in his usual open manner, as though the man were a friend and an equal.

"I trust Mason has spoken to you?"

Mr. Morris frowned. "Not recently. I haven't seen him in a month."

"Dash it all, we need an answer. Maids listening at every keyhole. I'll give my life for this country, but there's no need to be reckless about it. If he doesn't find you, then I will."

Emmeline, despite her rapt attention, couldn't make any sense of the passionate speech of the great orator.

Mr. Morris looked almost as perplexed as her. "What did you want an answer to?"

Henry looked scandalized. "Not here, man. Not where anyone can hear. We must be ready for anything."

"Anything? Has Mr. Randolph not returned then?"

"Tomorrow, if things go as planned. There's to be a grand fireworks display in celebration."

This much, Emmeline understood, though her mind was whirring from the rapid conversation. Mr. Peyton Randolph, Esquire, had presided over the Continental Congress. Everyone was eagerly awaiting his report and speculating on whether or not the ban on imports would be lifted.

"Look at that!" Henry said. "The storm's let up. Talk to Mason. I expect an answer." With that, Mr. Henry took his leave.

Mr. Morris stared after him for a somber moment. Then he shook his head and smiled. "I believe, Miss Gardiner, ye said something about yer hat."

She accepted his arm. The esteemed Patrick Henry was anxiously awaiting an answer, but first, Mr. Morris was going to help a young woman of no consequence find her ugly, lost hat. How peculiar that he esteemed her petty concern above the demands of a burgess. She would have protested, but she found herself loath to leave him.

Ten

RABBIE'S STORE

Quill found a muddy straw hat caught against a hitching post, trampled by horses, battered by hail, and covered in mud. It drooped as she picked it up. "Ohhh." The woe in her voice threatened to break his heart like the mew of a half-drowned kitten.

"Leave it."

"But it's my only hat. Without it..." Her voice trailed off, and she traced a finger down her delicate nose, her lips rounded in a pout.

He stared, suddenly itching to trace his finger down her nose and kiss her for good measure. He fisted his hands and stepped back. This was Charles' cousin. He shouldn't be longing to kiss her. Once this fancy passed, he would be glad he hadn't acted on his impulses. He took the hat from her and dropped it on the hitching post where some impoverished soul would find it. "Ye're my lass until ye're safe at home. I promised I'd care for ye and I will." The pronouncement sounded noble, but the truth was that he couldn't bear to leave her. After a miserable month of unrequited adoration, her smiles had finally turned his way like glorious beams of sunlight kissing the earth after a storm.

Tomorrow, he would think of her with the polite disinterest

her family would deem appropriate. Tomorrow, that would be easy, because this impossible fancy would at last have run through its supply of fuel and burned out. But this was today, and today he was entranced by the light and warmth of a flame too small to hurt anyone.

Miss Gardiner cast a last doleful look at the muddy hat but shifted the basket to the other hand and took his arm before he had the presence of mind to offer it. The hesitation to accept his escort, to accept the little touches encouraged by propriety, was not only gone, but reversed. Something had changed. Heavens above, something had changed.

They walked slowly. The street was littered with twigs, branches, and hailstones as big as pigeon eggs. Rays of sunlight broke through the clouds and shone off wet buildings and bushes. Williamsburg glowed as deep and rich as the colors in Màthair's oil paintings.

"Look!" She squeezed his arm and gestured with the basket. A double rainbow arced over the town. "Do you think Noah's rainbow was that big?"

"At least. His storm lasted forty days and forty nights."

"I wonder what God is promising us. It must be something big and beautiful."

Did God offer new promises? Since childhood, he had understood every rainbow to be a reminder of the promise made to Noah. That was the theology of rainbows. Scholars preferred Newton's scientific approach to optics, but she was musing on something more revolutionary than rays of light. Like a lad reciting his catechism, he repeated what every Christian child knew. "He promised Noah He would no' destroy the world by flood again."

"That's it." Each of the sunlight's seven sacred rays danced across her brow and the wild curls that had multiplied in the storm. Her face was as radiant as revelation. "We won't be destroyed when the king's troops come." She said it with such confidence he half believed her.

"Are the troops coming?"

She glanced at him in surprise. "We're at war, aren't we? It's only a matter of time."

Aye, they were at war. The king had dispatched troops. But he hoped that the quarrel would remain in New England and that Virginia would remain untouched. He was patriotic enough to disagree with Charles but not patriotic enough to hope for death.

He put aside his gloomy thoughts when he saw the windows of Rabbie's store. Each pane of glass was intact. At least his brother had been spared that difficulty. "Here we are."

She looked about them. "Where?"

He pointed to the lettering above the door: Robert Morris' Store. "We're going ta pay a call on my brother." He pushed the door open. "Afternoon, Rabbie. Do ye remember Miss Gardiner? I introduced ye on Twelfth Night."

Rabbie, dust cloth in hand, bowed in greeting. "Aye, I remember. Johnson's bonny cousin. Miss Gardiner, what made you take pity on my brother and be seen in public with him?"

"What? Oh, no! I assure you, he was the one who took pity on me."

Rabbie sent Quill an inquiring look.

"The storm caught her by surprise. I just took her ta shelter."

"Well then, what brings you here?"

"Miss Gardiner's hat was lost in the storm. She needs a new one."

"But I can't!" she exclaimed, much distressed.

"Dinna be daft," Quill said. "What did I tell ye? Ye're my lass this afternoon. Ye lost it on my watch. I'll not see ye hatless all summer." He tapped her nose. She blinked in surprise, but there was no need to keep his hands fisted at his sides when they had a chaperone. "Yer dainty nose would burn and 'twould be all my fault."

"I'm all out of British millinery," Rabbie said, in that infuriatingly perfect English he used in public, "but I have sourced some local craftsmen who are quite skilled at their trade." Not as tall as

Athair, he used a stepladder to get down two hats hung near the ceiling. He stepped back down and offered them to Miss Gardiner, who bit her lip. Was she worried about the expense? It was just a straw hat. Quill picked one up and dropped it on her head, then added the second hat.

She took them both off and studied them.

"We need a sturdy ribbon, or the wind will steal her hat away afore she gets home."

"I can do sturdy. I sold the last silk months ago. All we have is homespun."

"I like homespun," she offered.

Quill chuckled. One couldn't grow up with seven sisters and not understand silks and muslins. No lass preferred homespun when there were finer fabrics available. "Ye're a fine patriot. Ye'll make the Continental Congress proud."

Rabbie offered ribbons colored with local dyes: walnut brown, deep indigo, a softer blue, and drab, undyed cotton. Miss Gardiner's eyes lit up when the soft blue was presented. Then her jaw set, like a soldier bracing himself for battle, and she reached a tentative finger for the undyed cotton.

Quill reached across her. "Have ye ever seen such a bonny blue?" He unfurled the colorful ribbon and held it between them. "Almost as bonny as yer eyes."

She dimpled, clapped her hands to her cheeks, and dropped her gaze to the floor. He had flattered and flustered her all at once.

He was suddenly as cocky as a new barrister winning his first brief. "We'll take this one." He returned the ribbon to Rabbie, who raised his brows, glanced between Quill and the blushing lass, but blessedly kept his silence as he cut a generous length of ribbon, long enough to ornament the hat as well as tie it in place.

"There you are, miss," Rabbie said, handing it to her.

"Thank you."

While Miss Gardiner arranged the ribbon, Quill spoke to his brother. "Have ye seen Mason? I heard he was looking for me."

"Is he in town again?" Their brother-in-law's family had a fine brick home in Williamsburg. He came and went as his fancy dictated.

"Patrick Henry seemed ta think so."

Rabbie sighed and rubbed his brow. Patrick Henry was second only to Jack Mason when it came to radical patriotism. Henry had persuaded the Virginia Convention to raise a volunteer army. Leave it to Mason to drag the family through mud and fire to fight a threat that might never appear. Leave it to Rabbie to feel responsible about it.

Quill hated to see his brother worried. He turned the subject to happier matters. "Have ye seen Athair of late?"

"Aye. Just this week." Rabbie slipped from the king's English to the highland brogue they were raised on. "Ye willna believe what he had ta say." He lowered his voice and leaned over the counter. "He wants me ta marry. Now. With the ban on imports and business so poor."

"There were Dutch sailors in the bakery. Did they no—"

Rabbie cut him off. "I got linen thread, toothpowder, and some delftware. That's all. They didna have much else, and what they had I could scarce afford."

They must have had more. It made no sense for a merchant ship to make the crossing with an empty hold. Mayhap they had sold the bulk of their goods to the larger stores in Williamsburg and York Town and only offered Rabbie what was left.

Rabbie continued to share his grief. "Athair forgets a man needs ta establish his business afore he can support a family. I canna marry—" The door swung open and he straightened to greet a customer, only to have his pleasant facade crumble to annoyance when Jack Mason sauntered in.

Mason grinned. "Looks like I caught two birds with one stone."

Quill frowned at his brother-in-law. "Is Catriona in town with the wee bairns?"

"She is." He didn't elaborate on the health and happiness of his wife and children. "Rabbie, we need your storeroom. A Dutch ship just brought—"

Rabbie clapped a hand over Mason's mouth. Through clenched teeth, he whispered, "Three can keep a secret if two of them are dead," then glanced meaningfully over at Miss Gardiner, who had wandered to the other side of the store to tie her hat, as though anticipating the family's need for privacy.

"Quill," Rabbie said, "watch the store for me. I need to see to something in the storeroom."

"I need him, too," Mason said.

It was better to get this over with. "Miss Gardiner," Quill said, "do let us know if a customer enters."

Once in the storage room, Rabbie glared at their brother-in-law. "Are ye trying to get us all hung for treason? Have some sense, man."

Quill was still in the dark. "What is this all about?"

Mason beamed like a child with a new toy, not like a man bound for the gallows. "The Dutch just brought a whole shipful of arms: cannons, gunpowder, firearms, everything. We just need a place to hide everything for now, and this storeroom," he scanned the vacant shelves with pleasure, "is perfect." He frowned and walked over to a small puddle. "You'll need to fix your roof right away. The powder has to be kept perfectly dry."

Rabbie crossed his arms. "I'm not storing gunpowder."

"We already have the cannons hidden and most of the arms. Gunpowder is what needs to be stored."

"I will not endanger my family," Rabbie announced with furious diction.

"What family?" Mason asked. "You're a bachelor."

"I have a younger brother and seven sisters who are my responsibility if anything happens to our father."

Quill frowned. He wasn't a child. He could care for himself and a sister or two.

"Five sisters," Mason retorted. "The married ones don't count."

Quill countered, "They do if their husbands are executed for treason."

Mason waved away his concern. "My family will take care of her and the children if yours cannot. Now, as long as the weather clears, we'll bring the gunpowder on the morrow. The Dutch want it off their ship as soon as possible." Naturally, they would like to be rid of the volatile substance. It was a dangerous thing to transport and store.

"They will not bring it here," Rabbie said.

"But—"

"This is my whole livelihood. I sleep in this storeroom. I will not have it filled with powder that could explode if I drop my candle. If you want it stored so badly, risk your own neck."

Mason didn't take no easily. He argued his side until he was red in the face, but Rabbie held his ground.

"If ye'll excuse me," Quill interrupted at last, "I should be getting Miss Gardiner home." He wasn't certain how long she would wait before leaving without him.

"Not yet, you don't." Mason turned his glare to Rabbie. "Go tend your store. I would hate for you to risk your neck by over-hearing something sensitive."

Rabbie left Quill to deal with Mason's remaining demands.

"I'll get straight to business," Mason said. "Since Dunmore is in town, we have to prepare quietly. We need a place to meet."

"Any burgess would have a larger home than I."

"Only a couple have places in town. And those homes are crawling with servants who could spread rumors."

"Then use the Apollo."

"Same problem. Anyone could come in and out."

"What do ye want from me?"

"The Eagle."

"I beg yer pardon?"

"Your office, under the Sign of the Eagle, is perfect."

That office he shared with Charles, whose loyalist sympathies were too pronounced to tolerate sharing it with radical patriots.

"The answer is nay." Quill marched out of the storeroom, ignoring the protests behind him. It was one thing to share a dinner table with his radical in-law. It was something else to expect Charles to understand why their office needed to support the men who were forming an army to fight their mother country. He didn't understand it himself. The whole point of the ban on imports was to find a nonviolent solution to their differences with England. Rushing to arms when there was still a possibility a truce could be reached was foolhardy.

Rabbie and Miss Gardiner broke off talking when Quill walked into the room.

"Miss Gardiner. I'm sorry ta have kept ye waiting."

"It's not a problem," she said. "I'm sure you had something important to discuss. I should be getting home," she added. "Thank you for your time. And for...for everything." She was saying goodbye.

"Do ye think I'm as fickle as the weather? I willna leave yer side until ye're safely home, not with all these foreign sailors in town."

She accepted his arm. As they left the store and walked into the sunshine, he left the storm clouds of contention behind. This afternoon, he had a strange and wonderful feeling that she was his lass, and he was her lad. The feeling would pass soon, but he would savor it while it lasted.

Miss Gardiner broke the silence. "Is that the Mason that Mr. Henry was talking about?"

Quill looked at her intelligent face, wondering how much she had overheard and understood. "Aye. He's married to my sister Catriona. They have two wee bairns: Brodie and baby Jean."

She tipped her head and mimicked his inflection, "Bairns?"

"Bairns," he repeated. "Children. Brodie is a wee lad of three, and Jean was born this past Christmastide."

"I didn't know you were an uncle."

"I assure ye, 'twas through no fault of my own."

Her musical laughter assured him she wouldn't inquire further into Mason's business.

Too soon, they were at her front steps. She stepped back and swung the basket to her other hand. "I've taken so much of your day, and you've been so very kind. I don't know whether to apologize or thank you."

Witnessing her sweet gratitude fanned the flame in his heart to dangerous new heights. The shift didn't alarm him. Every flame blazed brighter before it died. "Dinna be daft. 'Twas my pleasure." He pressed a kiss to her cheek. It might have been a brotherly gesture, but he had never felt less like a relation than now, with her lips only a breath away. He pulled back before he did something he couldn't confess to Charles. "I'll let yer father know ye're home." That was the gentlemanly thing to do. "I suppose he's in the shop."

He took one backward step. Then two. With each step, the ache in his heart grew. He needed to know when he would see her again. "The fireworks are tomorrow. Will I see ye there?"

"I don't know if I'm going. I'll try. I would like to be."

"Then I'll be looking for ye." He tipped his hat and waited for her to shut the door before he turned to the workshop. Her father was about to discover that Quill had spent the afternoon alone with his daughter. He needed to guard his expressions as precisely as Rabbie guarded his speech.

Eleven

ARDENTLY

"Why are ye smiling?" Polly asked for the second time that morning.

"'Tis nothing," Quill said, hiding the offending expression behind a law book. He had given Polly a bland explanation for where he had been the previous day. His account was true, if incomplete, but this affair of the heart would be easier to sweep under the rug if no one suspected it had happened.

Charles opened the door to the office, and Quill dropped the book.

Polly ignored his peculiar behavior. "How is the Blue House?" she asked Charles. "Was it damaged by the storm?"

"We lost a few panes," he said as he hung his hat, "before we got the shutters secured. Susan's aunt is not pleased. She had just gotten the broken window in the dining hall fixed in time for the wedding. After that hailstorm, everyone needs windowpanes. It may be months before repairs can be made." His concerns were as practical and irrefutable as the optimism Quill countered them with.

"'Twould be a travesty in December, but this late in spring, open windows and cooling breezes are counted a blessing."

"Not if one's wife is recovering from the seasoning." Charles unlocked and opened his desk. "What about you? Did you close the shutters in time?"

"He wasn't there," Polly said with a trace of annoyance, "so I closed them."

Charles looked at his friend with a gaze that had uncovered any number of youthful follies, and the truth spilled from Quill like milk from a child's upset cup. "She had a headache and wished ta lie down afore dinner, with the curtains drawn and everything quiet-like, so I thought I'd take Gunpowder out for some exercise while she rested, but the storm blew up afore I made it ta the stable, and then—" He paused in his retelling. *Then* was the moment he had seen Miss Gardiner pelted by hailstones. He had given no thought to his sister and how the storm might aggravate her headache. His only thoughts had been for Miss Gardiner. She was alone. She was in danger. There was no way on earth or heaven he could have returned home at that moment. But how was he to tell that to Charles? Quill feared his fancy for his friend's cousin would reveal itself if he even spoke her name. He hadn't been able to hide his smile from Polly. What would Charles say if he knew his trusted friend had held his young cousin's hand, placed an arm around her shoulder, bought her dinner, uttered any number of little compliments, and enjoyed every moment?

"I took shelter in the bakery," he said, skipping over everything that had made the afternoon beautiful and glorious. "Then I went ta see how Rabbie had fared. He has a small leak in his roof, right over the storeroom, but his windowpanes are undamaged." He didn't say a word about Miss Gardiner, Jack Mason, or Dutch ships smuggling gunpowder and firearms into the colonies.

His conscience squirmed at the evasion. He told Charles everything. He always had. Well, almost always. He had kept his sisters' secrets. He also hadn't confessed to the horse racing, but that had happened while Charles was gone. He was here now, and his deep blue eyes had a way of penetrating Quill's thoughts, a trait that ran in the family.

He turned back to his desk, away from that quiet, steady gaze that invited confidences, and said, "Did ye hear there are ta be fireworks on the green when Mr. Randolph returns?"

"I did," Charles said shortly.

"Will ye be coming? Ye can show yer wife the best Williamsburg has ta offer."

There was a moment's hesitation before Charles said, "No."

"No?" Quill echoed, turning back.

"No. With the current tensions, it would be unwise to appear to support the Continental Congress by having a celebration when its president returns."

It had never occurred to Quill not to enjoy fireworks. He had attended last year's display to welcome Lord Dunmore's wife and children. Not a soul had suggested it would be unwise to appear to support the royal governor. Then again, so much had changed in a year. At Charles' wedding, he had overheard a man declaring that it would be unpatriotic to acquire a marriage license through the royal governor and that all Virginians, even the dissenters, should publish their banns through the Anglican Church.

Charles turned to his work without further discussion, and Quill followed his lead. That was something else that had changed in the last year. For years, he had floundered as a barrister, barely earning enough to cover his modest expenses. Despite having many acquaintances, he had few clients. The boy he had hired as a clerk had stopped coming into work. It hadn't mattered much, as there wasn't enough work to keep Quill busy, much less require a clerk to assist him. Then Charles had returned. Within a matter of weeks, his workload had doubled. His friend had always commanded trust and respect. By sharing an office, the community's esteem of Quill had risen quickly, and he found himself handling more important briefs and winning success in the courts.

All of this had been a miracle. Shortly before Charles' return,

Polly had come to town unexpectedly, and Quill had taken rooms he feared he wouldn't be able to afford. Then Charles had come and saved him, just like old times. Only this time, Charles hadn't known his friend had been in trouble. And Quill wouldn't tell him. He had spent his entire youth being rescued from a series of scrapes. To finally have the respect of his old friend in matters of business was worth more than a thousand briefs.

The morning passed quietly, with the occasional rustle of paper or question for his clerk. Underneath the dull work was a secret hum of pleasure. Miss Gardiner had blushed at his compliment, had taken his arm like she had a right to it, and had said, after he had kissed her cheek, that she hoped to attend the fireworks. It was impossible not to smile over cases of theft and forgery with memories like that.

In the early afternoon, when he had grown stupid from hunger and couldn't reason with the words on the page, Polly rose abruptly.

Quill yawned and stretched. "Is it dinner time already?"

"Do ye hear that?" She threw the office door open.

Church bells clanged in the distance.

"What—"

"Mr. Randolph has returned."

Quill glanced at Charles, who was corking his inkwell. Following his lead, he tidied his desk and locked the papers away. He would have been content to dine promptly, but Polly had promised to meet a friend on the green when Mr. Randolph returned.

After a brisk walk, they could see the crowd and the cavalry gathered at the end of the Palace Green. As one, it cried, "Huzzah, for Peyton Randolph, the Father of our Country!" It was true, then. Mr. Randolph had returned, and the fireworks would be tonight, and Miss Gardiner might be there.

What did it matter? It wasn't as if he would get to enjoy the fireworks with her by his side. His imagination, rather than accepting the dismissal, teased him with a comfortable image of himself doing just that, watching the wonder on her face and the reflection of a thousand lights in her eyes, her hand squeezing his arm with the thrill of it all. *Blast, bother, and bewilderment.* He wanted nothing more than to pursue this little folly and see where it led him. But reason had already shown him where it would lead: heartache for him and her, and losing a friend who had been his anchor through the turbulent years of his youth and childhood. He wouldn't court a lass whose family didn't approve of him as a suitor. And she was as bad for him as he was for her. A shy young lass with no dowry and no connections could do nothing to secure his place in society. Instead, she would be a bonny burden. She would one day make a fine wife for a man who didn't need a dowry or connections—someone who was capable and steady and knew where he was going. That kind of man could afford to follow his heart and choose an impractical bride. He wouldn't need to lean on his woman. She could lean on him.

Quill frowned for the first time since kissing her cheek. Thinking logically about matters of the heart soured his mood. If he had learned anything as a barrister, it was to use facts to build an argument. A year from now, this attraction wouldn't matter. He couldn't pine for this lass forever. There was a woman out there for him—someone as sensible and mature as she was sweet and pretty. One day, God would bring her across his path, and he would fall ardently in love with the rational creature.

He delivered Polly to the company of Miss Priscilla Ray, with whom she would spend the afternoon. He would meet them that evening on the green. Not for the first time, he wished he could muster a fancy for Miss Ray. She played a fine instrument and had a finer inheritance, but dancing with Miss Ray felt like dancing with his sisters. No deeper feelings were ever stirred.

His stomach rumbled, guiding him to Chownings. Along the way, he fell in with Patrick Henry and Colonel and Mrs. Hendriks.

"Word is," the colonel was saying, "he's going to leave. Thinks Williamsburg might threaten his family. Utter nonsense."

"Yes, my dear," his wife replied, "but only think how uncomfortable the palace must be until repairs are made. Hundreds of panes of glass, broken by the hail. Why shouldn't the Dunmores stay at Porto Bello until repairs are made?"

"I'll tell you why," Patrick Henry broke in with some heat. "We've been waiting for the Speaker of the House to finally return so we can discuss matters important to the future of the colony. But we can't finalize anything without the governor's approval."

"So get the governor's approval," Mrs. Hendriks said. "Porto Bello is a distance of what? Six miles? That's nothing. A man could be there and back in half a day."

Henry was fuming. "Half a day that could have been spent on more important things. It will take a week to discuss the conclusions of the Continental Congress. Twice that if even one of us is playing errand boy to his high-and-mightiness. It doesn't matter if *our* crops or homes were damaged by hail or wind, or tornado. We're honor-bound to be in Williamsburg at this time. And if we are, then the governor is. Let his family take refuge at the plantation if they like. May they be grateful for the extravagance of having two homes. But Dunmore's duty is here. If he abandons Williamsburg, then he abdicates his role as governor."

The royal governor was an essential branch of Virginia's government. Without it, the legislature would be rendered impotent. No matter their differences, they needed to maintain communication. If they did, they might just escape the dangers of civil war on Virginia soil.

"I have a horse," Quill blurted.

"What's that?" Patrick Henry asked.

"Nothing." Rational men didn't volunteer for taxing missions without fully considering the consequences.

"Morris here has a fine gelding," the colonel said.

"Say, that's an idea!" Henry said with enthusiasm, "I'll suggest it to Randolph as soon as I see him. If you're agreeable, Morris."

"I—" he began, then broke off. What would Charles do? Being an errand boy sounded mighty uncomfortable. That wouldn't dissuade him. If he believed a little sacrifice would keep the fractious colony together, he would do it. "Aye," Quill said with a sigh.

After a crowded dinner at Chowning's Tavern, he returned to the office.

Charles glanced up from his desk. "What took you so long?"

"There was a crowd at Chowning's." He unlocked his desk and stared at the papers. "They say Dunmore might leave for Porto Bello. If he does, the burgesses will need someone ta carry their papers ta his lordship." He glanced at Charles. "I volunteered."

Charles stared at him. "You did what?"

"I said I could carry the legislature's minutes and messages ta Porto Bello so the governor could read them and reply." When his friend still gaped at him, Quill shrugged. "Someone has ta do it."

"Yes, but that will take hours a day for heaven knows how long. Did that occur to you?"

"Aye. It did."

"Knowing that, you still volunteered. Why?"

"Ever since the Magazine Incident, the whole colony is falling ta pieces. I just want ta hold it together." He wouldn't join the radicals, risking their lives while threatening the peace. Instead of taking up arms with the Williamsburg Volunteer Company, he would take up paper and pray the documents were strong enough to bind the broken colony together. He would work for peace as ardently as some men prepared for war. What did it matter if only his horse looked heroic? Miss Gardiner didn't live along the path to Porto Bello.

Twelve

FIREWORKS & FAMILIARITY

The bard had failed her. Not one of his sonnets had prepared her for the warmth and light she carried in her heart, like the flame of a single candle. It had sparked to life sometime yesterday. Had it been the moment when he had called her name and run through the storm, or when he had taken her hand in his? She couldn't say for certain when it had begun. All she knew was the result.

She trusted Quillan Morris.

Trust. The word had as much charm as pickled beans. But to know you would always be safe with a man who would cheerfully assist you through your petty tribulations was a grand thing. Mayhap Shakespeare, being a man, didn't understand the magnificent beauty of having someone to turn to when things went wrong. She was just a girl. It was a great comfort to know that she didn't have to face every trial alone.

With that reassurance, she hadn't been much cowed by Mama's inevitable lecture not to dawdle through her errands or get caught in storms. Papa told her that Mama scolded her because she had been worried, then patted her shoulder and told her he was grateful Mr. Morris had been there to keep her safe and that their home was mostly undamaged.

The storm had broken two panes of the shop window, scattering toys and glass onto the floor of the wareroom. The hail had beaten down on the garden, snapping rosebud stems and stripping the peas from their vines. Nutmeg explored the devastation as thoroughly as a surveyor mapping the wilderness. A few apple branches had to be dragged out of the pasture, lest the old mare get sick eating the green apples. The west side of the house, facing the street, had lost several windowpanes. Emmeline carefully collected the glass and wrapped it in the oldest broadsides. If proper repairs couldn't be made before winter, there might be a way to glue the old ones together.

That had been yesterday. Today, she and Papa had dry-fitted the dining chairs together. With the promise of evening fireworks, the sun had hastened its journey across the sky. Her family walked to town in the rosy hour before sunset, when the world blushed under the sun's parting glance. By the time they reached the Palace Green, the light had faded from pink to gray. Hundreds of people crowded the green, but none were who she was looking for. Jenny might have been there. Mr. Morris certainly was. He had promised to look for her, but already there were so many people and so little light. He had probably given up on her.

"There are so many people," Henrietta said. "More than at Sunday meeting. But where are all the carriages?"

Mama scoffed. "Only a fool would bring a horse so close to fireworks. It would spook and run."

Papa, as usual, was more gentle with his words. "Best to leave the poor beasts in their stables."

Emmeline was starting to wish she had been left home with a book when the flash of a smile caught her eye. Mr. Morris had found her. He and his sister came over at once.

"Mr. and Mrs. Gardiner." His brogue was as mellow as moonlight on daisies. "Miss Gardiner, Miss Henrietta. I hope I find ye all in good health."

"Indeed," Papa said. "And you, Mr. Morris? Miss Morris?" He nodded to Polly. "I trust you are in good health."

"Aye, the best," Mr. Morris said.

There were a few minutes of pleasantries where Mama detailed their storm damage and Papa asked after theirs.

"Thank the Lord we were spared," Polly said. Addressing Papa, she turned the conversation, "Might I invite Miss Gardiner ta watch the fireworks with us?"

"So long as you keep her close. I don't want to lose her in the dark."

"We willna lose her, sir. I promise," Mr. Morris said, offering his other arm. She gladly took it.

He meandered with no clear direction or path, yet he found an acquaintance to introduce her to at every turn. She listened intently to their conversation, fascinated by the windows into the lives of such varied people. A man blamed the Gunpowder Incident on the colonial secretary, insisting the man had betrayed the very people he had been appointed to serve. George, the printer's apprentice, was enjoying an evening away from his master with boys his age. They boldly challenged Mr. Morris to arm wrestle. He handed her his jacket, cheerfully defeated them all, reclaimed his jacket, bowed with exaggerated courtesy, and then escorted Polly and Emmeline away from the mayhem that followed as the boys took to wrestling each other.

They next stopped to converse with a woman who speculated on when the next Dutch ship would come, and whether this time it would bring cloth.

"What do ye think, Miss Gardiner?" Mr. Morris said suddenly.

She startled, alarmed by all the eyes suddenly on her. She had been quite comfortable keeping her own counsel. "Well, I don't know when the ships will come or what they will bring, but I think salt is the greater necessity. Gowns can be patched, but without salt, how will we preserve meat and butter?"

The woman accepted her argument with grace. "Let us pray that the next ship brings salt and cloth."

It was now fully dark, save a few lanterns whose light dotted the green. Their meandering path seemed to be leading back to her family.

"Oh!" Polly cried. "There's Priscilla. I forgot to return something. Forgive me, Miss Gardiner."

Mr. Morris stepped forward, but Polly slipped her arm from his. "Dinna worry yerself," she said. "I'll find ye when 'tis over."

"As ye like."

In a moment, Emmeline and Mr. Morris were alone in the dark. They were honor-bound to each other until the fireworks ended. "I beg yer pardon, Miss Gardiner. I didna expect Polly ta leave us unchaperoned. Perhaps ye would rather return ta yer family."

"Don't you know? I was hoping to watch the fireworks with you."

There was a moment's silence. She had grown too comfortable with him and had said too much. It wasn't any more forward than yesterday when he had told her that spending time with her had been his pleasure. Then again, there were things a gentleman might say to a lady that a lady would never say to a gentleman. Was this one of them? Susan would know. Only fools spoke without speaking. When in doubt, Emmeline ought to keep her mouth closed.

At last, he replied, "The feeling, Miss Gardiner, is mutual." The words were as soft and sweet as a tea cake. Did he mean them? Or did his hesitation speak louder than the praise that had followed?

A breeze made her regret not wearing a shawl. In the cool of the evening, she leaned into his warmth, appreciating anew the arm that had sheltered her from the hail. Her shoulders were mottled blue and purple from the brief exposure to the elements. How many bruises had he taken for her? It was no use asking. In manly pride, he had brushed away her concerns yesterday and engaged in competitive athletics this evening. The boys hadn't stood a chance against him.

Why did he keep stealing glances at her? What was he thinking? And why did it feel so intimate to be on his arm now, when there were a thousand people around them? She wouldn't ask such indelicate questions. Instead, she introduced a topic of general interest. "I suppose Mr. Randolph returned safely."

"Did ye no' hear the church bells when he came inta town?"

"They rang the bells?"

"Aye. He's the very pride of Virginia. The cavalry had escorted him from his ship, cheering for the 'father of our country.'"

"Father of our country," she repeated. The title was stately and dignified. "I like that. Is the congress done, then?"

"For a season. The delegates have other responsibilities—families to care for and issues pressing to their respective colonies. Virginia needs its Speaker of the House here. Congress can find itself another president."

She laughed at his easy dismissal of a serious dilemma. "Is Virginia's legislature more important than the Continental Congress?"

"Some say aye and some say nay. What say ye?" Judges and juries were silenced by his opinions, and he wanted hers.

"Is the hand more important than the foot?" She was stalling, searching for words of wisdom worthy of his respect. "Our legislature is part of our charter and constitution. Congress is a temporary organization. It exists to protect each colony's charters and our collective constitution, but it will dissolve when the threat is gone. The Congress is only as important as the colonies and the constitution that it protects. If I had to choose one to sacrifice, that would be it."

"I believe, Miss Gardiner, that ye just won yer first brief." His eyes danced with the light of distant lanterns, but his gaze was steady. A thousand conversations mingled incoherently about them. They watched each other, silent as snowfall. A distant whistling rose above the voices. Mr. Morris blinked and turned his head, his face bathed in white light. An explosion like cannon fire shattered the air. She dove for security, burying her face against his waistcoat and clinging to his cravat. Cannons might fire, and hailstones smite, but she wouldn't face the danger alone. He would keep her safe. After a moment, his broad hand rested on her back. Encircled about in his care, her fears vanished like dewdrops touched by the sun's bright rays. The next time she was frightened, she would remember this moment, would long for Mr. Morris to hold her close.

Another whistle brought her to her senses.

"Oh! I'm such a goose." She leapt back, her face hot. "I forgot about the fireworks."

He tucked her hand through his arm, bringing her close again, though in a more dignified manner. "Dinna worry yerself. I rather liked it." It might have been sweet nonsense, but there was such sincerity in his voice that she accepted the reassurance. At any rate, she wouldn't allow her embarrassment to sully the beauty of the fireworks.

Lights showered from the heavens like a baptism of fire, illuminating the buildings that circled the green, founded and grounded on Virginia soil. The radiant church spire reached heavenward to the source of life and liberty. United with their countrymen—male and female, slaves and freemen, old and young—they gazed up; not at the oppressive darkness but at the light that dared to chase it back, that declared over the rooftops to fear not, for day always conquered night.

"I love this country," she confided, mesmerized by the display.

He placed a warm hand over her cold fingers. "So do I, Miss Gardiner. So do I."

At that moment, the flame in her heart burned brighter, reflecting the gold and white glory that covered the land they loved.

Thirteen

LESSONS & LACE

MONDAY, MAY 29, 1775

Emmeline straightened the last schoolbook. She had arranged them in a row across the table, in the order she intended to use them. They would begin with reading, then history, memorization, mathematics, and penmanship. She had spent the last week moving books on and off shelves, trying to whittle down the many joyous possibilities into lessons she could fit within the two hours that Kitty could be spared from her chores at Johnson Hall.

A breeze stirred the pages of Henrietta's copybook. Emmeline placed the inkwell on top. It was late May, and all the windows were open. Even the back door, which opened from the dining hall and faced the kitchen house, was propped open for a breeze. Henrietta sat on the wide covered porch, shelling peas with Mama. Sounds from the street carried through the open parlor windows.

A man's voice said, "You listen carefully and do everything she tells you to, understand?" That was Gideon, the footman for Johnson Hall. Mama had given Emmeline the same speech when she had begun dance lessons.

It was time for school.

She smoothed her starched apron and opened the door. "Good morning, Miss Kitty," she said in a sophisticated schoolmistress voice.

Kitty gave her a funny look, then averted her eyes.

"You may call me Miss Gardiner."

"Yes, ma'am."

"I'll be back for her in two hours," Gideon said.

"We'll see you then. Come, Kitty. We're having lessons in the dining hall." Once her pupil crossed the threshold, Emmeline closed the front door and led the way. Henrietta was standing beside the table. "Henrietta, this is Kitty. Kitty, this is my sister, Henrietta."

"How do you do?" Henrietta gave a little curtsy.

Kitty glanced at her, then said to the floor, "Fine."

"I'm twelve years old. How about you?"

"Eight."

"I was eight when I started lessons."

When she was eight, Emmeline read their entire shelf of Newbery books and moved on to the histories. There had been a time when she hadn't known her letters, a time before lessons, but she had been so young she scarcely remembered it.

"Sit down, please," she said. It felt odd to use her schoolmistress voice with her sister, but it helped her to feel like a real teacher. "Henrietta, you will begin with Plutarch's *Lives*." She set the heavy book in front of her sister and opened it to the first biography: Theseus of Greece.

Henrietta looked at it with disgust, like someone had suggested she follow a horse down a road and never mind about the droppings. "Mama doesn't make me read that. Do you expect me to read it all in one day? What is it about? Why should I learn it?"

"One question at a time," Emmeline said. "Plutarch's *Lives* is a collection of biographies about great men who lived about two thousand years ago. Begin the first biography while I work with Kitty."

Henrietta had the audacity to close the book. "I don't want to read about dead men."

"They're great men from ancient history."

"They're dead."

"Shall I get Mama? You know she told you to obey me for lessons." Emmeline opened the book again. "Start here." She jabbed a finger at Theseus and picked up the hornbook. Using her pleasant, yet authoritative voice again, she addressed Kitty. "Have you learned your Christ's cross?"

"My what?"

Emmeline pointed to the top of the hornbook. A cross marked the beginning of the first row of letters. "The alphabet. Can you tell me the names of these letters?"

"No, ma'am."

"Not any?" Emmeline couldn't hold back her dismay. She had hoped to begin the syllabary tomorrow and Newbery readers within the month.

Kitty's voice grew even smaller. "No, ma'am."

"Let me show you." She picked up a bit of straw to use as a pointer as she enunciated each lowercase letter, including both versions of "s," the ampersand, the five vowels, and the twenty-six uppercase letters. "Now it's your turn." She placed the straw in Kitty's hand. "Go on."

Kitty's eyes, fixed on the sea of letters, filled with tears. Her chin quivered. "I-I can't."

"Yes, you can," Emmeline said in her most encouraging voice. She wrapped her hand around Kitty's and guided the pointer. "We begin by the cross. The first letter is *A*. Say *A*."

Kitty sniffled. "*A*."

"This next letter is a *B*. Say *B*." And so it continued in the slowest, most miserable manner through the first four lines of the hornbook as the syllabary and the joy of actual books slipped farther and farther away. At last, they finished. She glanced over at Henrietta. "You can't still be on the first page."

"This is stupid," Henrietta said with the defiance only a younger sister would dare. "You're a terrible teacher."

Emmeline squeezed her eyes shut. She hadn't asked to be a teacher. But she had spent more than a week preparing with all her heart only to fail catastrophically on her first day, before they had even touched on mathematics. Why was this so difficult?

"Mama didn't make me read heavy books about dead men. She didn't make me learn the whole alphabet in one day."

Holding back tears, Emmeline returned Plutarch and the hornbook to their place in the line of books. A little too brightly, she said, "It's time for history." This, at least, was a book Henrietta had already been studying with Mama. She opened to the first story, which began the epic tale that led to the Battle of Hastings in 1066. She hadn't finished reading the first sentence when Henrietta interrupted.

"I learned that ages ago."

"Well, Kitty hasn't. And history is one of the few things you can study together."

Henrietta slouched so low in her chair that her loosely tied stays touched her chin. Emmeline bit back a correction and began the tale. The rhythm of words calmed her. It helped that Henrietta had stopped complaining, and Kitty was no longer crying. She got to the end of a section and looked up at her pupils. "It's time to recite the lesson. Kitty, you're the youngest. You go first."

Her dark eyes went wide in alarm. "Recite?"

"It means," Henrietta said before Emmeline could use her teacher voice, "that you stand up and tell us what you remember from what she just read."

"Oh." Kitty stood. After a minute, she said, "I don't know."

Emmeline looked back at the book. Was it possible she hadn't understood the story any more than she had known her letters? Kitty had said so little. How did Emmeline know her understanding wasn't simple? Like the pieman in the old rhyme, or like the child-like woman who helped the laundress down the road? "Was the story about Lord Dunmore herding pigs in a silk gown?"

Kitty giggled. "No, ma'am. It was about a king. He was dying, and people were scared because he didn't have a son and he needed to choose a new king."

"Well done, Kitty," Emmeline said with relief. "You may sit down. Henrietta?"

Her sister stood and gave a thorough, and somewhat embellished, retelling, which included the names of most of the men involved.

Emmeline set the history down. They would begin with that tomorrow. Then she opened Shakespeare and read a couplet through twice. Henrietta and Kitty repeated it with only a few mistakes. She handed Henrietta her copybook, where earlier that day she had written that very couplet in her neatest penmanship. "Copy that five times."

Paper was dear, and she didn't have a copybook ready for Kitty. They would move on to math. Since there were no numerals printed on the hornbook, she had written zero through nine on a pine shaving that curled. She placed a book on the upper edge, forcing it to lie flat. She glanced at Kitty, afraid of putting her to tears again. "Can you count?"

"Count what?"

Emmeline recognized her oversight immediately. There weren't even nine books in the room to count. "Just a minute." She ran out to the garden and collected a handful of sage leaves. She set them on the table in front of Kitty. "Count these."

Kitty slid the leaves across the table and counted to nine.

"How did you already know that?" Emmeline hadn't learned numbers until after she knew her letters.

"My grandfather taught me."

"I'm done," Henrietta said, sanding the wet ink.

"Good," Emmeline said. She moved the copybook aside to dry and handed her sister *Euclid's Geometry*.

"I can't do this!"

"You know most of your multiplication tables. This isn't much harder. Read the first lesson." Emmeline returned her attention to Kitty. "This is how we write numbers." She pointed with the straw, "Zero, one, two, three, four, five, six, seven, eight, nine."

"What's zero?"

"That's the number we write when there's nothing."

Kitty frowned. "Why would someone count nothing?"

"Because mathematicians are stupid," Henrietta said.

"Henrietta Gardiner," Emmeline said, forgetting her teaching voice and sounding just as scandalized as Mama sometimes did. "You mind your manners." Turning back to Kitty, she said in her calm teacher voice, "You'll understand later. Sometimes, nothing is just as important as something."

Just then, there was a knock on the door. "Excuse me."

It was Gideon. "Is Kitty ready?"

"Yes!" Kitty jumped up and ran to the front door.

By the time Emmeline returned to the dining hall, her sister had disappeared. This morning had been terrible. And she had to do it all over tomorrow. How had Widow Bray, God rest her soul, managed a class of thirty pupils? She couldn't even handle two.

She was gathering the books when her mother came in.

"How did things go?"

"Kitty cried, and Henrietta hates me."

"That bad? What were you trying to teach them?"

Emmeline spread everything across the table again and explained how each lesson had gone. "I'm afraid Kitty is going to cry every time I show her the hornbook."

Mama laughed. "Patience. They're only children. Learning takes time."

"But I could read at her age. And I loved Euclid."

"You started quite young. Henrietta doesn't have your enthusiasm for learning, and Kitty has likely never seen a hornbook before. Remember, haste makes waste." Her mother usually reminded Henrietta of that proverb when she was rushing through her chores. It hadn't occurred to Emmeline that it might apply to teaching.

"What should I do?"

"I was waiting to see if you would ask."

Emmeline hadn't asked her mother or God for help, but had relied on her own knowledge and whimsies to carry her through.

"For Kitty, start small. Introduce one letter each day. Show it to her in the hornbook. Build it with sticks. Trace it in the dirt. Have her stitch it on a sampler. For Henrietta, you're not wrong about Plutarch, though I'm not surprised she grumbled. But she needs to master her fractions before she's ready for geometry."

After Emmeline's grand hopes and plans, Mama's counsel was an unwelcome slice of humble pie. She could hardly pretend to be an esteemed professor when she was tracing letters in the dirt. Returning to her chores, she couldn't pretend to be an esteemed anything.

A neighbor called, so Mama left Emmeline in the kitchen, spooning filling into each pastry coffin. She wanted a dozen on the shelf. They would keep for weeks and make a quick meal when someone needed their hospitality. Emmeline pinched the dough, sealing each pie within its coffin as she resigned herself to humble pie. It would be better to trace letters in the dirt, one each day, than to see her pupils in tears again. It would be better to postpone the delights of higher learning and spend her days drilling unwilling students on multiplication tables and the alphabet. It would be dreary, but better.

Mama returned to the kitchen, looking smug. "She wanted the runt from our litter, and you'll never believe what I got her to trade us for it."

"What?"

"Well, it's no secret that when she got married, she quickly outgrew all her wedding clothes. Of course, she kept them, thinking that one day she could use them, but she already has three children and should give up hoping for ridiculous things like that. I'm so tired of seeing that faded old petticoat you wear all the time—" she gestured to the one she was wearing. It had been Mama's once, when it was a rich oxblood red. Over time, it had faded to a dull brick. Now it was Emmeline's.

"I talked her into one of her petticoats. The color isn't the least faded. It's like new."

Emmeline stared at her mother. "A new petticoat?" It wasn't really for her, was it? A new hat and a new petticoat in the same month? It was too much to be believed.

Mama smiled. "As good as new. Do you want to see it?"

"Now?"

"Now. Leave your pinner here so you can change."

So she could change. It really was for her, then. Something new that had been someone's *wedding clothes*. There was a dreamy elegance to the phrase. If she ever had the luxury of filling a clothespress with new clothing chosen especially for herself, there would be opulent florals, delicate lace, and no end to the ruffles. Getting dressed would be like gathering flowers to adorn the table —which color suited her fancy today?

She followed Mama into the house, trying on colors in her mind. There were so many beautiful colors in the world: soft sage, rosy pink, forget-me-not blue... Mama picked something dark off a chair and shook it out. The petticoat was solid indigo with nary a ruffle to soften the harsh silhouette.

"It's as good as new," Mama said, "and will never stain. You can wear it for years."

Years. She was sentenced to wear this until it was worn beyond patching.

"What do you think?" Mama prompted.

"It's so...serviceable." She rubbed the linsey-woolsey between her fingers. "It's quite sturdy. I really will be able to wear it for years." She blinked hard. "I'll change in my room." She hurried up the stairs so Mama wouldn't see her tears. Safely behind closed doors, she buried her face in her coverlet and sobbed. She was a goose to have expected anything more. She was an ungrateful wretch. But why, when there were so many beautiful things in the world, couldn't she have just one for herself?

"Dear Lord, why can't I have anything pretty?" The words, muffled in her coverlet, made their way to heaven and back. A thought, as soft as a rose petal, came to her mind. *But you do have pretty things.* A stillness came over her. Though she didn't have everything she dreamed of, she did have some pretty things. There was a beautiful little painting on her bedroom wall. On a shelf of the washstand was Aunt Vina's old hand mirror. Though the glass was broken, the birds and flowers of the pewter frame were quite beautiful. Hanging from a peg was the fine straw hat Mr. Morris had bought her. The ribbon was a coarse homespun, but it was patriotic to wear Virginia goods, and it was the prettiest shade of blue. His brother had cut such a generous length of it that, after measuring for the ties, she had been able to decorate the crown.

Determined to set her eyes on every beautiful thing in her possession, she opened the clothespress drawer where she had placed Granny's abandoned work basket. One day, she might have the time to spare to practice what little she had learned of the craft. Then she would be able to embellish even the plainest of gowns. Something peeked at her from under the bobbins full of thread. She pushed the bobbins aside and pulled out a length of white cotton lace, as long as her arm. Mayhap Granny had begun a shawl. It was a pity that something so beautiful was useless. Even Emmeline couldn't imagine a day when she would have time to complete such a lengthy project.

She held it up, imagining a lace trimming for her bed's tester, but there wasn't enough for that, either. She folded it in half, then in half again, before pausing. Might it be enough? Hardly daring to hope, she grabbed her blue gown from its peg and wrapped the lace around the cuff of one sleeve. Her breath stilled. There was enough of this beautiful lace to trim both sleeves of her best gown.

It didn't matter so much that she had an ugly skirt to do her chores in if she could wear a dress with lace on it to church and other fine gatherings. She clutched the lace to her heart and looked heavenward. "Thank you, Lord," she whispered. "Thank you."

Mama was expecting her, so she tucked the lace away to keep it safe for when she had time to work with it. Then she braved another look at the petticoat. It was just as harsh and ugly as it had been before. But Mama had been so pleased. Emmeline swallowed her pride and tied it on. The heavy fabric was long, hiding her ankles and brushing the tops of her shoes. From the waist down, she looked forty. She laughed. She would be forty when this finally wore out. At least Mr. Morris wouldn't see her in this ugly thing. She returned her blue gown to its peg and hastened back to the kitchen in the indigo petticoat, her spirits bright with the promise of a lace-trimmed gown.

Fourteen

DINNER AT JOHNSON HALL

TUESDAY, JUNE 6, 1775

"Mrs. Under—" Charles broke off with a frown. "I mean my father's wife—has invited Susan and me to dine at Johnson Hall." He spoke with weary resignation. Poor Charles. He deserved a better stepmother. A woman of warmth and understanding. A woman more like his late mother. Then again, he deserved a better father.

"I daresay ye should accept," Quill said, "though such a dinner is bound ta disagree with yer digestion."

"I must accept. I haven't seen my father since his wedding." Poor Charles. He would be obliged to dine with the disagreeable couple for as long as they all should live. "I was hoping," he continued, "that you would come." Charles had always hated attending social events alone. In their youth, he had declined every ball and concert that Quill had been unable to attend.

"I'll be there," Quill said, with the solemnity of backing a friend in a fight.

"Good," Charles said. "Oh, and Susan wants Polly."

Polly laughed at the crude invitation. "When is it?"

"Saturday."

"We can make it," she confirmed.

"Good. We'll meet my uncle's family there." Charles added, as though he hadn't just transformed an awkward family dinner into the most anticipated social engagement of the month. Miss Gardiner would be there.

The irrational fancy for the bonny lass had not died out with the hail and the fireworks. It would eventually. It must. Only then could he be free to follow his father's counsel to choose a wife. Only then would he polish his mother's betrothal brooch. In the meantime, he needed Miss Gardiner's sweet smiles and words like he needed food and rest after a long day's work.

~

SATURDAY, JUNE 10, 1775

Emmeline's shoes clattered unevenly on the bridge that led them to Johnson Hall. The heel of her left shoe had broken the day before, and she had crafted a replacement in the workshop. Her measurements had been hasty, and the new heel was taller than the old one. She would fix it once they returned home.

Below the bridge, a creek ran along the property's border, through a verdant wood. She would much rather take her meal here, sitting on the edge of the bridge with her feet dangling above the water, watching songbirds and butterflies dance in the dappled light, just as she had done years ago with Aunt Vina.

It had been three years since Granny last recognized her and eight years since Aunt Vina had passed. The great house had lost all its charm when it lost the light of two of Emmeline's favorite relations. It was unlikely she would see her frail grandmother today. Kitty would be tasked with keeping her away from company, even if that company was family.

After their walk in the midday sun, the house's entry hall was so dark it took her a minute to adjust to the change. She almost missed Gideon's smile as he took her hat. She had hardly ever seen him smile. Why now? Why at her? Her mind was as slow as her vision. Might it be because she was teaching his granddaughter? Teaching a child her letters didn't seem a very grand thing to her. Then again, Emmeline smiled at dewdrops on daisies. Not everything that brought joy was grand.

There was no opportunity to inquire. His expression turned somber, and he gestured for them to enter the parlor. The family painting that had hung over the mantel from her earliest memories had been replaced. Gone was the only portrait of Aunt Vina, replaced by a glossy new painting of her uncle with a sharp blonde woman and two young children. This was the family of Johnson Hall. Charles and his mother had been erased.

She curtsied when her mother did, careful to keep in her shadow. It had been more than a year since she had last dined with her uncle. While her parents had spoken with him, she had stood by the window, murmuring Shakespeare to herself. Her uncle had taken notice and decided she was not right in the head. Though she had never sought his respect, his loudly voiced opinion had frightened her. Her greatest hope for today was that dinner would be dull and uneventful; that Susan Johnson, née Bailey, wouldn't learn what her uncle thought of her. She would attract no attention. She would say nothing unless first spoken to, and then as little as possible. If the former Mrs. Underwood, now Mrs. Johnson, talked as much as she remembered, it should be quite easy.

"I trust you found everything in order when you arrived," Mama addressed Mrs. Johnson in a tone that did not allow for negation. As the one who had put everything in order, Mama knew the state of the house when the bride had arrived better than anyone.

"It was a dream. Chip had everything arranged just so for me." She placed a hand on her husband's chest in a manner too intimate for company. It stayed there for an awkward moment while Emmeline wondered who Chip was and why he had been given credit for everything Mama had done.

"Chip?" Mama repeated.

"Oh, dear me," the woman fluttered. "I forgot myself. Chip is what I call my dear husband when we're alone."

What a dreadful nickname for a grown man. Did the woman have no imagination? Literature was full of names better than Chip. If she couldn't improve upon the words of the masters, she ought to leave well enough alone and borrow from the wide repertoire of endearments the English language was full of: sweetheart, sweeting, darling, honey, lambkin, and ladybird. Her French grandmother had called Emmeline *mon petit chou chou*, which sounded charming even if it did mean "my little cabbage." Her late grandfather had called her pumpkin. Her mind was pleasantly engaged in the contemplation of sweet nothings when she heard a carriage. She drifted to the window, grateful Charles had arrived before she had been noticed. Behind the carriage, a gentleman swung down from a fine gray gelding.

She stared. What was Mr. Morris doing here? She had only expected Charles and Susan. The gloom that had hung over Johnson Hall for years was chased away by the sunshine one man radiated wherever he went. When he entered the parlor, his manners were so open and easy that she forgot her vow of silence long enough to return his greeting before returning to the shadowy corners of the parlor where she could listen and watch.

"Such a lovely gown, Susan," Mrs. Johnson was saying. "You must allow me to call you Susan. It would be too confusing to have two Mrs. Johnsons at once, and you know I was married first. It may only have seemed like a couple of weeks, but it already feels like we've been married for years. As I was saying, that is such a lovely gown. I may be your mother-in-law, but I am not so old as that makes me sound. I hope you will think of me as your older sister. I'm sure we can tell each other all our secrets."

Alarm was written all over Charles' face. He wouldn't entrust family secrets to his new stepmother and didn't want his wife to do so, either.

Susan smiled politely. "I couldn't possibly think of you as being that old. Do tell me how you find life here at Johnson Hall.

I believe you told me your previous home was north of the York River."

"Indeed, in Spotsylvania," Mrs. Johnson confirmed, then entertained them all with a description of all the people and places she had left behind.

Emmeline stood silently in the circle of ladies, mirroring Susan's posture and poise. There was no need to think of clever conversation or topics of general interest when Mrs. Johnson spoke without pausing for breath. All Emmeline had to do was listen, and her uncle would forget she was there.

At last, dinner was announced. The men all found their ladies —her uncle and his new wife, Charles and Susan, Papa and Mama. Mr. Morris offered Polly one arm and Emmeline the other and escorted them to the dining hall.

The table and chairs were works of art, crafted from Caribbean mahogany. The frames were more straight and square than the spindle-back chairs she and Papa had just completed, but that was the only plain thing about them. The backsplat of each chair was intricately carved with leaves and birds, and the curving front legs ended in sharp talons clutching ball feet.

They were abominably uncomfortable to sit in, but one didn't come to Johnson Hall for comfort. Emmeline seated herself with perfect posture. After so many dinners with Susan, she knew all her graceful movements and could execute them without looking down the table. So she smoothed the napkin on her lap and took ladylike bites of mashed turnips.

Mr. Morris was seated across from her. The freckles scattered across his face shifted with his smile like dappled sunlight on the forest floor. She returned his smile, wishing she could hear him speak, but he was too much of a gentleman to interrupt their hostess as she prattled on about all the precious nonsense her children had said only yesterday.

"My little girl just learned to say pretty. 'Mama, my pretty? Mama, my pretty?'" Mrs. Johnson demonstrated in a shrill voice. "It's so precious. I went to my room, and she had a smear of rouge on her nose and a tangle of ribbons on her head. I was so angry she got into my things until she said, 'Mama, my pretty?' How could I spank her for that?"

Mama was not impressed. "Indulge her now, and she will grow up thinking she's a delicate flower."

"Ah, well," Uncle Johnson said in a placating tone, "Emmeline's turned out quite pretty, even if you weren't able to indulge her."

Mr. Morris winked over a bowl of peas, with a complete disregard for the authority of fashion plates on the world of beauty. She dropped her gaze and smiled at her plate.

"You mistake me, brother," Mama said. "I meant that beauty is too often seen as the crowning glory of empty-headed young ladies. Too many girls of little intellect and no practical skills are married for their beauty, only for the couple to fall on hard times because the bride was unprepared for the demands of running a house."

"Practical skills?" Uncle Johnson scoffed. "No gentleman wants a bride who can work with her hands."

Emmeline's cheeks heated as she fought the urge to bury her calloused fingers in her napkin. According to Plutarch, the ancient Greeks had scorned manual labor to the point that an aristocrat was mocked if he played a musical instrument. That was thousands of years ago. In this age of enlightenment, it shouldn't matter if she had to weed the garden and milk the cow if she could dine with poise and read the wisdom of the masters.

And yet, it did matter.

Mama had lost many genteel friends when she married Papa. He owned land. He voted. He served on juries. He was honest and good. But upon Mama's marriage to him, she had fallen beneath the notice and concern of the gentry. If Mama, who was born and bred a gentlewoman, was looked down on by society, what did the gentry think of her daughter, who was raised on hard work? What did Susan and Polly think of her? What did Mr. Morris think? Emmeline's eyes stung as the conversation flowed forward like a river chasing the receding tide.

"There are many things expected of a gentlewoman," Susan said, countering Uncle Johnson's argument with grace and poise. "Needlework and musical accomplishments, for example. Her education will also include drawing, painting, and exposure to the arts."

"And," interrupted Mrs. Johnson, "the ability to plan and arrange social events, such as dinners and balls."

Emmeline was the only woman at this table whose education had not included all of the genteel accomplishments expected of ladies. While Mama had taught her fine penmanship, reading, and a few decorative stitches, there had always been too many chores and too few opportunities for other lessons. Emmeline would have loved to be tutored in drawing, painting, and music. She would have preferred lacemaking to darning stockings. But despite her earnest efforts to develop the skills of a gentlewoman, she wasn't one.

"Then we are in agreement," Mama said. "The education of young ladies is essential to their development. That is why—"

"Indeed," Mrs. Johnson interrupted. "I never said it wasn't. But, as there is no danger of *my* daughter growing into an empty-headed beauty, I can afford to indulge her on occasion."

Emmeline closed her eyes, silently praying that no one present understood the unexpected emphasis their hostess had placed on her daughter. She couldn't bear it if Mr. Morris, Polly, or Susan noticed the slight that had been placed on her intellect. It was plain to Emmeline that her uncle had shared his ill-founded opinion of her wits with his wife, who had flung it back at Mama.

"Beauty is as beauty does," Susan said. "Your daughter will have an excellent teacher in the art of planning dinners. The meal is so..." She paused, searching for a complimentary phrase. "Well balanced," she concluded.

Polly hid her mouth behind her napkin, her eyes dancing with amusement.

Papa, in an attempt to placate his hostess, said, "These turnips are some of the best I've had in years. Pray tell, how do you season them?"

"You mustn't think I made them," Mrs. Johnson snapped. "I don't dirty my hands in the kitchen. You think we don't have servants in a fine house like this?"

Mama's blue eyes lit with fire. "There is no shame in work, whether or not you have servants. I'm not ashamed to admit that my daughters and I make our own bread and till our own garden. Emmeline even helps her father in the workshop."

Please Mama. Stop.

Mrs. Johnson smirked. "I'm sure it's good for your daughter to be doing anything." She tapped her forehead.

"She only helps," Charles blurted, trying to save her from the scorn of genteel society. "A little. Here and there." Lord bless her cousin, he thought Mrs. Johnson was only shaming Emmeline for working with her hands.

"I'm sure she does what she can," Mrs. Johnson said. Then she raised her voice, "Miss Gardiner! Pass the turnips."

Emmeline, startled, looked up in time to see the woman pantomime the action. Eyes stinging, she passed the bowl. Her breath hitched, and she hugged herself, trying to steady her breathing. She could cry when she was alone in her room, but not here, not with everyone watching. She squeezed her eyes shut. *Please, Lord, make her stop.*

Mrs. Johnson did not stop. "We don't have bad blood like that in my family. I knew a family who—"

"Nor mine," Uncle Johnson interrupted. "My sister and I turned out just fine. Everybody knows it's too much reading, which muddles the mind. Poetry and novels and all that."

Emmeline's throat tightened, and she fought back a sob, her collarbone rising and falling with the wrestle. Mr. Morris sent her a questioning look. She gave a little shake of her head, not daring to answer lest her voice betray her.

Mama, with the poise of a gentlewoman, smiled at her brother and said, "An excess you're in no danger of."

"Quite right." Uncle Johnson stabbed his pork, pleased to have made his point.

Across from her, a chair scraped back, and Mr. Morris stood. "Excuse me," he said. "Miss Gardiner needs some fresh air."

Grateful for any excuse, she flew out the door before her red eyes could be noticed and remarked upon. The last thing she heard before bursting into the sunlight was Mama saying, "It's only Mr. Morris."

She was gasping for air with shallow, shuddering breaths, on the front steps, when he put an arm around her shoulders and guided her away from the house with its open windows to the relative privacy of a grove near the creek. He offered her his handkerchief. That simple act of kindness broke her resolve. She buried her face in it as all the tears she had been holding back burst forth with the fury of the Red Sea burying Pharaoh's army. She didn't want him to see her cry, which only made her cry more.

He patted her shoulder. "I hate ta speak ill of yer family but yer uncle doesna have sense enough ta fill a teaspoon. Men of nae sense have nae delicacy. They only understand crude humor and shallow motives. They dinna take pleasure in literature because 'tis filled with higher humor and deeper motives. They dinna understand the high and the good and the holy. 'Tis why yer uncle and his wife canna respect ye. Ye're made of finer stuff than they."

It was the kindest, most beautiful thing anyone had ever said to her. He had pulled back the curtain of silence she sheltered behind, looked into her soul, and pronounced it good. Her breathing was only a little shaky as she handed him the sodden handkerchief. The tears had come and gone as fast as a summer storm and left the world as clean and beautiful.

He pocketed the handkerchief. "I suppose we should return." He sounded as reluctant as she felt.

"I wish we didn't have to," she said. It would be humiliating to have everyone stare at her red-rimmed eyes and ask why she had left so suddenly. She wasn't certain she was ready to maintain her poise if her uncle made another insinuation about her intellect.

"If ye need more air, it would not be unseemly ta walk around the house once or twice afore returning."

In their haste to leave, neither had collected their hats. There weren't enough trees near the house to protect her nose from a sunburn. She didn't need Susan to tell her that walking in the sun with neither hat nor parasol was unladylike. "If you please," Emmeline said, "I'd rather stay in the trees. There's a patch of columbine not far from here."

Fifteen

A VIRGINIAN

He had come anticipating her smiles and instead had witnessed her tears. How was it possible that people as good as she and Charles had come from such a family? He glanced back toward the house. For one moment, Quill considered the propriety of remaining at the top of the gully while Emmeline searched for flowers. Then she slipped near the bottom. She gave a little cry and landed on her seat with the hem of her petticoat in the creek. It wasn't proper to plunge into a gully with a lass in the middle of a dinner party, but it would have been less proper to allow her to do so without an escort.

"Are ye hurt?" He was by her side in a moment.

"I'm fine. It's just a bit of mud." She rinsed her hands in the creek. "I don't usually run headlong into the ravine."

"Do ye call it a ravine? Charles and I called it that when we were boys and fancied ourselves explorers."

"I suppose that's where I learned it from," she said, standing and shaking her hands dry. Her indigo petticoat was six inches deep in mud. She brushed a curl out of her eyes, streaking her face with dirt.

He bit back a laugh and dipped his handkerchief in the creek.

"Allow me." He closed the distance between them. She took a step back.

"Ye have mud on yer face."

"Oh." The word was short and prim, as though she had just realized it wasn't proper to be alone with a man in a muddy gully during a dinner party.

"It's just me." He threw his arms wide to show he wasn't hiding anything.

The effect was as surprising as it was immediate. She tipped her bonny face toward him and shut her eyes. He closed the space between them, his heart still galloping from their race. Except for the dirt on her brow, she looked like a dream, the one he didn't tell Charles about, where he held her to his heart and kissed her. Dreams were dangerous things, like the will-o'-the-wisps from his mother's stories. Their fairy lights led travelers from safe paths and into death or danger. He swallowed. He had left the house as a gentleman, and he would return as one. He wouldn't kiss a lass he wasn't courting, and he didn't intend to court Miss Gardiner.

He pressed the wet handkerchief to her brow, beginning just above her straight little nose, and traced a line of mud above her blonde eyebrows, ending by one of the curls that framed her bonny face. The fashion was for curls like sausages: fat and long. Hers were small and delicate, as natural as the tendrils of a pumpkin vine that sprang back into place after a gentle tug. Surely, touching her hair was no more intimate than touching her brow. He reached a finger toward a bouncy curl, but she opened an eye, and he pulled back.

"All done?"

"Almost." He made a few short strokes across her forehead. "There. I'm afraid I canna do anything about yer petticoat." He stepped back, ceding the space she would expect now that her eyes were open.

She looked down with grim satisfaction. "The more it's laundered, the less I have to wear it."

"What does that mean?"

"I—" She shifted uncomfortably. "Nothing. Forget it."

"As ye like. He hadn't come here to make her uncomfortable. "Where do we find yer columbine?"

She looked around the gully. After a moment, her face brightened in delight. "There! Where the butterfly just landed. Aunt Vina loved columbine."

He followed her direction. A butterfly slowly opened and closed its wings, clinging to a delicate red flower. "Shall we pick it?" He reached for his penknife.

"I don't believe the new Mrs. Johnson is the sort of woman to appreciate wildflowers. Let's leave it for the butterflies."

"As ye like."

EMMELINE PLACED HER HANDS ON A LOW BRANCH AND hopped up. His hand darted forward to steady her, but she was already seated.

"Ye've got it?"

"I do." She wrapped an arm around the trunk. A breeze stirred her heavy petticoat. A robin whistled his song: *cheerily, cheer up, cheer up, cheerily, cheer up*. Dragonflies hovered above the creek. Nature was as untouched and untroubled by the murmurings at her uncle's table as it was by the reports in the *Gazette*. "It's like a sanctuary," she said in hushed tones. "I hope the war never touches this hallowed place."

Mr. Morris frowned. "I hope it ne'er touches Virginia."

"As do I, Mr. Morris. As do I."

He gazed thoughtfully into the creek. He hadn't taken the time to claim his hat when he had followed her outdoors, and his hair glowed in the dappled sunlight. The color was more radiant than all of Susan's jewels combined. How close could she get if she mixed her paints carefully?

"We are in a delicate situation," he said suddenly. "'Tis treason to ship and store arms to fight the king's men. 'Tis treason to even write a letter supporting the formation of an army, and yet our king is sending his warships to our harbor, and 'tis folly to remain unprepared. What are freemen ta do?"

She was honored that he would ask her such difficult questions, but he presented a puzzle she hadn't worked out. She considered it for a long minute, hoping to arrive at an answer both wise and clever. Nothing came to mind. Plutarch hadn't covered this. Neither had the *Gazette*. Feeling neither wise nor clever, she said, "I don't know."

To her surprise, he looked relieved. "Great minds have been arguing the point, but only the radical Tories and the radical Whigs pretend ta know what is right." He sat on a fallen log, like an old friend settling in for a long talk. "'Tis a contradiction, ta build an army ta fight against yer own king and country, in defense of yer country."

"Is it not also a contradiction for the king of a free people to be a tyrant?" She wouldn't have dared to say such a bold thing even to Charles. But for weeks, Mr. Morris had been wheedling little confidences from her and treating her most unusual thoughts with respect and consideration.

"A tyrant, Miss Gardiner?"

Once again, she would have been wiser to keep her thoughts to herself. She had said too much and had lost his respect. Determined to regain a measure of it, she offered a defense of her first statement. "Only a tyrant would declare war on his own people. Virginia has been loyal to the crown and constitution from the beginning. Virginia was loyal even through the upheavals of Cromwell. If, after everything, King George sends troops to tear the constitution from the hands of his servants in the Old Dominion, then is he not a tyrant?"

Mr. Morris pulled a slingshot from a pocket. "Ye make a strong argument." He nestled a green sweetgum burr in the sling. "But if the king is a tyrant, does that make it less treasonous for freemen to stockpile arms?" He closed one eye and aimed. "Or to build their armies?" He released, and the burr flew across the creek and into a bramble patch. "If anything, it makes the danger even greater. During the Jacobite 'Rising, even a letter could condemn a man to the gallows if it approved of such methods."

"I don't see how danger changes what is right and what is wrong. Either it's treason for a freeman to confront a tyrant or it isn't."

"His lordship would declare it treason." He picked up a stone. "Then again," he nestled it in the sling and took aim, "his lordship thinks his life is in danger every time someone disagrees with his policies." He let the stone fly, and it ricocheted off distant trees.

Emmeline gave a short laugh, then sobered. "That makes him all the more dangerous."

"Aye. If the war comes ta Virginia, he'll charge every man who opposes him with treason and see him hanged."

Goosebumps ran down her arms. Mr. Morris knew things about the world that she hadn't even considered. His conversation was as frightening as it was enlightening. She clung to a philosophy she had read in the *Gazette*. "The only thing worse than a civil war is giving up our rights without a fight."

He glanced up from nestling another burr in his sling. "Some of those rights belong only ta men, and yet ye care more about them than many men I know. Why?"

It was a simple question. The simple answer was that her heart burned for her country. Her blood stirred at the cry for liberty or death. But why did she care more than some men? She would never vote. She would never run for office or own property. At last, she said, "Women will never be more free than our men. When you lose, we lose more. The rights of Englishwomen have always been tied to the rights of Englishmen." She was proud of her little speech and couldn't understand why Mr. Morris was frowning at her again.

"The rights of Englishmen," he repeated.

"What other rights were we talking about?"

He raised a brow. "Only Englishmen?" He asked, his highland brogue as broad as the Palace Green.

What did it matter if his parents were Scottish? She wasn't fully English, either. The important thing was that they shared British soil. They had both been raised to honor the king and constitution. "British, if you prefer, though you know our rights came from England. That's what we inherited. That's what we're trying to preserve for the next generation."

Mr. Morris grunted. Her words had failed to please him. She didn't see why. It didn't matter that his parents weren't English. Her father, who could vote, was half French, but everyone considered him an Englishman. It was the language they spoke, the culture they inherited, and the land they called home.

"England," Mr. Morris said, taking aim again, "hung my grandfather." He released, and the burr struck a nearby tree with a solid thunk. He lowered his slingshot and looked up at her from his log. "England drove my father out of his native land. Did my rights come from England?" He shook his head. "If ye ask my father, England did its best to take them from him." He smiled wryly. "Englishwomen had best look elsewhere for their rights. I am no Englishman."

Emmeline was dumbfounded. She knew more about Cromwell and the Civil War than she did about the Jacobite Rebellion, and her pretty little speech had betrayed that ignorance. At last, she said, feeling contrary herself, "But you're not Scottish, either."

"Then what am I?"

She looked about the gully, lush with life springing from the soil. The columbine, sunflowers, and sweetgum trees were native. But in the garden, Dutch tulips had gone to bed, and English roses were waking up. They all grew in the same soil. "You're a Virginian, same as me. We all are. This is our land."

His hazel eyes softened, and she was rewarded with a smile she couldn't help returning. He held her gaze, and she was soon lost in the earthy mixture of greens and browns in his eyes, like the palette of a painter preparing a study of these hallowed woods.

"Emmeline!" Papa called.

"Coming!" She called back.

Mr. Morris leapt to his feet as though stung by a bee, ramming his slingshot into a pocket. He offered his hand. She took it and slipped off her branch.

His voice was anxious as he said, "I didna mean ta keep ye out long enough ta make anyone worry."

It was a funny, backward thing to say. "I thought I was the one keeping you out. And there was no need for them to worry. I was with you." There was no man she felt safer with, and not a soul whose companionship she enjoyed more. He was so easy to talk to.

Quill and Charles were spending the last night before term started at the Gardiners'. Mr. Gardiner had insisted that a pair of twelve-year-old boys would be no trouble and had put their trunks in the stable. He would drive them to school on the morrow.

"Come, see the workshop," Charles said in a rare burst of enthusiasm.

Mr. Gardiner stood at the workbench. He was tapping spindles into a comb-shaped board. Mysterious tools hung on the walls. The whole room smelled sweetly of wood shavings. Charles picked up a scrap and chipped away at it with a penknife. Quill copied him, but when the dog he was carving lost an ear, it looked more like a lizard. He abandoned it.

Shavings and chips littered the dusty floor of packed earth. He knelt and dragged his finger, tracing pictures in the dust. He drew a tree, a fox, and a bear. If he were traveling through the wilderness, he would need to make a campfire.

He pulled the flint from his pocket. Athair had given it to him for his birthday. He wasn't about to leave something that good at home when he might need it at school. The metallic sound of flint on steel was followed by a bright orange spark. He scooped some sawdust into a little pile and tried again. When the spark touched the pile, it turned into a little flame the size of a single candle. Then the flame stretched as wide as the dust pile and raced across the floor.

Mr. Gardiner cried out and dropped what he was doing. Spindles bounced and rolled free. He stepped over them and grabbed Quill's arm, yanking him away from the fire. He stomped on the flames. Charles threw a bucket of water, which mostly landed on Mr. Gardiner but succeeded in putting out the fire.

Mr. Gardiner glared at Quill. "Were you trying to burn the shop down?"

"Nay, sir," he said in a small voice.

"Trying to destroy a week's work?" He gestured violently toward some half-finished chairs.

"Nay, sir."

Mr. Gardiner's angry face blurred. "Then what in the name of all that is good were you trying to do?"

"I didn't mean ta. I just...I wasn't thinking."

MR. GARDINER WAS WAITING AT THE TOP OF THE gully. His eyes were as cold as a January sky.

"She was showing me the columbine," he said, wishing to heaven they had returned promptly to the miserable dinner.

"All this time?"

"Papa," Miss Gardiner said, "I'm sorry, but I couldn't bear to be stuck inside on such a lovely day."

The man softened. "Next time you need some air during a party, stay in sight of the windows." He gave Quill a sharp look. "Understood?"

"Aye, sir."

The Gardiners took their leave, and Charles took Quill aside. "When you said she needed air, we naturally assumed you would be near the house in easy view of the windows. That's your problem, Quill. You don't look before you leap. It's bad enough when you hurt yourself. This time, you hurt Emmeline."

"I hurt her? Did ye hear yer father? Yer stepmother? Her mother? They hurt her. I offered her an escape. Then I got her mind on other matters."

Charles raised his eyes heavenward. "Do not allow my father to hear you speak like that. When Uncle Rob went looking for her, my father said...how can I put this delicately? He thought you were having a lark at her expense."

Quill felt ill. "I would never—"

Charles held up his hand. "I know you would never hurt a girl on purpose. I defended you as well as I could. But sometimes. You. Don't. Think." His voice crescendoed. This wasn't the first time he had defended Quill. Neither had forgotten the time, years ago, when Quill had been on trial. A little folly had allowed him to be framed for something another man had done. "It shattered your reputation once. Not everyone has forgotten. And my father and his wife don't have a sense of delicacy or restraint. Imagine the rumor getting back to Emmeline. You can't tell me it wouldn't hurt her." He was right. Blast it, why did Charles always have to be right?

"I'm sorry," Quill said, and he was. He had been abominably well behaved. He hadn't held her in his arms, hadn't kissed her, hadn't even touched those delightful little curls, and yet he had lost her family's respect almost as much as if he had. It was enough to turn a gentleman into a scoundrel, except a scoundrel wouldn't mind hurting her. He would never hurt Miss Gardiner. He couldn't bear to see her cry.

Sixteen

FOLLY, FEAR, & THE FOWEY

MONDAY, JUNE 12, 1775

"Good morrow, Mr. Morris," Caesar said. "Just a shave?"

"Just a shave," Quill confirmed, sitting in his usual chair. He tipped his head back and closed his eyes while the barber draped a cloth over his chest and shoulders. His thoughts drifted to pleasant shores and implausible dreams while Caesar brushed the cool shaving cream across the fine stubble. In his imagination, his empty hours were not occupied with the worry of war. Instead, he was courting and kissing a suitable lass: one with a fine dowry and musical accomplishments, one who was no relation to Charles, who looked at him with adoration in her blue eyes, her wispy curls brushing his brow as she leaned close.

A sharp blade skimmed his face. Lost in thought, he almost didn't hear the door open and close or a man settle into the next chair, ordering another barber to give him a trim and a shave, but there was something familiar in his tone that intruded on his daydreams with all the grace of a stray dog interrupting a concerto. His sister's husband, Jack Mason, was in the chair beside him.

The last time they spoke, Mason demanded the use of the Eagle for secret meetings to discuss building an army. Following his older brother's lead, Quill had refused. It was too dangerous. But Miss Gardiner, without knowing his dilemma or his decision, had challenged him. Danger didn't decide whether something was right or wrong. Either it was good for a freeman to confront a tyrant, or it wasn't. Athair had risked his life to challenge a king. He had lost his fight, and yet Quill had always been proud of him. Why? He had admired his courage and his conviction. And somewhere deep in his boyish heart, he had believed his father had been right to defend his homeland.

Athair had been right, despite the foolishness and despite the danger. How was this civil war different than the Jacobite Uprising? There was no Bonnie Prince Charlie to gather round, but the threat of the king's men in Virginia was the same. Quill hadn't forgotten the terror of Athair's tales of the danger even after the Battle of Culloden was lost, as English soldiers cut through the Highlands, burning crops and houses, pillaging and murdering as they went. Was it wrong for Virginians to plan their defense, to import arms while they still could?

Nay, as much as he hated to admit it, Mason was in the right to plan and prepare. It was foolish. It was dangerous. It was treason. And Quill was honor-bound to aid him in the defense of their homeland. Caesar drew a blade up his throat. Death awaited traitors to the crown. Quill's chest tightened, and his pulse drummed in his neck so hard he feared the barber would nick it. If he went down this path, even Charles wouldn't save him from the consequences of his folly.

This couldn't be right. All good things came from God, and there was nothing good in a hangman's noose. There was nothing good in betraying the trust of a friend who had defended him through every hard time that had come his way. He still hoped the fractured colony would hold together, that the battles would remain in New England, that a little patience would bring about peace. And yet, the cold truth was that King George III had sent troops and warships to America, with the clear intent to fight against her. Virginia's peace was as fragile as a windowpane in a hailstorm.

Fear was uncomfortable, and Quillan Morris disliked being uncomfortable. In need of greater wisdom than he possessed and uncertain which of his friends and relations to trust, he prayed, rehearsing his dilemma. *Lord, what do I do?*

While Caesar patted his face dry, a proverb came into Quill's mind: Make hay while the sun shines. It wasn't from the Good Book. It was common sense from common men. Why, when he was seeking supreme wisdom, did his mind fix on that rusty old saying? Was this brittle peace a Godsent time of preparation? If Chesapeake Bay were blockaded, it would be too late to send for arms. They needed to prepare, to be ready in case the war came to their land. He needed to help Jack, but he needed to do it without the danger of the written word and the disapproval of his trusted friend.

The barber removed the cloth from his chest. "There you are, sir."

"Thank ye, Caesar," Quill said, tying his cravat over his throat. "I'll settle my account now if ye have a moment."

He paid with a tobacco note from last year's harvest, then handed Caesar a small coin. With a glance at his master, who was busy with a client, Caesar slipped his coin in a pocket and gave Quill a short nod.

Pausing by the door, Quill raised his voice. "Jack, I'll meet ye outside when ye're done." He leaned against the outside of the building, whistling an old tune and watching a boy run a hoop down the street.

By and by, Jack threw the door open. A streak of white on one cheek and a red nick on his jaw bespoke haste. "What is it?" Jack asked. "Have ye reconsidered?"

"I have." Quill waited for fear to reassert itself. Curiously, it did not. Taking it as a divine sign, he pressed forward. "These are my conditions: never mention me or the Eagle in any written communications. Only come after dark. Leave the office as ye found it. Only then can ye use my office."

Jack shook his hand. "Expect us tonight, half an hour after sunset."

After that, the morning flew by. He had half a mind to take Gunpowder out for some exercise south of town the moment Charles went home for dinner. Miss Gardiner would be pleased with his decision to aid Jack. Quill frowned over a brief. He couldn't tell her any more than he could tell Charles, though for a different reason. The fewer people who knew of his involvement in Jack's scheme, the safer his neck would be. So long as he kept his lips sealed on the subject, there was no danger in seeing her— no more than there always was. If he could brave a gully without kissing her, there was no reason he couldn't brave the road where she lived without succumbing to the temptation.

His happy thoughts were interrupted by the arrival of George Wythe, clerk to the House of Burgesses. He and Charles rose to their feet. Polly set her knitting down but remained sitting, a lady's privilege.

"At yer service, Mr. Wythe," Quill said with a bow. "What can we do for you?"

"Mr. Morris, is it? Henry told the House that you had agreed to carry their business to the governor."

Quill glanced at Charles. "Aye, that I did."

Mr. Wythe handed a thick package of papers. Quill accepted them and stared at the red seal.

"You'll find the governor onboard the *Fowey* man-of-war."

"Not at Porto Bello?"

"I'm afraid not. His lordship has made business as inconvenient as possible."

Inconvenient was right. Dumore's plantation was six miles to the north. York Town, where the *Fowey* lay, was twice as far: twelve miles a little south of due east. He would have to ride twenty-four miles today if he hoped to sleep in his bed tonight.

Though it had been done in haste, he had given his word to

assist. His honor would be questioned if he declined now. He glanced at Charles, who gave a nod.

"I'll leave straightaway," he said.

The first few miles of the ride were pleasant. Verdant trees shaded the road, and Gunpowder was as eager to be out of the stable as Quill was to be out of the office. Then the sun reached its zenith, and he was overwarm and without a canteen to wash the dust from his throat. It was strange to ride so close to his family home without stopping in for a visit, but he pressed on. As he rode through York Town, it was tempting to stop at a tavern or coffeehouse for a drink, but his conscience propelled him not to rest before he had delivered the papers. The House of Burgesses was counting on him.

He left Gunpowder in the care of a livery stable in York Town and walked to the pier with his leather document case, his legs stiff from a dozen miles in the saddle. Coming out from the trees, he stopped short to gape at the twenty-gun man-of-war in the York River. Her masts, though bare of sails, were as straight and tall as old pine trees.

The accused didn't fear the law until they stepped into a courtroom. Quill hadn't truly feared the power and might of Britain until he saw the *Fowey*. He had seen the officers, a few at a time, in their red coats on the streets of Williamsburg. He had read about the *Fowey* in the *Gazette*, where it appeared as harmless as black type across white paper. It wasn't a large ship, as far as warships went. But it was big enough to defeat the Williamsburg Volunteer Company the moment the word was given. He was nothing beside it.

He squared his shoulders. He wasn't there as a barrister of very little consequence. He wasn't there as the brother-in-law to a radical rebel. Captain Montague and Lord Dunmore knew nothing of that arrangement. He was there on official business for the House of Burgesses. He wouldn't be frightened away from his errand merely because of a boat. He strode down the pier until he met a pair of guards.

"State your business," one guard said.

"Mr. Morris here to deliver the House of Burgesses' minutes to Lord Dunmore."

"Come with me."

Quill followed the guard up the gangplank and past dozens of His Majesty's Marines.

"Wait here," the man said, leaving him on the open deck. He exchanged words with men guarding a door. After an interminable wait, the man gestured for Quill to approach and pass through the door. Lord Dunmore, elegantly dressed, waited in a chamber with dark wood furnishings. The guard announced Quill, then left.

"Mr. Morrison, is it?" The man studied his features with the care of a professor marking an essay.

"Morris, sir," Quill said. "Just Morris." Years ago, in Scotland, his father had been a Morrison, but had changed his surname before arriving in America. Quill had been born a Morris, as had his siblings.

"You look familiar. Have we met?"

"Nay, sir, though ye may have seen me at church." It was how Quill had been able to recognize Dunmore.

"Ah, that must be it."

Quill removed the papers from the document case and handed them to the royal governor. "Mr. Wythe gave these to me this morning. I came directly."

Dunmore broke the seal and thumbed through the papers. "Wait for my reply." He gestured to a chair and left Quill alone in the stuffy room. After a few minutes, a man brought Quill a tart beverage. Somewhat refreshed, he amused himself with the view of the river and woods from the high window. He hadn't expected Dunmore to sound so much like Rabbie, speaking the King's English with precision and the faintest hint of a brogue. He was one of them—another Scotsman trying to make his way in an English world. No wonder so many of the Scots merchants were loyal to him.

At last, his lordship returned. "Here is my reply." He handed him a sealed letter. "Deliver this to the burgesses."

"Aye, sir."

His lordship paused. "Where did you say you were born?"

"Here. In Virginia."

Dunmore's gaze sharpened. "Truly? I would have guessed you were born in the Highlands."

"My parents were. They immigrated before my brother was born."

"You have a brother? Where is he?"

"He's a merchant in Williamsburg."

That satisfied Dunmore. "The Scottish merchants are among the king's most loyal subjects. Give yer family my regards."

"I will. Thank ye, sir." Quill secured the letter in his document case and took his leave.

Gunpowder, refreshed from the livery's care, was as eager to see the road as Quill was to complete his errands. But after several miles, his urgency to return slackened. He had Dunmore's reply safe in his document case. What difference would an hour's delay make to the burgesses? Likely, they wouldn't reconvene until the morrow, even if he made haste. There was no need to play the martyr. Halfway to Williamsburg, he turned Gunpowder toward the comforts of Willow Haven.

Seventeen

WILLOW HAVEN

Quill opened the door without knocking. This home had been built when he was nine years old. There was the banister he had slid down as a boy and the dents in the molding from the times he and Rabbie had played swordfight indoors. In the parlor was a white-haired woman with a black lace kerchief. She glanced up from her needlework.

"'Tis about time," Great-aunt Moira said, as though he were late for dinner.

Quill laughed and kissed her wrinkled cheek. "Were ye expecting me?"

"Aye, ever since yer father gave ye that brooch. Come sit down and tell me all about her."

He sat opposite her on a cushioned settee. "Her? What lass do ye wish ta ken?"

"The one ye're courting, laddie. Who else?"

"Ah. I'm afraid I'm no' courting anyone."

"Whyever not? Has nae one of the town lassies caught yer eye?"

The lass who had caught his eye lived outside of town. "How can they when I have yer beauty ta compare them ta?"

Aunt Moira laughed. "Ye're a fine one with words. Use a few of them on a bonny young lass, and ye'll be courting in nae time."

"Quillan? Is my lad home?" His dark-haired stepmother entered the parlor, her face lighting when she saw him. "I thought I heard ye."

He rose and kissed her cheek. "Afternoon, Màthair. Business took me ta York Town and I couldna pass by without stopping in."

"Will ye stay 'til supper?"

"I'm afraid not. I've been gone most of the day already. I left York Town in such haste I didna stop for dinner."

"My poor lad. Ye canna leave until ye've eaten. Wait here, I'll bring something."

"Quill!" Marta squealed as she ran into the parlor, her mob cap askew over her brown hair. "Spin me, Quill!"

He scooped her up and spun in circles until she lost her cap and hair ribbon. He set her feet on the ground and dropped onto the settee, waiting for the spinning room to settle.

Marta walked as dizzy as a drunkard to collect her things. "Will ye come for my birthday? It's in..." her face scrunched as she counted on her fingers, "ten days."

"Ten days? And how old will ye be?" He tapped his chin. "I ken. Ye'll be sixteen."

"Nay. Anna is sixteen. I'll be eight."

"Eight? Are ye certain?"

She giggled. "Aye, I'm certain."

"Come here, lassie," Aunt Moira said. "Let me fix that ribbon of yers."

Màthair returned with a tray piled with enough scrumptious offerings to feed the family. She loaded a plate with salted meat, bannocks, and tea cakes and handed it to Quill. He balanced it on his knees as he broke and buttered a bannock while his step-mother prepared bergamot tea. Rumors of war faded as he ate. He was home, and all was right in the world.

Athair walked in. "Quill! I've been looking for ye since I saw Gunpowder in the pasture. What brings ye home?"

"Business took me ta York Town." He paused, wondering what effect his next words would have on his father. "Dunmore sends his regards."

Athair scowled. "What business did ye have with that old turncoat?"

Quill leaned back in the settee, explaining at length what the burgesses had asked him to do.

The frown softened, though it did not leave his father's face. "I suppose 'tis an honor," he said at last.

"Aye," Màthair said, serving the tea, "ta be trusted with something so important, 'tis a great honor for our lad."

Anna, Grace, and Hope joined the party in the parlor, exchanging news and stories until at last Màthair asked, "When did ye need ta return?"

"Soon." Glancing at the open windows, he saw the shadows had lengthened to early evening. He needed to make haste.

"I'll see that Gunpowder is saddled," Athair said.

Màthair began packing food as though he were journeying into the wilderness, not back to town.

"Come on my birthday," Marta said, "and bring me a present."

"Hush, Marta," scolded Grace.

"Come again," Aunt Moira repeated, "and bring me yer favorite lassie."

No one dared to hush Aunt Moira, so Quill laughed and kissed her goodbye.

He rode past the small house where he had been born. The building had come with this land that had enchanted his mother the summer she had first seen it. Lights like will-o'-the-wisps had winked in the willows by the creek. After witnessing so much death and destruction during and after Culloden, then fleeing with naught but each other and two heavy trunks, this land was a precious refuge, a safe place to bring their bairns into the world.

As their fortunes grew, Athair built the big house, and their land became a haven for their countrymen to work out their indentures. He passed a village of tiny shops and cottages. What would Miss Gardiner think of Willow Haven if she ever saw it? Would she be at home in his home? Aye, the lass would be as natural here as bluebells in the woods and bannocks on the table.

That pleasant thought kept him company through the sunset and gloaming, all the way back to Williamsburg, where he delivered Dunmore's papers to Mr. Wythe, stabled Gunpowder, and walked stiffly home. Polly was in the front room, reading by candlelight. She looked up when he walked in.

"There ye are," she said. "I hope ye dinna mind, but when I told Mason ye were away, he insisted ye had promised ta open the office for him."

Quill collapsed on the settee with a groan. Gooseberry leapt onto his lap.

"Was that wrong?" she asked anxiously.

"Nay," he said, absently stroking the cat's patchwork fur, "I promised him this morning, but once Mr. Wythe came ta the office, I didna give another thought ta the matter. Is he still there?"

She shook her head. "I locked up a few minutes ago."

"Good. Polly, promise me ye willna tell anyone about this, especially Charles."

Her brows knit together. "I promise."

"Not even in writing. Ye willna write about it in a letter or a journal or anywhere."

Polly's book snapped shut. "Quill, what's going on?"

It would have been hard enough keeping the matter a secret from Polly if he had been home. She already knew half of the matter. "I gave Jack permission ta use the Eagle ta discuss matters of defense. I meant ta be there."

Polly's eyes went wide. "Defense? Ye mean an army?"

"If there's an attack on Virginia, we need ta be ready. We need more than a militia. We need arms and ammunition. 'Tis treason.

There's no way around it. A condemning letter connecting me ta it could send me ta the gallows. I wish ta do what is right, but I dinna wish ta hang for it. I trust ye, Polly. Dinna breathe a word of this, not ta Rabbie, not ta Charles."

She placed a hand on her book and raised the other like she was preparing to testify in court. "With God as my witness, I promise."

That night, Quill dreamed the *Fowey* chased him down the Palace Green, cutting through the sod. Curling off the broadsides in waves as tall as the church steeple were bricks, earth, and trees. Miss Gardiner ran between him and the man-of-war. She held up the little book Polly had made her oath on, and the ship sank into the earth at her feet, the might of Britain subdued by words as insubstantial as paper.

Eighteen

LIBERTY OF SPEECH

TUESDAY, JUNE 13, 1775

Once Emmeline began teaching Kitty and Henrietta, it was agreed that she would help Papa in the workshop in the hours between when lessons ended and dinner was served. After dinner, she helped Mama with the kitchen and garden chores she wasn't able to finish in the early morning.

Late one Tuesday morning in mid-June, after a successful lesson featuring the letter *K*, Emmeline sat on her three-legged stool with the *Gazette* while Papa stood at the bench, crafting dovetails for the drawers of a document cabinet. With all the dynamic expressions she had mastered through reading Shakespeare, she read a speech delivered in the House of Commons.

"But, Sir, we are told that America is too strong for us and that we cannot make her submit. Idle and ridiculous idea! To suppose that a people without an army, and without the means of paying, feeding, and supporting one, are to be able, all of a sudden, to start up conquerors. If I was to believe the argument I have heard, in its real extent, I should suppose they were to conquer us."

She skimmed ahead, anxious to see what the vote had been. "They passed the Restraining Act," she said in a subdued voice. "The king signed it."

The bill had been an ongoing point of parliamentary debate for months. At first, the New England Restraining Act was only to apply to four of the northern colonies, forbidding trade with foreign nations and prohibiting them from fishing in the North Atlantic. Then, with little debate and no time to defend themselves, five more colonies had been added to the bill.

Papa sighed. "It includes Virginia?"

"It does." There would be no more Dutch ships braving Chesapeake Bay when this bill took effect. If the colonists continued to boycott British goods and Parliament forbade them from trading with anyone but Britain, what would happen to colonial merchants? The brother of Mr. Morris had too many empty shelves in his small store, even after the Dutch had brought their goods. What would happen to him? What would happen to the colonists who relied on merchants for the goods they couldn't grow and make themselves?

Looking for comfort, she said, "At least they don't prohibit us from using our own wood." That natural resource was abundant in Virginia. Local sawyers were taking advantage of all the damaged trees from the hailstorm: black walnut and pine, maple and oak. Imports could stop for years, and Papa would still be building furniture. Her family was safe.

"Indeed," Papa said, not looking up from the dovetail he was chiseling, "they haven't forbidden that natural right. But trappers aren't allowed to make hats with the furs they have trapped, and Virginians cannot export linen made from flax they have grown. Now, New England fishermen cannot fish in the open ocean. If the king can forbid fishermen from fishing, what is to stop him from forbidding sawyers from cutting wood? Or if he can forbid a flax farmer from weaving linen, what is to stop him from forbidding a cabinetmaker from building a cabinet?"

She folded the *Gazette* in silence. Papa's questions sobered her. If the freedoms of their sister trades had been chiseled away, their shop was just one strike of the mallet from joining them. It wasn't right. It wasn't fair. Laws should exist to protect people and to keep the peace, not to put honest workers out of business. They needed a hero to fight back, to protect their natural rights— someone to defend the innocent merchants, fishermen, and tradesmen. Someone to keep her family safe.

She put on her shop apron and lined up the little pine toys. There was a large collection of tops she had turned on the lathe, and a friendly cat that Charles had whittled before the wedding. Today, she was free to wield a brush, a hammer, or a pen. Would she always be? Were such freedoms truly in danger?

She uncorked a bottle of paint as verdant as the gully at Johnson Hall, then dipped the tip of a small brush in the bottle. She held the brush steady as she turned the top, creating a ring of green. Virginia was a land of many colors: red roses nodded their ruffled heads behind white pickets, joyful yellow sunflowers stretched over split-rail fences, rooted in the deep brown of rich soil, and brilliant blue skies followed every gray storm, but most of all, there was green. There was the golden green that whispered of spring, the deep blue-green of the shadowy woods in summer, the fields of green that promised a rich harvest, the silvery green that winked from high in the treetops. She had found every shade of Virginia green in one man's eyes.

She mixed a drop of red with the green on a dented tin plate, then added a stripe of the earthy green to the top. "Virginia is so far from London. What have we done to draw their anger to us?"

"Nothing," Papa said. "Nothing but speak an opinion that differs from theirs. Nothing but behave like freemen. Our Grand Charter guarantees liberty of speech. For over a hundred and fifty years, that freedom has supported a candid discussion of every issue this colony has faced. The most essential freedom is the freedom to disagree."

Emmeline glanced up from her paints. "Why should that matter more than our natural rights?" The freedoms denied in the new Restraining Act seemed much more punitive than words could ever be.

"Speech is a natural right. God gave us each a mind, a conscience, and the power to articulate what weighs on us. Only a fool seeks to silence those who disagree with him."

"Only a fool? Doesn't every man find disagreement to be disagreeable?"

"You studied Euclid. In geometry, is *A* farther from *B* or is *B* farther from *A*?"

She frowned. They had been discussing Locke, not Euclid. "They're the same."

"Correct. And so it is in every disagreement. The difference is as great on each side. Herein is the great mystery of government. The opinions of our elected representatives are as diverse as those of the voters who elected them. It is in the collision of truth and opinions that we create a unified voice."

This riddle was too much. "Sir?"

He frowned and glanced about the shop as though concrete tools would provide the abstract answer. His gaze returned to his work, and inspiration lit his eyes. "How do I unite four boards of differing lengths and facing different directions into one drawer?"

She glanced at the tool in his hand. "You chisel them and..." she paused, envisioning the tight dovetail created from the collision of metal on wood, "each gives away just enough to hold tight to the other."

"Good girl," he murmured, and returned to his work. Papa worked with his hands, but he was wiser than any of the king's ministers.

She uncorked another bottle of paint, feeling quite wise to have puzzled out his riddle. A contrasting ring of red was just what this top needed. Some differences were quite agreeable. She and Mr. Morris had disagreed in the ravine, but each had given a little space to the other's words. Might other wise men listen to the truths in her heart and mind if she dared to speak them?

~

Restless at work, Quill had left for an early ride before dinner. The road south of town was quiet. The Gardiners' home and gardens were quieter. He sighed. He might not see his favorite lass until they dined together at the Blue House on the morrow. He rode on for a mile before turning back to town. Approaching the Gardiners' home again, he slowed Gunpowder to a crawl, scanning every corner of the pasture and gardens for a bonny figure and a sweet face. His gelding took the liberty of pulling up grass that grew just beyond the pasture's split-rail fence. In that pause, something colorful caught his eye in the shop window. Upon inspection, he saw it was a merry collection of painted toys. Marta's birthday was coming soon. He ought to get her a gift. He dismounted and secured Gunpowder's reins to the pasture fence.

Hadn't Charles said his cousin helped in the shop, here and there? If he lingered, there was a hope that he would see her. He opened the street-side door and let himself inside. The shop had expanded since the last time he had entered it. The front room had a wood floor. On the wall to his left was a tidy line of dusted and polished tea tables, a cabinet-on-chest, and a clothespress. Along the wall to his right were two painted writing chairs, a settee with block-printed cushions, and, leaning upright in the corner, a child's coffin.

"Be with you in a minute," Mr. Gardiner called, his voice distant.

Quill crossed the wareroom and paused on the threshold of the dusty workshop. Miss Gardiner sat on a low stool in a back corner, intent on the movements of a fine brush with red paint. So that was what Charles had meant when he said she helped in the shop. She painted. He could have said as much. Even the most genteel ladies dabbled in paints. There was no reason to be secretive.

"Good day, Mr. Morris," Mr. Gardiner said, looking up from his work.

Miss Gardiner looked up with wide eyes and a mouth round in surprise. Quill grinned. The sound of his name had stolen her rapt attention.

"Good day," he said. "I was riding by, and I saw the toys in the window. It's my wee sister's birthday soon, and I thought there might be something suitable."

"Emma, could you assist him?"

"Yes, sir." She set her brush in a tin cup, then stood and smoothed her paint-splattered pinner. Quill couldn't help the way his eyes followed her hands across her waist and down her skirts. Her figure was just as fine splattered in paint as it was wrapped in her Sunday best. He glanced at her father, who hadn't noticed the open admiration, then retreated to the safety of the wareroom.

"How old is your little sister?" Miss Gardiner asked, following him to the window.

"She's turning eight."

"So young?" It wasn't the first time someone had been surprised that the youngest and oldest siblings in the family were separated by twenty years.

"She's my stepsister," he said, and picked up a Jacob's Ladder from the windowsill. Each block was painted with a different flower. He tipped the top block forward, painted with a rose, and it fell, leaving a block with a daisy in its place. "Do ye paint all of these yerself?"

"I do. I like to paint."

"So does my stepmother. She does beautiful landscapes. I have a few in my office."

"That sounds lovely. I don't do anything that fine. I just paint toys."

"Children need toys more than fine landscapes." He set the blocks down and picked up a fox the size of his thumb. It held its bushy tail high. Her hand had drawn a delicate smile. The friendly beast pleased him. Might it please Marta?

"Charles whittled that one, but I painted it. I had to mix three colors to get the coat right.

The fox was an earthy shade that wasn't quite red, orange, or brown. "'Tis perfect," he said. "Quite lifelike."

"Thank you. I think the color is rather handsome myself." She dropped her gaze and blushed. It gave her dimpled cheeks a lovely wash of pink. He was so enchanted by the effect that he almost missed the cause. He looked back at the wee fox. He had seen that color before. He saw it every morning in the looking glass. She hadn't tried to match a fox. She had mixed her paints to match his hair because she liked the color. The heat flamed up his neck and across his face, curling at the tips of his ears.

He set the fox down as though it were a tea cake hot from the fire and picked up a top, painted with flowers as blue as her eyes. He pinched the stem and flicked a finger across it. The top skittered off the windowsill and landed on the floor, still spinning merrily. "'Tis a fine top. Did yer father carve it?"

"No," she said, her voice whisper-soft. She bit her lip, then added. "I—I did."

He looked at the tops with a new appreciation. Some were big and some were small. The curves were of different thicknesses, but each top was smooth and balanced. Each one was painted with cheerful colors, some in bold stripes, others with delicate flowers or foliage. Miss Gardiner had the most delightful accomplishments. "Ye do fine work," he said. "Marta would love all of this. How am I ta choose just one?" He pulled the smallest coin from his pocketbook, a Spanish piece of eight, and handed it to her.

She stared at the silver wedge a moment, then said. "Then don't take one. Take two or three."

"Are ye certain?"

In response, she gathered up each of the three toys he had touched and handed them to him. "I'm certain."

He slipped the fox into his waistcoat pocket. Marta would be content with two toys.

~

Late that evening, wearing naught but her nightshift and lappet cap, she slipped into Charles' old room. She removed two precious sheets of paper from the writing table and gazed up at the full moon. A chorus of crickets and frogs filled the warm night air. The chores of the day fell away, and she cleared her mind, eager to meet her muse.

In her best penmanship, she began with the couplet that had come to her while churning butter.

What will we buy with a brave man's life?
What is worth the tears of the farmer's wife?

The words were her own, and they gave her a thrill. Her first poem. It was beautiful. Not quite Shakespeare, but finer than many lines she had seen published in the Poet's Corner of the *Gazette*. She waited for the beckoning of a muse, that little spark of light in her mind. In a moment, it came to her, like a leaf on the breeze.

The bravest blood of this generation—

That was good. She recorded it, dipped her quill in the inkwell, and then hesitated over the paper. A drop of ink splattered the page. She frowned and held the quill over the inkwell. Her muse had failed to finish the couplet. She must do it. What rhymed with generation? Veneration, celebration, obliteration, and desperation. They were all excellent words. One of them would serve her with distinction.

Will be spilled out of desperation.

That sounded pathetic, not heroic. She crossed it out and tried again.

> *Will be spilled for veneration.*

No. Just no.

> *Will be the cause of celebration.*

There had to be something better than that.

> *Will face obliteration.*

Every line was terrible. She dashed them out, smearing wet ink across the page and her hand. Forget the bravest blood. She would copy the poem out on a fresh page once it was complete. What were they fighting for? She could start there. This time, she arranged the words in her head, waiting to have a working pair of lines before wasting ink on them. After a time, she had several.

> *Justice and fairness before the law*
> *The virtues that the sages saw*
> *Blood runs red and courage dear*
> *Will help Virginians save it here.*

She read through her poem from the beginning. It rhymed well enough, but her meaning grew muddier as the words marched on. What were Virginians helping to save? She would have to expound on that.

> *Our birthright as Englishmen—*

She frowned. Mr. Morris had objected to being called an Englishman. She tried again.

> *Our rights on English soil*
> *For which we do toil—*

The meter was inconsistent, and the words were uninspired. How had the bard done it? She wrestled with words until the moon was high in the night sky. Then, she copied the page with her best penmanship, sanded the ink, washed her hands, and climbed into bed. Henrietta didn't stir when she joined her.

Emmeline slept past dawn and spent the morning racing through her chores, afraid of being held home when Mrs. Evans' carriage came for her. She began lessons by reading her poem to her captive students, watching eagerly for their reaction to her efforts, waiting to surprise them when she said that she was the author. Instead, Kitty fidgeted, and Henrietta yawned.

When she finished, Henrietta said, "What was that all about?"

"What do you mean?"

"It's like Plutarch. Lots of fancy words jumbled together that don't mean anything." Being compared to one of the greatest writers of the ancient world ought to have been a compliment. Henrietta meant it as a criticism.

"They mean things," Emmeline said.

"Like what?"

"Well, it's a poem about how Virginians would sacrifice their blood to preserve their rights. It's quite noble."

"If you say so."

Emmeline set the poem aside. Was it that bad? Kitty said nothing, but if the meaning was too complex for a twelve-year-old, she couldn't expect an eight-year-old to appreciate it. Henrietta was a poor judge of literature, but the printers of the *Gazette* saw poems every week. They would be better judges. She could submit it to them, and if it was good enough, they would print it. She would deliver it when she settled their account at the end of the month. If they printed her name in bold type, accompanied by her work, then she would know it was good.

Nineteen

DISTRACTION IN THE KITCHEN

WEDNESDAY, JUNE 14, 1775

A friendly fox smiled at Quill from his washstand as he worked the pomade into his hair. He followed with a light dusting of hair powder, ran a horn comb through his hair, then tied it back with a black ribbon. He checked the effect in a hand mirror. Miss Gardiner liked that color, just like she had enjoyed watching the fireworks with him. He knotted his cravat. Heat blossomed under the innocuous fabric. She had clung to his cravat, her face pressed against his chest, when the illuminations had begun. He tucked the tails of the cravat into his waistcoat and slipped the fox into the pocket. He grinned and shrugged on his jacket. The sooner he got to work, the sooner he could see her again.

He threw open his chamber door with a decisive air. "Are ye ready?"

Polly was standing by the front window. "I have been for ten minutes."

"Then what are we waiting for?"

Halfway across the street, Polly interrupted his whistling. "Why are ye so happy?"

"Why shouldn't I be?" He glanced about the street. A cart and wagon. A stray dog. Children chasing each other. "The weather's fine." He slid the heavy key into the lock. "And 'tis a Wednesday. Everybody loves Wednesdays." He threw open the office door and gestured for Polly to precede him.

She looked at him like he was daft. "Nobody loves Wednesdays."

"Oh. Well, they should."

She settled into her writing chair. Quill thumbed through his papers. Where had he left off yesterday?

"I suppose," Polly mused, "dining at the Blue House is something ta look forward ta. Is that it?"

"Aye," he said, unable to suppress a grin. "Dinner at the Blue House is always fine."

There it was. His brief for the Baptist fined for not paying tithes to the Anglican Church. Since the law required everyone to pay tithes, he would need to craft a moral argument, persuading the jury to make an exception. Yesterday, he had written, "If anyone will respect the higher laws of conscience, surely it is the church." It was a decent opening. What would Miss Gardiner think of it?

Polly interrupted his thoughts. "Is it the food or the company?"

Quill turned a page. "Is *what* the food or the company?"

"The reason ye love dining at the Blue House."

"Oh," he said, sobering. The last thing he needed was Polly's teasing. "Both," he said with nonchalance.

"Ah," she said, almost matching his casual tone as she opened the account book. "Of course ye dinna fancy anyone there. Our hostess is far too old. I'm yer sister. Susan is married. And dear Miss Gardiner is—"

He couldn't help the heat that spread across his face any more than he could stop a fire from racing across wood shavings. Polly glanced up in time to see him redden. Her eyes widened. His complexion betrayed him. It was too late to fully deny the attraction. He could only minimize it.

"'Tis nothing of a serious nature. Just a wee bit of a fancy. 'Twill pass soon enough."

She raised her brows. "Ye've done nothing ye would be ashamed ta admit in front of Charles?"

"Nothing has happened."

"Nothing? Ye were alone with her at the fireworks and Johnson Hall. Ye smile whene'er I say her name. Come ta think of it, ye're uncanny cheery after ye exercise Gunpowder. Ye've been sneaking off ta see her, haven't ye? Yet ye swear nothing has happened? Would she say the same?"

"Well—" Quill didn't have an opportunity to consider what Miss Gardiner might say because at that moment, Charles opened the door. While he hung his hat, Quill dragged his finger across his throat. This conversation ended. Now.

"Happy Wednesday, Charles," Polly said sweetly. Quill fought the urge to throw his inkwell.

Charles gave him a look that said, "What's up with her this morning?"

Quill shook his head. "How is yer family?"

Charles smiled foolishly. "She's fine."

"I'm glad ta hear it," Quill said.

"As am I," Polly said. "I'm sure Miss Gardiner feels the same." She winked at Quill.

In response, he dragged his finger across his throat. She needed to be as silent as the dead, or things between him and Charles were going to be very uncomfortable very soon.

Polly smiled cheekily. "Quill and I were just talking about how much we look forward ta dinners at the Blue House."

He leapt to his feet and gave her one more warning.

Charles stared at him. "Whose life is about to end?" At least someone understood the gesture.

"Hopefully no one." He placed his hands on his desk, scattered with papers. "Have ye ever defended a manslaughter?"

The next hour, he kept rapid notes while Charles explained every argument that might defend a man accused of manslaughter, and even more that would condemn him.

~

"I'm sorry dinner isn't on the table yet," Mrs. Evans said. "Maurice has a toothache." Her famous French chef was ill. Quill was famished. It took all of his efforts to stay on the other side of the parlor from Miss Gardiner. He needed a bracing meal or he would collapse under the strain of it.

"I'll help," Quill said. He could carry food as well as a servant.

"Well, I—"

"I'll go with Mr. Morris," Miss Gardiner said.

Polly looked expectantly at Quill. He ought to refuse her companionship. But he was already half-famished and wasting by the minute. His mind refused to articulate a rational argument for her to stay in the parlor.

"That isn't necessary," Charles said.

"If we are to eat, I'm afraid it might be," Miss Gardiner said. "I suspect I know my way around a kitchen better than he does." Then she slipped a hand into the crook of his arm and tugged him into motion.

Quill glanced back at Charles. His friend gave a reluctant wave of his hand as though telling him to go along, but be quick about it. Charles could see there was no arguing with his adorable cousin when her mind was made up.

The kitchen was a grave disappointment. It smelled of stew, but the only food in sight was a lump of raw dough and a basket of berries. His stomach growled. Nothing was prepared. Dinner was a long way off. "What can we help ye with?"

Maurice held a hand to his jaw as he spoke. Quill understood nothing. Either his toothache had impaired his speech beyond recognition, or in his distress, he had reverted to his native tongue. He glanced at Emmeline.

She raised both hands and pressed downward with her palms. "*Doucement. Doucement.*" Now she made no sense.

Maurice caught his breath and began again. The words came slower. Quill only caught scraps of Latin roots, but Miss Gardiner was nodding.

"Ye speak French?" He trusted her to learn anything a book could teach, but no book was adequate to convey the pronunciation and accent of another language. In the colonies, it was a rare lady who could speak French or German. He hadn't expected his friend's cousin to be one of the cultured few who could. When would she have had the opportunity?

Maurice scowled at the interruption.

"Yes. Hush," was all Miss Gardiner said, then gestured for Maurice to continue.

Quill held his tongue while his stomach rumbled. From the rafters hung strands and garlands of garlic, onions, dried apple slices, and herbs. It was some comfort to know they would starve surrounded by food.

She sighed and turned to him. "We don't have time to do everything he had planned. Everyone is expecting dinner now."

"The sooner we have dinner, the better." It was his life's motto.

She nodded slowly. "What can you cook?"

"Me?" He had never prepared a meal for company before. As a child, when he snuck into the kitchen, he would earn his pillage by slicing vegetables or stirring a stew. As a man, he hadn't had the opportunity to do more. His apartment didn't have a proper kitchen. Polly often set the table with cold cuts of meat from the butcher and bread from the bakery. In the winter, they might fry eggs or boil coffee in the fireplace. When Polly was feeling ambitious, he would haul a cast iron pot down the road where, for a small fee, the baker would cook it in his oven. Quill cleared his throat. "I can fry eggs."

Miss Gardiner looked at him expectantly as though certain his repertoire extended beyond that.

"And boil coffee."

She blinked twice. "Indeed."

He cursed the deficiencies of his education. All of that tutoring had been a waste. He couldn't prepare a dish worthy of company.

"Let's see what our other resources are." She made her way around the kitchen, looking in jugs and jars. "Milk, cream, butter, eggs, salt, pepper, and nutmeg." She looked at Maurice. "Is there cider? I could whip up a syllabub."

His face brightened. "Ah. *Oui.*" He pointed to the ladder and spoke rapidly in French.

"In the loft?" Quill asked. He couldn't bake, but he could climb. "I can get it." He was up the ladder in a trice and looking about the loft. In one corner was Maurice's rumpled bedding. A miniature painting and an ornate cross were nailed to the wall above the bed. Dried herbs hung in bunches from the ceiling. Barrels were stacked as high as the sloping roof allowed.

He tipped a barrel on its side and rolled it across the floor. Then Quill climbed far enough down the ladder to see what the others were doing in the kitchen. Maurice sat nursing his toothache. Miss Gardiner had tied his apron around her waist and was attempting to pin the narrow point of the triangular bib to her bodice. Quill returned his attention to the cider. With his feet on the lowest rung of the ladder, he coaxed the barrel toward him with his fingertips. One moment, it was hesitating on the edge of the loft. The next, it fell heavily into his arms. He stumbled off the ladder and fell hard on his tailbone.

The pain was blinding. He groaned and rolled to his back, the barrel pressing into his stomach. The sharp pain ebbed from him, hurting less with every breath. He opened his eyes. His guardian angel was leaning over him, her brows drawn together. A few wild curls had escaped her cap and bobbed about her face, like leaves in the breeze. He reached up and gave one curl a gentle tug. When he released it, the curl bounced back in place.

"Are you much hurt?" Miss Gardiner asked.

The question prodded his bruised pride. Her concern was pity, not admiration. She wouldn't dream of bending down to kiss him. He couldn't allow it even if she did. He had insisted to Polly that nothing had happened. His sister would know if that had changed, just as she had known he fancied her. Clenching his teeth, he rose to his feet and hefted the barrel manfully to his shoulder. "I'm fine," he said. "Where do ye wish for me ta put this?"

The concern was still on her brow. She didn't believe his bluff. She hesitated, and the tip of her tongue moistened her lips in a most distracting manner. At last she said, "On the table."

He set the barrel down where she had indicated, then offered a courtly bow.

Maurice pulled a cork and filled a tin cup as though resuming meal preparations, but he sat back on the three-legged stool and drank it.

Quill caught Miss Gardiner's eye. "I'm sure that was medicinal."

She smiled. "I hope so." Then she cocked her head. "Do you need some?"

"I'm better now, thank ye. I'll have naught save a bruise for my troubles."

She lifted a lid from a pot over the fire, and a tantalizing smell filled the kitchen.

"What's that?" he asked. "Ye canna have made a whole dish while I was in the loft."

"You're right. Maurice was preparing the filling for a savory pie. Since we don't have time to bake it in the crust, I thought it wise to reheat it as a stew."

She cracked an egg, carefully separating the white and yolk into separate bowls. He sat on a stool, his tender tailbone just off the seat, and watched her work. She cracked three more eggs, separating them deftly. Then she glanced up. "What?"

"Nothing," he said. The pleats of her white cap framed her face like a halo. Maurice's apron had never looked so soft and sweet as it did on her figure. Her eyes were deeper than the sea, and he would gladly drown in them. He rested his chin on one hand. "Ye look right bonny."

She glanced down at Maurice's apron. "I think you must have hit your head." If hitting his head was an excuse for speaking freely, he would embrace it.

Maurice held up his cider cup and said something that made her mouth drop open and her eyes widen.

Quill laughed. "I agree with whatever he said."

Her eyes grew wider. "I certainly hope not." Then she narrowed her eyes. "Do you speak French?"

"Nay, lassie, but the way ye blushed just now makes me think he must be right."

Her mouth dropped open again. "How dare you—" she broke off, smothering laughter— "think anything about me that would make me blush?" She turned imperiously. Going up on her tiptoes, she took another bowl from a shelf.

He sighed with contentment. "Did ye know," he said before he could think better of it, "ye're just as bonny from the back as ye are from the front?"

She gasped, whirled in place, and shook a spoon at him. "You, sir," she said primly, though her eyes danced and her cheeks dimpled, "are a distraction in the kitchen."

He grinned. "Believe me. The feeling is mutual."

The teasing faded as her gaze caressed his freckles, following them across his brow, down his nose and chin, and brushing up his jaw. Then those eyes of celestial blue looked into his soul with a light, love, and purity that could only be called heavenly. He was breathless. It didn't matter that they were on opposite sides of the kitchen. As incomprehensible as a chariot of fire, without a touch, without a word, she had pulled his soul to a holier plane.

She blushed and looked away. He blinked, as dizzy from her intimate gaze as he had been from his fall. They were on earth, in a kitchen, chaperoned by an inebriated Frenchman. He glanced at Maurice. He was smiling as though nothing gave him greater pleasure than watching Quill fall in love with the bonny lass who was doing his work. Maurice lifted his cider as if to toast a marriage. That sobered Quill. There was no wedding. This was a passing fancy. It had to be, though, for the life of him, he couldn't remember why. It would come to him later, when his reason returned. For now, they were responsible for getting dinner on the table. In a businesslike voice, he said, "What can I do?"

"I suppose you could beat the egg whites." She passed him a bowl and a beater.

"I'll beat anything ye ask me to."

Her eyes twinkled. "Then beat them until they're white and fluffy. I'll ready the other ingredients."

"Yes, ma'am."

The egg was beginning to look white but not fluffy when Charles came in. He looked from Quill to his cousin, measuring the distance with his eyes. Maurice was seated between them, drinking more cider.

"The syllabub will be done shortly," Quill said, not meeting his friend's eyes. "We can eat soon." He had assured Polly that nothing had happened that he would be ashamed to admit to his friend. When he had said that, he hadn't known how much could happen without a touch or a word. This enchantment was no fickle fancy. He was in love.

It wasn't shame that held his tongue. It was loyalty. Charles had made his expectations clear. A relationship with his cousin was forbidden. How could their friendship, already fractured from the political disputes, survive a betrayal of this magnitude? It wouldn't. Quill would be forced to choose between the loyalty of a friend and the love of his cousin. It was impossible.

Twenty

DISSENSION

Quill boarded the *Fowey* before the sun had crested the trees. After exchanging rehearsed pleasantries with the royal governor, he pulled a sealed bundle from his document satchel. "Here are the bills and resolves ready for yer perusal, sir."

Dunmore took the stack. "I see they've had a productive week. Let us hope they have finally devised a plan to reconcile with Britain."

"Aye, sir," Quill said. "Let us hope." Hope was why he was here, delivering papers, and why Charles had worked late, helping him prepare a brief. Hope was why the Continental Congress had declared July twentieth to be a day of fasting and prayer for a constitutional reconciliation with the Mother Country. Hope was why he continued to seek Miss Gardiner's company when reason told him he was foolish.

Dunmore excused himself, leaving Quill with neither amusements nor refreshments to pass the long hours of one of the longest days of the year. The sun was nearing its zenith when the governor returned. Quill stood and waited for his lordship to speak first.

Dunmore threw the papers on the table. "I cannot believe the House has made no attempts to reconcile with the Mother Country. On top of that, they have an ill-conceived plan to pay the militia for its services last year that I cannot approve. They insist there isn't enough coin in the colony and that the only option is to print paper credit."

Quill listened in respectful silence, not daring to agitate his lordship further. It seemed to him that if Lord Dunmore had a better plan for paying the troops he had mobilized last year on the frontier that he should have informed the House of it months ago. And if there was no better plan, then they would have to settle for paper money and take precautions against devaluing it.

He handed Quill a sealed letter. "Deliver this to the House promptly, Mr. Morris. Our time is drawing short."

"Aye, sir," Quill said. He was troubled by Dunmore's cryptic words. If time was drawing short, then hope was growing thin. The royal governor and the House of Burgesses were drawing farther apart each week. They no longer acted like branches of the same government, but like branches of neighboring trees, one old and strong, if a little sickly. The other was young and tender. Would they both survive the coming storm?

He bypassed Willow Haven and by two o'clock in the afternoon, arrived at the capitol building, where he delivered the message to Mr. Wythe. He lingered long enough to hear the letter read. Dunmore saw no objection to most of the bills, which he would sign once the House delivered them to him onboard the *Fowey*, but he refused to support the paper currency, professing indignation at the House's plan to support it by imposing a ten percent duty on slaves. Shouts of outrage filled the hall. Quill soon grew weary of the repetitive arguments and discreetly asked the clerk when he expected his services to be needed again. Assured it would not be until the morrow, he betook himself to the Raleigh for dinner. Then he went to the Eagle, vowing to work until the summer sun set.

The shadows were long when a boy delivered a note from Mr. Wythe. His services would not be required on the morrow. Their reply to his lordship would be delivered by Colonel Andrew Lewis, who had fought under his direction last fall and wished to speak to Dunmore in person about paying the brave men who had been injured on the frontier, fighting in the king's name.

Twenty-One

LETTERS

"Goodbye, Kitty. I'll see you Monday morning."

Kitty curtsied. "Goodbye, Miss Gardiner." Then she grabbed Gideon's hand and skipped down the road beside him.

Her studies had been slow, yet steady. Today, she had learned the letter *S* and reviewed all the letters that came before. In a fortnight, they would complete the alphabet and begin the syllabary and the Lord's Prayer printed on the hornbook. By the end of July, they might be done with the hornbook and move on to *Dixon's English Instructor,* with its complete syllabary and lists of simple words. Was it too ambitious to hope Kitty would be reading *Mother Goose's Medley* by cider season?

Emmeline placed her needlework basket beside Plutarch's *Lives* on the schoolshelf. Suddenly, as giddy as Kitty at the end of lessons, she flew up the stairs. Mama had asked her to settle their accounts today. She went to her chamber and threw open the clothespress. She lifted the winter blankets and put the stack on the bed. Hiding under where the blankets had been was her poem. The paper was as crisp and her penmanship as neat as she remembered it. This poem was the greatest accomplishment of her life. Soon, it would be printed in the *Gazette* with her name in bold type, and all of Williamsburg would know Emmeline Gardiner.

Her stomach turned, and her hand trembled as she picked it up for the first time in weeks. She carried it to the chamber on the other side of the stairwell like it was a borrowed jewel she was afraid to lose or break. She paced the empty chamber, reading the poem through, waiting for pride to chase away her nerves. Pride didn't come. She only saw the uneven meter and the muddy meaning that Henrietta had scorned. Had Shakespeare ever felt this sinking misgiving only to be comforted by applause?

She dropped the paper on the desk. She could do this. She could hand this to the printer as easily as settling an account. It would be foolish to change her mind because of Henrietta's opinion. Her sister was a poor reader and a poorer judge of literature. The printers dealt with words and poems every day. If her poem wasn't worthy of publication, then they wouldn't print it. There was nothing to worry about. She folded the crisp paper and sealed it with a moistened wafer.

She weighted the edge of the paper with a book and left the wafer to dry by the window while she changed into her going-to-town clothes: her best kerchief, a linen petticoat, and the floral jacket. The heat of summer had begun. Even if a thunderstorm rolled in, she would not regret going without a cloak. She tied the blue ribbons of her cherished straw hat. Was it only a month ago that she had been caught in a hailstorm and spent a delightful afternoon with Mr. Morris?

That day had been a revelation. Before then, her sketch of his character had been of a man of weak character and shallow mind. She hadn't noticed his lightness hid the finest soul of her acquaintance. So often with men, it was the other way around. Fine veneers disguised cheap wood. Who put a pine veneer over a heart of mahogany?

Quillan Morris did.

She collected the coin purse and slipped the letter into the market basket. Swinging it from hand to hand, she walked to town. It was summer by the calendar, but her heart was as jubilant as spring. He was a good man, and he loved her. He hadn't confessed his love in words but in straw hats, blue ribbons, and pastries; in shelter, escape, and companionship; looking at her in a way that made her heart melt like butter in a hot skillet. There had been words too, words that stopped just shy of a confession: little compliments, bold flirtations, and intimate conversations.

She had dreamed of love many times, but in all her dreams, she had done or said something so remarkable it had inspired the worshipful devotion of an imaginary man. What had she ever said or done to inspire love? It couldn't be music. She was incapable of an ethereal descant. Unless her middling attempts at the guitar were requested, she was the one listening with desperate admiration to far more accomplished ladies.

And yet he loved her.

She dreamed of appearing in colorful silks. He saw her often in homespun. He saw her without ruby lips or rouged cheeks.

And yet he loved her.

She longed to be a clever conversationalist. To amuse the company with her wit. She hated her own silences. How could she read so much and still have nothing worth saying?

And yet he loved her.

Her walk was almost a dance until she reached town and remembered to behave like a gentlewoman, at least while others were watching. Though she had no escort, she could walk in a dignified manner as she conducted her errands. She could have made her purchases from any dry goods shop. Mama wasn't particular about that. Emmeline chose to visit the Robert Morris Store. Again, it was devoid of customers, and the shelves were only half full.

"Good day, Miss Gardiner," Robert Morris said with a smile that reminded her of his brother. "How may I be of service?"

"Good day, Mr. Morris. I find myself in need of nutmeg, salt, a small sack of flour, and linen thread, preferably white."

"Then you've come to the right place," he said, turning to the shelves. "How is your family?"

"In good health, thank you," she said. "And yours?"

"Staying out of trouble, I hope." At her puzzled silence, he explained, "One of my brothers-in-law is a bit of a firebrand. Jack Mason. You met him, didn't you? When you were here with Quill?"

"I—well, I saw him. We were never introduced." Realizing that comment might be taken as a criticism, she added, "He seemed to have important things on his mind."

"Mason thinks anything on his mind is important. It's just as well Quill hasn't introduced you yet. He makes a tiresome acquaintance." He set the nutmeg, salt, flour, and thread on the counter. "Unlike present company."

She smiled at the easy praise, paid for her purchases, and wished him a good day. If she couldn't see her Mr. Morris today, at least she could see a man who reminded her of him. Next, she stopped by a fine brick home to notify the lady of the house that her document cabinet would be complete in a week and remind her to have payment on hand when it was delivered. With that, there was nothing between her and the printer's save a short walk. The basket weighed on her clammy hands, but the poem weighed on her soul. This would be the defining moment of her inconsequential life. Her heart beat faster, and her steps slowed.

Music filled the street, spilling out of an open parlor window. Emmeline drew near, listening discreetly just beyond the shutters. The strains of the harpsichord were joined by a woman's rich alto voice. The effect was so beautiful that it brought tears to Emmeline's eyes until jealousy spoiled her pleasure. What would it be like to sing and play until hearts and souls stretched toward beauty, goodness, and truth? She would never know. Mayhap she had musical talent. Had she devoted as much time to study and practice under a master, might she not be as poised and polished with her voice as she was at turning wood? Virginians didn't scoff at the trades with quite the arrogance of the ancient Greeks, but that didn't mean a chair or table would ever move hearts, no matter the skill and dedication of the craftsman.

She fingered the sealed poem in her basket. This was her one chance at greatness. This was her opportunity to move minds and hearts to defend their liberties. She would see her name in print, attached to her creation. The aroma of stew and bread mingled with unsavory city smells and twisted in her stomach. She had told herself the printers could decide if her poem was worthy of publication, but she had read many that she would have been ashamed to see attached to her name. She shook off her hesitation like a warrior facing battle. Now was not the time to quit. Courage.

She straightened her shoulders and walked into the office. "Good afternoon," she called. There was no answer. "George?" she said softly. It would be easier to face the apprentice than his master, especially after watching Quillan Morris defeat him in an arm wrestle. "George Cooper?"

After a minute, a tall youth with a boyish face came from the back room to the counter, wiping his inky fingers on his apron. "Yes, miss?"

"I'm here to settle my family's account for the month." Her voice quavered as though she had never done such a thing and was afraid of being laughed off the premises for paying a bill. She needed to control her voice before she spoke of what she had truly come here to do.

George pulled out the account book while she pulled two shillings from the coin purse. He took his time inspecting each coin for signs of filing, then dropped them on a scale.

It was time. Her heart pounded like a horse at a gallop. *Say something!* Her clammy fingers rested on the paper in her basket, but her throat choked on the words, and only the clatter in the backroom broke the silence. "Are you already setting the type?" Mayhap she could ease her way to the topic.

"Yes, miss."

"Then you have all the news for the week."

"I suppose so."

Her fingers pulled back from the paper. It was too late. They didn't have space in the *Gazette* for her poem. There was no point putting herself through an inspection and the judgment of professional printers and the entire community. They had already selected everything they would use.

George made a note in the account book and put the coins in a lockbox. He nodded to her, "Good day, miss."

"Good day," she faltered. Her heart sank with every step she took toward freedom. She, Emmeline Gardiner, was a coward.

What would her sacrifice have brought her country? It wasn't poetic enough to move hearts to patriotism, nor was it intelligent enough to persuade the mind. It was just as well for her country that she hadn't submitted her poem. The conviction didn't cheer her heart. She had discovered she was as cowardly as anyone and that her beloved writing—the one thing she had hoped to excel at —wasn't worth reading.

She choked back a sob, relieved to see no acquaintances on the street, but too proud to cry in front of strangers, either. She made it home without one tear shed. She composed her face before entering the kitchen and setting the heavy market basket and light coin purse on the table. While Mama looked over the purchases, Emmeline dropped her poem in the kitchen fire. Nutmeg meowed as flames licked across the paper, consuming the last traces of her folly. No one would ever see her name attached to the pathetic couplets. The cat pressed against her petticoats until she knelt and stroked his silky orange fur. The day had been as steady as a spinning cartwheel. Now that she was home, the turmoil in her heart slowed to a pace she could consider with the calm detachment of reason. There had been wisdom in her fear. Pride came before the fall. She was no poet. The entire scheme had been foolish. She was grateful none would ever know what she had almost done.

Our rights on English soil
For which we do toil.

How was English soil any better than the rights of Englishmen? Why did she, who had never been to England, persist in calling herself English, as though it were short for British American? English was the language she spoke, the founders of the colony, and the foundation of the legal system, but the colony was as diverse in people as it was in coin. They had been united in their loyalty to an English king. A king who didn't want them. Mr. Morris was right. They weren't English. They were American.

America was a land where a tradesman could earn respect and a lord could lose it. Character mattered more than inherited titles. It was a land where church spires reached the heavens. Her paternal grandmother had fled France, seeking freedom of conscience, and found it here. Yes, one was required to attend the Anglican church and pay its tithes, but that still left room for differing beliefs. Her grandmother had not been massacred or even put in the stocks for having a difference of conscience. Neither had Maurice. The soul was unfettered on American soil.

America was the birds in the spring and the bustle of foreign sailors in the shops. It was tradition and ingenuity, idealism and pragmatism, the old and the new. Words tickled inside her, begging to be set down on paper. When she had a free moment, she would steal up to her chamber and organize her scattered thoughts in the margins of old broadsides. Even if she never shared her words, it had felt good to record them. She was done with poetry, and she didn't want her name in the paper, but like Kitty tracing her letters in the dirt, Emmeline yearned to leave her mark on the world.

Twenty-Two

FIREFLIES & FANCY

SUNDAY, JUNE 25, 1775

Quill glanced over at Miss Gardiner. She was standing in the shade of the catalpa trees that lined the Palace Green, speaking with a friend, wearing the same blue muslin gown she wore every Sunday. It matched her eyes and tugged at his attention. He fought the pull she always had on him. Polly had warned him against toying with her affections, so he had taken his time to greet every acquaintance who had left church.

Colonel Hendriks burst out, "I tell you, he's planning an attack."

Quill wrenched his attention back to the colonel. "Are ye certain?"

"Why else would he be hiding on that warship when the legislature has begged him to return? I tell you, he no longer cares for the interests of this colony. Why else would he recommend the king send more warships to Chesapeake Bay?"

"Why indeed?" It was a puzzle to Quill that Dunmore could demand warships and then bemoan the Virginians for not making peace.

The colonel raised a hand to greet someone in the distance. "Excuse me, Morris. I need a word with Henry."

Quill had waited long enough. Surely he wasn't toying with Miss Gardiner's affections if he greeted her with the same civilities he had greeted half of Williamsburg with. She and her friend glanced at him as he approached and said their farewells.

"Goodbye, Emma! See you next Sunday!"

"Goodbye, Jenny!"

He greeted Miss Gardiner and, in the interest of civil conversation, asked, "Is Miss Jenny a good friend of yers?"

"Indeed," she said, glancing away, as though the civil question made her uncomfortable. "She lived with us for a year."

Quill blinked. This Jenny must be the lass Charles had rescued. After spending a year in the Gardiners' care, she was serving out her indentures as a lady's maid to Charles' wife. "She is fortunate to count ye as a friend."

"Thank you. I hope I prove a friend worth having." She bit her lip. "I was wondering—"

"Em-ma-line!" Henrietta called, running up to them. "It's time to go home."

"Tell our mother I'll be along presently." Once her sister was gone, she looked back at Mr. Morris. "I was wondering if you might like to join us for supper."

He couldn't have been more surprised if she'd kissed him. Surely it wasn't toying with her affections to accept an invitation. He hoped not, because he was too much of a gentleman to refuse her. "I would be honored," he said, and tipped his cocked hat. "Until this evening."

QUILL HAD NO APPETITE AS HE DIRECTED GUNPOWDER south of town. One meal wasn't a courtship, but this invitation had left him as unsteady as a top spinning on a windowsill, dancing on the edge of the precipice. What did her parents think of the invitation? Had they been privy to it before it was offered?

She must have been watching for him because she opened the pasture gate as he rode up. He directed the gelding to the back of the pasture, where he dismounted and relieved it of the harness and saddle. She seated herself on the fence, watching while he secured his saddle to one of the rails. Then she pivoted away, swinging her feet over the top rail and springing down on the orchard side of the fence. He clambered over the fence with less grace and followed her through the orchard, past the bee skeps and garden, and to the kitchen. He waited uncertainly outside the outbuilding.

"Is he here?" Mrs. Gardiner asked.

"Yes, ma'am. We just pastured his horse."

"Good. Take that pitcher and fill the cups."

"Yes, ma'am." She emerged from the kitchen carrying a redware pitcher. "I hope you like lemonade," Miss Gardiner said to him. "We're out of cider for the season."

"I love," he frowned and cleared his throat. "I love lemonade."

She glanced over her shoulder. "Coming?"

"I'll be along in a minute," he said, determined to brave her mother first. He stepped into the shadowy kitchen. The woman was arranging plates onto a tray. "Good evening, Mrs. Gardiner." He tipped his hat.

"Evening, Mr. Morris."

"Thank ye for having me ta dinner. May I carry that for ye?"

She looked at him shrewdly. He got the feeling he was being assessed for more than his ability to carry dinner, but after a moment, she simply said, "You may."

He took the tray from her and carried it up the back steps and through the dining room door, which was as open as the windows. Miss Gardiner was pouring lemonade into the redware cups.

"Where should I put this?"

She gestured to the table. "In the middle."

He set the tray down. With nothing to say and nothing to do, he held his hat and watched her set the cups around the table. Though she had been bold in her invitation, she had been demure since his arrival, barely speaking or looking at him. When the last setting was arranged, she finally looked up, but he couldn't hold her gaze. It dropped, brushed across his nose, down his jaw, and up the other side before meeting his eyes. He gripped a chairback for support. Heavens, he wanted to kiss her. The back steps creaked, and Quill collected himself in time to greet her father.

"Let me take your hat," Miss Gardiner said, tugging it from his hands and disappearing from the room, leaving him to face Mr. Gardiner.

"Charles said business is going well," the man said.

"It is," Quill replied. After a moment's pause, he added, "We've been working late to make up for the time I spend riding out ta York Town for the burgesses."

Mr. Gardiner was curious about his recent experiences carrying messages to Lord Dunmore and peppered him with questions, scarcely pausing for grace when the womenfolk joined them. It made the vexations of the month worth every mile to have Mr. and Mrs. Gardiner speak to him with respect. He was no longer the young boy who had carelessly started a fire or fallen headfirst into the pig's trough. He was a man of consequence, respected by esteemed members of the community. If he offered his suit to their daughter, they might be willing to consider it, even if Charles didn't argue his case.

When the meal was complete, Mr. Gardiner invited him to play checkers while the women tidied up. After a game, the women joined them in the front room. Emmeline took a guitar from a case. Her tunes were simple and her voice unpolished, yet she put his soul to rest better than music. What did it matter if she lacked genteel accomplishments? There would always be concerts at the Apollo, and he could get quite used to her simple music on a Sunday evening. Quill had only half a mind on checkers and was unsurprised when Mr. Gardiner beat him soundly in their second game. Then he sat back and listened to the music and taught Henrietta how to dance, and was enjoying himself so much that he was surprised to hear Mrs. Gardiner say, "It's getting dark. Can you make it back before the night watch?"

It wasn't possible that it was that late. They had only finished supper a few minutes ago. But the lavender clouds in the sky told him the end had come to one of the longest days of the year. "My brother-in-law, Jack Mason, is keeping watch tonight. He'll let me through. Thank ye for a fine evening, ma'am."

If he hadn't been watching, he might not have noticed the sliver of hesitation when she glanced at her daughter before she said, "You're welcome."

"Fireflies!" Henrietta cried, looking out the window. "Can I catch some?"

"May I?" her mother corrected.

"May I?"

Mrs. Gardiner unfastened the chattelaine from her waist and handed it to Emmeline. "Get a jar from the kitchen and hold onto it so Ettie doesn't break it. And remember to lock the kitchen."

"Yes, ma'am."

Quill followed the sisters down the back steps. "Thank ye for supper."

"You're welcome." Emmeline unlocked the kitchen and pulled an amber glass bottle from a shelf. "Thank you for coming."

"Hurry!" Henrietta cried. "They're in the orchard!"

Quill knew the fireflies weren't going anywhere, but once Emmeline had locked the kitchen door, he grabbed her hand and ran past the vegetable garden and the bee skeps to the old apple orchard. The keys and scissors swinging from the chattelaine clanged like bells. Once they reached the orchard, he reluctantly released her hand.

Panting and laughing, she took a moment to secure the chattelaine to her waist. It was the same one she had worn that stormy night she had warned him of impending tyranny, had worried over his safety, had wrapped his canteen to keep the cider hot, and had captured his fancy with the careless ease of a child catching fireflies. He had waited for that fancy to burn out, but days had turned into weeks and then months. The tinder had ignited kindling, and the kindling had ignited the slow-burning fuel-wood. If she had persisted in her indifference, the fire might have begun to fade, but she had, in her innocent way, taken to feeding the fire every time she was near.

And he, less innocent but no less pleased, encouraged it. Nothing gave him greater joy than her nearness. Nothing gave his troubled mind rest and conviction like a discussion with her. Nothing filled the quiet moments as easily as remembering the timbre of her voice or the light in her eyes. If this fancy ever burned out, if he had to persist living in a world without her, he would be left with nothing. The world would be cold, meaning-less, and empty. So why did he keep telling himself he was waiting for this fancy to end?

She untangled the keys, scissors, and pincushion. Delicate silver chains glittered down the curve of her hip. It wasn't the exaggerated curve donned by ladies of fashion but the gentle curve of a bonny lass who didn't need padding to accentuate her God-given beauty.

"I caught one!" Henrietta cried, running toward them.

In the orchard, a hundred stars wandered lazily through the apple trees, their lights waxing and waning like a breath and a sigh. A light flickered near him, no bigger than the flame of a candle. He cupped his hands together and caught it. "Miss Gardiner?"

After accepting Henrietta's, she brought the jar to him. He opened his cupped hands wide enough to slide across the mouth of the jar and flatten his palm against it. Two golden lights blinked through the amber glass. Emmeline placed her hand on top of his. He could have pulled away and allowed her to reclaim the jar, but it felt so good and so right to have her hand on his that he kept it there.

"We—my family," he clarified, "call them will-o'-the-wisps."

Emmeline repeated the word. "Do they have fireflies in Scotland?"

"Nay, but there are tales of creatures who use their lights to lead unwary travelers down enchanted paths. And this," he glanced at her hand on his and grinned, "is like a fairy story."

Her fingers curved around his hand. This—the promise of her steady companionship—was what he wanted. The life of a lone bachelor lost any attraction it had once held. He didn't want to go back to the man he was three months ago. What a dreary life he had once lived. He hoped never to forget how he felt when she was near, how his soul filled with light and hope and every heavenly virtue. Living starlight hovered around her, its glow dancing over her curls and sparkling in her eyes.

"Emma, come here! I've caught another!" Their naive little chaperone cried.

Quill slid his hand out from under Emmeline's with an exaggerated sigh, then looked at her and winked. Her smile reached her eyes before she went to help her sister. He whispered her name, too low for her to hear. *Emmeline.* Saying it gave him a comfortable thrill like the first notes of a favorite sonata. Why had he fought this attraction so hard and so long?

In this beautiful world, every good thing came from God. Was anything more beautiful and good than the way he felt when she was near? He loved her, and she loved him. It was folly to deny it. Charles wouldn't be pleased. He had made it clear that he didn't want anyone courting his cousin, not yet, anyway. Surely God didn't expect Quill to choose between the blessings of love and friendship. And if He didn't, then there must be a way to win Charles over. Quill would keep his friendship, and he would court Emmeline.

When a dozen lights glowed under her hand and illuminated her admiring face, he remembered that he was supposed to be on his way home. Her parents probably thought he was already. He hadn't meant to be deceitful; he just got caught up in the moment. One was never too old to appreciate the winking lights of June, especially when they led their courtship dance around one's sweetheart.

"I should be on my way home," Quill said. He hopped the split-rail fence by his saddle. Emmeline remained on the other side, holding her jar like a lantern.

"Ye'll release them tonight?" It seemed a shame to keep the shining little creatures trapped when they were looking for love.

"I'll put the jar by an open window. They can leave when they please." She rested the base of the jar on the fence, her fingers curving around its mouth. "Thank you again for coming. I enjoyed your company."

Her words of pleasure and admiration filled the empty corners of his heart. "Thank ye for yer company," he said. "It's my favorite."

She dimpled and dropped her gaze. Mayhap it was the magic of a summer's eve. Mayhap there were some kindly will-o'-the-wisps about who had led him, unwary traveler that he was, down this path. All he knew was that she was inches away. He pressed his lips to her forehead. It wasn't a real kiss. He needn't tell Charles. But the softness of her skin against his was real. The warmth that flooded his chest when she leaned into his touch was real. This enchanted moment was very real. He rubbed the tip of his nose against her brow. She stirred and in a moment her brow was against his, and the soft of her nose was against his. In a low voice, he said, "Good night, Emmeline."

A contented sigh escaped her. Then she whispered, "Good night, Quillan."

Even his name sounded better on her lips. This was better than a fairy story. The will-o'-the-wisps hadn't tricked him. They, through some Divine Providence, had kindly led him down a path toward his heart's desire. He would speak to Charles, and then her father, and the next fairy night they were together, he would kiss her properly, because next time, she would be his lass, and he meant to treat her well.

Twenty-Three

TEA FOR MRS. MORRIS

Polly was reading by candlelight when Quill arrived home. She glanced up as he entered. "The Gardiners take an awful long time ta eat their supper," she observed.

He grunted as he bolted the door. The last thing he needed while he was preparing to face Charles was Polly's teasing. He tossed his hat on the table and went to his bedchamber, where he hung his linen coat and waistcoat from a row of pegs. Despite the heat, he had been determined to remain properly dressed both at church and while visiting the Gardiners. Stripping off his shoes and stockings, he dropped onto the bed, his hands behind his head. A breeze meandered through the open window, stirred the bed curtains, and exited through the front window. The evening was too warm to close the doors. He would wait until Polly retired to her bedchamber before undressing further.

The candle flickered in the front room, and his bed curtains cast dancing shadows as the breeze teased them. What would Charles say? Was there a wise and responsible way to broach the subject? He would expect Quill to know that she had no dowry and to be prepared for the extra responsibility that came without it. Her family was in no haste for her to marry. Charles spoke of her as if she were a child, not yet ready to face the world. But Quill

175

wasn't asking her to face the world and all its ugliness. He would ask for her to face him, like she had that evening, leaning into his touch and offering her own in return. She had called him Quillan. His chest swelled.

The room grew lighter. He turned to see Polly standing in the doorway. "I would ask if the Gardiners are in good health, but I can tell by yer smile that they are."

Quill tried and failed to sober. His soul was as full of dancing lights as Emmeline's kitchen jar when they had bid each other goodnight. Smiling up at his tester, he managed, "Dinna say anything ta Charles."

"I didna say a word this evening ta anyone at the Blue House about yer supper engagement." She narrowed her eyes. "But I had truly believed it was just supper with the family. Was it more than that?"

"Aye," Quill said with perfect innocence. "I played several rounds of checkers with Mr. Gardiner, Emmeline played her guitar, and we talked until the sun set. Then Miss Henrietta needed assistance catching fireflies. It was a full evening."

"*Emmeline* played the guitar?"

Quill realized his slip but couldn't fully regret it. Though he did not welcome Polly's teasing, he would have to get past it. This time next week, he hoped to be courting Emmeline. If he pretended indifference now, it would only give her more to tease about later. "Aye, Emmeline."

Polly scowled. "This may be a passing fancy ta ye, but women, even young ones, dinna cared ta be toyed with."

Quill sat up and swung his feet to the floor. "I have never toyed with a woman's affections."

"Ye told me this was a passing fancy. Did ye tell her? Or are ye allowing her ta think there is depth behind yer little flirtations?"

"Ye dinna understand," Quill said. "I want her as my sweetheart. I wish ta court her."

"Court her?" Polly repeated in disbelief.

"Court her. Is there anything so wrong with that?"

"Well, she's young and has no dowry. More than that, ye told me this was a passing fancy. Nothing serious. It would be cruel ta play at courting and then drop her. Is that yer plan?"

"Nay, Polly. I ken what I said. I said it, not from any shallowness of feeling, but because I was trying ta be rational. I ken every reason she would make an unsuitable match. My life would be easier if she had a sturdy dowry and social connections. I've always hoped ta have fine music in my home. And I'm afraid Charles will be difficult. I've been fighting this attraction for months."

It began in the cool of April, on the eve of the Gunpowder Incident. Before that, his attraction had been shallow and fleeting. He had been annoyed every time Isaac Bailey had monopolized her attention and had been pleased to claim a smile or a dance from her, but those feelings had been forgotten each time they parted. Since April, his affections had been firmly attached to one bonny lass.

"Ye truly wish ta court her?"

"I dinna feel this way about anyone else. I never have. I love her, Polly." His confession hung in the air, plain and plaintive.

She sat beside him and squeezed his shoulder. "Then that's all that matters."

Relief filled his soul.

"I like Emmeline," she added, matter-of-factly. "I have no objections ta her as a sister. Athair won't object, either. He married Màthair right after she finished her indentures. Of course, she had been raised as a gentlewoman. Emmeline could use a little social polish, but that's easy enough. We could invite her ta spend Christmastide with us at Willow Haven. We could introduce her to our friends and neighbors. They accepted Màthair." She considered for a moment, then added, "What's next?"

"I persuade Charles. He thinks she's too young."

"She'll grow out of that," Polly said. "Besides, plenty of lasses are wed by her age."

"Wed? Slow down. I just decided ta court her, and if I'm ta

persuade Charles, then I need ta play by his rules. I need ta be slow and sensible."

"Slow and sensible," Polly scoffed. "No lass dreams of a suitor who will court her 'slow and sensible.'"

"Well, at least until I secure her family's blessing."

"Which ye will do on the morrow." Polly rose, taking the candle with her.

"I will—what?"

"Strike while the iron's hot," Polly said. "Speak with Charles afore ye talk yerself out of it. Good night."

Quill lay awake for hours, considering everything he might or might not say to persuade his friend.

HE AROSE EARLY AND DRESSED WITH CARE. HE WOULD be alone at the office when Charles arrived. That would give a favorable impression of his industriousness. Then he would broach the delicate business before turning their attention to their work. He explained his plan over breakfast.

Polly approved of everything except being left at home. "I'll stay quiet unless Charles is being difficult. Ye'll not even know I'm there. But if ye need a witness in yer favor, I'll be ready."

Quill assented. His desire to succeed surpassed his pride. "Dinna mention the horse racing."

"Do ye think I have no sense of occasion? Come, let us be on our way."

Quill's relief at reaching the office before his friend turned to dismay at the state of his desk. Was it this untidy every day? While Polly opened the window and settled into her work, Quill returned books to their shelves, sorted the papers that covered his desk, and organized them into drawers. With his desk clear of all save the brass inkwell, he was surprised to see how much dust had accumulated on the surfaces. He pulled a handkerchief from his pocket and wiped it clean. Cloudlike clusters of dust flurried briefly before descending.

"I'll sweep," Polly said, setting aside the account book.

Quill had been willing to overlook the dust on the floor, but he wouldn't naysay his sister's aid. Reaching through the window, he shook his handkerchief clean while Polly swept the dust and dirt into the street. The office hadn't been this tidy in months, possibly longer. He hoped Charles would notice.

Taking a seat, he stared at the empty expanse of desktop. There was nothing for him to do without returning some of those papers and books to his desk, but that might ruin the effect. He would wait. Charles would come soon. Quill would catch him in the golden moments between domestic felicity and the drudgery of work, when he was most agreeable. Watching the door and window, he fidgeted with the figure in his waistcoat pocket, then pulled it out. As always, it offered him an encouraging smile. This would all work out.

"What's that?" Polly asked.

"A fox." Quill set it beside the inkwell. The desk looked a little friendlier with that small figure on it.

"I see that. What's it from?"

Before Quill had a chance to reply, the door opened. He snatched the fox, stuffing it in his pocket, then turned with a smile. "Good morning."

Charles glanced at him with a stormy expression, slammed the door, shoved a key into his desk, and yanked open a drawer. "It may be for you," was all he said, before dropping into a chair.

Quill glanced at Polly. She gave a little shake of her head, which Quill interpreted as a warning not to broach such an important subject until this dark mood passed. He wasn't fool enough to need the warning, but he was worried for his friend. Something had shattered the peace and happiness Charles had enjoyed since his wedding.

"How is Susan?" Polly asked.

Charles' hand fisted, hovering over a brief until the knuckles turned white. When the color returned, he said, without turning, "She's in good health." Then he rested an elbow on the desktop and a hand sheltered his face from their view.

Polly bit her lip. It would be indelicate to pry further, at least from Charles. Quill attempted to settle into his day's work, but it was difficult to concentrate when his friend was hurting. What could have troubled him so? Mayhap it was a lover's quarrel, and they would make amends over dinner. That would explain his reticence to talk about the matter. Relieved by the simple explanation, Quill opened a book and began taking notes.

An hour or so had passed, the room quiet save for the rustle of paper, when he stretched and yawned. Voices outside the window caught his attention. Two sailors, one quite tall, with a familiar shock of white-blond hair, were looking into the office. A light of recognition lit the tall man's hooded eyes. He spoke excitedly to his companion in Dutch, gesturing to Quill. Then they opened the office door. Quill rose to his feet, as did Charles.

"Come in, gentlemen," he said. "I am Mr. Morris. This is my sister, Miss Polly Morris, and that is my friend and colleague, Mr. Johnson. Please, take a seat."

The sailors sat, and the tall one, who had offered Emmeline a "cookie cake" that day in the bakery, spoke at length to his dark-haired companion. Quill glanced around the room. Charles watched them warily. Polly leaned forward, as though she could understand their conversation if she listened closely.

At last, the dark-haired man addressed Quill in thickly accented English. "This is Captain Visser. You have met the captain before, no?"

"No. Nay. I mean, yes, we have met."

The man nodded. "I am Jan Dirksen, his, how do you say, one who buys? Super merchant?" He frowned, not satisfied that he had found the right word. Then he shook his head. "Captain Visser, he sees you. Wants to speak to you. But not much English."

Quill nodded politely.

"We sail in *tree* days." Like most foreigners, the man stumbled around words with the uncontinental *th*. "You are in good *helt*, no?"

"No. Aye. I am in good health, thank ye."

"And Mrs. Morris? Her *helt*?"

"My sister, Miss Morris, is also in good health." He waved to Polly, who inclined her head. Charles turned back to his desk.

The translator frowned. "No. Missus. Miss-ES. Your wife."

All the blood drained from Quill's face as Charles whipped around to face him. Quill fought the impulse to run for his life. To grab his trunk and disappear on the first ship he found. To vanish forever into the great unknown, where Charles could never find him.

After a strangled pause, Charles said dryly, "Oh, *Mrs.* Morris. Forgive us. You see, Mr. Morris was so recently a bachelor."

Polly choked and coughed. An exchange in Dutch further muddled Quill's mind. The *Gazette* had recently reported on a church in some faraway land. The floor in front of the altar had collapsed. The congregants had fallen with the rubble into the crypt below. That was what he needed. A collapsing floor. Instantaneously buried by ten tons of ancient stone.

"You choose well," Dirksen continued. "Your pretty wife— your *new* wife, she is in good *helt*?"

Polly and Charles looked at Quill with the rapt attention that questions of health never deserved. The air was thin. His head was light. He was trapped between the expectations of the Dutch sailors and his need to smooth things over with Charles. "Ah. Well, she's...the same." He nodded. That was an excellent word choice, allowing him to walk the split-rail fence between heaven and hell. "The same."

Polly dropped her pencil, the brass casing clattering as it hit the floor.

The translator nodded. "She was kind to the captain when he was lost. The captain is never lost at sea, but on land—" he threw up his hands and laughed. "He meant no offense to you or your wife. He did not see her ring. Did not know she was married. He thanks you for her kindness."

The translator nodded to Captain Visser, who removed a package from his jacket. Quill accepted it dumbly. It was light for its size and rustled within its paper. If he didn't know better—

"Not from England. Not from East India Company." The man winked. "Not break ban."

Quill was holding a package of smuggled tea. With the scarcity in the colony, it was worth a small fortune. "Thank ye. We havena had tea in months." He couldn't keep it, but he couldn't return it. The tea belonged to Emmeline for whatever kindness she had bestowed on the captain.

Dirksen nodded in smug satisfaction. "Kings rule land. Not rule sea." He and the captain took their leave. The moment the door closed, Quill dropped the tea on the desk and buried his face in his hands, refusing to meet the curious eyes around him.

At last, Charles spoke. "And here I thought I was the only married man in the room." After a pause, he added, "Who is she?"

Quill lowered his hands, focusing his gaze on a distant floorboard. "It isn't like that."

"Are you in need of an annulment? No charge for friends."

"I never said I was married."

"Funny," Charles said, "You didn't bother to correct him while he was here."

"He seemed so certain. And, well, *you* were playing along."

"Mmm. How was I to know you hadn't eloped last week? For all I knew, he was right."

"It was a simple misunderstanding."

"Which you did nothing to correct." Charles sighed. "Who kissed you this time? Or who were you kissing?"

"What? No one." He waved his hands wildly, brushing away the image the words created. "No one kissed me." He would have been delighted if Emmeline had, but there was no need to confess that. "And I didn't either." He refused to count the time he had kissed her cheek, or more recently, when he had kissed her brow.

Those weren't real kisses. They were just as close to real as he dared before he gained his friend's approval.

"What did happen?" Polly asked. "And who is that tea for?"

Quill slipped a hand into his waistcoat pocket. His fingers brushed against the little fox. He took a deep breath and then said, "I suppose he means it for Miss Gardiner."

Charles was appalled. "Emma is tangled up in this?"

"Well—" Quill hesitated, wondering whether it would be wisest to explain everything all at once, or if he should take the time to prepare a proper defense.

"And you allowed it." The disappointment in Charles' eyes stung Quill more than a teacher's rod across his knuckles. In a few words, he could have explained the misunderstanding to the Dutch sailors. They might have even laughed. Instead, he had reinforced a falsehood about Emmeline.

"Marriage is hardly a scandalous rumor," Polly protested.

Charles waved her off, intent on Quill. "I have stood up for you every time you've been in trouble because you are my friend. That's what friends do, isn't it? These are dangerous times. There are soldiers in the streets. Everyone is taking sides. What if someone threatens my family? Will you stand up for me? For them? Whose side are you on?"

"Yers," Quill said, fighting back guilt. Only a few nights ago, the Eagle had been filled with radical patriots who had arranged a break-in of the palace and removed the dozens of firearms displayed on the walls, arguing that if Dunmore could confiscate what was stored in the magazine, they could confiscate what was stored in the palace. If they didn't, those firearms would be used against them. Quill hadn't been in favor of the plan, but he had allowed the Eagle to be used to discuss it.

"Are you? If you won't stand up for my family when it's only uncomfortable, how will you have the courage to do so when it's dangerous?"

"I *was* standing up for yer family. Yer cousin was alone on the street when that hailstorm began. She needed shelter, so I brought her into the bakery until it passed. There were dozens of men in there, and she was the only pretty, young lass. Ye ken how men can be. The easiest way ta keep the sailors away was ta tell them she was mine."

"So why didn't you tell me about this when it happened?"

"I—" Quill broke off. He hadn't told Charles, at least in part, because he was afraid his friend would suspect a fleeting fancy. But the fancy wasn't fleeting, and Charles still didn't suspect. "Sometimes ye overreact ta things."

"I do not."

"Ye do," Polly said. "Remember that time ye told Quill ta never dance with her again?"

"He stood up with her three times in the same evening at her first ball. Rumors were bound to fly. And they did."

Polly waved his concern away. "Gossips will gossip. Susan and I settled the rumors. They didn't last long. No harm was done."

"No harm was done?" Charles repeated, incredulous. "You weren't there the next day. An old society matron came to call. My aunt insisted on entertaining her alone, so Emmeline wasn't burdened with the woman's dire warnings against you as a suitor and the aspersions against her virtue."

Quill felt ill. He had long been resigned to the fact that his reputation hadn't been restored in everyone's eyes, even after the courts had cleared his name. But Emmeline especially didn't deserve to be the subject of slander. "Why didn't ye tell me?"

"Did I need to? I warned you it would happen."

"So ye did," Quill said. This wasn't the morning to cross Charles a second time. He tossed the tea on a shelf. He wouldn't make his confession of pure love on the heels of slander.

Twenty-Four

DOUBT & FAITH

Emmeline's hand hovered over her sister's copybook as she read the beautiful lines again.

Doubt thou the stars are fire
Doubt the sun doth move
Doubt truth to be a liar
But never doubt I love.

The stars had come down from heaven last night to dance in the apple orchard. Quillan Morris had kissed her forehead and spoken softly. With such marked tenderness, she could no longer doubt his affections. He loved her.

She curved pages of the copybook, funneling loose sand back into the tin pounce box to be used again. Now that the ink was dry, it was time to put the writing supplies her sister had used during lessons away. She opened the box and put everything in its place: the blotting paper, pounce box, quill pen, and a corked inkwell. Only when she moved to place Henrietta's copybook in the compartment with the other papers did she hesitate. On top of the precious sheets of laid linen-rag paper was Emmeline's old copybook.

This wasn't the time for daydreams. Chores awaited her attention. She glanced at the back door, propped open for a breeze. She wouldn't be missed for another minute or two. The book fell open in her hand to a small composition. In a stolen hour Saturday evening, she had sat on the braided rug in her bedchamber, reading over the fragmented thoughts she had jotted in the margins of old issues of the *Gazette*. Then, like fitting spindles in a chairback, she had arranged those phrases in an elegant order until she had crafted a little essay in the back of her old copybook. There was no rhyme or meter, just the honest thoughts that burned in her heart.

"Emma!" Henrietta called from the porch.

She snapped the book closed and dropped it into the box. "What is it?"

"Mama says the pie will be done in a quarter of an hour, and you need to get ready to go to town."

"I will," Emmeline said, "as soon as I'm done tidying from lessons."

This pie was payment for some service. It meant Emmeline had to walk into the heart of Williamsburg again, just days after she had settled the family accounts and visited the shop of Mr. Robert Morris. This time her basket would be lighter on the return trip, and she needn't make so many visits. They needed nothing from the shop, Papa didn't have messages to send, and she had just settled the account with the printers.

Her eyes flicked to the corked inkwell. Did she dare? She didn't waste time deliberating, but set out a sheet of laid linen-rag paper and uncorked it. The moment she had signed her work, impulsively choosing for her pen name, "A Patriot," she sanded the wet ink, put away the writing supplies, and carried her half-dry composition up to her bedchamber, with a wafer seal. She was changing into her town jacket when Henrietta hollered that the pie was in a basket on the table.

"I'll be down shortly," Emmeline called back, tightening the laces of her jacket until it fit smoothly over her stays.

In a few minutes, she was walking to town, the hot pie swinging in the basket, the blue ribbon of her hat dancing in the breeze, and the paper folded, sealed, and tucked in her pocket. She had no visions of grandeur today, just an eagerness to share a few words with the world. Her fear of failure had been defeated by the security of anonymity. It had been prideful and foolish to attach her true name to an untried poem. Except for public figures, most people who contributed to the *Gazette* did so under a pseudonym. Christ had taught the wisdom of humility, that he who sat in the lower seats at a feast had nothing to fear but the honor of being raised to a higher seat, while he who claimed the highest seat risked being humbled.

For a young woman of no influence or formal education to use her given name was cocky, impudent, and brash. The people of Williamsburg might not give her credit, but by using a pen name, she allowed her work to stand on its own merits.

Two men with tomahawks at their sides guarded the road into town. They wore the hunting shirts of the Virginia Volunteer Company. "Who are you and what is your business in town?" one man asked, a stern expression on his face.

"Oh," she said, flustered. "I'm Miss Gardiner. I'm delivering a pie." She lifted a napkin and held her basket out to prove her statement.

"Smells good," the other man said. "Carry on."

"Thank you, sir." She dropped her gaze respectfully and passed them without incident. Her stomach rumbled. She needed to make haste, to deliver the pie before the printers went to dinner. She braced herself against the beauties in the shop windows and made haste with such determination that she didn't see Charles until he called her name.

"Emmeline! What are you doing in town?"

She sighed. Charles never approved of her traveling the country with no escort, but since he no longer lived with them, he couldn't escort her or run their errands. She could either please Mama or Charles, not both. "My mother sent me to deliver a vegetable pie to a family." She didn't say anything about her errand to the printer. She hadn't yet told anyone about it. She wanted to see if her words could succeed before she claimed them.

He took the basket. "Where do they live?"

She accepted his arm and directed him to the family, her mind racing. How was she to deliver her letter if Charles was intent on escorting her through town? How was she to get home if Charles was supposed to be returning to the office? They delivered the pie, and she hadn't yet thought of what to do.

"Come," Charles said. "Join us for dinner."

"I would hate to intrude."

"Nonsense. I think Susan will be grateful for the company."

They walked in silence. A line creased his brow.

Emmeline began to fear that she had caused it. "Are you well?"

A muscle in his jaw moved before he answered, "I am in good health."

"But low in spirit," she added.

He looked at her sharply, then his shoulders dropped. "It's nothing for you to worry about."

She squeezed his arm. At least she hadn't been the cause of his distress.

Unexpectedly, Charles said, "What *did* happen with that Dutch sailor?"

"Who?"

"Don't you know? The man, a Captain Visser, I believe, came to my office this morning inquiring after your health."

"Captain Visser? Oh! A tall man with pale hair?"

"You have met him."

"I have. He asked me for directions one day when I was in the front garden. Couldn't find his way back to town. I shouldn't have talked to him. That's one thing Mama is quite strict about. But it seemed harmless enough to point him on his way. But when I saw him again, he was determined to buy me a drink. The next time it was something at the bakery and—" she broke off, unsure of how much Charles already knew.

"And you were with Mr. Morris that time?"

"I was. I suppose he told you all about it."

"He said something. But what did he say to Captain Visser? The man was convinced you were married."

"Married? To whom?"

"Why, to our dear friend, Quillan Morris. Who else?" Charles smiled wryly. "You should have seen the shock on his face when the captain asked after his wife's health. I must know what Quill said to him."

Emmeline's face was hot. She wished she had seen Quill's face. He couldn't have been too upset about the confusion, not if he loved her. Or could he? "Let me think. That was back in May. Mr. Morris helped me find shelter during the hailstorm. We were waiting it out in the bakery. The captain saw me, and I panicked. I couldn't think of what to say or do, so I asked Mr. Morris for help. He didn't say we were married. I would remember that. I believe he told the captain that I was his lady. That was all."

Charles sighed. "The impulsive fool. Of course, he was trying to help."

Emmeline didn't appreciate her beloved being called names. "He isn't a fool. He may have a pine veneer, but he has a heart of mahogany."

Her cousin laughed.

"How is that funny?" She had been proud of that little imagery and was wounded to hear it so heartily mocked.

"I've heard him called many names before, but *pine veneer*?" He wiped his eyes with the back of his hand. "I'll think of that every time I meet an ugly man."

"Quillan Morris is not ugly," Emmeline said hotly. "I meant that his manner is open and unpretentious, but his heart is rare and good."

Charles sobered. "Listen, Emma. A man can have a good heart and still hurt the people he loves."

"He's your friend."

"Is he? Is anyone? Everything is changing, and I hardly know who to trust anymore." Charles, who had always been so steadfast, was vulnerable and uncertain.

"I think you should trust him," she said. "If you were in trouble, he wouldn't hesitate to help you. Give him a chance."

"You would argue in his favor? If that Dutch captain spoke English, half of Williamsburg would be gossiping about your supposed marriage."

"If the captain spoke English, we might have explained ourselves better. And there's nothing unseemly about marriage. It isn't the sort of gossip I should be ashamed to hear."

"You might think differently when you're a little older. Such foolish gossip might frighten off the few prospects you will have."

It wouldn't frighten off the only man she was considering marrying. "I want nothing to do with a man so foolish he will trust a silly rumor more than he trusts me."

When they arrived at the Blue House, Charles didn't wait on the front step. He opened the door and walked in like a man at home. His wife sat in the parlor on the settee, plying her needle on a miniature cap with whitework embroidery.

He bent and kissed her rosy cheek. "Susan, darling, how are you?"

"I'm fine." She placed her needlework in a basket. "We've had a very dull and quiet morning."

"Good," he said, and the relief in his voice puzzled Emmeline. "I hope you don't mind, but I brought some company."

For the first time, Susan noticed Emmeline hanging back in the foyer. Her face brightened. "Emmeline, do come in. What brings you to town?"

Charles answered for her. "She was running an errand for her mother when I saw her. Naturally, I brought her here."

"Well, I'm very glad you did. We'll have Graves drive her home after dinner."

Emmeline would be perfectly safe with the footman escorting her home. No sailors would deign to speak to her. But it would be impossible to complete her other errand.

It took longer to eat dinner than usual because she was the only guest, and there seemed to be an unspoken agreement to shower her with attention, which demanded she keep answering questions.

"Has the Committee of Safety spoken to your father?" Charles asked.

"Last week. They brought an agreement for him to sign."

Charles' jaw tightened. "And did he?"

"Yes." Sensing this might be a sensitive subject, she added, "We don't rely on imports much anyway. They weren't making him commit to something we weren't already doing."

Susan glanced at Mrs. Evans.

A question died on Emmeline's tongue. She wasn't impertinent enough to pry where she wasn't wanted, nor was she too dull-witted to infer the essentials. The Committee of Safety had come to see Charles, had expected him to represent the ladies of the Blue House, and the exchange hadn't ended well.

Susan turned the conversation to more cheery matters, and before Emmeline knew it, Charles was handing her up into a phaeton, and she was on her way home. "Graves," she said, and her voice trembled, "might we stop by the printers? I was supposed to deliver something."

He glanced at her empty basket and, for an uncomfortable moment, she feared he would begin asking questions, but he nodded and made a small detour, stopping across the street from the printer's.

"I won't be long," she said and hurried across the road.

George Cooper was crouched on the floor, rearranging the contents of the front bookshelves when she walked in.

"You needn't get up for me," she said. "I just was supposed to drop something off. I'll tuck it under the account book."

Closing the door behind her, she took a deep breath. Her heart was racing. She hadn't even dared to hand it to the apprentice. But it was done. She would be on her way home in a moment, and no one would be the wiser, but Graves wasn't waiting for her in the phaeton. He was in low conversation with a man beside a pony cart. She climbed up to her seat and watched their intense expressions until the pony cart man saw her. She looked away, and in a moment, Graves was climbing onto the seat beside her.

When they turned down the next street, she said, "Graves, would you mind not saying anything to Charles? About me going to the printers. It isn't anything untoward, but he seems to have a lot on his mind, and there's no need for him to worry about this, too."

"No need to worry, miss. I know how to keep a secret. I won't tell the Johnsons you went to the printers, and you," he glanced at her, "won't tell them I was talking with an old acquaintance. Neither of us was doing anything untoward, and there's no need to make the Johnsons—or anyone else—worry about us for no reason."

Pleased with the easy understanding they had settled between them, she enjoyed the luxury of an open carriage and a full belly. She didn't even feel flustered when the shirtmen demanded they state their business. Graves had a note from Mrs. Evans, and she had her empty basket. They were satisfied and waved them along. Many times she had walked this path alone and hungry, anxious to hurry home for a good meal. Today, she enjoyed the golden droplets of sunlight that slipped through the dense shade trees, their leaves dancing to the chorus of songbirds and cicadas.

Twenty-Five

FRACTURED FRIENDSHIP

SATURDAY, JULY 1, 1775

Late on another endless summer afternoon, a man entered the Eagle without knocking. Quill and Charles rose to greet him. With dismay, Quill recognized the radical patriot.

"Mr. Collins," Quill said with a slight bow, "how may I be of service?"

"As a member of the Committee of Safety, I have been given the responsibility of discovering who in Williamsburg is a friend to liberty and who is an enemy." His gaze fell on Charles.

"Ah," Quill said, "Well, my family has been careful to observe the import ban, and I—"

"I'm not here to question you, Morris. I'm here for Johnson."

Charles stood as still as a statue, his face ashen. He might be forced to sign a paper declaring his dedication to the cause of liberty and recanting any Tory sentiments he may have expressed. If he refused, he might have his name printed in the *Gazette* in a list of "enemies of freedom." He and Susan might be ostracized and harassed as a result. He might be imprisoned on dubious charges and remain in the public jail for weeks or months until a trial could prove his innocence. Quill raked a hand through his hair, and his gaze fell on an incriminating packet of tea that waited on the shelf above his desk. He had promised to be on Charles' side the day trouble came. That day had arrived sooner than he had anticipated. But what could he do? Quill sent a silent prayer heavenward. Just as silently, a ridiculous idea entered his mind.

In an unflustered voice, he said, "I'll be happy to answer any questions you have about his loyalties."

"That won't be necessary. Now, Mr. Johnson—"

"Works for me," Quill interrupted.

Charles and the committee man stared at him. "What was that?"

"Mr. Johnson works for me."

"He's a barrister, too," Collins said. "What nonsense is this?"

"This is my office, isn't it?" Quill asked, tipping his chin with a show of conceit. "Mr. Johnson and Miss Morris work here in my office. I will answer for them."

"Careful, Morris," the committee man said. "It's my job to weed out the enemies of liberty. You wouldn't want to be accused of harboring one." He paused with a hand on the doorknob. To Charles, he said, "Since your friend speaks so boldly for you here, I will defer speaking with you for the present, but consider carefully what you will say when I call on your home." The door slammed behind him.

Charles dropped to his seat and stared blankly at where the committee man had stood moments before.

"'Tis becoming as dangerous ta be a loyalist as it is ta be a patriot," Quill said. "They dinna leave a body much choice."

"You stood up for me," Charles said in a tone of disbelief.

Irritated by his friend's lack of faith, Quill said, "That's what friends do." His gaze fell back to the packet of tea. This office was becoming too public to store such things. He would have to find a way to give it to Emmeline before the wrong person discovered it and questioned his loyalties. "I wish I could have persuaded him of yer neutrality. I doubt he'll leave ye alone for long."

"You can't win every brief," Charles said. "But you bought me a little more time. Thank you." He turned his chair to face his desk and returned to his work as though he had forgotten the remaining threat.

Quill attempted to follow suit, but the trouble weighed on his mind. At last, they locked up and went to their respective homes for supper. Polly listened thoughtfully to Quill's tale.

"I'm sorry ta hear things are going poorly for Charles and Susan, but this is good for you."

"How is this good for me?"

"Dinna ye see? If a confirmed patriot is courting his cousin, it might protect Charles from suspicion."

"I doubt it," Quill said. "Her father is a landowner. He votes. If the committee doesna care about his political views, why would they care about the views of the man courting his daughter?

Polly sighed. "I see yer point. But ye did stand up for Charles and his family. Surely that counts for something."

"I suppose, but the committee isn't done with him. I canna ask ta court his cousin when he is in the midst of so much danger."

"But willna she be expecting ye ta court her?"

After the way he had behaved, she would. She had too much sense not to. But it was better to delay their courtship than to speak before he had all his witnesses in place. As Charles said, a man couldn't win every brief. He needed a solid case before he spoke, or he could lose her forever. "I'll court her as soon as things have settled down."

"That might take years."

"Not the war. I meant things with Charles. If ye had seen the way the committee man had threatened him, and how worried he was, ye would ken this is not the time ta broach such a delicate matter. A fortnight or two is all I expect."

Polly stabbed her supper. "I thought ye loved her."

"I do. But I've loved her for months and hope ta be free ta do so for the rest of our lives. What's a few weeks compared ta all that?"

"Forever, if she doesna ken why ye are sweet on her and yet will no' court her."

"Shall I avoid her, then?" Quill snapped. "Not speak ta her until I can offer my hand?" He hadn't meant to snap at his sister, but the strain was more than he could bear. He had refused to choose between the good and for what? He had foolishly hoped that carrying messages between the two branches of government would keep them bound together, but they grew further apart each week. One branch was determined to decay on the mother tree while the other had grafted itself to a tender sapling. Each pleaded with the other for reconciliation, while neither moved from the ground they had chosen. The same forces made it as dangerous to be a patriot as it was to be a loyalist and had strained his friendship more than he had imagined possible. It was too fragile to withstand the strain of betrayal. That's what it would be to secretly court Emmeline. He had to prove to Charles that he wouldn't drag her deeper into the danger that swirled around them, that he would never do anything to hurt her.

Polly's eyes flashed. "If ye canna court, that might be best. Dinna toy with her affections if ye willna see this through."

He wasn't toying with her affections. He was being a considerate friend. Irritated, he didn't speak for the rest of supper. After stacking his dishes, Quill threw off his outer layers and lay abed, his mind heavy with memories while he waited for the sun to set on the long day.

~

QUILL'S BLACK SCHOOL ROBES BILLOWED BEHIND HIM as he ran from the schoolroom, the first to escape. He scrubbed his face dry with his sleeve, hoping the boys hadn't seen him break.

Charles caught up to him. "Let me see your hands."

Quill lifted them, but the oversized sleeves hung to his fingertips.

The robe had been Rabbie's when he was Quill's age. Màthair had insisted he would grow into it. Charles pushed back the soggy sleeves. A fresh bloom of purple covered the fading yellow on the backs of his hands. An angry red welt ran across his knuckles.

Charles sighed and let the sleeves drop. "Did you have to answer the professor like that?"

It didn't matter that this time the answer had been correct. Quill had made no attempt to disguise his heavy brogue. The professor had declared him impudent and made an example of him.

"Aye. I'll no' talk like the enemy." Quill knew he was being obstinate. But somehow, these past few weeks had been easier to endure when he imagined himself a brave Highlander, fighting against the English at Culloden. The professors, with their foreign languages of Latin, Greek, and mathematics, were the enemy. It didn't matter that his equations never balanced or that he made paper darts instead of essays. It didn't matter that he peppered his English with as many Scottish words as he could. All that mattered was that his màthair was dead.

Charles shook his head. "He'll be angry again if you don't write your essay. Do you think you can?"

Quill curved his swollen hand, gingerly touching his fingers to his thumb. His knuckles throbbed with pain. "Nay."

They queued behind an older class for dinner. "Tell me what to write," Charles said.

"What?" Quill stared at his friend.

"Promise me you'll not provoke the professors again this week, and I'll help you with your essay."

"It willna work. Our handwriting is too different."

"Yours is just sloppy. It's easier to be sloppy than it is to be neat. But I'll only do it if you tell me what to write. I'm not composing it for you. And only if you promise to mind your tongue for the rest of the week." His blue-gray eyes were solemn and steady under a bruised temple. He had done that for Quill, too. Sunday afternoon, when a boy twice his size had insulted the Morris family honor,

Quill had charged into a fight. Charles had joined him. After a few blinding blows, Rabbie and Nathaniel had pulled them out.

Quill didn't know what he'd done to deserve a friend like Charles, but after that fight, he owed him everything. "Aye. I promise."

~

THE JULY SUN SET, LEAVING BEHIND A STICKY HEAT that clung to Williamsburg like honey to a bairn's hand. Quill left his jacket and cravat on the bed but, at Polly's insistence, put his waistcoat and hat back on. The streets were empty of all save the night watch. Music and conversations drifted from open windows. He itched to allow an evening breeze in the Eagle, but it was too important that their conversation not be so easily overheard or seen, so window and shutters remained closed.

Jack soon joined him, followed by Colonel Hendriks, Patrick Henry, and enough other radical leaders that Quill was obliged to give up his seat. He leaned against the desk, next to a lantern, listening to the arguments in the stuffy room, wishing Patrick Henry wouldn't sit at Charles' desk.

"Did you hear? Dunmore has abandoned his post. The *Fowey* and *Magdalen* left yesterday."

With Dunmore gone, there was no authority in the colonies to threaten the patriots with treason. The legitimate government was rendered impotent, as the legislative branch could pass no laws without the governor's signature. There was also no one to restrain the dubious authority of the Committee of Safety as it coerced the citizens to prove themselves "friends of liberty," whether they were or not. Until Dunmore—or another representative of the king—returned to Virginia, it would be far more prudent to be a patriot than a loyalist. He was safer. Charles was not.

Quill fingered the little fox in his waistcoat pocket. "He's going home?"

"No, just his family. They say Dunmore is going up to Boston to visit General Gage."

"Betray us to Gage, you mean," Jack said.

The colonel shook his head. "I say good riddance. But did he ever approve the militia's pay?"

"Nay," Jack said. "He refused to secure the paper credit on the grounds that he couldn't approve a duty on slaves."

"Why," Henry asked, "does England oppose our every attempt to slow the importation of slaves, an evil it will not allow on its own shore? I'll tell you. 'Tis because the Mother Country thinks the colonies exist to make her money. As long as it doesn't happen on her shore, she doesn't care what evils persist to fund her army and navy, which she will send on us."

"That's beside the point," Jack said. "I don't care what Dunmore isn't doing. It's what he's going to do that we need to prepare for. Will he persuade Gage to blockade the Chesapeake? If so, we need more powder and arms, and we need it soon."

"We need it now," Henry corrected. "By the time we send for more, Dunmore will have warships to prevent it from arriving."

"There's never enough gunpowder in a war," the colonel said.

"We're agreed that we need more," Jack said. "The only question is whether we buy it, steal it, or make it ourselves."

"Enough with the stealing," Quill said. "Besides, where would ye steal it from?"

Jack leaned forward and lowered his voice. "Every summer, the crown sends a supply of guns and powder to the Indians. If we could intercept one of those ships, we would be set."

A man standing in the shadowy corner said, "To intercept a ship, we need a ship. Where do we get one from?"

The meeting then devolved into a senseless discussion of how to acquire and man a privateer before returning to the more rational possibility of making gunpowder. Quill bit his tongue before reminding Jack that Athair had been making saltpeter, the main ingredient in gunpowder, for years as a crop fertilizer. Rabbie would not thank him for dragging the family into another rebellion. Debates over plans to arm their fellow citizens in the event of an attack raged on until midnight, when Quill reminded them it was now the Sabbath, and they finally dispersed.

He swept the dusty evidence of their gathering out the door and locked up. Earlier today, he had taken Charles' side. This evening, he had allowed the patriot leaders to discuss treason in the office he shared with his friend. Neither side would be pleased with what he had done, though he was only trying to keep the peace. He couldn't please them both. Was it duplicitous for him to be helping both of them? Or would he be able to bring the good of each side to the moderate middle? That was the side he wanted—the only side that wasn't clamoring for war.

Twenty-Six

THROWING STONES

SUNDAY, JULY 2, 1775

A fly settled on the pulpit. Mr. Price waved his hand. The fly stirred a few lazy inches before returning to rest where it had been. The rector didn't shoo it a second time. Ladies with flushed cheeks and shining brows were too languid to move their fans. In the balcony seats, schoolboys slumped against the railing, their eyes dull and listless.

Emmeline frowned at her prayer book. The July heat had settled on Williamsburg as heavy as a blanket, but that didn't explain why Mr. Quillan Morris hadn't glanced her way even once during the service. She had come to anticipate the pleasure of his friendly smile and stolen glances, the silent connection during services, and the unspoken promise that he would seek her out. She had boldly encouraged his attentions last week by inviting him to supper. By the time he had whispered goodnight, she believed he would be paying court within the week. Instead, he refused to look at her.

Services ended, and the congregation pooled outside like melting butter. She took her time arranging her prayer book and finding her handkerchief before leaving the pew. By the time she got outside, Mr. Morris was, as usual, in conversation with someone else. What was unusual was that he didn't even glance at her as she passed by, as invisible as a pane of glass.

She made her way to Jenny, her heart heavy with the conviction that Mr. Morris would not seek her out. The air was too indolent to stir the leaves of the catalpa trees that lined the Palace Green. A dog lay in the shade, panting with its tongue out. With no breeze, her petticoats trapped the warm air like a cast-iron lid on a stew pot. She patted her face and neck dry with the handkerchief and forced a smile. "Jenny, how are you?"

Jenny did not return the smile. "Fine," she said in a small voice.

Her conscience awoke to worries beyond her own. "You don't sound fine. What happened? Is your aunt well?"

"I told her to stay away from me." Jenny burst into tears. Heavens, everyone was out of sorts today. It must be the heat. If only a breeze would blow through and set everything to rights.

None did, so she patted Jenny's shoulder and asked, "Why in heaven's name would you do that?"

"I don't want them to notice we're related. She'll be safer that way."

"Safer?" Her mind was as heavy and sluggish as the air. She tried and failed to make sense of Jenny's words. "Is she in danger? Are you in danger?"

"I don't know. But I was dusting in the dining hall when some gentlemen came to call on Mr. Johnson early in the morning before he left for work, and couldn't help overhearing. They kept insisting he sign something. He refused, and they accused him of being an enemy to liberty."

Emmeline bit her lip. Charles didn't hold with the patriots, but he obeyed and enforced the law. Beyond that, he kept to himself. Just because he disagreed with something didn't make him a public threat.

Jenny blew her nose. "Mrs. Evans tried reasoning with the men, and then Mrs. Johnson, but they wouldn't listen. They said men had been tarred and feathered for less and that he was 'endangering everyone under his protection by his obstinacy.' I'm scared."

Emmeline blinked back tears. The patriots were supposed to be the heroes. They were supposed to be standing up for what was just and true. These men had just threatened her cousin, his wife, and household, and for what? Because Charles had been brave enough to disagree with words. Wasn't that what this whole conflict was about? The king was sending soldiers to punish Americans because some of them had been brave enough to disagree with words. Shouldn't the Committee of Safety and the volunteer companies be defending a man's right to speak his conscience?

"Disagreement isn't a crime," Emmeline said. "Charles is in the right. They must know it. They were probably just hoping to scare him into signing." Though she disagreed with her cousin's politics, she was proud of him for staying true to his convictions.

She looked over the row of carriages lining the green. Charles was handing Susan into the phaeton, like he did every Sabbath. The normalcy was soothing. If she was right, if the men were only making empty threats, then nothing of importance had changed. Her family was safe, and all was right in the world. Then a rock hit the carriage, and the world turned upside down.

A few yards away, a tall lad with a boyish face scowled at the phaeton and the person inside it. He swung his arm back, a large rock in his hand.

"George! No!" Emmeline yelled.

He glanced at her, but the loathing on his face didn't soften. He threw the rock. It flew over Charles' shoulder and past Susan's face, missing by an inch. It had come horrifyingly close to hitting one of them. Emmeline had predicted that war would come to Williamsburg. She hadn't predicted this. She was less frightened by the prospect of faceless soldiers fighting each other on the field of battle than she was by witnessing a boy she had done business with throwing rocks at Susan. There were distant shouts, but her mind was too stunned to comprehend them until Charles caught George's arm mid-swing. He pinned the boy's wrist against a tree, yanked the rock from his hand, and tossed it across the green. His cold fury was more terrifying than a heated tirade would have been.

"Touch my wife, and I will throw you in jail and prosecute your offenses before the highest court in the land. If you hurt her, I will hurt you. If you threaten her, I will threaten you. I will not hesitate to plead for the highest punishment the law allows. A day in the stocks is nothing. Men have been branded and sent to the gallows by my word."

Quillan Morris, who had been a furlong away before her cry, ran up to her. "Emmeline, what's wrong? Did he hurt ye?" His hazel eyes were intense, and her irrational heart wanted to say yes, just to hold his attention a little longer.

She shook her head. "He was throwing rocks, really big ones, at Charles and Susan."

"He could have killed her," Charles said.

George's face had lost all its color under Charles' threats. "I wasn't going to kill her," he said.

Charles was not appeased. "Even if you didn't mean to, manslaughter is still a felony. You would stand trial at the highest court in Virginia, and I would see to it that—"

"Easy, Charles," Quill said, in the tone one might use to calm a skittish horse. "He's just a boy." He waited while Charles relaxed his grip on George's wrist just enough for the color to return to his hand. Addressing the boy, he said, "Johnson is right. A rock that big could kill a person. I'd hate ta see a lad like ye in the gallows. Matter of fact, I'd hate ta see a lad like ye in the stocks."

George scowled. "I hate ta see Tories in Williamsburg."

Understanding settled in her belly with the weight of a rock. The threats had trickled from faraway palaces to familiar parlors. The fighting had begun, not on the battlefield between soldiers with muskets, but just outside the church by a boy whose heart had been poisoned by angry men.

After a moment's stunned silence, Quill said, "Dinna throw stones at a man for his beliefs. A country that silences each dissenting voice will never be free. And never throw rocks at a woman."

Words bubbled inside her, pressing for release, but she had no paper and was ill at ease vocalizing her thoughts with others. Quill would listen, but her words to calm George might irritate Charles, who was still angry. She glanced at Susan. A cluster of genteel folk surrounded her carriage, offering their support. Would they all leave if they knew why George had thrown the rocks? She looked back at the boy and his insolent scowl. She had seen him on many occasions and could not be satisfied with this new development in character. He should be better than this.

She focused on the top button of his waistcoat and said, "If you punish a man for disagreeing with you, then you're no better than a king who sends his armies to punish a disposition."

The words out, she looked up to see how her audience had received it. Charles was annoyed. Quill was surprised. But George had set the type that had published King George's declaration. That's who he was angry with, not Charles. And when she connected him to his enemy, all the fight went out of him like fire doused with water.

Quill saw it, too. "Take yer wife home, Charles. I'll handle this."

Charles hesitated, his narrowed eyes searching his old friend. He must have found what he was looking for because he gave a short nod, then left the boy in Quill's hands.

Quill turned his attention back to the boy. "Now, who are yer parents? I'd like a word with them."

George's jaw tightened.

When it was clear he would offer no guidance, Emmeline answered for him. "He's an apprentice for the *Gazette*."

"Thank ye, Miss Gardiner," Quill said. "There's yer family. Go to them and stay close. Stay safe."

Though she had hoped to witness how Quill handled young

George, she wasn't foolish enough to insist upon it. If the boy's anger continued to simmer, she didn't wish to become his next target. When she reached her family, they demanded a detailed account of what the commotion had been. She answered all their questions, but the heat of the day and her enduring thirst left her thoughts muggy. It wasn't until the evening shadows covered the raspberry patch that she had the clarity of thought to consider Quill's puzzling behavior. Unless she was very much mistaken, he had avoided looking at her during the sermon. He had been so studious in his avoidance of her that, had she not cried out when George threw the first rock, he might not have spoken to her that day.

He loved her. Even in her naive inexperience, she could see it —the way his eyes softened when he spoke with her, like her very presence touched a chord deep within his soul. He had run to her side at the sound of her cry, even more concerned for her safety than for Charles' and Susan's. He loved her. Such depth of feeling should lead to courtship. Instead, he was avoiding her. Why?

If she believed her uncle spoke for all gentlemen, then Quill didn't want her because she worked with her hands. But her uncle was nothing like Quillan Morris. It would be an insult to her beloved to believe her uncle spoke for him. But a gentleman's wife would be expected to have certain skills. Even if she couldn't paint fine portraits or play the harpsichord, she should be able to plan elaborate dinners for company. What did Quill know about her prowess in the kitchen? He had witnessed her cooking when Maurice had been ill with a toothache. Then again, there was nothing special about turning a pie filling into a stew. Anyone could do that. Did he imagine she would subject him to a lifetime of makeshift dinners when they expected company? She wouldn't, but he didn't know that. Were men really so simple and practical? She didn't want to believe it of Quill, and yet she could think of no better reason for a man to resist courting when he was so plainly in love.

The brambles caught on the linsey-woolsey skirt she had

changed into after church. The ugly thing was indestructible. She tossed a handful of sweet berries in her mouth. On the Sabbath, she only had to pick what she could eat. Tomorrow, she would have to harvest berries by the pail. An idea burst upon her like juice from a berry. She could give him a pie. It would mean another walk into town during the heat of the day, but she could manage that.

It would be a brazen thing to do. Gentlemen courted ladies, not the other way around. She had been bold enough to invite him to supper. The evening had gone well, but it hadn't borne fruit. She couldn't give him a pie when he had done nothing to reciprocate. She would only make a spectacle of herself. An evening breeze stirred the ribbon of her hat, as blue as the summer sky. He had bought her that hat and that beautiful ribbon. She owed him something for the gift. Mama would agree. There was nothing brazen in returning a favor. People exchanged and bartered goods all the time. Then he would know she could bake things of greater interest than reheated stew. There was no need for him to fight his feelings for her.

Twenty-Seven

RASPBERRY PIE

MONDAY, JULY 3, 1775

Quill was in a dour mood by the time Colonel Hendriks took his leave. He had been tired and hungry before the surprise visit and in no mood to endure the man's lengthy tirade on the state of the government. The only bright spot in a chaotic world was that he had made progress toward regaining Charles' respect. Though his attempt to protect Charles from the Committee of Safety had only delayed their interrogations for another day, it had proved his courage and loyalty. Then his friend had trusted him to manage the foolish apprentice while he took his wife to safety. Just one more success, and he would speak to Charles about courting Emmeline.

Meanwhile, he was attempting to follow Polly's challenge to not raise Emmeline's hopes before he had the courage to speak. Avoiding her company was as bad for his spirits as skipping dinner was for his belly. The days were going to be long and dreary until he spoke to Charles.

He locked his desk like a responsible man and put his cocked hat on, eager for dinner to alleviate some of the strain on his spirits. There was a knock, and the door opened. The sun behind his guest was so bright he couldn't discern her features, but he would know that silhouette anywhere. His traitorous heart tripped over itself. "Miss Gardiner," he swept off his hat in a playfully gallant bow, "to what do I owe this honor?"

She crossed the threshold, clutching a basket in front of her with both hands. She was a breath of fresh country air after a stuffy morning in the office. The open door was empty behind her. Surely she hadn't come to town alone. He wasn't as protective as Charles, but anyone with an ounce of common sense would be worried. Just yesterday, a boy had thrown rocks at his friend's wife. Some fool might extend the threat to his cousin.

Emmeline's eyes darted to his, then around the office, taking in each oil painting, book, desk, and chair. "I...well..." She was all nerves, which unsettled Quill.

"Let me guess," he said, trying to banish the mood with a measure of absurdity. "A man picked all the green apples from your orchard, and you need a barrister so brilliant he can persuade the court to decree that they must all be returned to you fully ripened."

Something between a scoff and a laugh escaped her, and she shook her head.

"No? Then Miss Henrietta eloped with the baker, and your father insists on an annulment."

Her mouth went round in shock, but her eyes laughed.

He leaned forward. "Miss Gardiner, you haven't been accused of forgery, have you?"

"Certainly not," she said primly, her cheeks dimpling as she held back a smile.

Whatever he had promised Polly about avoiding Miss Gardiner hadn't covered what to do if the lass cornered him in his own office. Dinner was on the table right now. It would be nothing to invite Emmeline to join them. "Polly went home ta set dinner out an hour ago. I was about ta go then, but the colonel caught me and—"

"Oh. I won't keep you then. I need to be going."

His heart sank.

She set her basket on the desk, took a deep breath, and looked at him solemnly. "The raspberries are ripe, you know." Her voice was high and breathy.

He tensed at the sound. What sinister evil had been hiding in the raspberry patch?

"And I—" her voice broke. She ran one finger along the edge of the basket.

His stomach dropped. Not that. Not to her. Blast it, but Charles had been right to worry about the bonny lass going about town and country without an escort.

She raised her chin and looked him in the eye. "We have a lot this year." The words spilled out. "And so when I made the pies, we had one too many. And I...I owed you something for the hat. I thought you might like one." She pulled a pan from the basket and handed it to him. It was still warm. She tugged the cloth away. The office was filled with the heady aroma of raspberry pie.

He had been braced for a sordid tale. He stared instead at a sweet pie. "You made me a pie?" That had to be the most idiotic thing he'd said all month. He was holding it, after all.

"Ye-es." She dragged the word out uncertainly. The poor lass had been afraid to tell him she'd baked him a pie. He laughed away the dark thoughts from where they still lurked in his mind. She flinched.

"Forgive me. It's just, I've never had a whole pie to myself." A whole, glorious, mouthwatering pie made for him by the most glorious, kissable lass in the whole world.

She twisted her hands. The vulnerable gesture twisted his heart. "I hope you like raspberries. They were," she waved a hand as though searching for a difficult word. "Ripe."

Avoiding her at church was hard enough. He could not very well be expected to avoid the lass when she caught him alone and unawares. Noise filtered through the open door. Carts clattered down the street. People shouted. Children laughed. It was all so very far away. Everything real, everything that mattered, was right there, in his office. He drank in her gaze like she was the last cup of tea in the colonies. Her eyes caressed his face in return, the same homely face he had once cursed in the looking glass. His heart melted like ice on a summer's day. He had to do something, quickly, to rein this in before he said something foolish. He needed to act friendly and disinterested. He needed to do something. Anything. So he did the first thing that came to mind. He kissed her cheek. "I adore raspberries."

Her shoulders straightened, and her hands stilled. "Good." She nodded. "That's all right then." She picked up the basket and stepped toward the sunlight. "I won't keep you."

"Wait," he said. "I will walk ye home."

"There's no need. See?" she added, gesturing to the window. "I brought Henrietta. I didn't come alone." Her little sister was waiting outside the office, her face flushed with heat.

"Then I will escort both of ye."

"But it's quite out of your way. I don't wish to inconvenience you over a pie."

"Miss Gardiner, please. I'll have no peace until I know ye're safe at home. Tensions are high in Williamsburg. 'Tisn't safe. Ye saw what happened yesterday. I wish I could say it had surprised me more than it did. I'm going ta walk ye home. Please, trust me."

She tucked her lips between her teeth and nodded. "As you wish."

"Oh, that reminds me." Quill grabbed the package above his desk and handed it to her. "Dinna open this afore ye're safe at home."

Her brow furrowed. She looked at him quizzically.

In a low voice that wouldn't carry through the open window, he explained, "Our friend, the Dutch captain, felt he owed ye something for whatever kindness ye did him. He wanted me ta deliver this ta ye."

She sniffed the package delicately. "Is this...what I think it is?"

"Aye, but the ban on imports is only against British goods. This was brought by the Dutch."

Satisfied, she placed the package in her basket. He locked up. If Charles returned first from dinner, all would appear as it should.

"What took you so long?" Henrietta asked. "It's hot and I'm tired."

"It wasn't so long," Emmeline retorted, "and we're all hot and tired."

"Come," Quill said, extending one hand to Henrietta. "I'll see ye home." Now that the little sister was holding one hand, it was only natural to offer the other to Emmeline. "Has anyone threatened yer family? I know Charles is having a difficult time of it."

"Why would Charles be having a difficult time?" Henrietta asked.

"Hush," Emmeline said. "Children should be seen and not heard." To Quill, she said, "We've had a few men speak with my father in his shop, but he's been a Whig for years. There have been no threats."

"I thought not. Ye'll tell me if that changes." He squeezed her hand.

"I will." Emmeline sighed. "Charles can't even vote. Why does it matter whether he's a Whig or a Tory?"

"It shouldn't," Quill said. "Even if he could vote, it shouldn't matter. What is a vote worth if ye're only allowed one choice?"

"True." They walked along in silence, swinging their clasped hands like a dance. "Jenny—she's Susan's maid—she overheard some men talking to Charles. They were trying to coerce him into signing something. When he refused, they threatened him and his household. They said men had been tarred and feathered for less."

Quill inhaled sharply through his teeth. "When was this?"

"She told me about it yesterday, so I imagine sometime last week."

Quill sighed. "A few days ago, a man from the Committee of Safety came here looking for Charles. I convinced him ta leave, but he threatened ta call on him at home. He should have told me they did." Just when he thought Charles' trust and respect in him had grown, he discovered he was wrong.

"So much has happened of late," Emmeline said. "He doesn't know who he can still trust."

"He can trust me. We may disagree on politics and policies, but not on his family's safety." He squeezed Emmeline's hand again and winked at her.

She smiled and blushed. "I told him to trust you," she said. "And I think he does, as much as he trusts anyone."

It was late in the afternoon when he finally arrived home for dinner.

"What took ye so long?" Polly asked. She glared at him across the table.

"Sorry." He set the pie between cold chicken and green beans. "I brought pie."

She scoffed. "Ye made me hold dinner so you could buy a pie?"

"Nay. I didna buy it."

"Then where did it come from?"

"Miss Gardiner." He raised his brows in what he hoped looked like confusion. He had done nothing yesterday to encourage her. He shouldn't know why she would give him, of all people, a pie.

They said grace. He helped himself to chicken and green beans. Then he slid an enormous slice of pie onto his plate. Warm berries burst across his tongue.

"So," Polly said sweetly. Too sweetly. "Ye were alone in the office with Emmeline?"

He inhaled the crust and bent to the side, coughing desperately into his handkerchief.

She tsked. "What will Charles say?"

He gasped for air and sat up, his eyes watering. "We were not alone." He coughed again. "She brought her sister."

Polly held his gaze.

He sighed. "What was I supposed ta do when she showed up with a pie? I thanked her politely and, in the name of safety, walked her and her sister home."

"So ye were alone in the office when Henrietta and Emmeline came in?"

He shifted uncomfortably. "Henrietta stayed outside, but the door was open. We only spoke for a minute afore I insisted I escort them home."

"How very proper. Of course ye didna kiss Emmeline."

The heat ran up his neck, across his cheeks, and to the tips of his ears.

Polly dropped her fork. "Ye did kiss her."

"Nay." His flush betrayed him. "Not the way yer thinkin'."

"What other way is there?"

His cravat was smothering him. All the heat of July collected together to press down on him in that moment. "Like I was greeting Màthair. Just a quick one on the cheek." He turned defensive. "She'd just given me an entire pie. I had ta do something."

"So ye kissed her like she was yer mother." Polly shook her head. "Honestly, Quill."

"What? Ye told me not ta lead her along."

"I told ye ta choose. Either court her for good and real or not at all. No lass wants a tepid lover."

Quill scoffed. His affections were as tepid as butter in a hot skillet, but the battle for her cousin's trust demanded patience and strategy. This wasn't the time to confess his longing to claim kisses sweeter than raspberry pie.

Twenty-Eight

THE FOWEY

THURSDAY, JULY 6, 1775

Mr. Wythe slumped into a chair and fanned his flushed face with a cocked hat. "I'm sorry to trouble you again, Morris, but I suppose you've heard the governor returned."

Quill choked back a sigh. "I did." He should have been happy that the rumors had proved false. Dunmore had not gone to Boston to beg troops from General Gage, nor had he fully abandoned his role in Virginia's government. The *Fowey* had returned to York Town only a few days after it had left. He had escorted his wife's ship no further than the capes. Quill wouldn't have expected Emmeline to sail across the open Atlantic alone. He would have seen her all the way home. "I suppose ye have something for me ta deliver." The sun was high in the sky, and parts of the road to York Town would have no shade.

"I do." He handed Quill a thick letter.

Charles frowned. "I didn't know the House had met again."

Mr. Wythe hesitated. "They haven't. This is from the Virginia Convention."

An uneasy silence filled the office. It was one thing to deliver messages from the House of Burgesses to the royal governor. It was another thing to deliver messages from a congress of patriots to a nobleman on a warship. Or was it? Quill continued to hope the conflict would be resolved with words, not war. That wouldn't be possible if the two parties couldn't communicate. He glanced at Charles. This was as much a service to the governor as it was to the patriots.

"To whom should I deliver his lordship's reply?"

"To the convention."

"Would ye mind telling the livery ta ready my horse? I need a few minutes ta prepare."

Mr. Wythe agreed, and after Quill had explained his rationale to Charles, collected his jacket and canteen, and escorted Polly to the comfort of a friend's home, he was pleased to find Gunpowder saddled and ready. The gelding pranced when Quill draped his linen jacket in front of the saddle and took the reins, eager to be on the road. Once they were beyond town, Quill let him gallop, enjoying the breeze the movement created, but it didn't last long before his horse slowed to a more conservative pace. Quill patted his withers. "Too hot for ye? That makes two of us." He took a drink from his canteen and hoped his horse had been properly watered that morning.

The sun beat down on them as they passed a tobacco field that had been cleared and planted up to the road, with no border of trees. Perspiration dripped from Gunpowder's neck. Quill was taking another drink from his canteen when his horse stumbled and the precious liquid splashed on his shirt. He wasn't even halfway to York Town, and they were both overheating.

"Come on, Gunpowder. I see some shade up ahead." He urged his horse on until they were standing in the shade of some old maples, panting. Continuing to York Town was unthinkable. He would ruin his horse if he rode there and back in this heat.

He dismounted and walked the remaining quarter mile to Willow Haven, leading his horse by the reins. He roused Billy the stablehand and instructed him in the care of overheated horses, something his father and the aging head groom had surely done a dozen times before. Someone offered him a drink of switchel, the earthenware container chilled in the stream. He drank it all, while one of his father's horses was saddled.

There was more shade between Willow Haven and York Town, and Quill was pleased his borrowed horse was not as taxed by the heat, since it would only have an hour or so to rest before the return journey. Still, he reminded the man at the York Town livery stable of the care his father's horse would need. Then he walked to the river.

The *Fowey* was indeed anchored again in the wide gray waters of the York River, but not everything appeared as it had on his last visit. Canvas tents nestled in the trees, less than a cannon shot away from the warship. Several shirtmen sat outside their tents, playing cards. Quill shook out his linen coat. It was rumpled from the journey and smelled like horse, but those were the hazards of summer travel. He put it on and approached His Majesty's Marines standing watch on the pier.

"State your name and purpose," one of the men demanded.

"Mr. Morris here ta deliver a message ta his lordship from the Virginia Convention."

"Wait here."

Quill waited under the glare of a July sun as hot as a simmering kettle. Clouds rose like steam across the sky. Sweat trickled down his neck. Sailors on neighboring vessels stripped down to their linen shirts, the sleeves rolled to the elbows. Water rolled under the pier. How heavenly it would be to sit down with his bare feet in the water, but a man was not free to do as he wished while waiting on nobility.

At last, the sailor returned to escort him onto the *Fowey*. "His lordship was having a bath," the man explained.

"Sounds refreshing." Everyone in Williamsburg knew that Lord Dunmore bathed often in the summer, his slaves pouring buckets of cool water over him as he rested in a tub. It was the sort of rumor whispered on hot summer days. It must be nice to be the highest-ranking man in the colonies. Nobility was exempt from the suffering heat that the common people worked through.

"Mr. Morris," Dunmore greeted him languidly from the comfort of his quarters. "It is good that I am so conveniently situated to Williamsburg. Twelve miles is no obstacle when the business is of importance. I told the burgesses so myself."

"Aye, sir." Quill didn't dare protest how inconvenient he found the twelve miles. It could have killed his horse. It also meant hours away from his business, missed meals, and relying on Charles to help prepare the briefs he didn't have time for. He felt a twinge of guilt, remembering all that his friend had done for him in the past weeks, despite the more alluring demands of a new wife. "The House asked me ta deliver this." He held out a thick letter.

"I will give it my immediate attention. Wait outside."

Quill had been dismissed like a common servant. He left the shelter of his lordship's quarters and was blinded by sunlight reflecting off the water. He leaned into a sliver of shade and waited, his eyes closed against the harsh light. This time, his lordship had not demanded that a man offer him refreshments. He wondered, idly, whether Dunmore's servants were expected to remember such mundane details as watering horses. They did not remember to offer Quill something, and he had emptied his canteen miles ago.

It must be nice to be so comfortable that one could forget that others were uncomfortable. Emmeline would never have done such a thing. She would offer a drink to any lost soul who came to her gate—even a tall Dutch captain who, for some reason, frightened her.

At last, Dunmore delivered his reply, and Quill was free to go. He got a cool drink from a coffeehouse, then rode straight for Willow Haven. He needed to return for Gunpowder, but he would wait until the relative cool of the evening to minimize the stress on his steed.

After returning the horse to the care of young Billy, Quill

stumbled into the house and dropped his coat on the bannister. He was so exhausted he was tempted to collapse on the stairs, but his stepmother, wearing a loose sultana, was there to greet him. "Quillan Christian Morris, what in heaven's name have ye been doing traveling in this heat?"

The room swam around him. He closed his eyes. "Dunmore. *Fowey.*"

She put a hand to his brow and tsked. "Just as I thought. Go ta yer room, take yer clothes off, and lie down. I'll send up something ta drink."

He didn't have the strength to agree or disagree. He gripped the banister and dragged his feet up the stairs. In his childhood bedchamber, he removed everything but his linen shirt and drawers and collapsed on the bed. Athair brought in a quart of switchel. Quill tried to refuse, but his father insisted he drink a cupful. Then he was allowed to rest, with the door propped open to encourage a breeze.

He woke, hours later, to a cool hand on his brow. "How are ye feeling?" Màthair asked.

He blinked. Her face didn't swim, and his head didn't pound. "A little better."

"Drink some more," she said, pressing a cup into his hands. "Slowly, or ye'll make yerself ill."

By the time he had drunk enough to satisfy her, the heaviness that had been pressing down on him all day had eased.

"We'll be having supper soon," she said. "Ye're welcome ta join us, if ye feel up ta it."

"I think I will."

She nodded. "I had the washbasin filled while ye were resting. Wash up and get dressed. Remember ta use the soap," she added, as though he were an obstinate bairn instead of a grown man.

"Yes, ma'am," he said meekly.

By the time he joined his family at the table, he felt almost himself again.

"Billy told me ye'd traded horses," Athair said. "I thought we would see ye again."

Màthair frowned. "Ye took better care of yer horse than ye did yerself."

"A true Morris," Athair said proudly.

She turned on him with a scolding finger. "That is not something ta be proud of."

He laughed and kissed her. She tried and failed to appear stern as she smoothed her hair, the gesture setting a pearl earring swinging. Those had been Athair's betrothal gift to her. The earrings looked far finer than the tarnished heirloom his father had given him.

After the plates had been served, Quillan asked, "How do ye clean silver?"

Aunt Moira held up her gleaming spoon. "A soft flannel cloth is all ye need ta keep the shine."

"Ta keep it? What if the silver is tarnished black all over?"

"Then ye use rottenstone or heartshorn."

"Or make a paste of whiting and water," Màthair added. "Why?"

"I was just wondering," Quill said, cutting his vegetables.

"I want ta meet her," Aunt Moira said.

"Meet who?"

"The lass ye've been courting."

He choked and coughed into his napkin. "I'm not courting anyone...yet." Escorting her home didn't count. Holding her hand while escorting her didn't either. He'd been holding her sister's hand, too. The fact that she made him an entire raspberry pie? It merely meant the adoration was mutual. Just because his aunt realized he was thinking about polishing up the betrothal brooch did not mean he had an announcement to make.

After a minute, Aunt Moira asked, "What color is her hair?"

"Blonde." The truth slipped out before he realized what he'd done. But his family didn't know her, so what harm could it do?

There were lots of blonde women in the world. "And curly," he added.

"And her eyes?" Grace asked.

"Blue," he sighed, though the common word didn't do them justice.

"Is she short or tall?" Hope asked.

"She's almost my height. And that's all I'm going ta say about her."

"Do I know her?" Aunt Moira persisted.

"Nay. I dinna believe a soul in this house has ever met her."

"That's because ye havena brought her ta meet me."

"I canna bring a lass I'm not yet courting so far."

"Not in this heat," Màthair said.

"'Tis only six miles," Athair said.

"For me, aye," Quill said. "But she lives outside of town." What would it be like to take a Sunday ride out to Willow Haven with her? He hadn't been able to take her to a bakery in Williamsburg without drawing Charles' ire. Things needed to be more settled before such an outing would be prudent, no matter how much Aunt Moira pestered him.

"I want ta meet her," Anna said.

"Me too!" echoed Grace. "What's her name?"

"Oh, no. Ye willna weasel anything more out of me."

"Does Polly know?"

She did, but she wouldn't betray him. Not after he had kept her secrets. Rabbie had met her once or twice, but that didn't signify. He hadn't confided in his brother. "I'll bring her as soon as her family allows," he said. Once he had Charles' approval to court, naturally, he would need to introduce her to his family. If Polly wasn't enough of a chaperone, he would ask Catriona to accompany them.

"When will that be?" Hope asked.

Soon, he hoped. Very soon.

After supper, Athair followed him out to the stable. "Do ye ken why I married yer màthair over an anvil?"

Quill had heard this story many times. "Because ye were in a hurry."

"Aye. Quite a hurry. But there's more than that. Scots for many years have married over an anvil. The Master Blacksmith takes two hearts, two souls, and welds them together. They become one heart and one soul. Nothing can hurt one without hurting the other."

"It must hurt abominably when one of those hearts dies."

"Aye. It hurts. Do ye ken why I married yer stepmother?"

Quill clenched his fist. White scars crossed his knuckles, a permanent reminder of the year his mother had died. He had been a lad of nine, and his professors punished him for misbehaving. After several long, miserable months, he had been hurt and confused to learn that his father was betrothed again. "The lassies needed a mother," Quill said. He had clung to the excuse. It was the only way to honor his màthair's memory. The only way not to besmirch the heroic status of his Athair. But he had always been afraid it was only an excuse.

Athair patted his knee and chuckled. "My laddie needed one every bit as much. Ye nailed the headmaster's door closed."

It had gotten a laugh out of his schoolmates. Their laughter had eased his grief.

"I ken she had a *màthair* heart," Athair went on. "And ye bairns needed that. But that wasn't the only reason."

Goosebumps prickled against his shirt. He didn't want to hear Athair confirm the truth. Not a truth that would shame his màthair's memory. He looked away. The boyish hurt was too strong in his heart.

"Yer màthair made me believe in marriage."

Quill looked back. His father was blinking tears from his eyes. "The good Lord didna make us ta walk this earth alone. The good book says so. 'Tisn't good for man ta be alone." There was a long silence. "Give yer màthair's brooch ta some bonny lass. Yer a man. 'Tis no' good for ye ta be alone. Have I no' shown ye so?"

"Nay, ye have," Quill said, his hands resting on the fence. "And I will. I just need a little time."

Twenty-Nine

A PATRIOT

The weather had mellowed to a commonplace July intensity by the time the next issue of the *Gazette* was printed. Emmeline skimmed through the broadside until she saw a piece attributed to "A Patriot." She tried to read it, to see if it was just as she remembered it, but the words blurred together. Her writing was in print. People all over Williamsburg would be reading her little composition; the same people who eagerly read parliamentary debates and foreign news would be reading and considering her ideas.

She hid her nerves and read the piece aloud while her father worked, then held her breath, wondering what he might say about it. He was one of the few men in the county who could vote. He attended elections and had witnessed debates among the burgesses. His opinion carried the weight of the most influential men in the colony. "What do you think?" Emmeline asked him.

"It is a wise man who can say so much, so clearly, in so few words, and a modest one who lets his words stand on their own."

She had meant to tell him it was her work, but the generous

praise made her bashful, so she folded the *Gazette*, put on her apron, and went to the workbench to help him.

~

Quill turned to the second page of the *Gazette* and found a piece titled, "On the Rights of Americans."

> *Many before me have spoken of the rights of colonial Englishmen. They have spoken of them as a birthright handed from father to son, like a lord bequeathing a castle on his firstborn.*
>
> *Though logical, this explanation is too narrow for the diverse population that builds our communities and assembles with the militia to defend these rights from foreign invaders.*
>
> *The French Huguenot claims religious tolerance. Landowners driven from Ireland participate in free elections. The Dutch, the Scots, and even the Spaniards who have settled among us claim the right to a fair trial by a jury of peers.*
>
> *Americans need not claim their birthright through a distant English ancestor. Our birthright comes as each immigrant is born again on American soil. It is renewed with the birth of each succeeding generation. We stand equal when we stand on American soil.*
>
> *A Patriot*

Quill read it twice, the words ringing in his soul like a church bell. This, so plainly written, is what he had been trying to explain to Miss Gardiner. His family, in fleeing English armies, had never desired to become English. But they were no longer Scottish. They had been "born again on American soil."

He showed the piece to Polly, who was almost as pleased with it as he was.

He showed it to Charles, who read it with a frown. "What Spaniard lives in Virginia?" He studied it again. "It isn't bad. The rights, of course, do come from England. And any immigrant must know he is living in British America, which the author ignores in his presentation. It's a sentimental piece. The author lumps all Virginian citizens together, claiming they inherit the same rights. He ignores the complicated laws surrounding Indians, the enslaved, and free Blacks. A barrister wouldn't have done such a thing. Still, it's an engaging little essay." He looked at it again. With a soft smile, he read, "Renewed with the birth of each succeeding generation."

"What is it?"

"Nothing. Nothing." He briskly folded the paper and patted Quill's shoulder. "You'll understand when you're older." He dropped the paper on Quill's desk. Charles had always considered himself an American Englishman. He was even married to an Englishwoman. He didn't understand what it was like to always be on the outside of such conversations, to finally have words to describe how he had always thought and felt.

Quill soon found other men impressed by it. Its concise argument was genius—it was easily remembered, quoted, and discussed. The article wasn't anti-British, but it was unapologetically pro-American. It inspired pride, patriotism, and unity among those who read it. Quill cut the article from its narrow column and carried it in his pocketbook, in case an opportunity arose to share it. Polly, who had neater penmanship, copied it so he could post it on the office wall: a reminder to himself and prospective clients that Lady Justice was blind, that every citizen had the right to equality before the law.

Who was the Patriot? Some prominent burgesses were suggested, but statesmen preferred to be as verbose as possible and would not have missed an opportunity to put their name in print. It must have been a more modest citizen, a voting gentleman of middling means, who had written a thoughtful and concise article and was humble enough to remain anonymous.

～

THAT SUNDAY WAS BETTER IN EVERY POSSIBLE WAY than the last one. Congregants were more alert, Quill smiled her way before the sermon began, and not a person was threatened before or after the meeting. Jenny's spirits had improved since the prior week, and Emmeline saw her bidding her aunt and young cousin farewell as she approached.

"How are you, Jenny? Have any more men come by the Blue House to threaten my cousin's family?"

"None," she said, "though I overheard the most shocking tale about his friend, Mr. Morris."

Emmeline, who had been about to scold her young friend for eavesdropping, halted when her beloved's name was mentioned. As the future wife of Mr. Morris, she had a proprietary need to know what was said about him. "Who is spreading tales about Mr. Morris?"

"Your cousin. Did you know he was on trial once? Not as a barrister, but as the accused?"

"I heard a little something about it," Emmeline said. It had been before Charles had gone to London eight years ago, and she had been deemed too young to hear the sordid details. She hated to encourage anyone to gossip about Quill, but she couldn't ask him for the story, either. If she was going to marry him, shouldn't she know everything about him? This would be the easiest and kindest way to learn. "Why would Charles bring it up now? The verdict was given ages ago."

"He was telling his wife. She had never heard of it, and Mr. Morris seems like such a nice person, not the sort of man you would imagine in the middle of such a scandalous affair."

Emmeline's stomach turned, and she braced herself for the worst. "I'm afraid I'm not familiar with the details."

"Well, Mr. Johnson is. He was called in as a witness—the only witness who was on Mr. Morris' side. They had known a young lady who was quite accomplished. She played three instruments and sang like an angel. But she was also a bit of a coquette, charming all the gentlemen."

Emmeline couldn't quell the jealousy that flared, but she did maintain her outward composure. She needed to hear the whole tale.

"Well, you know how much Mr. Morris loves music. The cunning sphinx—that's what Mrs. Johnson called her after she heard—she invited Morris to a little concert at her home. Of course, he couldn't resist such an invitation. But when he arrived, he was confused to find himself alone with the girl."

"There were no other guests?"

"It's worse than that. Her family was away for the evening. She had pleaded a headache to stay home and had lured Morris there. But she didn't know he had begged his friend to come as well. They didn't arrive at the same time, but Mr. Johnson was on his way; otherwise, there would have been no witnesses to what happened next."

"What happened?"

"She told him she had a new guitar that she wanted to show him, but she wasn't allowed to bring it into the parlor. So he followed her like a fly into a spider's web—that's what Mr. Johnson said—into the neighboring bedchamber, naively expecting her to actually have a guitar. Instead, she threw herself at him and started kissing him. He was so surprised, he just stood there like a statue until Charles walked in. Then she ran off and they left, agreeing to never return."

Emmeline was appalled that any woman would take advantage of Quill's gentle nature in such an egregious manner. "What an infamous way to behave!"

"But that wasn't the end of it! Two months later it became apparent that she was with child and when her father demanded to know who the father was, she insisted it was Mr. Morris and called the maid and footman in who had witnessed him visit that evening, but they must have known the whole story, because they neglected to mention that Johnson had come only a few minutes after Morris and they had to have known that. Well, the father demanded that Morris marry his daughter, and he refused, insisting there was no possible way that the child was his. The father brought the whole thing to court, but thanks to Johnson's testimony, they couldn't convict him. Only five months later, she gave birth to one of the biggest babies the midwife had ever brought into the world with jet black hair. After that, it was obvious that Morris couldn't have been responsible, but that she had tried to frame him."

"What a horrible thing to do to a man!" Emmeline exclaimed. "Doubtless she thought Mr. Morris would be a superior husband and father to the man who was guilty, but had she succeeded, how could she expect them to be happy together after abusing him in such a manner?" It had been foolish of him to follow her, but she could forgive a little folly. To have attempted to ruin his character and force him to raise a child that wasn't his was a kind of villainy that put Lady Macbeth to shame.

After Jenny took her leave, Emmeline was so deep in thought about Quillan Morris that she didn't see him approach and was startled when he greeted her.

"Are ye well?" Quill asked.

"Yes, quite well," she said, "only a little lost in thought." She would not cause him pain by telling him she had finally heard the old tale of the scandal he had been ensnared in. Still, she was grateful to finally know. She would have better tact now that she knew the story behind the trial. "And you? Are you well?"

"Quite well. I have been waiting ta hear yer opinion on this essay." He pulled a bit of newsprint from a pocket. "'Tis on a subject we were discussing a few weeks ago, but conveys my thoughts far better than I did."

She accepted the paper and saw, at a glance, that it was her writing. Did he suspect her? Was he teasing? She moistened dry lips. "I hope you don't mind. I—I didn't think to ask, since the words were my own. But I wouldn't have thought of it without you. I suppose I should have asked first, but I didn't really think they would publish it."

"The words were yer own," he repeated and took the paper from her trembling hand. "Ye wrote this? Ye're the Patriot?"

"Oh, dear." Her ideas weren't half as original as she had once thought they were. "You called me that once, and I—I rather liked it. I hope you don't mind."

Quill laughed, caught her hands, and kissed them. "I'm honored. I've been showing yer writing ta every person I've met. I had Polly copy it out in her best penmanship, and we hung it on the wall of the office. Ye've done me a great honor, finding the words ta argue my case. Thank ye, lass."

It didn't matter if the rest of Virginia never learned she was the author. Such a revelation could never bring the joy that Quill's warm praise had given her.

Thirty

TYRRANY BY TAR & FEATHERS

Quill's attention wandered to the paper tacked above his desk with tiny nails. Polly's finest copperplate script immortalized Emmeline's essay on American birthright. It seemed fitting to hang it beside the oil painting of Willow Haven, where he and Polly were born. He had feared his attraction to Emmeline was superficial—that he would wake up one day to rue the folly that had led him into an unwise marriage. Here was irrefutable proof that he adored more than her charms. He had encountered her mind, disguised in print, and it had filled him with wonder and delight. In the eternal wisdom of Shakespeare, he should "not to the marriage of true minds admit impediments." Her lack of dowry or social connections would be no obstacle, not when their minds and hearts were so compatible, as though God had created them for each other.

Each day, he awaited one more opportunity to prove himself to Charles, not as the foolish friend of his youth, but as a capable man of judgment and maturity. Any day now, and he would earn the blessing of his old friend. Then he would be free to call on Emmeline and kiss her without censure. Any day, now. He would see her later today. If Charles was in a generous mood this morning and the opportunity presented itself, things might be settled before dinner at the Blue House. Might there be a discreet way to steal his beloved away from company for a few words, and possibly a kiss? If Isaac hadn't spoiled it, the honeysuckle pergola would have been perfect. Mayhap it still was.

The door flew open, pulling him from his thoughts. Charles stumbled in, dressed for work with mismatched stockings of gray and black. His face was raw and red except around one eye, which shone blue and purple. He slumped into his chair without removing his hat. He made no move to unlock his desk and begin his work. Quill glanced at Polly, who looked as concerned as he felt. Something was very wrong.

"Charles," Quill said gently. Haunted eyes met his. "Are ye alright?"

His friend laughed. The sound had a sharp, biting quality. "I'm fine," Charles said.

It was plain as day that he was anything but fine. Polly jerked her head toward the door and went outside. Quill followed her.

Standing under the Sign of the Eagle, she said, "I'm going ta check on Susan."

"Ye dinna think they've quarreled?"

"Nay." Worry lines creased her brow. "I think...well, I'll tell ye if I'm right."

"I'll get my hat," he said.

"Nay. I dinna think Charles should be left alone in this state, and I dinna fear the Volunteer Company. If I'm not back within the hour, then I've decided ta stay with her. I'll see ye at dinner."

She was probably right, but Quill didn't trust a world that could upset his friend so thoroughly. Something was wrong, and he could only pray it would come out right. *Lord, keep her safe and help me ta help Charles.* He watched his sister until she was out of sight, then returned to the office.

Charles was resting his head against his slant-top desk.

"Polly's run an errand. Since she's not here, is there anything ye'd like ta get off yer chest?"

"No." The monosyllabic refusal was the most Charles-like thing to happen all morning.

"I've kept yer secrets afore."

Haunted blue-gray eyes met his. "I shouldn't have married her."

"What?" Quill would have been less shocked to hear Lord Dunmore was leading a band of privateers up the Chesapeake. "That's nonsense. Ye've never been happier." Marriage was the best thing that had happened to Charles. He frowned less and smiled more. He was less doubtful and more purposeful. Charles couldn't believe that his better-than-he-deserved marriage was a mistake. He would never allow his cousin to be courted if the best relationships only ended in misery.

Charles shook his head. "It was too soon. She survived the seasoning, but she never got her strength back. We should have waited."

Waiting was better than never. Grasping at hope, Quill asked, "Is she ill?" This black mood would pass as soon as she improved. It had to.

Charles dropped his head into his hands. "She shouldn't have been. None of this should have happened."

Quill dragged his chair across the room and sat, knee-to-knee, with the friend who had pulled him out of more scrapes than he could name. "Charles, this isn't the time for secrets. Start from the beginning, and tell me what happened. Trust me."

"They broke into the house around midnight," Charles said abruptly. Without giving Quill a chance to ask who "they" were, he continued. "I ran downstairs with a loaded pistol, but one of the men grabbed me from behind, and it misfired. They dragged me outside. I thought they would leave the women alone if they had me. I told Susan to stay inside. I begged her. Her aunt begged her. But she wouldn't listen. She can never sit still when someone is in trouble. She ran outside in her silk slippers, right up to the drunken mob, and demanded they release me. A man spat in her face and pushed her. She fell hard, then another man kicked her. She doubled over and didn't try to stand. Her breathing was...bad. Sharp. Uneven. And all this time, I was fighting the mob to release me so I could get to her. Graves finally came out and helped her back to the house."

The narration faded as though Charles hadn't the strength or the will to carry it to its conclusion. There was a long silence. At last, Quill said what Charles wouldn't. "Ye were tarred and feathered."

Charles gave a faint nod. "Then they pushed me down Duke of Gloucester Street in a wheelbarrow. There was a bit of trouble with the night watch, but one of them knew Jack, so—"

"Jack?" Quill repeated. "Catriona's husband, Jack? He was there?"

"That Jack. Yes, he was on watch."

Jack Mason had been at the Eagle two evenings ago. He had sat in Charles' chair, tipped back so all his weight rested on its hind legs, and laughed. Quill had welcomed him into the office and, though irked by the abuse of his friend's chair, had laughed, too. He couldn't recall what had amused them. He only remembered the laughter, empty and echoing. It sickened him.

"Polly went ta be with Susan," Quill said, as if this small kindness meant anything in the face of such vast injuries. "How is she? Did ye get a doctor?"

"It was too late. She lost the baby."

It took a moment for Quill to grasp what Charles was saying. His wife had been in the family way. The stress and injury of last night, coupled with her weakened state from the seasoning, had been too much for her to handle in that condition. Anger cracked like a whip. "Give me their names," he said, yanking his chair back to his desk and setting a sheet of paper atop the chaos.

"Their names?"

"Aye, their names. We're going ta bring the mob ta justice." He uncorked the inkwell, dipped the quill pen, and waited.

At last, Charles said, "Not this time."

"What?" Quill turned, dripping ink across the white page.

"The Committee of Safety has too much say, especially since the governor has fled town. There will be no justice. Not this time. Pursuing it will only put my family in further danger. I can't do that. I will do anything to keep them safe. I'm going to—" he broke off, as though reconsidering something rash. Then his shoulders set. "I'm going to sign the paper."

"And let the mob know they've won?"

"I wouldn't do it for my own safety. But if I had done this last week, they wouldn't have touched my wife. She wouldn't have lost the baby. For her sake, I need to silence my convictions."

They were supposed to be fighting for the constitution and protecting their home from an invading army. None of this was supposed to happen. Quill corked the inkwell. "I hate this," he said.

"So do I. But there's nothing we can do."

It was too late to prevent the events of last night. They couldn't seek justice. But he couldn't do nothing when his friend was in danger. Not after everything Charles had done for him. He grabbed his hat.

"Where are you going?"

"I'm going ta see Jack."

~

Catriona was pleased to see him. "Brodie was just asking about ye."

"I regret that I'm not here for the wee bairns. I'm here for Jack."

"The big bairn? He's asleep. He stood watch last night."

"That's why I'm here."

She raised her brows. "Jack said the night was uneventful. What happened?"

"Uneventful?" Quill shook his head. "Ye remember Charles Johnson?"

"Yer old school friend? Aye. His wife is a friend of mine. She invited us ta dinner the other day. Why?"

"While Jack was standing watch, a mob broke into their house and dragged Charles into the street."

Catriona's mouth dropped open. "Why would—"

"Ta tar and feather him. That's why."

"They didn't."

"They did. His wife, Lord bless her, tried ta plead with the mob." Quill paused, unsure if he had a right to tell more of their story.

"I admire her courage," Catriona said, "but I trust they didna take kindly ta the interference."

"They did not."

"Keep your voices down." Jack stumbled into the dining hall wearing nothing but his nightshirt, his arm blocking the light from his eyes. "A man has a right to sleep after standing watch all night."

Cat glared at him. "I've had enough of yer rights. I'll give ye a right. A man has a right ta think his own thoughts without being hauled out of bed in the middle of the night. A woman has the right ta plead for her family without a man laying a finger on her. I canna believe ye allowed that ta happen on yer watch—and ta a friend of mine!"

Jack raised his arm to squint at her. "Who?"

"Mrs. Susan Johnson and her poor husband."

Jack waved her accusation away. "He's a Tory. Everyone knows it."

"She isn't. And what does it matter if he is? He alerted the town the night of the Magazine Incident. The man had a right ta sleep last night."

"Cat—Kitten," he wheedled, "don't be angry. I didn't know it was him. It was dark, and men all look the same when they're covered in tar and feathers. I certainly didn't know they hurt his wife. I'll speak to the men. I'll tell them never to do it again."

"Ye better," Quill said. "Or ye can find another place ta hold yer meetings." He wouldn't risk his neck to help men who would threaten his friends.

Catriona placed her fists on her padded hips and glared at the two men. "What meetings?"

～

EMMELINE WROTE BY THE LIGHT OF THE FULL MOON, pouring her righteous indignation into the margins of last week's issue of the *Virginia Gazette*. That afternoon, Graves had delivered a sealed letter from her cousin.

Charles, peaceful, steady Charles, had been tarred and feathered last night because he was believed to be a Tory. Susan, beautiful, kind, and elegant, had been spat upon and handled violently. He wanted to warn his uncle to take every precaution, in case his family was also in danger.

Beginning beside the announcement of George Washington being named commander in chief of the new Continental Army, she began her essay, encircling the broadside with her fevered thoughts.

> *Liberty or death is on every tongue, emblazoned*
> *over the heart of every volunteer to the mighty cause.*
> *But whose liberty and whose death do we speak of?*
> *It is liberty to all, not a handful of aristocrats on*
> *a far-flung isle. And the death we speak of is not*
> *foolish or vengeful. We offer ourselves as a blood*
> *sacrifice to preserve our neighbors' liberty.*
> *Yet these mighty words have been profaned by*
> *drunken mobs, crying liberty while hauling innocent*

men from their wives' embrace to punish a difference of opinion with tar and feathers.

The passion of a mob is blind to reason—it destroys a neighbor's liberty as easily as his property. It will sacrifice a neighbor's life in its cause. But it is a perverse liberty that allows criminals to escape justice. Liberty does not reign when a mob has taken power.

Yet this is the sorry condition of Virginia's capital! The brave and true cower inside each night while drunken mobs rule the streets.

We can have no victory over invaders while our capital suffers in such a manner.

How can our brave soldiers march to battle when they fear for the safety of loved ones at home? Such a thing is unthinkable. Our citizens must be united before our cities are safe. We cannot entrust all our unity to our representatives in Congress and neglect the troubles in our own garden.

We decry the heavy hand of despots and tyrants —let us also decry the heavy hand of a drunken mob. It, too, is an enemy to liberty.

We must first vanquish the despot in our hearts and homes. Second, confront him in the streets. Only then can our brave soldiers be true friends of freedom, ready to stand tall on the battlefield with the cry, "Give me liberty or give me death."

Emmeline hid the *Gazette* under her clothespress and climbed into bed. It was a pity Papa wouldn't allow her to walk into town alone anymore. Even Henrietta was deemed an unsuitable companion. There was too much danger right now. Quill and Charles had convinced him of that. They hadn't convinced her. If liberty was worth the price of death, then wasn't truth worth a little risk as well? What if her words had the power to silence a mob? Instead, she would have to remain silent, because to go alone after she had been forbidden would dishonor her parents.

From today forward, she would only go to town accompanied by her family for church, or when the carriage came to take her to dinner at the Blue House. Her eyes flew open. Graves had stopped by the printer's before and had kept her secret. She could ask him again. The Patriot had something new to say.

Thirty-One

EMMELINE'S HOLIDAY

Emmeline dragged the tip of a piece of straw across the hornbook while Kitty named each letter of the alphabet. After reviewing the sounds each vowel made, they moved down the hornbook to the syllabary.

"Ab, eb, ib, ob, ub," Kitty read each syllable clearly. "Ba, be, bi, bo, bu." Then she repeated the Lord's Prayer with a little help. "Our Father, which art in heaven, hallowed be thy name. Thy kingdom come. Thy will be done in earth, as it is in heaven. Give us this day our daily bread. And forgive us our debts, as we forgive our debtors. And lead us not into temptation, but deliver us from evil: For thine is the kingdom, and the power, and the glory, for ever. Amen."

When they reached the end of the prayer, Emmeline dropped the straw on the table. Kitty had finally mastered the hornbook. Next, they would move on to the full syllabary contained in *Dixon's English Instructor*. That was a challenge for the morrow. Today, she wanted to savor the awe and pride she felt at witnessing her pupil's success. Where were the fireworks? The cannonfire? The music and dancing? There should be a public celebration for this momentous occasion. Kitty had learned her letters. Her young pupil would be sounding out words by cider season.

"You did it, Kitty. You did it!"

Kitty grinned. "Am I done with my sampler?" All of her letters were neatly stitched, with her name at the bottom.

"You're done with the letters on it. Would you like to add a border of flowers like mine has? Then it would be something pretty to hang on the wall. You don't have to decide right now," she added before her pupil could decline. "But you are done with the hornbook. I made some teacakes to celebrate. I left them in the kitchen. Wait a minute for me."

She was returning to the house with a little basket of teacakes when she saw the restless heads of two matching horses in the road. She didn't recognize the horses and couldn't imagine whose carriage was stopped in front of their house. She leapt up the back steps as a knock sounded. "Excuse me," she said to her pupils, setting the basket on the table and hastening to answer the front door. To her astonishment, Polly Morris was there.

"Polly," she said, forgetting all her manners in the surprise of the moment. "What are you doing here?" Her eyes drifted to the fine carriage, an unfamiliar coat of arms on the door.

"What am I doing here?" Polly repeated. "The courts are in session. 'Tis unwise ta distract the jury with a female clerk, so I've very little work ta do. The weather has been too sultry for social niceties, so 'tis better if I dinna spend that time calling on friends. The short of it is, I have decided ta go home, ta Willow Haven. Would ye do me the honor of accompanying me?"

Emmeline was so awed by the unexpected invitation that for one blissful moment, she forgot that she must decline. Then all of her responsibilities fell back on her shoulders. She had a cow to milk, a garden to tend, lessons to teach, meals to prepare, and wood to turn. "Oh," she cried, the remorse pure and painful, "I would love to, but I cannot."

"What would you love to do?" Henrietta asked, wandering into the room with a half-eaten teacake.

"Miss Morris has invited me to be her guest and accompany her to visit her family."

"Oh. Did Mama say no? I thought she was gone. Is she back already? Is it for a long visit? Is that why she said no?"

"Mama is a mile away just now, remember?" She had taken a crock of fresh butter to exchange for a bundle of rags they would sell to the printer.

"Then ask Papa," Henrietta said with infuriating simplicity. "He's more likely to say yes, anyway."

Even though she knew Papa would decline, it seemed rude to Polly to persist in her refusal without asking her parent. "Come, wait inside. I'll just be a minute."

After offering Polly a teacake, Emmeline went to the workshop to explain the matter to her father.

"You may go," he said.

"What? But there's so much to be done. Who will milk the cow, teach the lessons, weed the garden—"

"Emma," he interrupted. "Even the finest schools have holidays. Tell Kitty that I need a word with her grandfather, and I'll let him know she won't have lessons for a week. As for the rest of the chores, if we cannot manage a week without you now, what will we do when you leave us for a home of your own? You're a gentlewoman's daughter. Go act like one."

Afraid the answer might change if Mama returned before she left, Emmeline accepted Polly's help packing her clothing into an old laundry sack. The footman raised a brow but didn't comment as he placed the old sack beside a locking trunk with shiny brass hinges. The carriage rocked into motion, turning in a tight arc.

"Are we returning to town?"

"We'll have ta pass through it. Willow Haven is off the main road between Williamsburg and York Town."

Belatedly, Emmeline remembered her essay. If she had thought to bring it, she might have asked to stop by the printer's to deliver it. Instead, it would have to wait for her return. She hadn't known they were going through town. It was for the best.

She would have been terrified to confess her writing endeavors to Polly, but she should have summoned the courage for Charles. Sweeping her guilt under a rug to be examined later, she said, "Willow Haven is a pretty name."

"Aye. Wait 'til ye see it." She then captivated Emmeline with the tale of her father's role in the Jacobite 'Rising, his escape, and how he had begun a new life in Virginia. She described her other sisters, her mother, and her great-aunt. While she talked, Emmeline wondered whether it had truly been Polly's idea to introduce her to their family, or whether it had been Quill's. Unless distance prohibited it, most women met their suitor's family before they were betrothed, but she hadn't anticipated the opportunity to come so soon and suddenly.

There was an undeniable connection—wordless secrets communicated in little glances—but she couldn't say with any certainty that courting had begun. She had imagined there would be more words, more gestures, and more time spent together. Being suited for each other didn't make him a suitor, not if he wasn't making an effort. But as the miles rolled behind them, her confidence in him grew. He wouldn't have arranged for her to meet his family if he wasn't hoping to marry her. What did it matter that the opportunity had presented itself before he was formally courting? Or might he be waiting for his parents' approval before moving forward? There was little to impress his family with in her laundry sack of apparel. She would have to be on her best behavior this week because she had no other way to impress them.

They turned off the road to York Town into a shaded wood. "I apologize in advance for anything Aunt Moira might say ta ye," Polly said. "She isna afraid ta voice her opinions. And if she asks ye about Mr. Ingram, ye dinna know him."

"I don't know him," Emmeline replied, her honesty tainted with curiosity.

"Good," Polly said, waving her fan. "Ah, look. That's the house I was born in. The overseer and his wife live there now. And that's the village," she pointed to a cluster of small shops and homes. "Màthair worked in the village kitchen afore she met Athair."

Taking some comfort in their stepmother's humble origins, she admired the grand house built on a small rise. An old maple tree shaded one side, and an ancient wilderness bordered the extensive property. Emmeline stepped down from the carriage and into a storybook, all quotidian cares forgotten.

Assured the servants would tend their luggage, Polly led her through the foyer and into an elegant parlor. An elderly woman sat in a wing chair, her hands resting on a jeweled cane. Her white hair was veiled with black lace. A silk kerchief was arranged in artful tucks and gathers around her pale throat. Pinned to the bust of her bodice was an enormous brooch that glittered like dragonfly wings. She lifted her chin as they walked in.

"Aunt Moira," Polly began in an overly sweet tone.

"'Tis about time," the woman said. "I haven't seen ye since—"

"A year," Polly interrupted, with a glance at Emmeline. "I haven't been home in a little over a year. But I'm here now, just as I promised."

"A year," Aunt Moira repeated in disgust. "I'll never forget the day ye left withou—"

Polly interrupted her aunt again. "May I introduce my friend, Miss Emmeline Gard—" She broke off when a woman with dark hair, powdered to a smoky gray, swept into the room and embraced her.

"Polly! Home at last!"

Emmeline, feeling like an intruder on an intimate family reunion, took two discreet steps to the side. She suddenly remembered her mismatched heels and, for once, wished she had worn the linsey-woolsey petticoat. As she still hadn't hemmed it to a proper walking length, it would have hidden her shoes from notice.

Aunt Moira stroked the head of her cane. "I was about ta tell

Polly how unseemly her behavior has been. An entire year unchaperoned in the city."

"I'm not unchaperoned," Polly said, her words more bold than her gaze, which didn't meet her aunt's eyes. "When I'm not with Quill, I'm calling on friends in the most respectable manner."

"I'm just glad ye're home, my dear," the woman said, and Emmeline wondered what it would be like to have such an affectionate woman as a mother. "It doesn't matter what happens. Ye can come home at any time, do ye hear me?"

"Aye, Màthair." Polly seemed a little uncomfortable. "May I introduce my friend? This is Miss Emmeline Gardiner."

Emmeline curtsied.

"Am I acquainted with yer family?"

"I don't believe so, ma'am."

"She's a close cousin of Charles Johnson," Polly said. "Ye remember Charles?"

"Aye, though I havena seen him in ages. He was a good lad."

"Take off yer hat," Aunt Moira demanded.

"I'm sorry?" Emmeline said, unsure she had heard right.

"Take off yer hat. I want ta see yer hair."

Afraid to offend the matriarch of the family, Emmeline set her hat on the tea table and removed her round-eared cap as well. "I'm afraid it is a little wild today," she said.

"Blonde and curly." Aunt Moira drew the descriptive words out with satisfaction. "And she's just the right height. Ye might have told me, Polly."

Polly narrowed her eyes. "Told ye what?"

Mrs. Morris answered first. "How beautiful her hair is, being so blonde and curly." She sent a warning look to Aunt Moira. To Emmeline, she said, "Do sit down, my dear, and tell us all about yerself. We're so glad ta finally meet ye."

Emmeline had never talked so much about herself as she did that hour, answering the many questions Aunt Moira and Mrs. Morris put to her. What could this mean but that Quill had told them about her? Why else would they have anticipated meeting her?

Polly took her on a short tour of the house, ending in the bedchamber they would be sharing. "This used ta be Quill and Rabbie's," she said, and Emmeline could imagine a slingshot hanging from the bedpost as the brothers lay across the rag rug on their stomachs, marching lead soldiers into battle.

Given permission to make herself at home until dinner, Emmeline retraced her steps to the entry hall, studying each oil painting, then paused outside the library. The broad mahogany desk and chair warned her that the chamber belonged to the master of the house. She didn't dare cross the threshold, but she couldn't tear her gaze away, not when an entire wall was covered in bookshelves with more books than she had ever seen in her life. She whispered the titles like a prayer. They were arranged in friendly clusters—a few faded clothbounds stacked under a seashell bigger than her fist, a parade of well-loved leatherbounds beside a small sculpture of some distinguished Greek or Roman, newer leatherbounds awaiting the master's attention, and a large rock that shimmered in the afternoon light. She had never seen anything more beautiful than that room.

"Would ye like ta borrow one?"

She gasped and turned to face her host, embarrassed that she had been caught gawking at his library. "Athair, I—" she broke off, realizing to her further mortification that she had presumed to call him by the familiar name his children used. "I beg your pardon. I meant to call you Mr. Morris."

"I would be honored if ye would call me Athair." He patted her shoulder. "A man can never have too many daughters."

If she married Quill, then she would become this man's daughter, by law. Was he thinking that?

"Miss Gardiner, is it? I heard ye were fond of reading. He stepped into the library and around the vast desk. "What do ye prefer?"

"Oh," she said, stalling for an answer that would impress him.

"Well, everything?" That was no answer. She stepped into the library and tried again. "Shakespeare and Herodotus. Plutarch and Dante." With each author she named, she found herself a little deeper in the room. "The English translations, of course. I never mastered enough of the classical languages to read the originals."

He studied her with a look of mingled wonder and amusement. Uncomfortable with the attention, she studied his desk. They had built a similar one last fall, though the finish work had been less elaborate and the color a little lighter, as they had used local maple, not imported mahogany. At last, Athair said, "Sometimes the best opportunities are granted ta those who least appreciate them." He turned to the shelves. "I do have English translations." He unshelved the parade of well-loved leather-bounds and set them on his desk. "There's *The Republic*—"

"What's that?"

"See for yerself." He handed the book to her.

She turned past marbled endpapers to the title page. "This is by Plato," she said stupidly.

"Ye've read him?"

"Not this. I've read *Death of Socrates*. I didn't know he wrote anything else." She bit her tongue. There was no need to brandish her ignorance.

"He wrote several things. I recommend *The Republic*. The ideas have helped form many a government. Of course, ye are welcome ta any title ye please."

She hugged the book to her heart. "I'll start with this. Thank you. Thank you so much."

Over dinner, she met the youngest Morris girls. They had been upstairs in the schoolroom when she arrived. Sixteen-year-old Anna wanted the details of every ball Emmeline had attended, and was a little disappointed to learn there had only been two before patriot restrictions against extravagance had been pushed. Grace and Hope giggled and chattered about an abundance of nothings. The youngest, Marta, was delighted to learn that

Emmeline had made her birthday presents and begged permission to leave the table to retrieve them. After she finished her plate, permission was granted, and Marta soon returned with a top and Jacob's ladder.

"There was a fox, too, wasn't there?" Emmeline asked after witnessing a demonstration of how well Marta could operate the toys.

Marta's face scrunched. "A fox? Nay."

"Is that where that came from?" Polly asked suddenly, drawing everyone's attention. After a flurry of questions from her family, she simply said, "Quill keeps that in his waistcoat pocket." Then she laughed. "Once he forgot it on his washstand and left the office in the middle of the morning to retrieve it. He never told me where it came from."

Emmeline fought back a smile as her face heated. "I only painted it. Charles carved it."

"Blonde and curly," Aunt Moira said smugly. "I knew she was the one."

"Wait," Grace said, "Is Quill cour—"

"Hush," Màthair said. "Dinna pester her."

After dinner, the family went to their chambers to wait for the heat of the day to fade. Polly dressed down to her underpinnings and fell asleep. Emmeline removed her stockings and kerchief before losing herself in the borrowed book. She only made it a few pages before the sticky heat pulled her attention away. Over dinner, Athair had reported that it was ninety-two degrees on Fahrenheit's thermometer, and that the horses were appropriately cared for. Mathair said she was grateful the courts would prevent Quill from traveling that afternoon. It wasn't good for man nor horse to be active when the air was so close to blood temperature.

She dipped a handkerchief in the water pitcher and then ran it across her face, her arms, and even her ankles. Then she stretched an arm through the curtains, where a faint breeze offered a little relief. It felt so good that her head followed, and she found herself in a world of shimmering green maple leaves. There was an inviting crook between a sturdy branch and the trunk that promised a comfortable seat. She glanced back at the bed. Polly snored softly.

She tucked the back hem of her petticoat into her front waistband, knotted the precious book in her kerchief, and climbed out of the window. The branches closest to the house were a little shaky, but this wasn't Emmeline's first tree. Her bare feet curled around the bark, and she reached her arms wide to steady herself on neighboring branches. Soon, she was safely cradled against the sturdy trunk. Hidden high in the branches, she savored the breeze that wrapped itself around her bare skin. Unknotting the book, she soon found where she had left off.

Many pages passed before she was pulled from her reading by the sounds of movement in the house. She held still, waiting to be missed and discovered, wondering what Polly would think. After several minutes had passed, she grew curious and peeked inside. The fluttering curtains framed an empty room. She dropped the book softly to the floor and climbed inside, her reading sanctuary as secret as a robin's nest. She shook her petticoats free of tree bark and was tidying her appearance in the looking glass when the youngest of the Morris girls came in, her feet bare and her hair wild.

"Miss Gardiner," Marta said, "Can ye fix my hair ribbon?"

"Bring me a brush or a comb and I can." After only a few hours, she had forgotten her fears that she might not belong at Willow Haven. Quill's parents had been welcoming and attentive. His younger sisters were curious and admiring. Even the forbidding Aunt Moira had, for reasons Emmeline didn't understand, approved of her. She was a gentlewoman's daughter. No one had made her feel like anything less.

Quill's stepmother had once been an indentured servant working in a kitchen, and now was the notable housewife of this grand and beautiful home. At Johnson Hall, being a lady was as much about what one didn't do—cook, or clean, or work with one's hands—as it was about etiquette and a refined education.

At Willow Haven, it didn't matter that Emmeline was the daughter of a cabinetmaker and that her fingertips were calloused from work. Somehow, she was as at ease at their dining table as she was at Papa's workbench. The family was as curious about her work as they were about her heart, mind, and soul. At last, she had found a welcoming place where she could dovetail the disparate parts of herself into one whole.

She had come home.

Thirty-Two

INNOCENT & FREE

With a strike of the gavel, the courtroom stirred to life. Quill didn't fight the grin on his face. Winning a brief made him feel like a schoolboy on holiday. He had Charles to thank for his success. While Quill had been carrying messages for the burgesses, his friend had made sheets of notes in preparation for the trial. Charles was the only man in the courtroom still seated. He was reading over his notes for his next brief, which wouldn't be presented for hours.

"Charles, everyone is leaving." His friend stirred and tucked the papers in his document case. Quill led his freshly vindicated client outside. A convicted man was being pushed into the stocks. His client looked away. He had been at risk of that and more. Quill clapped a hand on his shoulder. "Come, let's celebrate being free men. I'll buy ye a drink at Chowning's." He looked over his shoulder as the stocks were locked in place. Freedom was for the innocent. If only King George and Lord North spent a little more time in the courts. They needed the reminder. Never had Quill witnessed a jury condemn a man for his disposition. Free men were only punished when their actions went against the law. They weren't punished for their private thoughts and convictions as long as they conformed their actions to the letter of the law.

Mayhap the king was like Lord Dunmore, quick to suspect his subjects were plotting evil against him, and quick to punish them before they had acted. But that wasn't how the law worked. A man was innocent until he was proven guilty. A man was free to choose, to act. Only when and if his actions violated a law was he punished and his freedom curtailed. It would be ridiculous for his client to also be spending the day in the stocks simply because another of his countrymen had been found guilty. But that was how parliament had voted to punish Boston. A small group of men had thrown the tea. They were never caught and punished. Instead, troops had been sent to occupy the whole city.

He shook off the heavy thoughts. He had won this brief, and the court was adjourned until after dinner. He would enjoy himself. The streets were filled with vendors who renewed their hawking as people poured from the courthouse. A man beside a cart full of fabric called, "The finest Virginian homespun! Get your patriotic fabric here! Blue stripes! Brown stripes! Fine indigo. Suitable for shirts, shortgowns and petticoats."

A young woman rocked a baby and called more softly, "Fresh eggs, sweet peas, carrots, and honey!"

The merry chaos called to him, but he had promised to buy drinks. There was a short line to enter Chowning's. Other barristers had gathered there with their clients. While they waited to enter, Charles' eyes darted about. Only a week ago, he had been paraded down this street in a wheelbarrow, covered with tar and feathers, punished for being true to convictions that differed from what had become popular. Once they were seated in the corner, Charles eyed the crowded room with distrust.

When their waiter set the mugs on the table, Quill raised his. "May justice be blind, and the innocent always be free."

After one drink, they went their separate ways. Quill bought a loaf of fresh bread, which he ate while wandering the street, enjoying the bustle of the market. People hawked their wares. He saw a ribbon as blue as Emmeline's eyes, embellished with flowers. Such a gift was for courting. True, he had bought her a ribbon for her hat, and a new hat as well, but he had had a ready excuse for that. But to just walk up to a lass with a pretty little thing for her that he'd purchased only because it reminded him of her, that was only for courting. He was still waiting for God to show him the way, to pave the path forward with kiln-fired bricks and strew it with flowers. Or, at least, to give him a sign that Charles was ready to approve his suit.

For now, he just needed to see her as often as he could. With no sister to report to, no one would be the wiser if he slipped away from the crowds to see her this evening. He had missed her at church, and Charles had convinced Susan not to hold their usual dinner. The town was flooded with people while the courts were open, and he feared lest some danger should befall his cousin. Quill wouldn't argue against keeping Emmeline safe, but he missed her.

This wasn't courting—warm smiles and stolen glances, the joy of her company, polite little kisses—aye, this wasn't courting, but it wasn't quitting, either. He fingered the ribbon. It was perfect for her, and ribbons kept well. He could tuck it away with the brooch. He would give the ribbon to her as soon as he had Charles' blessing. The brooch he would save for betrothal. He paid and was putting it into his pocket when someone grabbed him by the arm. The ribbon fell to the ground.

"Got you, MacKenzie," a man growled.

Quill scowled up at the stranger. "I beg yer pardon—"

"Scottish born, speaks broad, double-breasted waistcoat, shoes in good condition, about twenty-eight years old, runaway joiner."

Runaway. Quill's blood ran cold. He had seen that advertisement several times on the back page of the *Gazette* for the well-dressed, well-educated Scotsman. He hadn't given it much thought at the time. He certainly hadn't imagined someone would mistake him for a runaway servant. "I'm not the man yer— you are looking for." He flattened his brogue, attempting to sound as English as possible."

"That's what every runaway says. Bob!" He shouted across the market. "Got one."

Blast. If this man were in the business, nothing short of a five-pound bribe could help him now.

The two men dragged Quill toward the wagon. He dug his heels into the dirt. His jacket ripped at the shoulder seam. "I'm not a runaway," he cried. Then his eyes fell on a familiar face. "Charles!"

It took only a second for Charles to comprehend the situation. He pushed through the crowd. "Unhand him!"

"No, sir. We found him. We get the reward."

"There is no reward for him. If you do not unhand him, I, Charles Johnson of Johnson Hall, barrister at law, will drag you before the general court, and by the time my prosecution is complete, you will count yourself fortunate to be spending a day in the stocks."

"He has gotten lots of people in the stocks," Quill added helpfully.

Charles spared him an annoyed glance.

"But this man is a runaway. "He's the right age, the right height—"

"The wrong hair color."

"What?"

Charles was all business. "If you're looking for the runaway Scottish carpenter with the double-breasted waistcoat, you should know he has dark hair cut short."

For the first time in his life, Quill thanked the Creator for red hair.

"Could be a wig," Bob said, and yanked his queue.

"Ow!"

"Satisfied?" Charles asked. "Or do I need to prosecute you for kidnapping a free man?"

The men released him. Quill put a hand to his head. His hair was wild. One of the buckles he'd clipped above his ears hung sideways. "Thank ye, Charles. I'm impressed ye remembered the description so well."

Charles shook his head and pulled a paper from his colorful pocketbook. It was a clipping of the very advertisement from the *Gazette.*

"I didna know ye took such a keen interest in runaways."

"I don't. Unless the runaway sounds a little too much like a friend." He tucked the paper back in his pocketbook.

"Ye thought this might happen?"

"I was worried it would. You do have a knack for scrapes." He frowned at Quill, taking in the torn jacket and unbound hair. "You look awful. Tidy up before your next brief."

Feeling as humble as a lad who had lost his first fight, Quill picked up the ribbon and shook the dust from it. He returned home, fixed his hair and exchanged his jacket, and made it back to the court halfway through Charles' prosecution of the man who had eloped with a young woman of twenty years. "The law is clear. No contract entered into by an individual under the age of twenty-one shall be binding. Without her father's permission, the marriage contract is void." His argument against the elopement continued strong and clear. The court ruled in his favor and declared the marriage void, and ruled that the unborn child would be raised as a ward of the church.

Quill's palms were damp as those words shook free old memories of another trial. He had been the accused. Charles had been his witness, had saved him from the shame of the false accusation and the misery of a loveless marriage. But his relief had been mingled with guilt as the young woman who had accused him sobbed in her mother's arms, her belly large with child. She never disclosed the name of the man who had abandoned her. A few months later, she gave birth. Somewhere in Williamsburg, that child was also being raised as a ward of the church. The young woman had vanished years ago. Some said she had run away to the frontier, others that she was living with distant cousins in the sugar islands. Some said she had died of illness. Others said guilt had driven her to an untimely death.

Quill didn't hear the words Charles murmured as he gave a handkerchief to the distraught lass. He didn't hear the next case called. An acquaintance elbowed him and gestured to the bar. Quill rose, but his hands shook so badly he couldn't read the notes Polly had copied out for him. He improvised, but his stammering words didn't save his client from the public humiliation of the pillory.

That evening, he dropped the ribbon on his small dining table where it mocked him through his lonely meal of cold coffee and stale bread. Gooseberry rubbed his leg. He dropped a hand and stroked his head. "This would be easier," he confided in the cat, "if he weren't such a good friend." He sighed. "I suppose today was another mark against me. How can he trust me ta keep his cousin safe if I canna keep myself out of trouble?"

Thirty-Three

HIDDEN GIFTS

The days passed like a dream. Emmeline woke with the sun and spent the early hours in the company of Anna, Grace, Hope, and Marta, until they went off to the schoolroom. Then she accompanied Polly on a morning walk. When the sun crested the ancient trees, they retreated to the parlor where Emmeline read while Polly practiced her instrument, and Aunt Moira did needlework. Treated like a beloved relation from the hour she was introduced, Emmeline claimed the privilege of addressing the guardians of Willow Haven as if they were her family, reasoning that when she married Quill, they would be.

After dinner, the house was quiet while the family rested through the hottest hours of the day. Once Polly was asleep, she climbed out to her favorite branch to read until the house awoke, when she would creep unseen through the open window, delighted to have kept her secret one more day.

The next week, Catriona Mason arrived with her two young children. Three-year-old Brodie wore a white frock and peered at Emmeline from around his mother's petticoats while his baby sister, Jean, clung to her mother's bosom.

That evening, they gathered in the parlor. Màthair sat on the floor, helping Brodie to build a house with wooden blocks while

Marta tried to use her top as a chimney. Athair read a broadside imported from London. Aunt Moira tatted lace. Emmeline sat at the tea table, helping Grace and Hope to trim their bonnets, listening to the story Anna read aloud.

Polly, who was sorting through a large pile of music, said, "I expect Quill will come tomorrow."

Anna set the book down. "So soon?"

"Soon?" Polly echoed. "We've been here since Thursday last. On the morrow 'twill be Wednesday."

"I hadn't realized," Emmeline murmured. Though she had looked forward to seeing Quill in his ancestral home—ancestral wasn't the right word, but it sounded grand—his arrival would mark the end of her stay. She would leave this enchanted story-book world and return to her never-ending chores.

"Will ye leave?" Hope asked.

"Leave?" Marta's top spun off the house, but she failed to notice. She ran across the room and flung herself at Polly. "Ye and Miss Gardiner are staying, aren't ye?"

"Only until Quill comes," Polly said.

Marta shook her head. "He can stay, too."

Polly sighed and patted her sister's shoulder. "I'll visit again, as soon as I can."

"And ye'll bring Miss Gardiner?"

"Or Quill can bring her," Aunt Moira said without looking up from her lace.

Unsure how to respond, Emmeline became very interested in the precise placement of ribbon on Hope's bonnet.

Anna yawned. "Cat," she said, as her sister walked into the room, cradling a sleeping baby, "read the next chapter."

"If I sit down, Jean will wake."

"I can read," Emmeline said. All eyes turned on her, and her stomach dipped. But by the time she had found the chapter indicated, everyone had turned back to their own tasks. The room quieted as she began. She lost herself in the story until the end of the chapter woke her to her surroundings.

"She has a fine reading voice," Aunt Moira pronounced.

If the praise had come from Màthair, Emmeline would have doubted it. But Aunt Moira was blunt and unafraid to offend. She only said what she truly meant. Emmeline had a fine reading voice. She could die now, knowing she had offered something to the world.

⁓

THURSDAY, JULY 19, 1775

The morrow dawned bittersweet. Emmeline dressed with care and packed her bag before breakfast. Had Christian in *Pilgrim's Progress* been as grieved to leave the pleasures of Vanity Fair as she was to leave Willow Haven? He couldn't have been, for his pleasures had been shallow and vain. She had had a taste of heaven and was obliged to return to earth.

It was better to think of the joy of seeing Quill. From little things the family had said, Emmeline had gleaned that he had spoken of her in a way that led them to believe his attentions, his fancy, and his hopes for the future were fixed on her. Had he arranged for Polly to invite her for the week? It seemed the most likely explanation for Polly to single her out as a particular friend, but she hadn't dared to ask. Would he court her openly after this? Would he skip past that step, as Charles had done, and propose marriage?

A whirlwind of possibilities circled her mind, making it impossible to read. She set her book on the tea table and studied an oil painting in the quiet parlor. Green hills ended abruptly at cliffs over the stormy sea. She had once been to Chesapeake Bay. The sandy beach had stretched for miles in either direction. The playful waves had lapped at her ankles and drenched her petticoats. This painting showed a different sea. Mighty waves broke against the cliff, big enough to swallow a man whole.

"Do ye like it?" Màthair asked.

Emmeline startled. She hadn't heard anyone enter. "I've never seen anything like it."

"Most Virginians haven't. I sketched this landscape when I lived at Applecross, near the Isle of Skye. I painted it years after I left. The colors are from memory."

"It looks like you're right there. I can feel the spray on my face." After a moment, she added, "I only paint toys." Despite Quill's assurances otherwise, her art seemed common and insignificant compared to the beautiful paintings this woman had done.

Màthair studied her. "When I was young, I loved nothing more than drawing and painting. I would spend hours filling my sketchbook. I didna notice the rain or the time as long as I had something ta draw. Then, when I was yer age, I stopped."

"What? Why? Ye have a gift."

"'Tis a story for another time. At the time, I didna have much choice. When the opportunity came again, it felt like catching my breath after being held underwater. That's when I understood. My gift came from God. He didna just create the physical world —the sun, the flowers, and our mortal frames. He created our spirits. When He did so, He planted in each of us a gift or two. He made me ta be a mother, but he also made me ta bring joy ta others through my art. It pleases Him when we use our gifts. They aren't meant ta be hidden away."

Emmeline couldn't imagine these beautiful paintings being hidden in an attic or a root cellar. They beautified the walls of every room they appeared in, from the parlor to Quill's office. "Your paintings are like windows to heaven."

"Bethankit, but ye will find that is true of every divine gift. Use yers, and others will see a tiny reflection of His majesty and goodness. Dinna hide yer light under a bushel."

Màthair spoke as though Emmeline were hiding something grand, but she wasn't. She couldn't paint like this. Her musical accomplishments were middling, at best. Her apparel was common. What light was she hiding? If she had a gift like this, she would shine it from the rooftop. *What gift?* Her heart cried. *What divinity do you see in me?* The words swelled inside her, fighting to be free. She clamped her lips on the rough-hewn questions. Sawdust had no place in the wareroom. Bold questions were out of place in the parlor.

The morning crept along. She expected Quill to appear at any moment. Every moment, she was disappointed. When the case clock struck twelve, it was agreed that he must be waiting for evening or might not even come until the morrow. Haunted by all the unread books she would leave behind, Emmeline renewed her efforts to finish the one she was on. After dinner, the family retired in their usual manner. As soon as Polly dozed off, Emmeline climbed out to her reading branch.

This nook was a secret she was hiding, but it was no divine gift, at least not the kind Màthair had been speaking of. She rested her bare feet on the branch, leaned against the trunk, and opened a small book. Reading was something her soul hungered for, but she didn't see how that was a gift to be shared, unless God meant for her to teach others to read, like Kitty. Quill and Charles had seen that ability in her before she had developed it. Emmeline sighed. As much as she loved learning, most days teaching was little more than another chore, like milking the cow or setting the table. Still, the joy of seeing Kitty finally master her hornbook was real. Were all gifts like that? Did artists and musicians ever tire of the work they put into their craft?

Writing was a little like that. Sometimes the muse was there, and sometimes it wasn't. But when Quill had thanked her for her work, for finding the words to express his thoughts, had she ever felt such joy? The light she was looking for had been reflected on his face. With a twinge of guilt, she remembered the essay she had written after Charles was tarred and feathered. It was hiding in the clothespress under the winter blankets. Might her plain-speaking prose be the divine gift Màthair had spoken of?

Emmeline closed the book and slipped it into her pocket. For once, her thoughts were too restless for reading. This was her last day here. She didn't know when she would return to the loving family she had found or the little wilderness that separated Willow Haven from the common world. She stood on her branch and listened to the leaves rustle their ancient song. The wind tugged at her petticoats as though asking her to play. She laughed at the whimsy. What could be more delightful than to follow the breeze and explore the woods?

With some effort, she leaned far enough in the window to collect her shoes and stockings. She knotted them in her kerchief and puzzled out a staircase of branches that ended about five feet above the ground. She hesitated, but the ground looked soft. She put on her stockings and shoes, then leapt, bending her knees so deep they almost touched the ground. She dusted off her petticoats and looked back up. The tree worked well enough coming down, but she couldn't make it back up again, not without a stump or a ladder to get her started.

She would have to ask Quill if he had ever managed it. For now, she was stuck. There was no ladder or stump awaiting her convenience. The only way back to the bedchamber was through the door and up the creaking stairs. She was committed to her adventure.

Not far from the edge of the woods ran a merry little creek. She left her shoes and stockings on the bank and stepped in. The water was delightfully cool, if a bit muddy. She squelched along, her petticoats held aloft, as minnows darted around her legs like arrows and dragonflies hovered above the water. Tomorrow, she would return to her life of practicalities and chores.

What would it have been like for the prisoners in the *Allegory of the Cave* to be forced to return to their cave after they had finally experienced the sunlight? That's what going home felt like. It shouldn't. She had a good home and a good family and was proud of the work they did. But every book there she had read several times over, and she was seldom praised for doing her chores or anything else. And she saw now how hungry she had been for more knowledge, more wisdom, as well as any praise.

She waded past corked jugs nestled in the water and came upon a mossy log that spanned the creek. She sat on it, the hem of her petticoat trailing carelessly in the water. She kicked her feet, watching the water droplets fly through the air like diamonds. Every home should have a creek or a river. Even Mama would agree. It would be so nice to have a place to cool their drinks on hot days, so long as one didn't drink too fast.

Tilting her head back, she soaked in the sound of rustling leaves and the babble of the creek. She would worry about chores again once she was home and not a moment before. Then her hands would be busy every hour of daylight, and she would find a way to deliver her little essay and discover whether it stirred hearts as much as her first one had.

Her thoughts returned to the small book in her pocket. It would be so luxurious to read with her feet in the cooling creek. She brushed a curl from her brow, and a drop of water streaked across her forehead. She looked at her hands, at her petticoats limp with water, and at the innocent creek burbling below. A small accident could ruin the paper. It would be shameful to have destroyed such a beautiful trust through recklessness, and she did, truly, wish for Athair to like her.

If only she were back in Quill's tree. She couldn't get there without trailing wet petticoats through the house and disturbing someone's rest, and she couldn't answer questions without betraying her secret reading branch. It would destroy the magic of this moment, this little part of the world that belonged to her for just this moment. She sighed. The tree would have been an excellent place for a breeze to dry her petticoats. Then her eyes fell on another branch, and she smiled. She had found another reading tree.

Thirty-Four

THE OTTER

Quill completed his last brief by mid-morning. The sun was still bearable. It wasn't too late to ride out to Willow Haven. He could enjoy dinner with his family and return that evening, when the sun was behind the trees. He hurried down the courthouse steps like a schoolboy on holiday and almost ran into Mr. Wythe.

"I beg yer pardon," Quill tipped his hat and made to step around him.

The clerk held up his hand. "Actually, I was looking for you, Morris."

His hopes for the day extinguished like a fire doused in water. Remembering his manners, he said, "How may I be of service?"

"I hate to bother you again, but—" his voice trailed off, and he held out a packet of papers.

"For his lordship?"

"Yes, I'm afraid so."

Quill sighed. He had once hoped to keep the two branches of government together by riding messages between them. That hope had died. The House of Burgesses hadn't met since June. This message would be from the Virginia Convention that was meeting in its stead. He accepted the papers out of respect for Mr. Wythe. "When do ye need a reply?"

"Tomorrow will do, unless Dunmore says it's urgent. I suspect this may be the last time."

"Good," Quill said, with more force than he intended.

Mr. Wythe raised his brows. "We are, of course, grateful for the service you have provided."

Quill waved the formal gratitude away. "I am only disappointed it has done nothing to heal the divide."

"I begin to wonder whether the breach might be beyond healing. I pray I am wrong. Congress has designated tomorrow as a day of fasting and prayer for a constitutional reconciliation. General Washington still hopes to reunite with the Mother Country." Wythe referenced a private letter recently published in the *Gazette*.

Even Washington hoped for peace but prepared for war. He had accepted the position as commander in chief of the Continental Army. If anyone were sent to the gallows at the conclusion of the conflict, a colonial general would be the first man to go. Surely Washington knew that. Yet Virginia's hero from the last war had accepted that possibility. He hoped for peace, but would be executed if it came.

Quill bid Wythe farewell and headed to the livery stable. As he walked, his fingers found the little fox in his waistcoat pocket, tangled in ribbon. Where was Emmeline when he had a contradiction to discuss? He hadn't seen her all week and would much rather steal away for a tête-a-tête in the apple orchard than face Dunmore again. His heart and mind raced ahead, eager to claim her affection, to begin courting in earnest, but this week had not provided the opportunity to discuss matters with Charles.

The sun was at its zenith when Quill approached the *Fowey* for what he prayed was the last time. There was more than one warship anchored in the York River. The sixteen-gun HMS *Otter* was moored alongside the *Fowey,* nearly doubling British might in Virginia. The canvas tents, nestled among the trees near the riverbank, had also multiplied. Armed shirtmen paced up and down the shore, as though warning the redcoats that they didn't belong on Virginia soil and would be dispatched if they disembarked.

One of the shirtmen approached Quill. "Are you from the *Otter* or the *Fowey*?"

"Neither. I'm from Williamsburg."

The man's glare softened to wariness. "If you're not a sailor on leave, what do you want with them?"

"Mr. Wythe, clerk to the House of Burgesses, wished for me to deliver a message to the governor from the Virginia Convention."

"May I see it?"

Quill hesitated. He didn't wish to rile an armed and restless militia. "I am under instructions to deliver this ta the governor," he reiterated. "Has there been trouble from the warships?"

"Landing parties have been stealing livestock and other provisions. We're trying to prevent further incidents."

"Then I pray for yer success," Quill said. "Now, if ye dinna mind, I have nae wish ta prolong this unpleasant business."

The shirtman nodded and allowed him to pass, but as Quill approached the gangway, the marines standing sentry pointed their bayonets at him.

"State your name and business," one demanded.

"Mr. Morris here to deliver a message to Lord Dunmore." He hoped they would demand he hand over the letter and tell him to move on. He had no patience to stand in the sun while his lordship enjoyed a cold bath.

"Dunmore ain't here."

"Not here?"

"Try the *Otter*," the sentry said.

The sentry of the *Otter* repeated the interrogation. Then, to Quill's disappointment, they allowed him to board. A liveried footman met him outside the governor's new quarters. He led him inside, to where Dunmore sat at a large table, reading foreign broadsides. The footman announced him. Dunmore set aside the papers.

Quill offered a reluctant bow. "Your lordship, the Virginia Convention has sent ye a message." He handed it to the governor, who took it, excused the footman, and broke the seal. Dunmore settled into a cushioned chair and read. Quill knew better than to sit in an earl's presence without an invitation. So he stood and waited, his presence forgotten, watching the wind whip waves crosswise to the river current and ripple the canvas of the volunteer army's many tents.

An age later, Dunmore dropped the papers to the table and scowled out the window. At last, he noticed Quill was still there. "You're not a burgess," he said abruptly.

"Nay, just at their service—and yers," he amended before giving offense.

"A service that has failed in its mission. The House has made no attempts at reconciliation." He frowned at the volunteer army pacing the shore. "The local rabble shouts challenges to my men every evening. Now this convention makes impertinent demands. Matters cannot continue like this."

"Will ye follow yer wife and family ta England, sir?"

Dunmore shook his head. "My duty is here. I do not expect to see my family for a long time." He clasped his hands behind his back and looked toward the shore. "You may have heard of an old acquaintance of mine, a Colonel Washington. He now calls himself a General." The earl sighed, like a heavy weight was settling on him. "It seems I must prepare for war. I must be ready for when the rebel Virginians attack."

"I beg yer pardon, sir, but Virginians are not planning ta attack." The militia camp was there to deter pillaging. Even Jack's bold moves to acquire firearms were only preparation for defense.

Dunmore's eyes narrowed. "Do you presume to know more about Virginia's military than I do?"

Quill's breath froze in his lungs. Dunmore was the last man he would confess his military involvement to. "Nay, sir."

"Good. I have fought for Virginia. Now I must fight against her. It is time to gather people and supplies. You have until the morrow to get your affairs in order."

"Sir?"

"You heard me. Get your affairs in order and report back here. We have work to do."

"Me? Ye want me?"

"I don't *want* you. I am ordering you, in the name of the king."

To refuse an order of such magnitude was akin to treason. But the war had not yet come to Virginia, and already the redcoats were stealing livestock. Dunmore had already requested warships to blockade the Chesapeake from trade. He wouldn't hesitate to inflict famine on the people of Virginia. What was next? How many battles would be fought to subject Virginians to the will of Parliament? And would the earl stop at battles? English soldiers had not been content with their bloody victory at Culloden. They had swept through the Highlands, plundering and pillaging as they went, burning homes, murdering the men, and ravishing the women.

And Dunmore demanded that Quill assist him in his detestable work.

"But, my family," Quill said pathetically, "They need me."

"I wasn't aware you were married."

Blast it. Where was Mrs. Morris when he needed her? "I'm not yet, but—"

"Good. Keep it that way. We cannot afford distractions."

Quill took a step away from Dunmore and closer to the pier and freedom. "What time should I return on the morrow?" He took another step back.

"Soon enough that I don't doubt your loyalties—or your family's. Be on board by noon."

He attempted to buy himself time. "I need ta pack. I need ta notify my clients and settle my accounts. I need ta say goodbye ta my family." It was a lot to accomplish in less than a day.

"Then I suggest you make haste."

Quill bowed deeply. "Yer servant," he murmured. Then he turned and walked off the man-of-war under the watchful eye of His Majesty's Marines. These men would do anything the earl told them to, as surely as they would follow any orders from the king.

In a daze, Quill walked from the ship when he wanted to run. He mounted Gunpowder and rode through York Town. The streets were as quiet as the birds in the afternoon heat, but he couldn't shelter in a tavern until the long shadows of evening. This was his last day as a free man. He had until the morrow to get his affairs in order. Then what? If he returned to the *Otter*, he would be completely under Dunmore's control. He had to run.

There was no time to return to Williamsburg. There wasn't time to say goodbye to Emmeline or to explain things to Charles. There was no time to pack a proper bag. He needed to put as much distance between himself and the *Otter* as possible. He would ask Athair for help. Gunpowder could rest until the cool of the evening while he gathered whatever supplies his father could spare. He would ride until nightfall and then rise early on the morrow, following the great wagon road west until he was beyond the reach of any man who would enforce an order made in the king's name. It was the only way he could maintain his freedom.

Thirty-Five

BLUEBELL IN THE WOODS

The house was quiet as Quill threw his coat and cravat over the banister. He had only worn them today to show respect for the court and the governor. The court was now closed for the season, and he hoped never to see the governor again. The linen waistcoat over his shirtsleeves was dignified enough for an interview with his father. The dining hall and library were vacant. Only Polly was in the parlor, calmly knitting like the world wasn't about to end. She glanced up at him. "There ye are. We were expecting ye all morning."

"Where's Athair?" he asked, rolling his sleeves to the elbow. "I need ta speak ta him as soon as possible."

"I havena seen him since dinner. I expect he's still abed, unlike Emmeline."

"What?" Since he didn't have time to tell Emmeline goodbye, he didn't have the patience to be teased about her.

She smiled smugly. "I should be yer favorite sister."

"If I admit that, I'll have trouble by the dozen."

"Ye mean half-dozen," Polly said.

He turned to the door, determined to wake Athair from his heat-induced slumber, but at that moment Marta ran barefoot into the parlor, a green ribbon streaming from her fingertips. "Polly, tie my hair," she said.

"I thought ye preferred Miss Gardiner ta do that." Polly took the ribbon and rebraided her hair.

Understanding broke on him like the crack of a whip. "Emmeline's here?"

"Did I no' tell ye?" Polly looked far too pleased with herself. "Last I saw her, she was reading in yer old bed."

Quill took one step toward the stairs and stopped. "On my bed," he repeated.

"I couldna bear ta be crowded with the wee ones all week. That was afore I fell asleep. I think she's in the nursery now. Quill, are ye listening?"

He was gaping at the stairs like he'd never seen a step before. At least he could tell her goodbye. It was the one ray of sunshine in the gathering storm. *Thank ye, Lord.* Would it be wrong for him to run up the stairs to see her at ease in his bed? Would the memory bring him comfort in the coming days—or would it be a painful reminder of what might have been?

"She isn't!" Marta cried. "I wanted her ta tell me a story and she never came in and I looked all over the house. She's gone!"

"Hold still." Polly tied the ribbon firmly. "Are ye sure she is no' anywhere inside?"

"I'm sure."

"Then she must be outside," Quill said. "I'll look."

"I thought ye needed ta speak ta Athair." Polly's eyes danced.

"I do. But I need ta speak ta her as well. Find me when he's ready."

"I'll get my shoes," Marta said.

"We'll wait here," Polly told her. "I'll read ye a story while we wait for Quill."

He hastened outside only to pause on the front step, wondering where to look. If he'd known she was here, he would have been as alert as a sentry as he rode in, looking for any sign of her presence. As he hadn't, he had to guess where she might have gone. The sun beat down on him.

When they had escaped dinner at Johnson Hall, she had declined his offer to walk around the house in the full sun, preferring the shade of the gully. He strode to the shady wilderness that gave Willow Haven its name. Willow branches hung like curtains separating the garish sunlight from the shadowy calm that an old creek meandered through. A dozen feet downstream, he saw a pair of shoes that had been left beside the water.

He would have recognized that mismatched wooden heel anywhere. Determined to return the shoes to their owner, he picked them up. Her stockings were tucked neatly inside, but one garter ribbon slithered to the ground. Everyone wears garters, he reminded himself as he picked it up and tucked it inside her shoe. But this wasn't everyone's garter. It was Emmeline's, and he had touched it. He shook his hand, trying to brush away the feel of her garter ribbon against his fingertips. Of course, she wore garters. He had never doubted it. But now he knew they were rosebud pink.

He dipped his hand in the creek, splashed the cool water on his face, and ran a wet hand behind his neck. Water trickled down his spine. He dipped his hand again, splashing his face and throat in a battle against the sticky July heat. It didn't matter what color her garters were or if she had been reading in his bed. He wasn't here to chase fancies. He was here to say goodbye.

Sobered, he headed downstream. There were no muddy footprints to follow. He could only hope she wasn't far. His free hand slipped into his waistcoat pocket and found the fox. At least he would have that to remember her by. The creature was tangled in the ribbon he had tucked in there the other day. He had meant to save it as a gift to celebrate the day he began courting her. He had been a fool to wait so long, to try so hard to please his friend. With or without Charles' blessing, there would be no courting now. He had to flee, and she had to stay. He had forfeited the opportunity to say anything to Emmeline but goodbye.

Would she be waiting for him when he returned? Would he return? Uncertainty swirled and churned like a raft adrift in a tidal river. "Lord, I thought ye blessed the peacemakers," he prayed aloud as he walked. Mayhap the blessings only came to those who succeeded in making peace. His attempts had failed. Or were the blessings only found in heaven? "At least bless me and my family as I escape Dunmore. May we remain free and safe. Emmeline, too. And Charles. Is it too much ta ask that what might have been may yet be?"

The Almighty hadn't answered his question when Quill rounded a bend and saw a flash of blue in a tree. There was his bonny patriot. She sat reading on a branch as thick as the trunk of a neighboring tree. Her petticoats stirred in the breeze, nodding like a bluebell, and her toes were as round and pink as a cluster of unripe blueberries.

He set her shoes down, straightened, and swept his cocked hat from his head. "My lady," he said, and performed a gallant bow.

She looked up from a book, delight radiating from her countenance. "You found me."

"And yer shoes," he said.

She blushed. "I couldn't very well wear those in the creek." She tucked the book in a pocket. "I hope I didn't keep everyone waiting, but when you didn't come this morning, we didn't expect to see you before the evening. I'll be right down."

"Dinna trouble yerself," Quill said, possessed with a boyish urge to prove himself. "I'll come up." He peeled off his shoes and stockings and hoisted himself up. Within a minute, he had climbed up to meet Emmeline. Standing across from her, he gripped the branch above for balance. "I was surprised ta arrive home and hear ye were here."

"You didn't know?" Dismay and disappointment shadowed her features.

"Should I have?"

"No, I thought, mayhap, you had..." She shook her head. "Never mind. It doesn't matter." She didn't meet his eye.

There wasn't time for him to puzzle out her disappointment. He was just happy she was here. "I couldna have prayed for a better miracle. I was afraid I wouldna see ye again."

She looked at him now, her face clouded with concern and wariness. "You talk like you're dying." She looked him over from his head to his feet, but there was nothing to see but his legs, bare below the breeches, and his arms, bare below the shirtsleeves. Her inspection lingered just long enough to bring a blush to his ears.

"I was supposed ta be here hours ago, wasn't I? Let me tell ye what happened. I finished my last brief early this morning and was hoping ta come straight here, but Mr. Wythe found me and asked me ta deliver a letter ta Dunmore. I had agreed ta deliver messages from the House of Burgesses ta the governor, but the House hasn't met in weeks. Instead, the Virginia Convention wanted ta notify him of their resolutions. I had hoped, when I began this service, that it would bring the estranged branches of government together, or at least prevent them from breaking apart." He shook his head. "Each time, they were more opposed ta reconciliation."

"Come." Emmeline patted the sturdy branch beside her. "Make yourself comfortable."

He accepted the invitation. The branch wobbled slightly as he settled onto it, and he reached an arm behind her for balance, pressing his palm flat against the trunk. A breeze brushed her curls against his cheek. He could stay here like this for hours. He could sit beside her for days. Let the king and colony fight it out. All the peace he needed could be found at her side. If only he could tell her that. If only—

"And then?" Emmeline asked suddenly, disrupting the stream of his thoughts.

"What?"

"What happened after Mr. Wythe asked you to deliver a letter? Did you do it?"

"Oh," he said, recalling his mind to the tale he had begun. "Heaven help us, but I did deliver that letter."

Her brow furrowed. "Why is that such a bad thing? What was in the letter?"

"I never saw. But Dunmore will have nothing to do with such things in the future. He is preparing for war. And he ordered me, in the name of the king, to assist him—to fight against my countrymen. He expects me ta board the *Otter* on the morrow afore it weighs anchor."

Her eyes widened, and a small gasp escaped her. His hand dropped away from the coarse tree trunk and wrapped around her, pulling her tight as though her nearness could soothe the ache of their impending separation. She rested her head on his shoulder. They sat there in mutual contemplation of an uncertain future. A squirrel scampering across a neighboring tree dislodged a leaf that floated lazily down to the creek. The gentle current carried it along its winding path, where it would flow into the York River. It looked so peaceful and innocent. It had been easier, at first, for him to agree to something that seemed to please everyone. He couldn't have guessed where it would lead him, any more than one could suppose such a quiet creek would flow into a vast tidal river where a man-of-war awaited his return.

At last, she said, "You can't go to him."

"Aye, but there will be consequences when I dinna return."

"I know," she said softly. She didn't need to say more. She respected his decision as much as she was grieved by the necessity of it.

"I'm leaving tonight." With his free hand, he pulled the ribbon from his waistcoat pocket. "I meant ta save this for a happier occasion."

She reverently took the ribbon and traced a finger down the climbing roses. "It's beautiful."

He nudged her shoulder with his. "'Tis why it reminded me of ye."

She blushed, but her eyes smiled as she wound the ribbon around her hand. "Now it will remind me of you."

He pressed a kiss to her brow, then bowed his head until his nose pressed against hers. "I dinna know how long I'll need ta be in hiding. It may be weeks. It may be months. Or longer." Together, they released a sigh, their breath rising and falling as one. "Am I a coward for running?"

"For refusing to fight against your countrymen? For defying an edict of the royal governor? Nay. You've chosen the braver path."

Her trust made him a little more confident that he could brave the coming days. Now he should return to the house and speak with Athair. There were only a few hours before he needed to leave. The time for sitting on fences was past. There would be no coming back from the choice he had made. Still, he lingered on a branch ten feet in the air, holding Emmeline's hand and resting his head against hers, taking comfort in the soft sound of her breath. Hesitation had robbed him of choice in more pleasant matters, but if God gave him another chance, he wouldn't hesitate to speak his heart.

A voice, veiled by leaves, tugged at his attention, "Emmeline? Quill?" Polly called, her voice growing closer. They sighed together. Then he kissed Emmeline's brow. "Come, we need ta discuss plans with my father." He reached for a neighboring branch.

"We?"

"Aye, we. I'll not leave yer side a moment afore I have ta."

A smile lit her face, and he almost asked her how long she would wait for him.

Thirty-Six

THE PRICE OF FREEDOM

Quill waited for Polly to lead the way back to the house so he could walk by Emmeline's side. Thankfully, his sister refrained from questioning them. If there was one thing he lacked, it was answers. If there was one thing he had in abundance, it was the sense of belonging to Emmeline, and she to him. As they walked through the woods of Willow Haven, a line from her essay "American Birthright" came to mind.

We stand equal when we stand on American soil.

It didn't matter that his parents were Scottish and hers had been born in the colony. It didn't matter that he had studied at William and Mary while she had studied at home. Her mind and heart were equal to his. He hoped they would be united on American soil, once this trial was behind them.

Athair was waiting for them in the library. "Polly said ye had something ta discuss?" He glanced at Emmeline with a hopeful smile.

"Aye," Quill said bitterly as he and Emmeline took their seats on the settee. "Ye ken I've been delivering messages between the Burgesses and Dunmore?"

"Aye," his father said, a line between his brows. "What happened?"

Quill took a shaky breath. He hated to prove his father's concerns had been right. Emmeline squeezed his hand and gave him an encouraging smile. He squeezed back and launched into his tale. It was a little shorter this time as she helped him get to the point instead of distracting him with her curls. Then he offered his plan. "I thought it would be prudent ta escape ta the wilderness for a time. I'll get as far as I can in the gloaming, then wait for the moon ta rise. 'Tis a quarter moon. That will be enough light ta travel by if I stay on the main road. Then I'll spend a few hours in an ordinary, and set out again at first light. I'll be hours away afore Dunmore realizes I'm not going ta return. I'm hoping he will have more important concerns than launching a full pursuit."

Athair sighed. "I regret that it has come ta this. I had hoped, when he arrived, that he would leave our family differences in the past. I regret ta see my child troubled by my old enemy."

Quill shook his head. "He doesna know I'm more than ilk ta ye. Dinna blame yerself."

"Ye talk like a Virginian," Athair scoffed. "In Scotland, clan loyalties run as deep as the ocean. Sharing a name means sharing an enemy. Old Murray knows that." His father rose and walked over to a large map of Virginia that hung on one wall. "Yer plan ta head west is sensible. Ye ken I own a piece of that wilderness. 'Tis a recent investment. I was looking for a man ta increase its value by planting an apple orchard and building a small home. There are no buildings on the property. Ye'll have ta make yer own shelter and live off the land. Take the old wagon. We'll fill it with flour, tools, and apple seeds. If ye were no' in such haste, I would send a milk cow with ye. I might send one in the spring."

"In the spring? I was hoping this would be forgotten within a few months at the most." He glanced at Emmeline. "I dinna wish ta spend the rest of my life alone in the wilderness."

"Ye might no' have ta be alone," Athair said with a mischievous smile. "There's an anvil out back. We could—"

"Nay," he said, cutting off his father's proposal. Anvil or not, no ceremony would be legally binding without her father's permission. Anyone present during Charles' successful prosecution knew that. And no sensible father would allow his daughter to marry a man who was fleeing from the governor.

Athair grunted. Quill got the impression his father had a rather romantic idea of this whole adventure and was disappointed his son didn't see it in the same light.

"Well, let's plan yer route," Athair said. "There's a road through the Blue Ridge Mountains by the town of Winchester. Ta get there, ye'll need ta head north ta Fredericksburg. Ta get there..." His voice trailed off as he traced the path south to Williamsburg. "From Williamsburg, 'tis twenty-eight miles ta Gooch Ferry where ye can cross the Pamunkey River. Once ye cross, Mills Ordinary is only six miles more. How far have ye taken Gunpowder today?"

"Eighteen miles. He's resting now, but I dinna believe we can make it another thirty-four miles in one night."

"Forty," Athair corrected. "'Tis six miles from here ta Williamsburg."

Quill shook his head. Pushing Gunpowder nearly sixty miles in one day was unthinkable, especially during the heat of summer and at the beginning of such a long journey, but he needed to get beyond the reach of Dunmore's men before they initiated a search. He would go as far as the limits of human and equine endurance allowed. "I dinna believe I can make it ta the ferry tonight," he said.

Emmeline studied the map carefully. "The crossing looks awfully close to the York River. Might the Marines be there? Might they be looking for you?"

"'Tis a possibility," Quill said, "but I doubt it. The *Otter* and *Fowey* are moored at York Town," he pointed to a bend in the river miles to the southeast of where the Pamunkey flowed into the York. "Dunmore will want all the sailors ta report back ta the ship afore it leaves. He wants me there by noon tomorrow. I imagine the sailors have similar orders and those who were on leave are already returning ta York Town. Only a deserter would stray as far from the ship as Gooch Ferry."

"If ye can make it ta Chisivels Ordinary tonight," Athair said, pointing to a small mark along the road between Williamsburg and the river, "then leave at first light, ye should be ta the ferry afore the sun crests the trees."

There was a tap on the door. "Aye, what is it?" Athair asked.

A maid opened it. "A message was just delivered for ye, sir. From the governor, sir."

Quill's pulse quickened even before Emmeline squeezed his hand. He had been so certain the governor didn't know who his family was. He didn't know where they were. Yet why else would his father receive a letter from Dunmore on the same day Quill had received orders from him? Athair waited for the door to close before breaking the red government seal. His brows raised as he silently read. Had a spy followed him to Willow Haven? Had the Marines asked after his family? He had been foolishly optimistic to believe he could run away—that his family would be untouched by his folly.

Athair grunted, his eyes still on the paper.

"What is it?" Quill asked. "What does he say?"

Athair handed it to him and stood, hands clasped behind his back, facing the map. Quill and Emmeline, heads bent together, read the letter.

Felicitations to Mr. Duncan Morrison,

Imagine my surprise on recently discovering that the supporter of the false prince was not hanged with the rest of the traitors in 1746, but has been living a life of comfort and prosperity on a plantation located only a few miles from the capital of His Majesty's Old Dominion. Justice demanded a forfeiture of life and property for those who attempted to usurp the crown for another. Instead, you have lived in remarkable comfort and sired many children.

You have evaded justice most impressively for nearly three decades.

There are two choices before you. Either you will give your son to me in the service of His Majesty, King George, or you will forfeit your livestock and other property, as listed below. I expect you to deliver your choice to me tomorrow before noon.

Your Servant,

John Murray, Earl of Dunmore

Below the elaborate signature was the list.

2 Horses
10 Muskets with Bayonets
4 Half-Barrels of Gunpowder
10 Bushels each: Indian Corn, Wheat
10 Barrels of Whiskey
A Goodly Quantity of Vegetables, Fresh or Pickled
20 Hens
5 Pigs
10 Turkeys
1 Milk Cow

Quill had never been so thoroughly trapped. Either he boarded the *Otter* on the morrow and be forced to assist in preparations for war against his countrymen, or his family bought his freedom by supplying Dunmore for the coming war. It wasn't right to charge a man with treason after nearly thirty years of peaceful, productive living. It wasn't right, but might it be legal? Charles might know. Quill had never seen such a brief. But he didn't dare appeal to the law for redress against the governor's accusations any more than Charles dared to charge the men who had tarred and feathered him. There was too great a possibility that his father would be put to death, and all of his property seized. His sisters would be left with nothing in this world. Without a dowry, they would struggle to contract marriages with suitable gentlemen.

Dunmore had him cornered.

"Morrison? The false prince?" Emmeline repeated, her brow furrowed in confusion.

"When my father was a young man—" Quill began.

"We dinna have time for tales," Athair said. "We have a lot of work to do if we're to meet Old Murray's demands by noon tomorrow."

~

"OH, BUT YOU CAN'T!" EMMELINE CRIED. FATHER AND son turned to her, surprised by the passionate outburst. Who was she to tell them what they could and couldn't do? "I—I beg your pardon." She dropped her gaze to her hand clasped in Quill's. He had brought her into what could have been a private meeting. Was that not an invitation to speak her mind? She was the girl who planned to marry him. The consequences of this meeting could affect her as much as anyone.

"Have ye no respect for the royal governor?" Athair asked, a hint of amusement in his eyes.

"More, I believe, than Lord Dunmore does, or he would not have fled his post. By fleeing Williamsburg and hindering the legislature from acting, our governor has, in effect, dissolved the government. He has abdicated his role as a representative of the king and has placed himself in a state of nature, no longer deserving of reverence, but a common man like any other." Her speech was met with silence. Afraid she had said too much, she blushed and looked away. "At least, that's what Locke would say."

Quill nudged her elbow with his. "I like it better when ye say it." She looked up. His steady gaze was warm and admiring. She hadn't lost his respect by speaking up. She had only surprised him.

"What ye're saying," Athair said, "is that as a common man, he has no authority ta make the demands set forth in this letter."

"Yes, sir."

"Unfortunately for us," Quill said, "there are hundreds of sailors in the York River. I would wager most of them have never read Locke and those who have didna understand it. They will follow whatever orders Dunmore gives them, whether or not he is overstepping the bounds of his authority. Even if we have right on our side, they have might. We canna fight them."

"You could still run," Emmeline said, but both men shook their heads.

"Nay," Quill said. "I thought I could run when I thought he knew nothing of my family. I was wrong. If I run, my family will be punished in my place. 'Twould be better ta surrender myself than ta risk the safety of so many others."

She sighed. "I cannot bear the thought of you at the mercy of such a man. We must think of another plan."

Athair frowned. "Ye canna run, ye canna return ta him, and I will not give strength ta a man planning an attack on my country-men. Yet we canna defy a man intent on destroying us."

"'Tis impossible," Quill said. "We canna win, no matter what we do."

"We canna win," Athair agreed, a slow smile lighting his face, "but if we bury the treasure, neither will he."

Thirty-Seven

LOVEBIRDS

"If we—what?" Emmeline asked, bewildered.

"Bury it, hide it, move it somewhere safe," Athair said. "We divide the best livestock and the best horses amongst the neighbors' pastures and replace them with their worst nags. Same with the food. Ammunition is a little trickier. We'll have ta keep a little powder—wet it, so it's spoiled, and take the locks off a couple of muskets. We willna let them find the rest. If we convince them that Quillan is gone and I am doing my meager best ta cooperate with his demands, they may let it be."

"Hide it?" Quill repeated. "That seems unnecessary. We're supposed ta deliver the goods ta the *Otter*, at least, if the militia allows us ta do so. They have quite a presence on the river. Moving and hiding everything sounds like a lot of work. We just need ta fill some wagons with spoiled food and drive sickly livestock down the road."

"'Tis just a precaution," Athair said. "If Dunmore sends his men ta investigate Willow Haven after the delivery, then they can report that we sent him the best we had."

Quill blanched. "Ye dinna believe he will send his men here?"

Willow Haven was too peaceful to be troubled by the mundane concerns of life beyond its boundaries. Was it possible that armed men could come down the drive, their bayonets flashing as they threatened the peace and prosperity of this heavenly home? It was as unthinkable as the printer's apprentice threatening Charles and Susan in the church yard. Yet that had happened.

"I hope not," Athair said, "but 'tis best ta prepare for the worst. I willna let the king's men anywhere near Elspeth and the lassies, nor will I supply them with the goods they need ta fight against us and our countrymen."

"What about Quillan?" Emmeline asked. "He's the man the governor wants, so he's in more danger than the rest of the family combined."

"I'll not hand him over," Athair said.

Emmeline still didn't like the idea of Quill remaining this close to York Town while they were disappointing Dunmore. The governor knew this was his family home. If his men had informed him of that, might they also have discovered his lodgings in Williamsburg and Rabbie's store? He would be much safer at her home, spending a quiet day in the guest chamber. "Wouldn't it be safer for him to run away—for a few days, at least? If they're displeased with how you are fulfilling their demands, might they try harder to take him? I think he would be safer if—"

Quill scowled. "I'm not such a coward as to leave my family to face the king's men in my stead."

"Of course not, but—"

"Dinna fash yerself," Athair said to both of them. "I will face the king's men. The family will be nowhere near Willow Haven until the danger has passed. We have friends enough in town ta take them in for a day or two."

"I willna run," Quill said stubbornly.

"As long as ye hide good and proper, that's fine. Miss Gardiner, we'll have ta send ye home—"

Her disappointment must have shown on her face because Athair laughed and said, "Or ye could hide with Quillan. Whichever ye please."

"Oh." Her face grew warm. She was disappointed that Quill would stay while she would leave. At home, she would have no way of knowing whether he was safe and no way of assisting him through the danger, but hiding in the woods or a kitchen loft without a chaperone was not the solution she had in mind. "No," she said primly. "That wouldn't be quite proper."

"I'll no' be putting ye in danger," Quill said. "Please, return ta town with Polly."

As much as she hated to leave him, it was neither proper nor practical for her to stay when the other women left. She nodded.

"Then that's settled," Athair said. "I'll speak with yer màthair. Ye can tell the rest of the family." As they were leaving the library, he shook his head and muttered, "Elsie is not going ta be happy about this."

Polly was practicing the spinet in the parlor. She looked up as they walked in.

"Could ye gather the womenfolk?" Quill asked. "Everyone but Màthair. I have something important ta discuss."

Polly glanced between them. "Everyone but Màthair?"

"Aye. Athair wanted ta speak ta her."

"Irregular, but not unseemly," Polly said as she left the spinet. "It will take me some time ta gather everyone else." She winked and closed the parlor door behind her.

Quill stared at the door. He would never object to a few minutes alone with Emmeline, but his sister was acting as though they were newly betrothed. It was absurd to think a private interview with his father would result in such an understanding when everyone knew it was *her* father's permission he needed. Then again, Athair had scarcely seen them together before suggesting they elope—a suggestion Quill had cut off before it had fully formed. Had Emmeline bewitched his entire family? If only

Charles had been as easy to convert to the cause. He would have begun courting her weeks before.

Instead, he had to be satisfied with a few minutes alone together before preparing to face Dunmore's threats. Would it be such a terrible thing to kiss a lass he wasn't formally courting? Would she mind? Charles would, but Charles wasn't here, and Quill found himself caring less and less what his loyal friend would think, at least regarding Emmeline. He would begin courting her the moment the danger passed and he could offer his suit as a free man.

His bonny lass paced the room, as though she had forgotten he was there. That was his answer. He was the only one wondering if this moment of privacy was a good time for kissing. Suddenly, she stopped and said, "I hate that you'll be here when the king's men come. I hate that I have to leave you. How will I know the danger has passed? When will I know if you're safe?"

"I'll come ta ye the moment I'm free," he said. "Trust Athair. If anyone can outwit the king's men, 'tis him."

"If?" The word wobbled between freedom and captivity, pleading for hope, yet fearing devastation.

He closed the space between them until those beautiful eyes blurred into a sea of blue and rested his brow against hers. Her nearness was as natural as breathing. She was tangled in his heart. Life without her was as impossible as the day sky without the sun or the woods without trees.

He took her hands in his. "Pray for me. For us." It would take a miracle—a rapid succession of mighty miracles—but if God was good, they would be together again, and soon. The war would pass them by, the fields would be heavy with grain, the harbors would fill with merchant ships, and Emmeline would be by his side. The coming years would be full of peace, prosperity, and her.

She nodded, the soft of her nose rubbing pleasantly against his. "I will. I promise."

He closed his eyes and savored her nearness—a breath away from a kiss—until a sound in the foyer reminded him they wouldn't be alone for long. He took one step back as the parlor door opened. Emmeline dropped her eyes but not his hands as three of his female relations invaded their sanctuary. Aunt Moira leaned on her jeweled walking cane as she limped to her chair. Catriona took the other wingchair with Jean on her lap. Polly took the seat at the spinet with her back to the keyboard. The eager glint in their eyes told him they would welcome news of a betrothal, especially if it meant a hasty wedding over an anvil. Emmeline had charmed every last one of them.

He sat on the settee, and Emmeline, who was still holding his hand, sat beside him.

"Well, lovebirds?" Polly prompted.

Lovebirds. She must have seen them sitting on that branch together. The blush that heated his face ran down his exposed forearms for everyone to see. He fixed his gaze on one of Màthair's oil paintings. It was a landscape of a creek running past willows and bluebells. "Where ta begin?" He had already told his full tale twice and was growing weary of it.

Emmeline squeezed his hand and calmly announced, "The royal governor is leaving York Town tomorrow on the HMS *Otter*. He demands Quillan accompany him—" several gasps interrupted her, "—or that the family supply him for battle preparations. By noon tomorrow, either Quillan boards the *Otter* in the service of the governor, or we deliver supplies, purchasing his freedom."

Irate exclamations followed her announcement.

"Nay!"

"Tell me it isn't so!"

"It canna be true."

"Aye, 'tis true," Quill said. "Ye need ta leave for a day or two, just in case the king's men come calling on Willow Haven."

"Surely ye willna go with them," Catriona said. "Jack might—"

"Athair and I have a plan," Quill interrupted. He still hadn't forgiven his brother-in-law for failing to protect Charles and had no desire to become indebted to him. "We're going ta hide all the valuables in our neighbor's barns: grain, firearms, whiskey, livestock, and horses, and we'll replace them with spoiled grain, broken firearms, and long-toothed nags. Then Athair offers them everything he has. They leave, satisfied that they've ruined us, and we stay, satisfied that we've cheated them."

"I dinna like any of this," Polly said.

Catriona gave her a look that reminded everyone who the responsible older sister was. "We need ta put on a brave face for Màthair. Ye ken how she feels about the king's men."

A dozen questions followed, and he worried they wouldn't have time to execute the plan because they were so busy talking about it, but at last Catriona rose, saying, "My wee bairns are better travelers in the morning than the evening. We'll leave for my townhome at dawn. I'm going ta pack." She paused by the threshold. "Miss Gardiner, ye're welcome ta stay as long as yer family can spare ye."

Emmeline shook her head. "Thank you for your kindness, but they'll be expecting me already."

"If ye'll see her safely ta the Blue House," Quill said, "I would be much obliged."

"But Charles—" Polly began.

Quill shook his head. Though this brush with danger would do nothing to persuade Charles that he would be a prudent suitor for his cousin, it would be impossible to keep it a secret. "He might as well know the danger we're facing."

"Is that all?" Aunt Moira asked, looking like a dowager queen who was much displeased with her court.

"All?" Quill repeated. "Would ye rather Dunmore send out a warrant for my arrest?"

She scoffed. "Ye tease us with good news and then only give us bad."

"I didna tease—"

"I was young once. I'm no fool." Aunt Moira leaned on her cane and looked pointedly at Emmeline. "When ye are my age, ye will understand that joy doesna come from a lack of obstacles. It comes despite the obstacles." She patted Emmeline's shoulder. As she shuffled from the room, she added, "Some things are worth fighting for."

He released a deep sigh. It wasn't often his great aunt tested his nerves. It wasn't folly that delayed him now, but wisdom. Emmeline deserved to be courted by a man who wasn't wanted by the most powerful man in the colony. After months of waiting, they could endure a few more days. If Athair's plan worked, he could be calling on her this very Sunday.

If.

"I packed this morning," Emmeline said, pulling him from his reflections. "May I help you 'bury the treasure?'"

He laughed. "Did ye wish ta hide me or the horses?" He had meant it as a light, teasing question, but the ache to hold her close and kiss her had been growing by the hour. There was nothing proper in his hope that she would be the one to tuck him into whatever small, dark space he would hide in while the king's men searched the property.

"Not you." She said it a little too forcefully and looked away, blushing. "Let's help hide the horses or anything else."

An unexpected wave of relief washed over him. There were proper ways to kiss a sweetheart and, God willing, they would have all the time in the world to explore those possibilities. "Let's start with the horses." Together, they walked into the sunlight.

Thirty-Eight

MOVING BUSHELS

A man leaned against the stable, sharing the afternoon shade with an enormous sow and several of her progeny, watching as a boy poured slops into a feeding trough. The young swine squealed and trotted over to their meal. The man looked up as Emmeline and Quill approached.

"He's a mite deaf," Quill said in a low voice. "Spent his youth in a smithy, shoeing horses. Pray, excuse our raised voices." He then, half-shouting, introduced the groom to her, who nodded respectfully. As a guest of the Morris family, her position as a gentlewoman was assumed by all she met, even the Morrises, though they knew her father was a tradesman. She hadn't needed to hide her calloused fingertips or her interest in weighty books to gain their respect. At Willow Haven, the incongruous parts of her heart, mind, and soul had come together like opposing sides of the same drawer.

"Mr. Morris," the groom said, just as loud, "I mistrust ye be needing yer gelding again. 'Twould be better ta wait another hour or two afore we saddle him. Yer athair would agree with me."

"I've nae need for Gunpowder afore the morrow. Speaking of which, all the womenfolk will be going ta town. We'll need a carriage ready at dawn. All the other horses will need to be hidden in the neighbors' stables tonight."

Quill explained their troubles to the groom, who was almost as horrified by the threat to his master's son as he was by the threat to his horseflesh, though Dunmore had only demanded two of the many fine specimens. He was impatient to hide them in the neighbors' stables, but that would have to wait. First, they needed the horses to pull wagons.

The groom argued, and Emmeline anxiously watched the shadows. There were only a few hours left before sundown. This was the time for action, not talking. She hated to be idle when there was work to be done, but she wasn't familiar enough with the ways of Willow Haven to begin on her own.

At last, the groom acquiesced. "I'll ready the wagon, sir." He turned to the boy who, after pouring the slops, had lingered in the shade, listening. "Billy!"

The boy startled at his name. "Sir?"

"Take word ta the village that we need all the men they can spare."

Billy seemed pleased to be included in the important matter. "Aye, sir!" He ran like a fox from the hounds.

Relieved that the work would finally begin, Emmeline asked, "What are we moving first?"

Quill frowned. "I was hoping Athair would return by now. It depends on which neighbors are willing ta hide which goods. Muskets with bayonets, gunpowder, Indian corn, wheat, whiskey—"

"We're running out of time," she said, interrupting his list.

He cast his eyes about the farm, as though expecting to see the answer written on the walls of the outbuildings. "Let's save the pigs and hens for the village boys. I expect they'll enjoy the chase more. We can begin by loading the grain."

Emmeline gathered her skirts and ran. After a moment, he caught up with her and they raced past a smokehouse, a dairy, and a corn crib, to the granary. The grain barn looked far too big to balance on the mushroom-shaped stone pillars that discouraged rodents from climbing up and in, but it remained steady as a boulder when Quill slammed both hands against the door of the outbuilding a moment before she collided into him.

"Sorry," she said shortly, then leaned against the doorframe for a moment, gasping for breath, her lungs burning, breathing so deeply her ribs pressed against her stays, and she feared she would burst the lacing.

"Are ye well?" Quill asked, panting with his hands on his knees.

"I am," she said, though her lungs still burned. This wasn't the time for petty complaints. Quill, Willow Haven, and all of Virginia were in danger. She would do everything she could to save them.

Still panting, he opened the double door. A dirt path wide enough for a wagon cut through the middle of the barn. From the high ceiling hung a contraption of ropes and pulleys. Like handing a lady into a carriage, Quill helped Emmeline up to the raised wood floor. She turned and reached down, offering both her hands. Amused, he allowed her to help pull him up. Then he led the way to a ladder.

"After ye," he said.

She hesitated. Climbing trees had been unladylike enough, but Quill hadn't been standing below while she climbed up, and he had allowed her to descend first. Ladies like Susan might not have developed rules of etiquette involving ladders and trees, but Emmeline was far too modest to climb with her hem directly above a gentleman's head, knowing that under her petticoats, her legs were bare from the knee up. "Not up a ladder," she said.

Quill blushed as though just realizing what he had suggested. "I didna mean—of course I would never—that is ta say, I suppose I should go first." He turned his red face away and climbed the ladder to the loft.

Emmeline glanced about to be certain there were no men about who might follow her up the ladder, then hiked the front of her petticoats almost to her garters and climbed up. When she reached the solid floor of the loft, she gave a little gasp. As she dropped the hem of her petticoat, she forgot about matters of modesty and etiquette. The loft was stacked to the roof with barrels and bags full of wheat. A fine flour-like dust covered the floor. It was a wonder that the loft didn't bow under the weight of the barrels and bags so full of wheat that kernels burst from the seams and spilled to the floor. There was more than enough grain to feed several families through the winter, and it was only July. "There's so much," she said, awed.

Quill chuckled. "This is for everyone at Willow Haven, not just my family. I suppose 'tis good Dunmore made his demands now. We'd have a hard time hiding everything once the harvest is done. The first crop of Injun corn will be moved into the cribs soon, though not as much as last year."

"Why not?"

Quill cocked his head. "The hailstorm, lassie. What else? The damage in the fields was heavy—we lost a third of that crop."

She approached one barrel and was distressed to find it empty. If all the barrels were empty, then there wasn't half as much grain as she had first thought. "A third?" She repeated. "Will Willow Haven have enough for winter?" She had been enjoying the bounty of the family's food for a week, with no thought for the coming winter. And Dunmore was demanding ten bushels of their precious stores.

"Aye. Athair is too clever ta be beaten by a little hail any more than a sudden change in the import and export laws. This year, he planted wheat instead of tobacco. 'Twill be enough ta make up for what was lost."

"Is any of it spoiled?"

"I believe some critters got in ta that," Quill said, pointing to one corner. "We brought in some cats, and some of the village boys joined the battle. Though we won the war, no one has been eager to eat grain filled with animal droppings and dead critters."

"Then that's what we give Dunmore," Emmeline said, with grim satisfaction. "Are there ten bushels of it?"

Quill frowned, counting by pecks. "At least thirty-two pecks," he said. "I canna be sure until we move them. It may be as much as forty." There were four pecks in a bushel, so if they had forty pecks of spoiled grain, they would satisfy Dunmore's demand of ten bushels.

A wagon rolled through the open doors, stopping under the pulley system. Several men followed the wagon in and opened the double doors on the opposite wall. A breeze stirred the air. "Master Morris," one of the men said, looking up, "what would ye have us do?"

"We're going ta move our best grain ta the neighbors' barns ta hide it from the governor. I'll need another man or two up here ta help me load the pulley, and others ta help unload it in the wagon."

They were soon joined by two tough and wiry men, who spread a heavy net on the loft floor. Quill hefted a bag of wheat into the middle of the net. Emmeline followed suit. The bags were heavy, but not heavier than the dining table or the clothespress she had helped Papa with that year. She dropped hers with a satisfying thud. When she returned for another bag, one of the wiry Scots stretched out an arm, blocking her path. "There, miss," he said. "There's no need for a lady like yerself ta be dirtying yer hands. We've got it."

She looked at the bags and barrels full of wheat. Dunmore would love to take them all, strengthening his soldiers and sailors who didn't belong here while Virginians went hungry. "I'm stronger than I look," she said, sidestepping his outstretched arm. God had made her as much a tradesman's daughter as she was a gentlewoman's. She was accustomed to wrestling with coarse materials and heavy goods. If her lowly talent might save Quill, she wouldn't sit on a bushel and watch the men work. She hefted another bag onto the net.

The Scotsman looked at Quill for guidance. He placed a bag on his shoulder. "If my lady wishes ta help, I'll nae stop her."

The men accepted his verdict, and they fell into a rhythm loading the net. After a time, they hooked the net to the pulley and lowered it to the wagon. There were a few minutes to rest, then the empty net returned to the loft, and they returned to work.

Her arms were burning, and they were filling the wagon with a final load when Athair rode in on a fine bay. He expressed his approval and updated them on their progress. "The village boys are driving the fowl and swine ta the neighbors', and another wagon is half-full of Indian corn."

Even with all the help, it still took several wagon loads to move everything. When it was dark, the horses were unhitched, and the wagon, filled with thirty-eight pecks of spoiled wheat, was left in the barn. Emmeline's back was stiff, and her arms burned with fatigue. Any other night, she would have fallen into bed without supper, but she couldn't bring herself to leave Quill so soon. Not when she didn't know how tomorrow would go or how soon she might see him again.

After supper, they sat side-by-side on the parlor settee. A manservant had come in and lit the candles until the parlor was as bright as a ballroom. Her head bobbed, and Quill pulled her close. She sighed contentedly, then yawned. Suddenly, she remembered something.

"What about Gunpowder?"

"We've already taken care of it," Quill said.

"Not that gunpowder. Your horse. You weren't planning to leave him in a neighbor's pasture, were you?"

"That was the plan."

"But might the Marines recognize him?"

"I didna ride him onto the *Fowey*."

"Of course not," she said quickly. "But are you saying that no one saw you ride into York Town?"

"Nay, lass. I came and went in full daylight."

"So they have seen him. What if they recognize him in your neighbor's pastures? They'll suspect the plan."

"I suppose," he said slowly. "But from a distance, he's just a gray gelding. And where else would I hide him?"

"I thought—" she hesitated, then gathered her courage and tried again— "I thought I might take him. My home isn't along the highway to York Town, and you know he's always been quite content in our pasture."

Athair looked over just then, sending a questioning look to his son, who blushed as red as a rose. Emmeline grinned.

THE PENDULUM IN THE CASE CLOCK SLEEPILY COUNTED out the hours while the candles burned low. Though it would have been prudent to retire after supper, he hadn't been able to pull himself from Emmeline's side, at least not until Athair finished reading his paper.

"What's this?" Emmeline asked, tracing a finger across the back of his hand.

"'Tis nothing," he said.

She studied him thoughtfully. She was too clever to believe scars appeared without an injury. For a moment, he thought she might press him for the tale. Instead, she raised his hand to her lips and kissed it. Breathless, he watched as she caressed the scars of his childhood.

During a season of misbehavior that followed his mother's death, he had been the frequent recipient of school discipline. The wounds had healed long ago, and angry red scars had faded until nothing was left but pale stripes—a permanent reminder of the dangers of flouting authority. He had learned his lesson but was fast forgetting it. She took his other hand and studied it by candlelight, tracing the scars and pressing kisses to them.

He might have sat up all night with her on the settee, but when the case clock chimed midnight, Athair loudly folded his paper and announced that it was time to turn in. Today was the day. In a few hours, she would go to town with the rest of the family, and he would wait to see how Dunmore responded to their plan. They sighed, and Quill walked her to the foot of the stairs. For a moment, they were alone, and he rested his brow against hers. "Good night, Emmeline."

"Good night, Quillan." Her brow furrowed against his. "Are you certain you'll sleep well? Polly and I could move."

"I'll be fine." The pallet Màthair had made up on the floor of the library would be far more comfortable than sleeping in the bushes along the highway like he might have done, had they kept to the original plan. Besides, he wouldn't be able to fall asleep in a bed that smelled like Emmeline. "I'll see ye in a few hours." He kissed her brow. She squeezed his hand and walked up the stairs, disappearing inside his bedchamber.

That night, he prayed, not kneeling beside his bed, but standing at the base of the stairs that led to her. *Please, Lord, grant us success tomorrow. May we remain free. And if we are, may I be free ta make her mine.*

Thirty-Nine

SPOKEN FOR

THURSDAY, JULY 20, 1775, A DAY OF FASTING AND PRAYER FOR A CONSTITUTIONAL RECONCILIATION WITH THE MOTHER COUNTRY

The first ray of sunlight cut through the trees. Dewdrops shone like diamonds. Quill shifted Emmeline's bag to his other shoulder and caught her hand. The gesture cast a long shadow across the grass. She and the other women would be far from Willow Haven if Dunmore's men came to call. They, at least, would be safe. Even the women down in the village had been encouraged to take a holiday and make themselves scarce until evening.

Màthair had been quite distressed when she learned of the governor's demands. When she was just a lass, British soldiers had killed her family and destroyed her home. She had pleaded with Athair to submit to the demands rather than risk a fight, but he had only kissed her and promised to keep her and the other women safe. If the worst happened, they could appeal to Rabbie or Jack for anything they stood in need of. But he promised to do his best to make certain the worst didn't happen.

Emmeline had been far more optimistic. This would work. It

299

had to. They had right on their side, didn't they? The Lord would protect them. So he clung to her hand and her faith, quelling the chill in his heart. Màthair's fears were from childhood memories in a faraway land. They had nothing to do with a Virginia morning full of birdsong. This threat would pass like dewdrops vanishing under a rising sun. He would remain a free man. His family would be safe. Willow Haven would remain unscathed. And he would pay a courting call on Emmeline that Sabbath and kiss her in the gloaming.

He drew her into the quiet space between the stable and the smokehouse to bid her farewell, but when her soft blue gaze met his, the uncertainties of the day fell on his chest like a bushel of wheat. He might never see her again. For a long minute, they stood there. She held his hand, yet his heart ached as though they were miles apart.

When her face blurred, he wiped his eyes with the backs of his hands and did what fools and wits had done countless times before and since. He quoted the Bard. "'The wreck of all my friends, nor this man's threats, ta whom I am subdued, are but light ta me, might I but through my prison once a day behold this maid.'" He had never set out to memorize that line. It had never been assigned to him by a tutor or professor. Instead, he had once, in a spirit of playful flirtation, read it to a bonny lass, not suspecting that she had already captured his heart, that he would daily crave to see her and be near her.

"I'll pray for you," she said solemnly, "every hour until you come."

He dropped her bag to the ground. "And I willna keep ye waiting a moment longer than I must." He would come the moment the threat had resolved. Tonight. He hoped to come tonight. He would speak to her father and beg for leave to court her. That plan filled him with as much trepidation as defying Dunmore did, but some things were worth fighting for. She was one of them. He stroked a finger down her nose and enjoyed the rapid flicker of emotions across her face: surprise, a blush, pleasure, and adoration. What a miracle that such feelings were mutual.

He leaned forward to rest his brow against hers, but their hat brims bumped together. He laughed at his clumsiness while she fought back a smile and straightened her hat. He lifted his by the crown, turned his head to duck under the brim of her hat, and kissed her cheek. God willing, in a matter of a days, they would be kissing as sweethearts. He would remember to remove his hat first.

The steady rhythm of horse hooves pulled him from his thoughts. They would soon have company. Afraid to embarrass her, by allowing witnesses to their intimate moment, he stepped back and murmured, "Wait here." Then he slung her bag over his shoulder and walked out to distract the groom and stablehands with a discussion about horses, but the groom wasn't there. Instead, he found himself facing two men wearing striking red coats over white waistcoats and breeches, looking down at him from horseback.

He stopped short. "Good morning, officers," he said loud enough for Emmeline to hear. "We were just preparing the final things for the delivery. Everything will be on its way ta York Town soon." This wasn't the plan. If the king's men came at all, it should have been after the women were safe in town. He was supposed to be hiding in the woods. It was too late now.

"Morning, Morris. I'm Lieutenant Allred, and this is Ensign Tanner. His lordship thought you might be needing an escort so's you don't get lost on the return. Or, if you would rather make a donation to the cause, it's us that'll make certain everything makes it there undamaged."

The lieutenant's eyes widened. "Speaking of undamaged donations," he said in a luxurious drawl.

Quill's stomach dropped. Emmeline hadn't hidden behind the stable and run for the house. He turned and despaired to find her standing behind him. Lieutenant Allred dismounted and stepped toward them. Quill threw his arms wide, using his body as a barricade. The man would kill him before he touched her.

The lieutenant turned to his comrade. "Didn't his lordship ask for a girl to make his bed? I just found me a peach ripe for the picking."

Quill went cold. Sweet Emmeline, prisoner on the *Otter*, would be forced to play mistress to the most powerful man in the colony. If they succeeded in dragging her on board, nothing short of a naval battle could free her.

"She's spoken for," he said, hoping to protect her from these men as easily as he had protected her from Dutch sailors. It was almost the truth. An unspoken understanding bound them together. All he had to do was speak to her father, and it would be true.

The man snorted. "Who do you think you are, the king of England? It don't matter what you or any other man says. His lordship's an earl. An earl! And he's spoken for her—or will as soon's he sees her."

Was life like this in Britain? Did men of rank and title roam the countryside, claiming whatever struck their fancy with no regard for the laws of God or man? Lord Dunmore's wife had barely sailed, and he was already looking to keep a mistress—to coerce a maid young enough to be his daughter into his bed. The man could have every horse in the county and all the grain in the granary, but he would never lay a finger on Emmeline.

The fire in his soul that he had ever kept banked in the name of goodness and civility, roared to life. "Touch her and die," he growled. Over his shoulder, he said, "Get to the house. Now. Barricade the door."

For one long moment, she stood there, pale with fright, and he understood the terror Charles had felt when his wife had faced a mob.

"Emmeline!" His desperate cry broke her frozen posture.

She turned and ran. Watching her flee around the back of the stable, Quill wasn't prepared for the lieutenant to strike him in the crook of his elbow. As the officer darted past him, Quill caught his jacket and tackled him to the muddy ground where the big sow had wallowed the day before. Before the man had time to regain control, Quill hooked his arms through the man's elbows, pulling them back like a useless pair of chicken wings. The man cursed and flailed, but he obviously hadn't spent his youth wrestling schoolmates twice his size.

Every muscle was engaged to keep his weight pressed against the man who was grunting and cursing like the swine he was. Between the grunting and cursing, a high sound caught his ear. A feminine cry of distress. It was then that he remembered the other officer.

"Blast." Where was the militia when he needed them? Just another man or two on his side was all he needed. But there weren't enough of them to protect the colony properly. They weren't there to ward off this attack. He released Lieutenant Allred and leapt to his feet before the man could react. Running around the stable, he saw Emmeline had made it halfway to the house before being caught. Ensign Tanner's fists clenched around her upper arms, and Quill ran faster, determined to put his own fists in the man's eyes. Emmeline dug in her heels and leaned back as far as the man's cruel grip on her allowed, but with every step he took back, he yanked her toward him, and she stumbled forward to regain her balance. Only a few more paces and they would reach the horses.

Suddenly, she picked up her feet so the ensign was supporting all her weight. The unexpected change tipped him forward, and her knees hit the ground with bruising force, but the look of defiance she gave the man made Quill's heart swell with pride.

Ensign Tanner could no longer stand upright while dragging her dead weight forward. "Blast you, girl!" He released one of her arms and drew a fist back to box her ears or blacken her eye as Quill came up behind him.

Not willing to allow either injury, he hooked an arm through the man's before he could strike. Then he kicked the back of his knees. They buckled. In the fall, his grip on Emmeline's arm failed. Quill threw his weight at the man's back. Together, they crashed to the ground as Emmeline scrambled backwards. Perhaps the Biblical angel who wrestled with Jacob was on their side, because their fall missed pinning her by mere inches. Only her petticoats were crushed.

"Go!" Quill cried.

This time, there was no hesitation. She yanked her petticoats free, gained her feet, and ran. She had almost reached the front steps when someone struck him from behind and, as his vision clouded, he lost sight of her. The fight had become two against one. Praying that the doorbolt would hold long enough for her to retain her freedom, he turned his attention to the two men intent on beating him.

There was no question of winning. He had sacrificed his freedom and his future the moment he had tackled a redcoat. And yet, he would do it again. At every threat and every opportunity, he would take his place between the lass he loved and the men who would hurt her.

While the lieutenant knelt on Quill's left arm, the ensign shifted to the right, pulling himself out from beneath Quill. As he came free, Quill tucked his feet under his hips and pushed back, tipping the lieutenant to the side. For one last, blissful moment, he was free. He clenched his fists and punched the ensign in both eyes.

Forty

UNCOMFORTABLE

Emmeline slammed the door and slumped against it as she secured the bolt. Her heart was racing in her throat as she gasped for air. A stitch burned in her side. She had made it to safety, but what about Quill?

Athair thundered down the stairs. "What is it? What happened?"

"The redcoats," she gasped. "They're here. They have Quill."

He scowled and stormed into the library. Emmeline could hear the sound of books being dropped and drawers being yanked open, only to be slammed closed. Had the man taken leave of his senses? His son was in trouble. He needed help. After a minute, Athair reappeared in the foyer. She stumbled aside into a stack of luggage so he could throw the door open. He paused on the threshold, his eyes dark and serious. "Close all the windows. Bolt the door. Dinna open them for anything."

"Yes, sir."

He gave a curt nod and ran down the steps. She watched her obedient hands bolt the door, locking the good men out with the bad. Would Athair be able to reason with the men? Could he still outwit them?

Màthair ran down the stairs. "What's happening?"

305

"Athair said to close the windows," Emmeline said, hastening to the parlor. The window stuck on its way down. She grunted and strained at it. In their time of trial, this was the small task she had been asked to do. She couldn't fail.

"Where is he?" Màthair asked, closing the other window with effort.

"With Quillan, I hope." The muscles in her arms still burned from moving the grain. Added to that, a dull ache encircled them where the officer had gripped her bruisingly hard. Her knees were so tender she felt them with every step. None of that mattered—not with Quill in trouble. She dropped her weight, almost hanging from the frame as it slid closed. Kneeling on the parlor floor, she added, "The king's men came early. It's too late for us to flee or for Quillan to hide. They already have him." A wild desperation propelled her to her feet and hastened her to the dining hall. Closing the windows was the one thing she could do to help. It was as noble as running to the house so he could better fight her attackers.

At least one of them was a hero.

"Why would they take Quillan?" Màthair asked, following her to the dining hall and closing another window while she talked. "They're supposed ta take the wheat and whiskey and so on. They said they would leave the family alone if we gave them that. And we were at least going ta pretend ta be willing."

"They took him because," Emmeline began, as they moved to the library, where precious books littered the floor, "because he wouldn't let them take me." Her voice broke, and tears filled her eyes. Quill hadn't hesitated to endanger his liberty when hers had been threatened. While she loved him for it, she feared what the consequence would be.

"Oh, my dear girl," Màthair said, pulling her into an embrace.

"He had to attack the redcoats," she explained as a sob swelled in her chest. "He had to. But now—" She broke off. There would be consequences for attacking the king's men. Màthair didn't ask the question that burned her conscience—why had she been so quick to run when he was in danger? Why had she been so quick to accept that he would protect her when that protection might cost him his freedom? She was no fighter. She was an Athena, not an Amazon. She could read and talk of great heroes and warriors, but that didn't make her one. She couldn't have saved Quill. She couldn't even have saved herself. She had run because she couldn't fight.

They secured the remaining windows on the ground floor and tidied the library. All was secure from the good and the bad. The heavy fall of little feet came unsteadily down the stairs.

"Brodie?" Màthair called softly, then gasped as she saw him trying to open the front door. "Stop that."

"Time to go," he said as he rattled the latch. "Mama said, 'Time to go.'"

"Later," she said, and picked up the squirming boy. "It will be time to go later, won't it, Cat?" She nodded meaningfully at the woman descending the stairs.

"Aye, we will go later." She gave her stepmother a quizzical look and followed her into the parlor.

As Emmeline pushed the pile of luggage in front of the door, she wondered what had become of her bag. There had been more important things to worry about, but Mama would not be pleased if she returned home with only the clothes on her back. A hiccuping laugh escaped her. Mama should be grateful if she got home at all.

QUILLAN MORRIS DISLIKED BEING UNCOMFORTABLE, SO lying facedown in the dirt with a man's heavy boot across his shoulder blades was an unwelcome experience. He didn't have a clear view of his attackers as they grappled for his hands, which he fisted under his belly. Once they bound his wrists, his life as a freeman would end. He would be their prisoner. Then what? Would they take him to the *Otter* and leave his home and family untouched? That had been the agreement—one offered before they had threatened Emmeline and he had tackled His Majesty's Marines.

Boots were pressed against his side while hands wrapped around his bicep, inching his fist toward the open. Quill refused to surrender his freedom so easily. He kicked his heels until they hit something that cursed at him. The weight on his shoulders doubled, and the toe of a boot hit his forehead.

"Filthy Scot," the lieutenant spat. "How dare you lay a hand on His Majesty's Marines?"

It had been a foot, but Quill wasn't one to be pedantic. "Ye threatened my woman," he ground out, then added, "Does his lordship know how ye feel about Scots?"

"He's an earl. Nobility don't count."

A fire burned in Quill's heart, consuming the petty concerns that dominated his life and leaving him with white-hot certainty of his course. Never again would he bow to a nobleman. He would fight for Emmeline, for his home, for freedom from the oppressions of other men. He would fight for the hope of this land—that it would become what she believed it already was—a land where all men stood equal before the law and God, no matter how noble or common; where they were judged by their choices and not their ancestry. They would all be Americans, and one blessed day, that would be all that mattered.

A weight pinned his legs down—likely the lieutenant was sitting on them. Before Quill could wrestle his ankles apart, a rope bound them together. Even if he threw off his attackers, he wouldn't make it one step toward freedom before they caught him again. There was another kick to his head, and in the blinding pain that followed, one wrist was caught and bound. He kept his free arm tight against his body, the fist under him where they couldn't reach it, but it didn't matter. It was two of them to one of him, and they hauled him against the split-rail fence. With a persuasive sword against his throat, they succeeded in tying his wrists together, the lower rail of the fence going between his arms.

He was trapped. He couldn't even fight the dew that soaked through the knees of his linen breeches. He was powerless to keep the officers away from the house and could only pray that they never made it inside.

"What is this nonsense?" Athair's voice thundered as he came into sight, scowling at the disheveled men. Twin bruises were blossoming around the ensign's eyes. The lieutenant's face had fared better, but his once snowy breeches and waistcoat were smeared with dirt and manure. The swinelike appearance was appropriate for the kind of man who would abduct an innocent maid.

"Is no' my livestock in the pasture? My grain piled in wagons? My guns and powder ready? Take it all, but leave my son."

"Your son attacked us," the lieutenant said fiercely.

A flicker of surprise crossed Athair's face. "I'm sure there was some misunderstanding. My son would never—"

"Nay," Quill said, glaring at the officers, "there was no misunderstanding. They said they were going ta abduct Emmeline and put her in Dunmore's bed. I objected."

Athair looked at the men again, as if appraising their injuries. A light glinted in his eye, and Quill realized his father was proud of him. Addressing His Majesty's Marines, Athair said, "Ye willna touch any woman under my care. Do ye understand?"

The lieutenant curled his lip. "You aren't in a position to be giving orders. Do you understand?"

"Dunmore is an old acquaintance of mine," Athair said. "We attended Eton together. I understand him quite well. I understand that when he learns ye've betrayed and deserted him, yer careers will be ruined."

"We're not deserting him," the ensign said.

"Ye're not?" Athair's eyes danced with merry malevolence. He took a step closer to them, the toes of his shoes inches from where Quill knelt. "When yer bodies are found in a wagon accident up by Gooch Ferry, disguised as farmers, with yer uniforms half-hidden under a deluge of goods ye've taken from Willow Haven in his name, nothing ye say will convince him ye didna betray him and desert him. I believe death is still the punishment for deserters?" Athair half-queried, resting an arm on the fence. "Now, I'm prepared ta give the governor supplies, as he requested. If ye're prepared ta leave my son and my women alone, my wagons are at yer disposal."

The lieutenant scowled. In one last, feeble show of dominance, he pointed to Quill and said, "He stays here until it's all loaded."

"As ye like," Athair said, as though it were of no matter. He rested a hand on the fence. "Let me assist ye. The grain is already loaded in a wagon and waiting in the barn." He pointed his free hand. The men turned to look, and something struck Quill's knuckles so hard and suddenly that he almost cried out, but his father was already walking away, leading the men with him.

Once they were out of sight, Quill arched backward until the rail pressed between his shoulder blades and his fingers brushed the grass. They curled around a wooden handle. Running a thumb along the edge, he realized he was holding a folded penknife. With great dexterity, he opened it and pressed the blade against the rope.

In a movement as effective as digging a grave with a spoon, he rocked the blade against his bindings. If he could free himself before they were done, he would go to the house and protect the women. The men had chosen to tie him up and follow Athair rather than pursue Emmeline, but that might change once they had the other things they had come for. A sharp pain cut through his thoughts. He had knicked his knuckles with the knife. Inhaling through his teeth, he transferred the handle to the other hand. At least he knew the blade was sharp. Now, if it would only cut the rope instead of his skin. After a few minutes, a cord snapped. He strained against the ropes until they dug into his flesh, but he couldn't burst the remaining cords. Sighing, he resumed the awkward and tedious process of sawing through his bindings.

Dishonorable men were most trustworthy when fear made

them circumspect. Did they fear Athair's threats enough to accept the spoiled goods? Might it be that easy? Might he and Emmeline walk free with nothing worse than a pounding headache and a few bruises? He hoped they would, but his captors had already proved they were not to be trusted.

And so, Quill knelt in the wet grass, sliding the blade across his bindings, praying the Lord would protect them.

Forty-One

TOGETHER

Emmeline absently ran the edge of the parlor curtain between her thumb and forefinger, over and over again. Though she couldn't see Quill or his father from here, she could see part of the drive that the men would take when they left Willow Haven. No one had come or gone since she had begun her vigil.

"What's taking so long?" Marta whined.

"Patience," Catriona said, as though Marta were her daughter and not her sister. "They're probably hitching the horses to the wagons. That's bound ta take some time."

They were all struggling to be patient. Polly had placed a thick stack of music on the harpsichord. She turned it over one piece at a time. Whatever she was looking for, she hadn't found it the first four times she had gone through the stack. Aunt Moira sat in her wingchair. A piece of needlework was forgotten on her lap. Grace and Hope had their workbasket out. They had made cockades from the scraps, but the loops came out uneven, so they unpicked the basting threads and started over. For the first time since she had come to Willow Haven, Emmeline missed having something to busy her hands with.

Màthair touched the frame of a small landscape painting. A

sea of heather surrounded a fine country home. "I never thought the king's men would threaten my family here."

Emmeline bit her lip. Athair could have kept his family safe by meeting Dunmore's demands. He might have done so if she hadn't objected so vehemently. Quill wouldn't have needed to attack His Majesty's Marines if she had waited in the house for the carriage. He was in danger because she had spoken up. Her vision swum. She dried her eyes with a handkerchief.

Were the men loading the wagon? Would the Marines accept the spoiled grain and inoperable firearms? Or would they recognize they were being cheated? Would they be angry? What kind of revenge might they take? Would they beat Quill? Press him into the king's service? Had he already been punished for protecting her?

Please, Lord, she prayed silently, *don't let them win. Not this battle or any other. Protect Quillan. I'm proud of him—proud of his honor and courage—but I don't want him to be hurt or captured.* Her petticoat had a swath of mud from when she had dropped to her knees. Her arms were tender and bruised, but that was a small injury compared to what the men had threatened her with. Quill had, once again, taken bruises that were meant for her. If only she could see him, could know that he was safe and free, that whatever injury he had endured would heal quickly.

"I canna see anything," Anna said, frowning out the other parlor window. "I'm going upstairs."

"Nay," Màthair said sharply. Anna's eyes went wide, Aunt Moira's brows raised, while Catriona's furrowed, Brodie looked up from his blocks, Hope and Grace looked up from their sewing, Polly dropped the stack of music on the harpsichord keys, and Jean whimpered. Màthair sighed. In a gentler voice, she said, "We need ta stay together. Until the men leave, until yer father and Quillan return, we need ta stay together. I canna lose ye." Her voice broke, and to Emmeline's amazement, tears ran down her cheeks.

Catriona handed her stepmother a handkerchief and put an

arm around her shoulder. "We'll stay together," she said in a soothing voice. "This will all turn out in the end."

Polly opened a glass cabinet and removed a miniature, which she handed to Màthair. Cradling the little painting of her husband in her cupped hands seemed to calm her. "He will keep us safe," she said.

Emmeline didn't dare take Quill's miniature from the cabinet. Instead, she slipped a hand into her pocket and clutched the ribbon he had given her the day before. "I believe in you, Quillan," she whispered into the curtains. "God is on your side. Together, you can do miracles."

~

His hands cramped.

He strained against the rope, but it held tight. At this rate, the Marines would be boarding the *Otter* before he freed himself. He shifted his weight, relieving the pressure of the fence rail that had been cutting across his arm. The squeak of a wagon wheel caught his attention, and he dropped the blade into the grass before it rolled into view, heavy with grain, powder, and guns—but not heavy enough.

"These muskets are useless without their locks. What happened to them?"

"What? No locks? I suggest ye visit a gunsmith in York Town and have them fixed. His lordship will be expecting the muskets to have locks."

"And do you expect me to believe ye only had three half-barrels of whiskey?"

"Ye've seen all my outbuildings. That was the last of the whiskey, the wheat, the corn, everything. And with the hailstorm this year destroying so many crops, 'tis going ta be a hard winter. Have ye no conscience?"

"Hard winter my foot. In a fine house like that, you have no more than this?" Realization dawned on his face. "That's where you're hiding it all, isn't it?"

"All what?"

"The locks for your guns, the barrels of whiskey, the fine women. Everything. Well, if Dunmore don't get it, nobody will."

Before he had time to guess at their meaning, one man kicked Athair from behind so his knees buckled, and the other hit him over the head with the butt of a musket before tying him up, while Quill strained at his ropes.

EMMELINE PRESSED HER FOREHEAD AGAINST THE GLASS cabinet. A row of miniatures smiled back at her, but she only had eyes for one beautiful, smiling face. All would be well, she told herself again. It had to be. If only she could see him from these windows. She returned to her vigil, hoping to see Quill walking back to the house, his freckles stretching in a delightful smile, and froze when she met the eyes of a man in uniform a few feet away, his arm swinging forward. There wasn't time to articulate a warning. She gave a little cry as a rock flew from his hand. She threw her arms in front of her face as the rock shattered a window pane, and everyone else cried out.

She lowered her arms in time to see Catriona, a babe in one arm, scoop up a sobbing Brodie and run for the stairs, followed by the other women. She glanced at the window as another pane shattered, then ran up the stairs like a lost sheep fleeing from a wolf. She followed them into the nursery, and Polly slammed the door closed behind her.

"You're bleeding," Màthair said, and Emmeline looked around the room to see who she was talking to. Catriona was in the rocking chair with Brodie, patting his back and murmuring a lullaby. Aunt Moira sat on the edge of a bed, gripping her cane so tight her knuckles turned white. Anna and Grace sat beside her. Hope looked out the window. Marta wriggled under the bed.

Polly was wedging a chair under the door handle. Jean looked at them all through the spindles of her cradle, intrigued by the sudden appearance of so many people in her quiet nursery. There was no blood anywhere.

Emmeline startled when Màthair grasped her wrist and turned it over. A shard of glass pierced the palm of her hand, and blood trickled down one finger and onto the polished wood floor. She blinked as the glass was pulled out and one of Jean's clean linens pressed against her throbbing palm.

"There now," Màthair said, "that's better."

Better? She forced a grateful smile and nodded. The voices of unfamiliar men echoed in the house. Quill and his father wouldn't have just let the enemy break into their home. What had happened to them? Had they been captured or killed? The possibilities were as unthinkable as her fate should they drag her onboard the man-of-war. Belowstairs, something slammed and broke and shattered. She longed to run, but there was nowhere to run to.

Instinct pulled her as far from the door as she could go, though reason told her the few feet she could put between herself and the enemy would make little difference when the time came. They would have cleared the glass in the parlor window by now. At any moment, they would hear feet thundering up the stairs. What had happened to Quill and Athair that had allowed this man to get past?

She pressed the linen against her palm and looked out the window, framing a lacework of leaves that danced to the tune of Catriona's lullaby. The view reminded her of the one from the guest room, but these were the thin outer branches. She reached through the open window and stroked a bough too green and delicate to support even a baby's cradle. When she had longed to escape into a literary world, it had never been to that peculiar lullaby in *Mother Goose's Melody* where the world was too weak and foolish to protect even a baby. "Should we close these windows?"

"And be trapped in here?" Polly asked, pressing her shoulder against the door and clutching a pair of scissors like a dagger. "Nay, leave it open."

It was ridiculous to feel safer with the window open. It wasn't as though they could escape the danger by jumping out. Then again, they were in no danger of the men reaching them through the window. Even if they found a ladder, they could only reach the boys' room, and why do that when they could crawl through the broken parlor window? She felt foolish for even asking the question.

She ought to be like Polly, choosing a weapon and preparing to fight, but the nursery was no magazine. It had soft blankets. The only hard thing was the furniture. The only sharp thing, besides the scissors Polly wielded, was a cushion of pins. She wrapped her hand around the top, pushing the heads of the pins into the cushion. An army of sharp tips emerged from the bottom like thorns. This was the best weapon she could find.

She strained her ears, but though there were distant sounds below, none of them had the firm echo of a man's tread on the stairs. She prayed they were only pillaging the house, that they wouldn't come up the stairs. That the nursery door would be secure.

Brodie's sobs quieted as Catriona sang softly, *"Tha mi sgìth 's mi leam fhìn, buain na rainich, buain na rainich."* Though Emmeline didn't understand the song, she took comfort in the rise and fall of the words, just as Polly took comfort from an open window. If the men were here for them, wouldn't they already be up here, pounding on the door?

She had begun to hope the worst was over when Anna said, "Do you smell that?"

Catriona abandoned her lullaby. The breeze carried the faintest scent of something burning.

"Dear Lord, not that," murmured Màthair. Her face lost all color. "Anything but that."

Forty-Two

ESCAPE

Quill strained against his bindings. It was no use. The only escape was through the awkward use of the penknife, which was more effective at nicking his flesh than cutting the rope. Meanwhile, what were the redcoats doing? What was their bitter revenge? Stories of the terrible months following Culloden flooded his imagination. His whole life, Athair had told those stories, and they had been as fantastical as Gulliver's Travels. A lawless time, where soldiers plundered, raped, tortured, and murdered those they had conquered. Listening by the fire, he had taken comfort knowing that such things would never happen in peaceful, law-abiding Virginia. Now they filled him with horror, fueling a desperate need to escape. He transferred the penknife from one cramped hand to the other. *Lord, keep her safe. Keep them all safe. And let us escape.*

Athair, slumped beside him, was in a rare state of despair. "I swore nothing would happen ta her or the lassies," he said. "I've promised her since our wedding night that I'd always keep her and the family safe, especially from the king's men." He gave a bitter laugh. "By the time we married, I was sure they had given up looking for me. I thought I was so clever—that they would never

318

look for a Mr. Morris in the colonies, that they would give up when they didna find Duncan Morrison in Scotland. What Scot would abandon his clan name? They would never suspect such a thing. But Clan Morrison was tied ta the land we left behind. And this, Elsie, ye and Rabbie, the lassies, and our displaced countrymen, this is our new clan. This is Clan Morris."

And Clan Morris was under attack. Scottish blood flowed hot through his veins, and Quill understood how his ancestors had dared to defy the British and defend their lands and their lasses. The knife slipped again, and a sharp pain told him where the blade had landed. Exhaling through clenched teeth, he resumed his efforts. So focused was he on cutting the unseen bindings that he didn't notice Billy walk up to them until he spoke. "What happened? Did they tie ye up? I ken they were bad'uns. We waited by the road for them, but they didna come, so I came back so's ta see what happened." He climbed over the fence. "Ye have a knife? That must be hard, cutting yer own rope."

"It is hard," Quill said, with little patience. "Mayhap ye could do better."

"As ye like," Billy said, taking the knife from him. In less than a minute, the lad had cut through the ropes. Quill stared at his raw wrists. Several cuts shone with fresh blood. But he was free. And with that freedom, he would run straight to the men who had captured him, ready to renew the fight and risk everything again to defend the ones he loved.

"I'll free my father," he said. "Billy, we need ye ta alert the men of the village. There's trouble at the great house. We may need their help."

Athair added, "And if there are any women left, tell them ta flee, now."

"Aye, sir! Count on me!"

Quill knelt behind his father. The ropes had been tied in haste and would be easier to unknot than to cut. He dropped the penknife and worked with his fingers, amazed at how quickly the knots came undone, now that he was free to work them from the outside. As he worked, he said, "Lord willing, soon this will be just another story where ye escape and outwit the enemy."

"Nay," Athair said. "This will be yer story."

Quill could almost picture grandchildren around his knees as he told them the tale of how he and their mother outwitted the redcoats.

Throwing the rope to the ground, Quill ran ahead of his father, desperate to see what the officers had done. He soon saw smoke billowing from the lower windows. The house was on fire. Had the women been captured? Or were they still inside?

POLLY WRESTLED THE CHAIR BACK AND PEEKED OUT the door. A wall of smoke blocked their view. "We're trapped," she said, her voice unnaturally tight.

"No, we aren't," Emmeline said. "Come on! We'll climb down the tree." She threw open the door and darted into the boys' room.

The women followed her reluctantly. "It's too high. We can't reach the ground."

"I've done it," Emmeline said as she tore off her shoes and stockings. "I'll help you."

"What if we fall?"

"Throw the mattress out the window." She, Polly, and Anna stripped the bed and wrestled the mattress through the window, where it broke through the branches and fell to the ground as solid as a book. Then Emmeline tucked the back hem of her petticoat into the front waistband, climbed out, and found familiar footing. She clung to a branch tightly with one hand and held the other out. "Who's first?"

Anna took her hand and allowed herself to be guided down the tree, following the path Emmeline had puzzled out the day before. She took an awkward leap onto the mattress, then looked up and laughed. "Come on down, the water's fine! And throw me my shoes!"

A shower of shoes rained from the window. While Emmeline climbed back up, Aunt Moira told Anna, between coughs, where to move the mattress. Màthair handed the matriarch a lace-edged handkerchief, which the woman placed over her mouth to filter the smoke.

Polly accepted Emmeline's help, but once her feet were on a steady branch, she insisted she could climb the rest of the way down by herself.

"Can ye carry Brodie?" Catriona asked.

"I think so."

At first, the boy wouldn't let go of his mother's neck, but then he clung to Emmeline. He was a lot heavier than he looked. Worse than that, it was hard to see around him for her footing, and she only had one free hand for climbing, as the other was holding him. They made it halfway before she misplaced her foot and slipped. She grabbed wildly with both hands for a branch while Brodie cried and clung to her neck. Her heart hammered as she hung in the tree, swinging her foot to the next secure branch. "Good boy, Brodie," she said in a shaky voice. "Hold tight." She seated herself on the lowest branch, close to the trunk.

Polly stood on the mattress and reached for him. "We're almost done," she said soothingly. "I'm right here. Let go, we can do this." Brodie reluctantly allowed himself to be passed to his aunt. Polly couldn't quite grasp him before Emmeline let go, and they tumbled back onto the mattress. Before Brodie had a chance to cry, Anna scooped him up and ran for the woods, disappearing behind a curtain of willow branches.

That was three down.

Grace and Hope went down almost as bravely as Polly had, but Marta needed coaxing and carrying. The moment she tumbled onto the mattress, her dark-haired sisters grabbed her hands and ran for the woods.

Emmeline's legs burned as she climbed back up, but she wouldn't rest until everyone was safe. "Hand me Jean," she said.

"Nay, I'll take her." Catriona fiercely tied her baby to her chest with a shawl. She wouldn't trust Emmeline with her children, not after she had nearly dropped Brodie, but she did accept her hand and guidance all the way down. When she reached the lowest branch, she sat, untied the shawl, and used it as a sling to lower Jean into Polly's upstretched hands.

"Aunt Moira, ye should go next," Màthair said.

The old woman shook her head. "I'm too old for this. I'll take the fire."

"Dinna say such things. The house can burn. But I'll no' lose my family ta another fire."

Aunt Moira pounded her cane on the floor, like a petulant carpenter trying to hammer a nail in one go. "I'm staying put."

Something flashed in Màthair's eyes. "Aunt Moira, climb out that window or I will push ye."

The old lady's jaw dropped. "How dare ye speak ta me like that?"

"Hand me your cane," Emmeline said. Màthair handed it over before her aunt could stop her. "All clear?"

"All clear," Polly cried.

Emmeline dropped the jeweled cane onto the mattress. The old lady looked furious—so furious she put one foot out the window. Emmeline had to grip the branch above her head to walk close enough to the house for the old woman to climb on her back like a child. "Hold tight," she said as her legs trembled on the unsteady branches. Carrying Aunt Moira down the tree was even more terrifying than carrying Brodie. Her old bones wouldn't survive a fall, and her memory wouldn't forget this day. Standing on the lowest branch, Emmeline coaxed the woman off her back. Then she asked for the shawl again. Polly threw it to her. Emmeline knotted one end around the branch above her and tugged it firmly. "Climb down this."

"What? I can't climb."

"It's only a few feet," Polly called, "then I'll catch ye."

The old woman looked back up at the smoke-filled room. Perhaps realizing that, at this point, down was easier than up, she grasped the shawl. Her grip was loose, and her hands slid down the fabric, but with enough control that Polly was able to catch her. The terror on Aunt Moira's face was soon replaced with triumph when she stood with her bare feet on solid ground, leaning on her cane.

Màthair waited by the window. Though she had been most distressed by the fire, she had insisted on seeing her loved ones to safety before escaping it. She was less spry than her daughters, but she didn't cling to Emmeline either. Emmeline waited while Polly helped her stepmother down. She would make her leap when the mattress was clear, collect her shoes, and run barefoot into the woods.

"Emmeline!" Quill cried. She looked up. He was leaning out the bedroom window, the worry on his face as plain to read as type on paper. He had run into a burning house to save her.

"Quill!" She scrambled back up the tree. She had to get him away from the danger. His face was covered in cuts and bruises from his fierce defense of her safety and freedom. She reached both hands to lead him out and was surprised when he pulled her inside. She tumbled headfirst into the room in a tangle of petticoats and was still trying to find which way was up when he pulled her onto his lap and held her in his arms, rocking like a cradle.

"The fire!" Emmeline said with urgency. "You have to get out."

"Shh." He brushed the curls from her face. "'Tis almost out. Ye're safe now." He took a shuddering breath. "I'm sorry we couldna keep them from the house."

Safe. At his assurance, her aching muscles relaxed into his arms. For the first time since the men arrived, they were safe. "How are you free?"

"I told ye," he said, "If anyone can outwit the king's men, 'tis Athair."

"But you're hurt." She reached a hand to his face, swollen, cut, and bruised.

He shook his head. "'Tis nothing." He traced a finger down the inside of her arm. "What's this?"

She frowned. An ugly red scratch ran from elbow to wrist. It must have been the tree. "That's nothing. I don't even remember getting it." She would be sore for a week, but no harm had come that wouldn't heal with time.

"Did they...did they hurt ye?"

"They never made it up the stairs."

"Thank God." His arms tightened around her, but he kept rocking, as steady as the pendulum of the parlor clock.

"My hand got a piece of glass in it when they broke the window, but it was just a little piece, and Màthair took care of it."

He pulled her hand from his jaw, frowned at the cut, and pressed a kiss to it. If she weren't so exhausted, she would return the favor. There was a bruise on his forehead and a scrape on his cheekbone that deserved attention. Mayhap there would be time later. For now, it felt heavenly to rest in his arms, knowing that she was safe, he was safe, and he loved her.

She sighed contentedly against his waistcoat. "My hero."

A faint laugh was followed by soft kisses on her forehead, her cheek, and her nose. She savored his affection, storing it up like a bountiful harvest before a lean winter. Once again, he had taken the bruises meant for her and insisted it was his pleasure. There would be more battles than this, real ones, and she wouldn't hold him back from serving. Not if he wished to. In the lonely days to come, she would treasure this moment, knowing he still fought to keep her safe, that he loved her, that he would protect her.

Little footsteps clomped up the stairs. Quill released a deep sigh, and the kisses stopped. She rubbed her forehead against his waistcoat in protest.

"Miss Gardiner, where are ye?" Marta asked. The footsteps

stopped abruptly. "Oooo," then she added, "The fire is out, so we can use the stairs again, but the parlor smells funny. Come see!"

Emmeline sighed, grabbed a bedpost, and pulled herself to her feet. Then she offered a hand to Quill, the one that was only a little scraped from climbing trees, and helped him to his feet. "We're coming," she told Marta.

The little girl turned and scampered down the stairs, not looking to see if she was being followed. Quill embraced the moment, and Emmeline, kissing her brow one last time before taking her hand and following his little sister.

Forty-Three

HOME

In the parlor, every windowpane had been shattered, and the fringed remains of the curtains were as charred as the once pretty paper that covered the walls. Màthair's beautiful paintings were ruined. Emmeline's feet, still bare, found puddles of water covering the charred floor.

Athair had both arms around his wife. "Everyone is safe," he said. "That's what matters." He looked around the room. "The fire didna make it far afore we put it out. I'll buy ye new paper and upholstery. Any kind ye fancy. The old ones were looking a mite shabby, anyhow. But I am sorry about yer paintings."

Emmeline went to the glass cabinet. The wood was scorched, but only one pane had broken from the heat. The miniatures had escaped, unharmed. She removed Quill's and held it beside his face. It was a very good likeness, down to the clusters of freckles— a little denser across his nose and cheeks. He blushed under her scrutiny.

"Keep it," he said, wrapping her fingers around the little frame.

"Oh, but I couldn't," Emmeline objected. "It's part of a set. I'm just pleased the miniatures are unharmed, especially after the loss of your beautiful family portrait."

"Keep it," Màthair echoed. "Heaven knows ye've earned a memento. I'll make another."

"Yes, ma'am," she said, awed into excessive politeness. She hadn't dared hope for a likeness of her beloved. "Thank you, ma'am." She could keep the miniature, though she wasn't sure where she would put it. Mama would ask questions if she placed it on the parlor bookshelf. Henrietta would ask questions if it went on their bedroom wall beside their samplers. If Emmeline wanted to keep the likeness away from her family's teasing questions, she would have to tuck it in the clothespress with her stockings and shifts. Her face heated at the prospect. The more she blushed, the bigger Quill's smile became, until she couldn't help smiling back.

"Come," Athair said, "the upholstery in my library is neither charred nor sopping wet. Let's continue our discussion in there."

No one objected to his suggestion of increased comfort. Emmeline sat beside Quill on the library settee and tucked her bare feet under her. Athair sat behind his desk and pulled his wife onto his lap in a manner far too familiar for company. But after everything they had been through together, mayhap she wasn't company. They had been pleased when she had addressed them from the first day as though she were another of their many daughters. She rested her heavy head on Quill's shoulder. He wrapped an arm around her, and she snuggled closer. Sooner or later, she would be part of this wonderful family.

Athair, arms around his wife, leaned back in his chair, and reported the events of the morning with businesslike efficiency. "I've sent some men from the village to make certain the king's men return to their ships. They'll let us know when they've sailed."

"Will they be back?" Emmeline yawned. "The king's men, I mean."

"I made arrangements to keep them away," Athair said.

"What does that mean?" Polly asked, joining them.

"It means that, unfortunately, they got what they came for. The whole list."

"What?" Emmeline said, suddenly wide awake. After all that, after hiding the goods, after the men had bruised her arms, after Quill had fought them so bravely, after the fire, those men had won. The injustice stung. She blinked back tears. "After everything we did—"

"Dinna fash yerself." Quill's breath tickled her hair. "A barrister canna win every brief. Soldiers dinna win every battle. Ye were brave, my bonny patriot. And ye're safe. I'd do it all again," he added, wrapping her in a fierce embrace, "I'd fight every last redcoat in Virginia ta keep ye safe."

Hot tears ran down her cheeks and moistened his shirtsleeves. She had found her hero. And she prayed that when the battles reached Virginia, she wouldn't lose him. "I love you," she whispered, so softly he might not have heard.

"And I, ye, lass."

On the other side of the room, the family discussed the events from the day, but she was too weary to contribute. An hour ago, she had been ready to climb mountains. Now she was as exhausted as if she had climbed an entire range. She cradled the miniature on her lap and closed her eyes, savoring the comfort of Quill's arms around her. At first, she drowsily followed the conversation, but it ebbed and flowed and made little leaps that her mind, half-asleep, was too clumsy to follow.

At one point, Polly was explaining how they had thrown Aunt Moira's cane out the window, and the next, Quill was saying, "I'll bring in the mattress."

Their father snorted. "Stay there. Any fool can see she likes ye better than a mattress."

"The poor dear," Màthair said. "No wonder she's tired. She carried half the family down that tree."

"Ye be good to her," Aunt Moira said. "I like her."

"I will." Then he added, so softly only she could hear, "always."

~

IT WAS EVENING WHEN THE MORRIS CARRIAGE CAME TO a stop in front of Emmeline's home. Quill, who had insisted on keeping watch all the way, handed Gunpowder's reins to the groom and opened the carriage door.

"Thank you," Emmeline said. "There's no need for you to come in. I'm certain you and Polly are anxious to be home."

"Dinna be daft," Quill said, swinging her bag over his shoulder and offering his free hand. "I willna leave yer side until ye're safe with yer family."

"Aye," Polly added. "What would yer parents think of us?"

What would the Morrises think of her parents? Mama was bound to have worried over her prolonged absence, and when Mama worried, she scolded. Emmeline opened the door. "I'm home." Her voice echoed in the quiet house.

Quick footsteps came from the back porch, and Mama met them in the front room, followed by Henrietta.

"It's about time," Mama said. "Taking off without a word to me. We've been expecting you for a day and a night. Kitty came for lessons this morning, and I had to send her home. I've been beside myself with worry."

"I apologize for the delay," Quill said. "We were waiting for word that the York River was clear of men-of-war."

Mama was not appeased. "As that river is in the opposite direction, I fail to see how an entire fleet of warships would prevent your timely return."

"There's a lot to explain," Emmeline said, wondering how to condense a tale that seemed so fantastical now that she was safe at home. Nothing so outrageous or interesting would dare to happen under Mama's watchful eye.

"There better be," Mama said, glancing at Quill. "Charles said Mr. Morris finished his last brief yesterday morning. We expected him to have you home by nightfall."

Polly spoke up. "Circumstances out of Quill's control arose. Mr. Wythe needed him ta deliver a final letter to the governor, and then Dunmore sent men ta press Quill into the king's service, raid our barns, and set fire ta our house. I'm grateful Miss Gardiner was there. She saved my life. She saved my family." The praise was a wild exaggeration. The menfolk had put out the fire before it had reached the bedchambers, but if they hadn't been there, it might have become true.

A curious look crossed Mama's face. Henrietta's eyes went wide, and she hopped on one foot, a sure sign that she was eager to say something and could hardly wait for company to leave so she could ask questions.

"There's a lot to tell, but I'm sure the Morrises are anxious to get home," Emmeline said, prompting them to say their farewells.

The moment the door closed, Henrietta burst with questions. "Did their house burn down? Did your clothes catch fire? These ones didn't. But you have dirt on your skirt. Did anyone get burned? They didn't look burned. How did you save them? Did you put out the fire? Why didn't they help?"

"I believe I arrived just in time for supper," Emmeline observed. "Let's get it on the table and call Papa in, and then I'll tell you what happened." She didn't have silk ballgowns or fine musical accomplishments, but she had her words, and she would share them in her own way and in her own time.

Forty-Four

TAKING SIDES

FRIDAY, JULY 21, 1775

Quill removed his hat as a footman led him to the dining hall.

Colonel Hendriks sat at a table surrounded by papers. His lame leg was resting on a neighboring chair. He didn't move from this comfortable arrangement, but beamed up in greeting. "Morris! Good to see you, boy. Knew you'd come round eventually. What changed your mind?"

"Dunmore made the mistake of threatening my family." And his home and his lass, but the colonel didn't need to know everything.

"Came to a fight, I take it?" The colonel said, assessing his injuries. "I hope they look worse than you. Who did he send?"

"His Majesty's Marines. I fought an ensign and a lieutenant." Determined to avoid starting rumors, he didn't mention Emmeline's presence.

Colonel Hendriks was delighted. "Two to one, and they were both officers. I knew you had a fighting spirit."

"Thank ye, sir. I'll serve wherever ye can put me. I dinna care

331

whether that's with an independent company or a volunteer company."

"That's the spirit, but haven't you heard? The Virginia Convention dissolved both of those."

"What? Now, when the need has never been greater?"

"Aye, the need is greater. Too great to rely on unskilled volunteer companies. We're raising sixteen battalions of minutemen who will drill more often than the militia and be ready to serve at a minute's notice. And, we're raising two regiments of regulars who will commit to a full year of service."

"Virginia regulars?" Quill repeated. Only the British had regular soldiers.

"That's right. It's about time our commonwealth had trained soldiers. Patrick Henry will command the first regiment. You know him. Colonel Woodford will command the second one. He's a good friend of mine. We fought together alongside Colonel Washington—now General Washington—during the French and Indian War. Henry's a good man, but lacks experience. I recommend Woodford."

"I'll have to sleep in a tent," Quill said, considering all the ways being a regular might be more uncomfortable than serving in the militia had been, "even in the winter. I'll have to leave my office and my rooms and my comfortable bed and say goodbye to my family and—" He broke off as his heart sank. He would have to leave Emmeline for a full year. The other sacrifices were nothing next to that.

"Lord willing, you'll have until September to get your affairs in order. It will take time to gather men from across the colony. Until then, you'll muster every two weeks with your county militia.

"That leaves some time for courting," Quill said, the words escaping before he had time to consider the wisdom of saying them aloud.

The colonel laughed. "Court all you like. We'll need women willing to follow the regulars when they move camp."

As much as he ached to keep his bonny patriot where he could see her face every day, a camp of rough soldiers was not the safest place for such a bonny lass. Besides, Charles would be distressed enough that a patriot soldier was courting his cousin, without the threat of dragging her into the war. "I canna promise a woman, but I'll join the Virginia regulars."

"Excellent choice, my boy. Now, where do I put you? The commissioned officers have all been appointed—men with battle experience, you understand. But I can't have you enlist as a lowly private, not after fighting two of the king's officers. And as a man of letters, too..." He drummed his fingers on the table. "I'll tell you what. Another young chap from William and Mary came by this morning. Probably a friend of yours. I put him in as a sergeant. I'll do the same for you. Sign here. We may be able to grant you a commission in the coming year, but it's a fine start."

Quill signed, then took a moment to read the fine, looping script. "Ingram? Nat Ingram? We'll serve together?" He had scarcely exchanged a word with his old schoolmate since last July.

"You know him? I thought you might. All you college boys seem to know each other." The colonel made a note. "There. I've put you in the same company." He smiled, as though he had done them both a favor.

Quill brushed aside his discomfort. Being in the same rank and company as Ingram would be no greater a hardship than spending winter in a tent or mustering in the sleet. They had made it through their William and Mary days without animosity. They could drill shoulder to shoulder and fight on the same side of a war without their recent differences getting in the way. It wasn't as though any of his sisters were going to be camp followers.

～

QUILL SHOOK MR. GARDINER'S HAND, RELIEVED TO have the difficult conversation behind them. "Thank ye, sir. I'll be good ta her."

"She could do worse," Mr. Gardiner said. It was hardly praise, but he had given his permission. Mayhap he would warm to the idea, given time. "When does your regiment muster?"

"September."

"In time for winter quarters," he looked at him thoughtfully, then sighed. "I suppose you would like to see her."

"If I may." This had been the longest week of his life, and Sunday was still an age away. He couldn't bear to wait until then to speak with Emmeline.

Mr. Gardiner gave him one last, measured look. Then he nodded. "You may." He gestured out the back shop door. "Don't do anything to make me change my mind."

"Thank ye, sir," Quill said. "I'll no' make ye regret this."

Emmeline was on the wide back porch with Henrietta, Kitty, and a stack of books. She glanced up and met his gaze with a smile. "You came," she said.

"I promised I would. I see ye're occupied with yer pupils."

"I am, but we're almost done with lessons. Would you mind waiting a few minutes?"

"Not at all," he said. If the next couple of months went as he hoped, he would be asking her to wait a year. A few minutes was nothing.

She returned to her lesson, helping Kitty read a syllabary aloud from *Dixon's English Instructor* while Henrietta read silently, a fat book open across her lap. When the lessons were complete, he gathered the books and carried them to the dining table. "I was hoping we might take a walk? I suppose yer pupils could come along as chaperones," he added, mindful of her father.

"I would like that."

The heat of the day followed them down the shady lane. Kitty and Henrietta fell behind, gathering wildflowers to weave into crowns. "What did you wish to discuss?" Emmeline asked.

"I have something ta tell ye and a question ta ask."

"Oh?"

"I'll do the telling first, because it might change yer answer."

Her brow furrowed, but she waited for him to continue.

"I stopped by Colonel Hendriks' home earlier today." He took a breath. "I told ye I would fight every redcoat in Virginia ta keep ye safe. I meant it. I went ta the colonel intending ta join either the Williamsburg Volunteer Company or the Independent Company. But they've both been dissolved."

"What? Now?"

"Aye. Instead, we will have minutemen and regulars. I'm going ta be a Virginia regular in the second regiment. On my honor, for a whole year, I will be a soldier. I have until September ta get my affairs in order, then I'll report ta Colonel Woodford."

"I'm proud of you," she said.

He shook his head. "I dinna wish for war. I pray for peace. But if war comes, I am prepared ta fight. I love this country too much." He moistened his lips. "I love the people who live here even more." He waited a long moment before broaching the topic that had tantalized him for months. "Now that I've told ye my decision, I need ta ask ye yers."

"Mine? She picked up a feather and twirled it. "I can't be a soldier, but I can fight with my quill," she said, her eyes twinkling.

"Och, lass. Ye canna tease me so. Write all ye fancy, but dinna tease me. Not when I've waited so long."

She sobered. "What is it?"

"Might I begin courtin' ye?"

She released the feather. "I thought you would never ask."

"I wanted ta do things right. I wanted ta be certain."

"And are you?"

"Only of what matters most. I canna say what will happen in this war. I canna say if yer cousin will forgive me for—for any of this. But I am certain of how I feel when I'm with ye. And I wanted ta know if—if ye might feel the same way. If we might spend more time together, knowing we feel the same, hoping and praying the future works out for us."

"Yes," she breathed.

"Yes?"

"Yes, please. Yes."

The road was clear of carriages, and their escorts were still weaving their crowns, a comfortable ten yards back. He took her hand and led her behind a broad tree trunk.

"What is it?"

He removed his cocked hat. "I was hoping ta kiss my bonny lass."

She blushed pink up to her curls, which were damp against her forehead. He rubbed his nose against hers. "May I?"

She answered with a quick, shy kiss. He dropped his hat in surprise. She had kissed him first. He would treasure that memory to his dying day. His bonny lass had kissed him first. How had he ever doubted that Emmeline was a lass he could love for always? She had a way of meeting him—his mind, his heart, and now this. Her lips brushed the scrape along his cheekbone, and his pulse quickened.

Two days ago, he would have been driven mad by her nearness, but now, Lord bethankit, he was free. Free to stand true on Virginia soil, meeting her level gaze. Free to kiss her and court her. Free to fight for everything and everyone he loved. But first—

He untied the blue ribbon at her throat. Several curls tumbled free from their pins as he lifted her hat and hung it on a neighboring fence post. Her eyes danced as she fought back a smile—the effort causing her cheek to dimple and her lips to pucker adorably.

He cupped a handful of ringlets, as soft as flower petals and as light as thistledown. The curls spilled from between his fingers, bouncing as they fell. Was Eden ever as lovely as this moment? The sky was a celestial blue, reflected in his sweetheart's eyes. Everything good and beautiful in their summer paradise had come from God—the sweetgums and maples, freedom and future, and her. Knowing the sacrifices he soon faced, he still chose Emmeline and the land that they loved.

At long last, he kissed her. It wasn't goodbye, and it wasn't goodnight. It was a glorious greeting, a firm decision, a sacrifice made, and a side chosen. Even in that paradisiacal garden, where everything planted was good, the first man had been offered a choice. Despite the cost, he had chosen his woman. Mayhap man wasn't meant to spend eternity alone in a garden of leisure. God knew he would fall. And in His mercy, He planned salvation from the beginning—salvation born of woman.

Her lips softened, and he leaned into her redeeming touch. She was his, and he was hers. No friendship was more dear; no freedom was more cherished. After a long moment that wasn't nearly long enough, he pulled back. Her breath was warm on his lips as he listened for travelers down the country lane. The morning was quiet, save for the distant laughter of their wee chaperones. There were no witnesses to spoil the sweetness of their first kiss.

She must have agreed, because a moment later, she leaned into him with a kiss as sweet as raspberry pie. The fire that had long smoldered in his chest stirred and grew, the heat rivaling the summer sun. He had found a lovefire that would never grow cold. One slow kiss followed another as a breeze wound a cooling path around them.

A contented sigh escaped her, and he rested his brow against hers.

"I love ye, my bonny patriot," he confessed, "and I think I always will."

Forty-Five

CHARLES & SUSAN

Charles glanced up as Quill returned to the office. "Did yer errands go well?" he asked absently.

"I accomplished what I set out ta do." He had enlisted in the army, gotten Mr. Gardiner's permission to court Emmeline, then held her and kissed her like he had been longing to do. The only thing left to do was inform Charles of the sides he had taken, though it would probably be wisest not to tell him about the kissing just yet. After an awkward silence, Quill said, "Will ye ask me what my errands were?"

Charles set his quill pen down. "If I ask, will you give me an honest answer?"

"I dinna believe I have ever lied ta ye. I might not tell ye everything, but I dinna lie."

Charles handed Quill a button.

"What's this?"

"I was hoping you would tell me. I trust it has something to do with the way the chairs rearrange themselves in my absence, or why I've spied candlelight through the shutters after dark, or why Jack Mason has been lurking at the end of the street on nights I work late."

Quill dropped the button. Charles knew about the meetings. He had known all along—or at least, suspected.

His friend looked at him with those blue eyes that could see right through a man. "What have you been doing? What rebel mischief have you entangled yourself in?"

"I'll tell ye, but there's something ye need ta understand first. I will never betray ye or yer family. Not ta the Committee of Safety or anyone else. But I love this land. I love the freedoms it promises and the people who live here. If the king sends the fight ta us, then I will fight ta protect my family and yers from the evils of despotism. I went ta speak with Colonel Hendriks this morning." He paused. "I am now enlisted in Virginia's second regiment."

Charles flinched.

"There were no commissions available, so he made me a sergeant," Quill said, as though his friend had been worried about his rank. "I know ye willna be fighting alongside me, but dinna ever doubt my loyalty. If I die in the cause, I wish ye ta know that I was fighting for ye, not against ye."

Charles started to say something, but Quill silenced him.

"There's one more thing. Ye may be as angry about this as the other. I'm courting Emmeline."

"What?" The word was sharp and urgent. "How long have you been—"

"Today, Charles. I started courting her today, after I spoke with her father."

"What are you thinking? You've just thrown your life away on the rebel cause. What do you have to offer her? A tent in a dirty camp? The fleeting safety of being allied with the winning side? The heartache of seeing you injured or killed in the cause?"

"Enough," Quill said. "Do ye think I havena thought of all that?"

"I don't see how a man can think of all that and make the decisions you have made. You were a marked man before becoming a soldier. Emmeline might have died this week, and on your watch."

"I know," Quill said, wondering how much Polly had told Susan. "I was there. And I would have died ta keep her safe. Where do ye think these bruises came from? Dunmore didn't just want whiskey and gunpowder. He wanted a girl ta keep his bed warm now that his wife is gone."

Charles inhaled sharply, but Quill continued. "Did Polly tell ye that? They tried ta capture Emmeline, ta force her ta return with them. I attacked His Majesty's Marines, knowing I could be imprisoned, or worse. I did it because I value her safety and freedom above my own. I love her, Charles. I've been fighting it for months, because I knew ye didna wish for her ta have suitors yet. I hoped that the day might come that ye would decide I was worthy of her. Ye've always been my friend. I didna wish ta lose that."

Charles raked his fingers through his hair. "You've been sneaking around, holding meetings with radical rebels in my office." After a moment's silence, he added, "Tell me you aren't."

"It's our office," Quill corrected, "and I'm not a radical. But I have been allowing meetings here."

"If ye're not radical, why host illegal meetings and join an army of traitors?"

"I want ta keep my home safe. I want ta keep my family safe. I want ta keep Emmeline safe. Is that so radical?"

"The way you're going about it is."

"I ken ye must be angry—"

"I'm not angry. Worried. Frightened." Charles gave a short laugh. "I can never stay angry with you, not even when you plunge into the most impulsive, foolhardy schemes." He hesitated, then solemnly added, "When they come after your neck for treason, find me. I won't let them take you. And," he took a deep breath, "be good to her."

Quill stared at his friend. That was it? That was the terrible, horrible, impossible conversation he had been dreading for months? Charles knew about the meetings. He knew he was joining the patriot army. He knew Quill was courting Emmeline against his wishes. In return, he offered to betray the king to save Quill's life.

"There is a friend that sticketh closer than a brother." He had seen that proverb somewhere in the Good Book. Here was that prophesied friend. While the branches of government splintered apart, while the constitution crumbled, while neighbors became enemies, he and Charles were still friends. When he married Emmeline, they would become family, almost brothers. Better than brothers. Quill wiped his eyes.

Charles stared at the emotional display. "What's wrong?"

"Nothing," Quill said. "I was just afraid, for a minute there, that I was going ta lose my closest friend."

"After all the scrapes we've been through together? If you're trying to lose me, you'll have to try harder."

"I assure ye, I've never tried ta lose ye. Friends?"

"Friends," Charles repeated, then cuffed his shoulder playfully. "Even if I have to drag your sorry hide through the pearly gates."

Quill laughed. It was good to be friends.

❧

EMMELINE POURED THE SAND BACK INTO THE POUNCE tin and read her essay.

> The king and his ministry will soon send the war to Virginia. What then? Who will rise as the hero to defend our homeland and our rights as free Americans?
>
> This fight is too great and the battle too strong for any one man. We need every heart to be willing, every mind to be firm, every hand to defend. The coming conflict will try men's souls and require the best that

every man can offer—not just men, but women, and even children will have their parts to play. And they must play them well or there will be no victory, for—

There was a sound at the front door. Emmeline left her essay on the table and answered it. To her surprise, Mrs. Susan Johnson was there, the overskirts of her chintz gown gathered high over a linen petticoat. She greeted Emmeline warmly, and after a few civilities, introduced the reason she had come.

"I understand your desire to marry—how do I put this delicately?—more comfortably than your mother. And a young woman of understanding could never be content with an ignorant husband."

Emmeline inclined her head. Someone must have informed Susan that Quill was courting her.

"A lady of your temperament must also desire a husband with genteel manners. Charles has a natural sympathy toward an old friend, mind you, but there is no need to marry the first gentleman you meet. You're at a lovely age to make connections and understand not just books, but people."

Emmeline was dumbfounded by Susan's concerns. Books were full of people. Their habits, philosophies, deepest thoughts, and emotions. The best and worst that people were was recorded in history and literature. She may not have had all of the opportunities of a gentlewoman, but she was not uneducated about the virtues and vices common to mankind.

"You may be afraid," Susan continued, "due to your station in life, that no other gentleman will come your way. I think your relationship with myself and Charles should assure you that is not the case. I had hoped to have you stay with us once we have our own home and my health improves. You have always been like a sister to Charles, and I had hoped, with your mother's permission, to bring you into society as such. There will be many opportunities for you to meet other gentlemen. There is no need for an intelligent, amiable, and, might I add, beautiful young woman to settle on the first gentleman who pays her court."

"You do not approve of Quillan Morris," Emmeline observed, pocketing the flattery to be enjoyed later. "Is there a defect in his character that worries you?"

"Quillan Morris is a well-educated and agreeable gentleman. But that is not uncommon among the middling and upper classes. A young lady of your tender years and inexperience shouldn't rush into her first opportunity for marriage."

"Thank you for your concern," Emmeline said politely. Then she did something she had always been too awed by Susan to do before—she spoke up. "Thus far, he has said nothing about marriage, only that he wishes to pay court, a possibility I have considered for months. I am well acquainted with his character and esteem him highly. And he is better acquainted with my character than anyone. If it does come to marriage, I believe we shall suit each other quite well."

She didn't have to hide her flights of fancy from him any more than she had to hide that she was a cabinetmaker's daughter. With any other gentleman, she would have to be careful to present herself as a gentlewoman's daughter and nothing else. Was it foolish to hope for a husband who loved every part of her? A husband who wasn't ashamed of her parentage and skills? She didn't think so.

"Well, if you're certain," Susan said, "then I have nothing more to say on the matter, but to wish you happy. If there's ever anything I might assist you with, please don't hesitate to ask."

"Thank you," Emmeline said, relieved that Susan had accepted her decision. Then a sudden thought occurred to her. "With the current tensions, I am not allowed to visit the shops anymore. Would you be so good as to go in my stead?"

"Indeed, yes. I will gladly purchase anything you—"

"Oh, that is kind," Emmeline interrupted, embarrassed by the generosity of her offer, "but I was hoping you would deliver something to the *Gazette*."

It could not have been often that a lady as fine as Susan Johnson, née Bailey, was asked to perform such a common service as delivering letters, but she accepted the errand as gracefully as she poured tea and played the harpsichord.

After Susan's carriage rolled away, Emmeline tidied up from the day's lessons and joined her father in the workshop. There was something satisfying about sending one's words out into the world, much like the satisfaction of seeing a dining set arranged in its new home.

"I wonder," she said to Papa as she unfolded the latest broadside, "whether there might soon be a demand for campaign furniture. If you don't need my assistance today, I thought I might begin making a folding chair with wood from the scrap pile. I know at least one gentleman who will soon be in need of one."

Epilogue

WEDNESDAY, SEPTEMBER 27, 1775

Emmeline poured a basket of apples into an oak tub. They had been picked the week before and were soft and mellow. Using a cudgel, she smashed the fruit into a pulp. Once it was done, it would be scraped into the cider press. Most family farms didn't have their own press, but Papa could build anything he set his mind to—and anything Mama set her mind to, besides.

From the wide back porch, she could see Henrietta in the orchard, shaking branches until the apples fell to the ground like oversized hailstones.

"Good afternoon, Emmeline," Jenny said, passing by. Emmeline blinked in surprise. She hadn't expected to see her friend today.

"Afternoon, Miss Gardiner," Kitty said, pausing for a hasty curtsy before running after Jenny, who seemed bound for the orchard.

"Afternoon," Emmeline called.

A moment later, at a more decorous pace, Mama joined her on the back porch. "Mrs. Susan Johnson just left."

"I didn't know she was here," Emmeline said, disappointed to have been left to work alone when pleasant conversation was going on in the parlor.

"She brought Kitty and Jenny. I sent them to help Henrietta pick apples." Laughter carried to them. The girls were having a merry time of it.

Emmeline continued pounding the cudgel against the soft apples. "I told Kitty we wouldn't have lessons until the apple harvest was over and the cider was put up for the year."

"That's why she came," Mama said. "She wants to hurry the harvest along."

"It is?" Emmeline was surprised by Kitty's enthusiasm until she remembered something. "I did promise her she could begin reading *Mother Goose's Melody* when we resumed lessons."

"She has made good progress in her lessons," Mama said. "She and Henrietta, too. You're a good teacher." She paused for a moment, then added, "Susan had a proposal for me."

"Oh?" Emmeline stirred the pulp with the end of the cudgel and unearthed several whole apples. She smashed them.

"To begin with, she has invited you to spend a fortnight with her in October, to give you a season when the courts are in session."

Emmeline looked up. "That is quite generous of her." She sighed and looked at the row of baskets, heaping with apples, on the porch. "It's a pity it's too soon for another holiday. Several officers have left orders for campaign furniture, and I can't abandon Kitty's lessons again when she is finally ready to read in earnest."

"Wars aren't won or lost on folding chairs," Mama said. "If you cannot complete them before you leave, then either your papa will do so, or they will have to wait. As for Kitty, she lives with Susan now, remember? You can bring your books with you and have lessons there."

"But, I have nothing to wear. I mean, nothing suitable for the kind of company Susan will expect me to mingle with." She looked down at the stained pinner that she wore to protect an old shortgown.

"There's no need to be extravagant during wartime," Mama said. "Many fine ladies are showing their patriotism by wearing homespun. However, Quillan's mother, Mrs. Morris, has quite generously sent Susan several of her old gowns, suggesting they might be made over for you."

Stunned, Emmeline forgot the cudgel in her hands. Màthair's gowns were as lovely as a fresh-picked bouquet. None of them was a harsh indigo or a serviceable linsey-woolsey. She was a gentlewoman and an artist, and her gowns showed both sides of her, with fine fabrics and a finer palette of colors.

"This is a wonderful opportunity," Mama continued. "You will take lessons from Susan on how to be a gentlewoman. Then you will apply those lessons at social events under her chaperonage."

"Lessons," Emmeline repeated. She had always been good at lessons.

"Yes, lessons. When I was a little older than you, I learned that my education had failed to prepare me for the responsibilities I had undertaken in becoming a tradesman's wife. Fortunately for you, it is easier to learn how to plan dinners for company when you know what ingredients and work go into all of the dishes than it is to have to learn how to cook after you marry."

Emmeline blushed. "We're not betrothed," she said, though Quill had, on occasion, hinted at their future together. "And he reports to his regiment on the morrow."

Mama smiled. "That reminds me. I thought I heard someone speaking with your father and—ah, there he is."

Emmeline looked up as Quill exited from the back of the workshop. He was dressed as a soldier, with a walnut-brown hunting shirt over brown breeches. He was no knight of the Round Table, but he was real. Her heart, though aching over their coming separation, swelled with pride.

"Mr. Morris," Mama said, "how nice to see you. I understand you will soon report to your regiment."

"Aye, on the morrow. I've just gotten the last of my things in order." He glanced at Emmeline. "Well, almost the last. Might ye spare Miss Emmeline for a few minutes?"

Mama took the cudgel from Emmeline. "Run along, you two. But not too far, and not for too long. And don't do anything unseemly."

"Yes, ma'am." Emmeline removed her pinner and left it on the porch railing. Quill offered his arm, then led her to the country lane that ran past their house. To Emmeline's surprise, Mama didn't send Henrietta, Kitty, or Jenny to follow them.

Maples and oaks flamed above the lane like living bonfires. Sunlight filtered through the leaves like stained glass. Parliament couldn't stop the seasons' eternal progression any more than it could prevent two hearts from growing together. A leaf fell, dipping and diving, until it landed on Quill's cocked hat. Emmeline plucked it off. It was nearly the same color as his hair. She twirled it in her fingers. It was a fine leaf, worthy of pressing in a book—a bit of color to pull out and admire on a dreary winter day when she despaired of seeing him again.

"Yer wareroom is looking a mite bare," Quill said, slowing his pace. "Did ye sell out of campaign furniture again?"

"We did. I have a couple of camp tables that I mean to finish after all the cider is put up. Papa was going to help, but a man saw the loom he was making for Mrs. Finlay and put in an order for one just like it. I suppose the colony needs fabric as much as furniture." She glanced at Quill's uniform. The edges of his hunting shirt were left raw to feather into a fine fringe. The design was said to soften the silhouettes of longhunters, allowing them to hide in the woods. Would the regulars need to spend much time in hiding?

The long shirt was tied loosely over his civilian clothes, allowing her to see the heart of his waistcoat. When had knights abandoned chainmail? If only Quill could wear archaic armor under the hunting shirt. Wool and linen would do little to defend against bullets and bayonets. She bit her lip. "Are you certain you have everything you need to be comfortable?"

He laughed. "I didna join the regulars so I could be comfortable. But my sisters have knitted wool stockings by the dozen, Susan has outfitted me with enough herbs to open an apothecary, Charles surprised me with a heavy wool blanket, and my bonny lass crafted a bedstead that, when folded, fits into a portmanteau. I'll be the envy of all the soldiers." He paused. "There's been something I've been meaning ta ask ye, Emmeline."

"What is it?"

He turned to her, clasping her hands between them. "In a year's time, Lord willing, I'll complete my military service. When I do, will ye marry me?"

Would he be alive then? Would he be well? Would the patriots be branded as traitors, forced to flee into the wilderness or foreign lands? She set aside her questions, ones which they had no way of answering, and without hesitation said, "I will. I would love to." When the time came, she would welcome him with open arms and cover with kisses every bruise and scar that had come as he defended the land that they loved.

"I have something for ye." He released her hands to unwrap a handkerchief, revealing a silver brooch. Two shining hearts twined together, sharing a single crown. "'Twas my màthair's betrothal brooch. Now, 'tis yers."

"It's beautiful," she said reverently, too awed to touch it, afraid her fingerprints might sully the silver.

"'Tis why it reminded me of ye."

She smiled. "Now it will remind me of you." She would need the reminder when his regiment left Williamsburg. In the meantime, though his first duty was to his country, she hoped to see him often during the fortnight she stayed with Susan in October.

He pinned the brooch high on her shortgown. "How is it that while one country split in two, two hearts became one?"

She considered his question, searching for a clever answer.

Though she had read the wisdom of the ages, none of the great poets or philosophers came to her aid. "I suppose I don't know. But I am glad."

"As am I." He studied the brooch. "I suppose I should apologize for the crown. I canna say what Athair was thinking. He was part of the Jacobite 'Rising when they married. He has never been fond of the king of England. Mayhap he meant it for the Bonnie Prince."

"It's for the King of Kings," she insisted. "Even if our earthly king betrays us, the King of Kings will not." Their entwined hearts were trusting that. "I'll pray for you. For us. That we'll be together again."

~

QUILL WRAPPED HIS ARMS AROUND HER. HOW OFTEN, while his regiment was stationed in Williamsburg, would he be at liberty to call on his betrothed? Whatever it was wouldn't be enough. She rested her cheek on his shoulder. Her fingers brushed across the raw edge of the cape of the hunting shirt.

"Ye like the uniform, then?"

"No," she cried, lifting her head. "Well, yes, but—" she paused to rub the tip of her nose against his. "You've always been a hero."

"That, my bonny patriot, is the most nonsensical thing I've heard all month." It wasn't so very many months ago that she had accused him of betraying his country for a little comfort. She may have forgiven him for his failure to prevent the Magazine Incident, but she hadn't always thought him a hero.

"It's true," she insisted. "I might not have seen it at first, but you always have been." She blinked back tears. "Forgive me. I am proud of you. I'm just afraid of what's bound to come."

He rubbed her nose thoughtfully. "What is bound ta come?"

"I don't know for certain, but you may be forced to leave Williamsburg. There may be battles. You might—" Her voice tightened.

"Och, lassie. No matter what comes, ye'll be in my heart and I'll be in yers." He touched the brooch she wore. "We'll say our prayers and put our faith in the King of Kings."

"No matter what comes," she said, and stroked her fingers across his brow and down his cheek.

He chuckled. "What are ye doing?"

"I don't want to forget."

"Ye have my miniature." Thanks to his blessed stepmother, he now had one of her, too.

"I can look at it. But I can't touch it." Her fingertips rested at the corner of his mouth, teasing him. There was a famine coming, when he wouldn't be able to see her or touch her, when he would battle the fear that he might never see her again. So, he caught her hand and kissed each finger. Then he tossed his hat on a fencepost.

"What are you doing?"

He grinned. "This soldier was hoping to kiss his bonny bride before going off to war."

Emmeline looked pleased, flattered, and a little shy. "Bride?"

"Aye, lass." After a moment, he added, "Ye did promise ta marry me."

"I did, but *bride?* It makes me sound like springtime and roses and like you—" She broke off, blushing.

He could only guess what she might have been thinking about him that would inspire that maidenly blush. "Like I love ye more than life itself?" He took her hands in his. "Like I'm counting down the days and months until I can be your husband? Like I canna wait ta stand up with ye before God and man and make our wedding vows?" He rested his brow against hers. "All of that is true. And ye do remind me of springtime and summer and every beautiful flower the Good Lord created."

After a moment, she whispered, "I love you, too."

There was nothing deeper that words could say, so he whispered his love in kisses as slow as the wink of a firefly, and she sweetly returned each one. A breeze stirred the trees, and falling leaves danced around them. There were many good things in this beautiful world, but few were worth living for. Fewer were worth dying for. The reality of their pending separation ached too deep to be soothed by a gentle kiss, so he wrapped her in a fierce embrace. She buried her face in his hunting shirt, the brooch pressed against his waistcoat. They clung to each other, their hearts beating as one.

He might return in a year. He might return with scars or wounds. He might not return at all. Yet despite the ache, despite the cost, some things were worth living for, worth fighting for, and worth dying for—like freedom, friendship, and the woman he loved.

Historical Notes

Last Monday, between 2 and 3 o'clock, we had three severe hail storms, from the west, which quickly succeeded each other. The first lasted very near five minutes, and most of the stones were as big as pigeons eggs, some much larger. A great number of windows were broke, particularly at the palace, which lost upwards of 400 panes. The gardens likewise sustained a good deal of damage; and we hear that the storm was very violent at Green Spring, and sundry other places near town.

— PURDIE'S VIRGINIA GAZETTE, MAY 26, 1775, SUPPLEMENT, PAGE 3

In researching 1775 Williamsburg, I relied heavily on the three newspapers printed concurrently in Williamsburg, all under the title *Virginia Gazette*. Sadly, printer Clementina Rind passed away in 1774, but not before publishing a pamphlet entitled "A Summary View on the Rights of British America." Historians inform us that the anonymous author was none other than Thomas Jefferson.

Though this novel was years in the making, looking back, it seems there was little I needed to invent for my novel—a rich historical setting already existed for my fictional characters[1]. The hailstorm really happened (above is one account). The advertisement for a runaway Scotsman was real. So were the cheering and fireworks to welcome "Peyton Randolph, the father of our country," home after he served as President of the Continental Congress.

Other cameos of historical characters include: Lord Dunmore, George Wythe, Patrick Henry, and the enslaved barber named Caesar.

March to Independence: The American Revolution in the Southern Colonies 1775-1776 by Michael Cecere helped me make sense of the Dunmore's comings and goings, and provided a balanced look at the rumors that flew around Virginia as people worried that war would come to their colony.

Historians believe the reason Dunmore fled Williamsburg in early June, after having so recently returned to it, was that one of the printers of the *Gazette* warned him that a copy of a private letter Dunmore had sent to England months before was about to be printed in the Gazette.

It seems to have occurred to the royal governor that Virginians would not respond favorably when they learned he had been encouraging the king and parliament to send warships to block the Chesapeake.

Yet the House of Burgesses publicly lamented Dunmore's flight. They were not so rebellious in June of 1775 as to pass laws without the governor's signature, and they reluctantly agreed to conduct Virginia's business through letters. At the end of June, while censoring Dunmore, the House passed a resolution insisting that they would risk their lives and properties to "maintain and defend [George III's] government in this colony, as founded on the established laws and principles of the constitution."[2]

In his refusal to support a bill that would have paid the soldiers who had fought under him in the 1774 battle known as Dunmore's War, his lordship said, "as it imposes duties upon slaves imported, I cannot assent to [the bill]."[3] This was not the first time British officials had vetoed a Virginia-born plan to charge such a high duty on imported slaves that it would sharply decrease the number of new slaves brought to the colony.

Though modern historians glorify Dunmore for offering emancipation to patriot slaves who fought under him, he was no abolitionist. Nor did he have a history of providing for the soldiers who fought under his leadership.

While he resided on the HMS *Fowey* and later the *Otter*, landing parties stole livestock and provisions from the locals, further disintegrating trust between Virginians and the British might that had once protected them.

Under the heat of a Virginia summer, the government of the Old Dominion wilted. The governor abdicated his role, and the House of Burgesses, the oldest English representative government in North America, met for the last time.

Each side believed the other was planning an attack, and each side prepared for the battles to come.

Notes

HISTORICAL NOTES

1. The one exception to historical accuracy in the setting was the allowance for the General Court to meet in July. According to research published by Hugh F. Rankin in August of 1958, "The General Court met twice a year, on April 10th and October 10th, provided those dates did not fall on a Sunday. In that event, the session was begun on the following Monday. The court sat for twenty-four days (Sundays excepted) or until the docket had been cleared." He notes that the first Tuesdays of June and December were reserved for the courts of oyer and terminer. I hope the reader will forgive me for misleading them within the novel, as my earlier attempts to discover when the court was in session had failed, and the book was nearing completion when I succeeded in finding a trustworthy source.
2. From a meeting of the House of Burgesses, Saturday, June 24, 1775, as reported in Purdies's *Virginia Gazette*, June 30, 1775, Supplement, page 1
3. Dunmore's reply is reprinted in Purdie's *Virginia Gazette*, June 23, 1775, Supplement, page 2

Acknowledgments

Thank you to my alpha, beta, and gamma readers:

Keira Dominguez

Debra West

Anna Hall

Jessika Caruso

Rebekah Haynes

You helped me see the story through the eyes of the readers, showed me what worked, and advocated for a story with more kindness and a more satisfying first kiss.

Because I don't speak Dutch, I reached out to the Uncrushable Jersey Dress Facebook group and asked if any fans of mid-century romance author Betty Neels could tell me, in Dutch, what the tall, vast, Dutch captain says to himself when he is asking Emmeline for directions.

"Betty" Sandra Wylie suggested "*Ik raak altijd verdwaald op het land,*" which translates as, "I always get lost on land." This echoes something his translator will later say for him and was perfect for this scene. Thank you, Sandra, for helping the story feel a little richer.

About the Author

Stephanie McRae is a descendant of American patriots, including one soldier who died at Valley Forge. She is also the wife of a US Navy veteran. While their family of seven was stationed in Virginia, they took many opportunities to visit Colonial Williamsburg. It was during one of these trips that the seed for her first historical novel was planted.

Also by Stephanie McRae

Heart of the Revolution

The Lady and the Loyalist

The Hero and the Patriot

Short Romances

Wager for a Kiss

Marry Me at Willow Haven*

---

* This novelette is currently only available to newsletter subscribers